VALENTINE

Sorcha Black

Belfry Publishing

Cover by
Justice Serai

Editors for Valentine
Lina Sacher & Nerine Dorman

Editors for Villain
Justice Serai & Nerine Dorman

Formatting
Polgarus Studio

To Mack from Kink Monsters for letting me borrow his idea.
To Jory for all the shit I put her through.

Chapter One

The girl's hair flowed like a copious frost waterfall, drifting around her, as white as staring directly into the sun. Her jaw was square, stubborn – too masculine for a woman. She was cold and sharp, and more lovely than any human had a right to be. Power rolled off her like tendrils of snow drifting across the road in midwinter, but no one else saw it here, in their school full of Typicals.

No one else even noticed her.

He stalked her through the hall. Every nerve in his body burned, fine-tuned to her location. People swerved around him as though they felt his compulsion and were loath to cross its sullied, dishonorable path.

It was a big university, but how had he not noticed her before?

His cock had led him to her, an insistent weathervane. A fearsome desperation made him wonder how deeply his morality ran. The thoughts she inspired were anything but moral.

If he stayed behind her, where she couldn't see his power, he could watch her all day without her noticing him. Except that would mean skipping Research Methods, and he had one of those ridiculous professors who graded attendance.

The beauty moved around the corner and vanished into the throng of Typicals. His heart resumed its normal business of beating and moving blood away from his cock and back to his brain.

He talked himself down on the way to class. For just a moment he imagined what he'd allow himself to do if he was a less scrupulous man.

He'd find her again. He'd find out where she lived. And then he'd do what any self-respecting villain did with a pretty girl.

Keep her.

*

"Seriously, Alison?"

Jory's roommate slathered cold, wet eye makeup on her while simultaneously jerking around in time to the dubstep that blared through their minuscule dorm room. By the time she was done, Jory would look as if Picasso had attacked her in a dark alley.

"We're getting you laid tonight, oh Queen of the Lizard People. Your look is too serious. If I trash you up...just a little..." She put the final touches on what felt like an epic amount of eye gunk. "Then we'll have those high heels pointed at the ceiling in no time."

Jory sighed. "Alison. I have a boyfriend. You know this. I'm not going to hook up with some random guy just so you can feel less judged. I swear I'm not judging you."

Alison sniffed the air and made a face. "Do you smell that? Smoke. I think your pants are on fire about that whole boyfriend thing. I'm calling bullshit, once and for all. We've shared a room since September, moron. I'd know if you were talking to anyone. Ever. Let alone some imaginary hottie in Arizona."

Fuck. She'd never been a good liar, but dating wasn't that simple for people like her.

"Alison, I..."

The pretty brunette lowered her voice to a whisper, her gaze sharp. "I don't care if you're Atypical. You're not going to die a virgin on my watch!"

"Maybe I was lying about the boyfriend, but I'm *not* a virgin." Jory arched a brow. She hadn't had a lot of sex, but it still counted, even if it had been in high school. It hadn't worked out well. Losing control was supposedly fun for people, but when she lost control, things got unpredictable. Almost freezing her boyfriend's dick off had cast a chill on the whole idea of dating.

"Whatever. Close enough. How many people have you slept with?" Alison started to tidy away the paint trays then paused to hand Jory a mirror.

She took it, but didn't look right away. If she looked like an escapee from a grade school makeover party, she wasn't sure how she'd sneak off to wash her face without Alison bludgeoning her to death with one of her textbooks. "I refuse to answer that question."

A Typical couldn't possibly understand that Jory's life wasn't really her own. Aside from the coursework for her Atypical History program, she also had her ever-developing powers to contend with and combat training to think about. Men weren't even on her radar.

If she didn't do well at this round of combat training, or if anything went wrong, she might never get chosen for a team. If that happened, she'd end up being the same as a Typical – with a Typical job, and a Typical life.

Becoming a hero was her entire life's goal, but she might need to start making other plans. Most of the people her age who'd gone to Atypical schools were already matched with teams. After Atypicals hit about twenty, getting chosen became almost unheard of. If she didn't get picked in this round or maybe the next, she'd need her degree to fall back on. Teams needed to mesh before they were completely mature, or the members would be too set in their ways to work as a unit. At least that was true in the court of public opinion. If things didn't fall into place in the next few months, she'd be fucked.

But yeah. Apparently guys were supposed to be number one on her list of priorities.

Alison rolled her eyes. "Don't look at me like that. This is for your own good. I'm not trying to be a bitch. It's winter break. All of our assignments are in. Nothing left to do but have fun until everyone heads home." She pulled Jory to her feet. "Come on. Between that dress of mine and the boots, you're going to have men drooling on you all night."

"Ew." She lifted the mirror and the woman who looked back looked…hot, polished. Like a character from a reality show about college students trying to get laid. Crap. If this worked the way Alison wanted it to, tonight was going to be a long string of annoying men who thought sexual aggression made them sexy.

"See? Didn't I whore you up nice? Now quit fucking around and let's go before all the hot guys decide who they want to go home with."

Jory tried to lag behind and get lost in the crowd of socializing women that congested the dorm halls, but Alison kept a firm hold of her hand and got her out to the car without any chance of escape.

Inspiration struck. "Wait! I forgot my bag."

"Nice try. Get in the fucking car before I beat your ass."

Whatever happened to the days when the girls her age avoided her? Damned college open-mindedness. She'd told Alison she was Atypical one day, hoping to scare her into minding her business, and instead Alison had made her a pet project. Apparently, she'd grown up with a cousin who was Atypical, so unlike many people she had no aversion to Jory. Damn it.

"How are we getting back?"

"Taxi. I'll give you money if you really did forget your purse. I wasn't about to give you the chance to go hide like last time." The girl gave her a sidelong dirty look. "You're lucky I understand you a little, or you wouldn't have *any* friends here. You might think you're better off alone, but scaring people away doesn't make for a very meaningful life."

"But sleeping with a stranger will?"

"It's a start. We have to get you past the first hurdle before we get fancy."

A line was forming outside the club by the time they got there. Starting the evening at eleven p.m. seemed ridiculous considering that was usually the time she went to bed. When she went to the training facility during break she'd have to get used to sleep deprivation again, but for now she'd enjoy her eight to ten hours every night.

Alison parked the car a block away and they walked to the club, Jory feeling conspicuous and over-sexualized in the tall leather boots with the too-high heels. Maybe Alison thought they were "fuck me" boots, but to her they were more "attract unwanted attention from slimy men" boots. The honking cars were probably a bad sign.

They waited in line for all of three minutes before the bouncer picked them out and waved them in.

"It happens all the time." Alison shrugged. "Who am I to argue that that kind of compliment?"

While waiting for their drinks at the bar, some man paid before Alison even had to pull out her wallet. The vultures descended. Her roommate looked as if she was in her element, holding court to a throng of almost impolitely interested men, whereas Jory accepted their attention awkwardly. For Alison's sake she tried, but there were just too many, and they were all shouting different conversations over the throbbing club music. Pretty soon her head was throbbing in time with the noise, and she cringed at the amount of other people's spit she could feel on her face.

After a third drink was pressed on her in too short a time, Jory excused herself to go visit the restroom. Alison tried to insist on being her chaperone, but after getting delayed several times by insistent men, Jory gave up on her friend and made a break for it.

She'd almost made it when she was grabbed from behind and some guy started dancing with her, grinding against her ass, laughing in her ear as though they were having a great time together. When she pushed away from him and glared, he held up both hands, as if he'd made a mistake, and faded back into the crowd of dancers. What was it with these guys? They all acted like she was just there to amuse them, and for heaven's sake, they all looked alike! It was hard to remember which ones to avoid.

She turned back toward the restroom and fell off her heel. Just when she thought she'd caught herself in time, she toppled over and landed in the seat of an empty booth.

An almost empty booth.

A sinfully attractive man looked up from a book. To her dismay, her mouth opened and closed a few times before anything came out.

"I-I'm sorry. I fell."

He gave her a friendly smile. "You okay?" Pretty. Reading a book here was a little weird, but there was something about him… His eyes. They were the darkest she'd ever seen – completely black, without even a sliver of white.

Atypical.

Maybe it was the beer she'd had, or maybe he was dampening his power, but she'd almost missed it. But why would he try to hide his power in a room full of Typicals?

Great. Now she felt even more like an idiot. If he'd been drunk and Typical, he would have forgotten her immediately after she got up.

"Yeah, I'm okay." The words came out breathier than she would have hoped, but it hadn't sounded too dumb.

He nodded pleasantly and looked back down at his book. Jory tried to read the title, but his fingers and the table hid it from view. Why would he be reading in the middle of a loud club?

Feeling as though she was getting creepy, she got up from the chair.

"You're going?" He looked back up at her, and the bottomless depths of his eyes held her in place.

"Yes, I…uh…I was just headed to the lavatory when your chair was nice enough to catch me." Lavatory? Ugh. Smooth. Now it sounded like she was in middle school. She gave herself a mental shake. It was the creepy eyes. They'd thrown her off.

"Mmm." He nodded absently. "Come back when you're done." He went back to his book and his unruly black hair obscured his face.

Great. He was the same as the rest of them. Bossy and assuming.

She rose from the table and made her way to the facilities, determined to go home after that. Alison came out to the bar by herself all the time, so she didn't need to feel bad about abandoning her, and she'd be damned if she was going to go back to that Atypical's table so he could be bossy with her. Some Atypicals really thought they were too good for other people.

There were so many women in the restroom that it was hard to get through the door. Maybe they'd all realized it was safer in there. She'd had enough of lecherous men for a lifetime. Why did Alison seem to love their attention so much?

Or maybe Jory was missing something.

When she was done, she had to psych herself up to go back out into the fray.

As she neared the Atypical guy's table, preparing to avoid eye contact, something changed her mind – or the part of her mind that controlled her feet. She was standing in front of his table before she knew what she was doing.

What the hell was she doing back here again? She tried to take a step back, but her feet wouldn't obey. She waited, seething, knowing he was doing something to make her obey him. How dare he use his powers to manipulate her behavior? Anger throbbed in her head, spurred on by her headache.

She could feel him ignoring her. The book title said something about sociological research methods. After a minute he closed the book and laid it aside, then turned his attention back to her. The eyes made her forget all the accusations and smart-aleck remarks she'd been preparing.

"Hello, Jory. Thank you for coming back." The music seemed quieter here. She could hear every word he said even though he hadn't raised his voice.

"You know damn well I didn't come back because I wanted to."

He chuckled, the sound sending a shiver along her skin while also pissing her off. "Yes, I know, but I promise you it wasn't my doing. The same thing happened to me the first time I saw you at school."

Had he said her name? He'd seen her before?

"Who are you?"

"Valentine." He leaned back in the curved bench seat, draping his arms across the back, like it was his throne. The dark hair and eyes against his tan skin were striking. Such a pretty man, yet not at all feminine.

She didn't know any Valentines – if that was even his real name. "Do we know each other?"

"A little now. Names at least." His mouth quirked as though at a private joke, but this time something sinister lurked around the pleasant façade.

"So if you didn't drag me back over here, what happened?" Would sitting make her seem less nervous? Standing around was making her feel as though she was waiting for his permission to sit.

He shrugged. "I honestly don't know." After a sip of his beer, he looked her over as though he really hadn't bothered before. "By all means, sit."

Jory sat, trying to look calm and aloof, but also trying not to fall off her boots again while pulling enough dress under her butt so that her skin didn't touch the cold vinyl chair. Men never had these problems.

Valentine folded his hands on the table. They were rough and callused – odd for a college student. He must have had a job doing some sort of labor on the side, or maybe he had Atypical combat training on the weekends. He leaned toward her, and she was infinitely glad the round table between them was so big. Frissons of something uncomfortable drifted over from him. She wished it was something helpful, like terror or disgust, but it was more like the knot she got low in her stomach when she watched really good porn. Lust. Not the average kind she got when she talked to a hot guy, but the kind that made her feel the need for some private time.

He was watching her with an expression that suggested he was suffering right along with her.

"Why did you come here tonight, Jory?"

"To hang out with my friend Alison and have some fun. You?"

He shook his head. "The real reason, and then I'll tell you mine."

Oh, jeez. Like the truth, truth? Fine.

"Alison thinks I need to get laid. She wouldn't lay off until I came along. She seems to think I'll pick up a stranger and go home with him."

His eyebrows might have raised somewhat, but it was hard to tell if it was her imagination. "You do that sort of thing regularly?"

"What? No!" The words were out of her mouth before she realized it was none of his business.

"I didn't think so. Atypicals tend to be careful about who they fuck."

She could feel her cheeks heating. The word 'fuck' falling from his lips had been orgasmic to her ears. She imagined him leaning her over the table right here, and sinking his cock into her, as though he didn't care who saw. Her nipples were uncomfortably hard.

"So why did you come here? To catch up on some light reading?"

"I knew you'd be here. I thought it would be less frightening for you if I

7

spoke to you in public, at first."

A cold trickle of dread trailed through her innards. This was too creepy and weird. Was he stalking her? No. It felt bigger and less controllable than that. If she hadn't known she was coming tonight, how had he known she'd be here?

"So…uh…you're taking sociology?" *Make polite conversation and get the hell away from this guy, Jory.* There was some weird shit going on here tonight.

He snorted. "Yes. My master's degree."

What was so funny?

"Are you going to talk about the weather next?"

Jory frowned. "Normally when you meet someone, you have a conversation that starts out with harmless things," she pointed out coldly.

"About school? The weather? My astrological sign?" He was mocking her. "Well, my name is Valentine Ott, I prefer the winter, but fall will do, and I'm an Aquarius. On a more relevant note, I'm twenty-three, Atypical, I went to Atypical school until university, and I have a facility with rope."

His attitude sucked, but he was a hell of a lot more interesting than the other guys she'd met tonight. Maybe even all semester. At least they could talk abilities.

"Rope? I've never heard of anyone having powers that involved rope." By the look of him he didn't use it for Boy Scout sorts of reasons.

He ignored that. "Your name is Jory Savage, I'm guessing you like springtime, budding flowers and small forest animals, you're a Gemini. You're twenty-one, Atypical, went to Typical school, and your powers have something to do with the cold. Your weakness is your hair."

She stared at him. How the fuck did he know all of that? And the hair thing? How had he figured that out when she'd only known a few months?

"You didn't say what your weakness is."

His smile was alarming.

"Come here." He patted the bench seat next to him.

"Why?"

"Because you want to."

Fuck. She did, but she was also afraid of what would happen when they got closer.

Jory's body vibrated with the tension of staying where she was and not going to him. His face was emotionless, as though he watched an experiment where he had no interest in the outcome. She had the impression that he cared a lot more than he was letting on.

"If I go over there, what's going to happen?"

He arched a brow at her, and it made her insides all shivery, as if her body wanted to please him and her brain was getting in its way.

A vision of him using his rope to tie her to this table flashed to mind. Her panties were gone. She writhed, caught, unable to get away from him. He lowered his pretty face between her legs and…

The gasp that escaped her brought her back. She blinked at him. Had he planted that idea with his power or was it her sex-starved body being a pervert? She could smell her own arousal. If she went over there, things were going to get…unpredictable. That was bad when you could accidentally freeze a room full of innocent bystanders.

"I…don't think that's a good idea. I've been gone a while. I bet my roommate is getting worried."

Valentine's expression turned mocking, but it was hard to tell if he was laughing at her or himself. "If you change your mind and want to talk more, I'm a TA in the sociology department."

She nodded jerkily and rose from the table, clutching the edge of it while trying to make herself back away.

"Let's cut the crap, shall we? I know what you want, Jory. Maybe more than you do. Whatever this draw is between us, I don't think it's going to go away until we fuck." He paused. "There's a chance it will, but fixing it my way will be much more pleasant. At least for me."

She took a step backward, teetered on her heels, and grabbed the back of the chair. What if he was right? Or what if this was just a weird power of his and it would stop as soon as she walked away? Her body was screaming at her to stay. Or to skip the sitting and talking and…what? Bring a guy like this to her dorm room? Have Alison and the guy she picked up screwing like ferrets in the next bed? Freeze them all to death when she lost control?

"You smell like you want to be fucked, Jory."

Oh god. "I have to go now," she whispered. She took another step back. He chuckled. "Is your mommy calling you?"

Cheeks burning, she broke eye contact and turned away. The noise of the room came flooding back, assaulting her ears. She walked methodically back to where she could see Alison sitting on a guy's lap, surrounded by other guys. She'd beg Alison to loan her some money and go straight home.

Feeling braver after a few minutes of being hit on by safe, boring men,

Jory glanced over at Valentine's table, half expecting him to be sitting there with another girl. It would make her feel better if he was. Or if he'd left. Or if he'd gone back to reading.

No such luck.

He was sitting there quietly. Watching her.

Chapter Two

It wasn't until Valentine found himself standing outside Jory's dorm room window in the sloppy, wet snow that he had to admit things were getting out of control. At night he'd go to bed with the best of intentions to sleep through his usual five hours, then wake up about two hours in, his hard-on pleading for relief. Every dream he had was about her, and they were never about making dinner together or long walks on the beach.

The snow melting in his hair and dripping ice water down into his collar was a wakeup call as he stared at a dark window – even to someone as fucked up as he was.

He walked on, realizing his footprints in the snow shouldn't stop there and turn around, in case someone called the cops about the crazy stalker outside the dorm.

Really, he should be thinking about going home about now. His family would be waiting for him, since it was almost Christmas, but it was hard to leave without seeing her again and trying to fix the asshole first impression he'd made.

Jory wasn't a club girl. He'd figured that out without the other clues about how she seemed to hate the attention she got from the men there, but he'd still come on too strong because of the uncontrollable…craving he had for her. He knew she felt it too, and that had made him less careful with his words. He wasn't the world's most tactful man, even at the best of times.

Nothing he'd tried eased the ache. If he could just get his dick into her, the torture would stop.

After walking a loop around the school, he headed back home, trying to focus on the sound of the snow slopping around his feet, the feel of it seeping into his shoes.

He could pick a girl up at the club, or find someone on one of the kink sites to meet up with, but something told him that would be about as satisfying as using his hand. No amount of fantasizing would replace the real thing. The shock and fear in her pale blue eyes, the scent of her arousal... He groaned and readjusted his rapidly hardening cock.

Think about anything else. Think about grading papers. Think about the family business. Think about Christmas.

All of those thoughts slid away, and there was just her, on her knees, her face tear-streaked. Sweetly begging for him. Fuck – he needed to get home.

Valentine let himself into the side door of the ugly factory, and stomped up to the loft. The place had been hopping with people when he'd rented it, but the designer had gone under and the workers had lost their jobs. During the day, with the natural light streaming in, a few of his entryway windows looked out over the silent sewing machines, which now wore cloaks of dust. If the building sold and the new owners wanted him out, it would be a pain finding something like this again.

He threw his sodden coat on the rack, not caring if it dried overnight. There was nowhere to go the next day anyway. His shirt was next, still chill and damp from the snow that had melted into it. Squelching shoes and wet socks followed. Was it still coming down?

The nearest window to the street showed the snow still coming down in heavy clumps, like winter was trying to bury the ugly world in something clean. At this rate his car would need to be shoveled out.

As he neared the window, to look into the street, the hallucinations began.

Jory, in a white nightgown, covered in snow, staring up at his window.

God – he was going mad.

She caught sight of him. Her shoulders slumped and she covered her face with her hands then hurried off back down the street, leaving puddle tracks behind her.

Real. Fuck. And where the fuck was her coat?

Unreasonably pissed, he jammed his shoes back on, grabbed his coat, and ran down his stairs two at a time. He pelted down the street. The little idiot was going to get abducted dressed like that – or get frostbite at the very least.

Valentine caught her before she turned the corner onto the next main street. He grabbed her arm and spun her around, hoping like hell he wasn't delusional and accosting a stranger.

"What the hell are you doing out here dressed like that? It's fucking winter."

She blinked up at him like a confused child.

"I don't know. I woke up from a…dream. And my feet just took me here. Something keeps pulling at me and it won't leave me alone." She looked upset and helpless, and the tight grip he had on her arm must have been painful.

He let go of her, shucked off his coat and draped it over her shoulders, his gaze drawn to the way her pretty tits were heaving and the melting snow had made the nightie cling to her puckered nipples.

"Come up to my place," said the wolf to the lamb. "We'll get you warmed up then I'll drive you home." He wasn't lying. He wasn't. He had to give her back to her life.

She wasn't for keeping.

Jory stumbled after him in the snow, clutching his hand. "There's something wrong with me." She whimpered and his cock felt like it was going to burst.

"There's nothing wrong with you. You're just horny," he grumbled. "Why are you wearing a nightgown?"

"I've been horny before. This is different." She tried to pull her hand free, but stopped when he didn't immediately let go. "And I like nighties. Half the girls in the dorm sleep naked. What's wrong with wearing something that covers everything except my head and feet?"

"You're like a pervert magnet."

"I guess that's how I ended up outside your house." Her laugh was nervous, but the attempt at humor made him smile back at her.

"Yes, you've come to the right place." They were at his door and he opened it and led her up the stairs.

"Why don't you live on campus?"

"Too many complaints about the screams coming from my room." He waited for her to laugh or for her eyes to widen, but the implication seemed to go over her head. "Seriously, though. I just needed my own space. No nosy neighbors here."

In the foyer, she peered through the window into the work area below. "No neighbors at all. You could crank your music and walk around in your underwear all day, if you wanted to."

Or bring girls back to his place and do horrible things to them.

Valentine took the coat from her shoulders, both to be a gentleman and to get another look at her curves through the translucent white fabric. Jory was small, but had more than enough tits and ass to ignite his imagination. At

13

only about six feet himself, he was still almost a head taller.

She pulled her feet out of her boots, which made a wet sucking noise as they popped free.

Jory looked back up at him and he only realized where his gaze had settled when she crossed her arms across her chest, as though she was cold. She was blushing.

"Let me find you something dry to wear. You must be freezing."

"Surprisingly enough, I don't really feel the cold." She laughed and gave him a lopsided smile that made him smile back again. He wasn't really a big smiler, but she kept catching him off guard. "But something dry and less see-through would be nice."

He sighed. "I guess the Saran wrap I was going to offer you is out of the question then."

Jory rolled her eyes.

"Hey, you're the one who called me a pervert. I have a reputation to uphold. Come with me." Heart in his throat, he entered the main room, which took up the entire floor, other than the bathroom. Having her in his apartment was making this far too dangerous. His tenuous hold on control might not last with her in here and almost naked. Controlling himself was never an issue, and the fact that it suddenly was, specifically with this girl, was unnerving.

"T-shirt? Button down? Track pants? Boxers?"

"Um." She stared at him while she fiddled with the bow on her gown. A fucking bow. Did she even know what she was doing to him? No. The fact that she didn't seem to know made it that much more charming. "Maybe a t-shirt and track pants, if it's not too much trouble?"

He retrieved the requested clothing out of his chest of drawers and handed them to her.

"You can put them on in there." He indicated the bathroom. "Or just change here. I can assure you I wouldn't mind in the least."

Jory took the clothes from him then clutched them to her, staring at him as though she was in a trance. "I'll go in there." She nodded to the bathroom, but her gaze had slid down to his bare chest. "You must have been cold out there with no shirt on." Frowning, she stepped toward him, hand raised.

Valentine braced himself, gritting his teeth to control the wave of lust that washed over him as her shy fingertips brushed along the muscles of his chest. They drifted over his ribs. Then lower. She looked mesmerized, as though she'd forgotten she was touching a person, and only followed the instinct to touch.

When she reached the waistband of his jeans, she seemed to realize what she was doing. Her eyes flitted up to his face and she tugged at her lip with her teeth.

Oh, honey. You have no idea who you're playing with.

Val pulled the loaner clothing out of Jory's hands and stepped toward her. "First things first." He turned her around and ran a hand over her hair. She hissed then whimpered as he took firm hold and separated it into two sections. Before she could protest, he braided each side, listening with interest to the way she moaned as though he was rubbing her clit. Her hair was just as sensitive as he'd thought, but he needed it bound to limit her power. He grabbed two short lengths of string from his pocket, wrapped them around the bottom of her new braids, and watched as the ends of the twine wove themselves together with a touch of his finger.

Perhaps he was safe from her power now, but that mostly meant he was less safe from himself.

He turned her back to face him. The long white braids framed her face, but showed more of it than usual. The innocence of the hairstyle suited her. Her eyes were wide, but rather than objecting to anything, she appeared to be waiting.

Fighting to restrain himself, he brushed his lips gently against hers. *Give her time to push you away. Don't rush her.*

Jory kissed him back immediately, hooked her fingers into his belt and pulled him closer, kissing him more desperately. He walked her backward and pressed her against the wall, tangling his fingers in her braids and holding her still while he took charge of the kiss. She moaned into his mouth.

He pulled back. "Jory."

"Huh?" Her lashes fluttered open, revealing her submissive gaze.

"Are you into kink?"

"Wha…? I don't know."

She didn't know? Crap.

Jory was on her toes now, trying to get him to kiss her again.

"How many people have you slept with?"

She sighed and leaned her head back against the wall. "Why do people keep asking me that? One, okay. Just one."

"And?"

Her groan spoke volumes. "Three times. The first two hurt. The third one didn't turn out well."

Didn't turn out well? Had someone walked in on them? Had he gotten off too soon? Had his dick fallen off?

"Why?"

She bit his chest, right above his nipple. The pain went straight to his cock.

"It was good. He took his time. I lost control, though."

"What happened?"

"We had to go to the ER. I gave him a little frostbite. On his dick."

Valentine chuckled even though he tried not to. She narrowed her eyes at him.

"Sure, laugh." She growled. "I've been celibate since senior year, and I've only had sex three times – two of which were quickies at house parties."

He kissed her again then tugged on one of her braids. "This should fix that."

She pulled the braid around to examine his handiwork. "How do you do this with the string?"

"I'm not sure." He shrugged. "I've just always known how. Like breathing. If the rope is synthetic, I can't do anything with it, but if it's made of something natural – even partially – then I can usually make it do what I want."

"Do you have to touch it?"

"No."

"Show me." Her eyes sparked with interest.

His power usually terrified Typical girls, and the few Atypicals he'd been with either hadn't been into bondage or had known him too long to be impressed. A little almost-virgin was probably going to freak out, but he had to admit that he liked the idea.

He went to his closet where he retrieved two coils of rope he'd been fooling around with earlier. They were new coils, but obedient. He moved her to the center of the cavernous room, and put the coils at the foot of his bed.

"I'll show you what they can do, but if you want me to stop, just say so."

She nodded, smiling as if she was at the circus waiting for the clowns to come out of the tiny car.

At first he had one end of each coil rise in the air, to get her used to the idea. When that didn't startle her, he thought of how the power looked when it rolled off her, and had the rope mimic the movements.

"Beautiful!" Her lips were parted. It was hard to admit to himself that he was enjoying showing off. Having a talent for rope was about as fascinating to most people as collecting stamps. It may have been interesting to the person doing it, but the onlookers, if they weren't collectors themselves, were generally only looking to be polite.

A few times he let the end of a rope skim past her ankle, but after the first couple of times it didn't startle her.

"See, rope isn't as flashy as a fireball or being able to fly, but it has its uses." He sent the ends snaking up each of her legs, circling, constricting slightly, raising the hem of her nightie as it went.

She gasped and blushed, then tried to hold down the gown.

"What's the matter, Jory? Do you want to stay an almost-virgin forever?"

After a moment's hesitation, she stopped fighting his rope, and the obedient things dragged her gown up until he got a good look at her creamy white thighs and the pale blue panties with white cartoon cats on them.

Valentine almost swallowed his tongue. He didn't think he'd ever undressed a girl who was wearing anything other than lingerie or nothing under her clothes. The fact that Jory had likely put these on with no intentions of being seen in them, made seeing them that much more intimate.

"Do you always wear little girl panties?" He smirked and reveled in the pinkness of her normally pale cheeks.

"I like things that are fun. Obviously, I didn't go to bed thinking I was coming here." She looked down at her bare toes. Her shoulders were rounded.

"They're pretty. May I come closer?"

She nodded but looked sulky. "If you think they're pretty, why are you being a dick about it?"

Valentine barked a laugh. "I'm always a dick, snowangel. You'd better get used to the idea." He walked up to her and silently commanded the rope to hold her in place. "These panties are actually a perfect match for your night gown."

She shivered at his smile, but she didn't say a thing as he reached out and ran his finger along the top edge of her underwear, over the bump of her hipbone, to just above her pussy. Although she whined quietly, she didn't object. Touching her when she was dressed like this made him feel like even more of a pervert than usual. Most of the women he brought home were dressed to pick up or to go on a date, not dressed like a girl kidnapped from a Victorian Christmas card.

The ropes coiled around bits of her gown, hauling it up like the curtain on a stage, higher until her pink-tipped breasts were exposed to him.

She trembled, waiting, her eyes luminous, and her breaths shallow. She visibly struggled to dampen her reactions to what he was doing, but he could almost taste her fear and excitement in the air. Surprisingly, she didn't attempt to cover herself with her hands.

When she swayed on her feet, he flicked a finger, which sent rope to trap her arms and pull them outward horizontally from her body, and spread her legs slightly while he was at it.

She tugged at the bonds, testing them but not panicking, every squirm and yank making her tits jiggle.

Damn. Every curve and contour of her sweet body was making him impatient to take her. Even the texture of her skin was made specifically for him to mark.

He wanted to fuck her so badly, it was putting him at a disadvantage. He much preferred hooking up with women he could dismiss if they wouldn't do what he wanted in bed. For her, he'd even settle for vanilla.

"Now you're completely at my mercy." He gave her his best wicked smile, which made her brow crease with uncertainty. "You can see how useful rope can be, even if it doesn't make anything go boom."

She held her body rigidly, waiting. Waiting for him to touch her?

Was her body arched slightly toward him, offering herself to his hands, or was that wishful thinking? He paused, watching her. The longer he waited, the more pronounced the thrust of her breasts and the desperation in her gaze.

Nervously, she licked her lips. "What are you going to do?" she whispered.

"Anything I want to." He forced himself not to ogle her breasts and marvel at the tiny way she was built. Her curve of her ass was made for his teeth, but admiring her too long would betray how much he desired her. "What are you secretly hoping I do?"

She frowned in apparent dismay. "Do I have to say? Can't you stop if I tell you I don't like something?"

Carte blanche? He'd have to see what he could coax her into trying.

"I guess we could do things that way."

She shifted and her gaze dropped. "It's just – I can't tell you what I like because I don't really know."

Part of his brain felt as though it was melting. "Fair enough. If you want me to stop doing something, you say 'red,' okay?"

"Why not just have me say no, or stop?"

"Some girls like to be able to say those words and have their partner ignore it. I'm used to the word red, but we can make it no or stop if you want."

She looked perplexed. It was completely charming. Had she been living under a rock?

"Red is okay."

"Okay." With shaking hands, he unlaced the bow at the collar of her nightie, as he'd been longing to do, and let the ropes catch her more securely, holding her so she couldn't move much of anything. Watching her expression turn to panic and disbelief was delicious.

"But aren't you going to let me go so we can..." She struggled for a word, but he saved her the trouble.

"So you can use me like a dildo and sneak back to your dorm? No. In this arrangement, I'll be the one doing the using, Jory."

Again, he waited for her to complain, or even to tell him to fuck off, but she said nothing while her gaze said everything.

Unable to wait any longer, he let his fingers drift over her skin, moving up toward her breasts. She thrust them out farther, but he moved his hand back so she only got the most teasing of touches. He persuaded her pretty pink nipples into peaks, enjoying the way the girl waited impatiently for every brush of his finger, yet jerked as though shocked when he made contact.

Curious, he walked around behind her, inspecting the body he was being given to play with. He trailed his fingers over the globes of her spectacular ass and her breath caught as she clenched her bottom.

"Has anyone every touched you here?" Valentine traced the spot between the back of her thigh and her ass, entertained by the way she struggled against his ropes, trying to get away from his hand. He followed the curve of her ass, up her panties, to her anus, and was delighted by her indignant squeal.

"No! No, why would they want to?" She shied away from his inquisitive fingers, but he only followed her. There was only so far she could go. "I know people do *that* in porn, but no one I know likes it."

"I hate to break this to you, but some of them are lying." He chuckled and swatted her ass. She squeaked then sighed. "You like being spanked, little girl?"

"What? No, I – you caught me off guard."

Leisurely, he moved back in front of her. "So, if I was to tell my ropes to let you go, and walk you over to the bed and put you over my knee, pull down your little girl panties and spank your bottom until it was stingy and pink, you wouldn't like it?"

She gasped, but the way her lips were parted suggested she wasn't as horrified as she let on. Or that if she was, it was more at her own interest than at his suggestion. "I'm a grown woman. You can't do that."

"Oh, but I can." He chuckled at her dismay. "And I probably will, at some point, if you disobey me."

"If I…?"

The poor thing was having trouble keeping up.

He cupped her breasts, each a handful, not sure why doing something so vanilla was turning him on the way it would have back when he'd been a virgin. The silkiness of her pallid skin was fascinating and addictive. He caught her nipples between his fingers, pinching and rolling them, until she was squirming and moaning for him.

"Are you going to be a good girl and do what you're told?"

Her color was high and although she averted her eyes, she nodded. Maybe he was a bastard for coaxing her into submitting by using her own body against her, but he didn't feel entirely scrupulous around this girl.

Valentine slid his finger from her bellybutton down over her panties, finding the divot between her pussy lips and pushing the thin cotton up until it formed to her. He ran his short fingernail over the bump of her clit a few times, loving how she whined for more when he moved his fingers lower to check how aroused she was. Wet right through. She was more than ready for him.

He slipped his hand into the front of her panties, aware she was holding her breath. "I'm going to touch you, and you're going to tell me if you like it."

"Please," she whimpered, the word little more than a desperate sound. Her skin was flushed and hot to the touch, her gaze glassy. He'd only ever seen this level of sexual arousal in women he'd teased for ages, but as easily as he'd drawn this reaction from her, he was suffering the same way.

Impatiently, he used two fingers to separate her pussy lips, her slick heat against his fingertips making him groan inwardly. He tapped gently at her clit and she screamed for him, fighting his ropes.

"Please what?" His voice sounded strained, even to his own ears, but his cock was throbbing for her. Why were they so damned hot for each other? It had to be the connection, and the way he could always sort of feel where she was, even if he couldn't see her.

"I don't know!" she whined. "There's something wrong with me. I'm so...so..." She sobbed. "I can't wait anymore and you keep making it worse. I need you! Now! Please make it stop."

He smirked. "Stop? You want me to stop? Are you saying red?"

"No, no. Fuck you, Valentine!" She was fighting his ropes now, hard. Every exhalation was a loud whine. "If you don't want to help me then let me go. I don't like being laughed at. Let me go and I can fix this myself."

He quirked a brow at her icy glare. "No. You're my captive, and that means I get to torture you if I want to. And I do. Besides, you know you can't actually fix it yourself. You'll go home and rub against your hand, then in a few hours you'll be back here begging for my cock again, won't you?"

She whined, defeated.

"So if you want help, you'll have to do what I say. You'll have to ask nicely. And just because you ask nicely for something doesn't mean you're going to get it. Spoiling bad girls just makes them more spoiled."

A fat tear spilled over and rolled down her cheek. Fuck. Tears were such a turn on.

"Please?"

"Please what?"

"Please make it better?"

Hell.

He paused, desperate to use her, struggling to regain control. Maybe he had her restrained, but the feelings he was having were out of control. Having her so hot she was begging for him wasn't enough. He needed more, but what?

"Say 'please use me, Sir.'" As soon as the words were out of his mouth, he felt like an ass. He'd never pushed for titles in any of his D/s relationships, so why was he doing it with a girl he barely knew?

He needed it from her though – needed to watch her pretty mouth say he was in control. Hell, he didn't feel in control at all, and it scared him.

When she hesitated, he leaned down and kissed the inside of her hip, then sucked there until there was an ugly hickey. She was fighting to get her pussy closer to his mouth by the time he was done.

"Say it or you get nothing more."

"But why?" Her face was blotchy with emotion.

"Because to get what you want, you have to give me what I want. They're just words."

"No." The word left her mouth like a breath. "They're not just words. Not to you."

Time to play hardball. With a thought, the ropes fell lifeless to her feet. He caught her elbow before she stumbled, knowing she was relying on the restraints for support even if she hadn't realized it.

Her knees buckled, but she regained her balance without much help.

"What are you doing?" she asked plaintively.

"Letting you go." He shrugged, flicking a finger at where he'd laid the spare clothing he'd lent her. "Go change and I'll drive you home. I wouldn't want you to think I was keeping you against your will."

Chapter Three

"But…" After all that Valentine was just going to let her leave? She couldn't leave! If she walked halfway down the block, the heat between her legs would set her panties on fire. She retrieved the clothing he'd lent her then turned back to him. That stupid blank mask was back on his face, in place of an actual expression.

"But what? I told you what my price was, and you refused to pay it. There's nothing more to discuss."

"So that's it? It's your way or the highway? No negotiation?"

"It was a simple request." He arched a brow and the small sign of disapproval made Jory's knees wobble.

Why did he have to be so gorgeous? And so impossible?

How many straight guys would balk at having sex with a willing girl? Maybe she wasn't a supermodel, but she knew she was pretty enough to attract attention, even if she was a little pale. Maybe she wasn't his type. Maybe he'd seen her mostly naked and changed his mind? Refusing to say that one sentence couldn't seriously be a deal breaker for him, could it?

"Change," he barked.

Startled, she dropped the clothing on the floor and pulled the nightie off before she could decide whether it was a good idea.

"Oh fuck." Valentine ran a hand through his long, unruly hair. He stared for a moment then shook his head. "I meant for you to go into the bathroom to get changed, not strip for me."

Mortified, Jory turned away and fumbled with the t-shirt and, for about two decades, she struggled to get it over her head and her arms through the holes. It smelled like laundry soap and Valentine, and if he weren't standing right there watching, she'd stuff her face into it and just breathe him in. He smelled good enough to eat.

"Put your hands on the bed," he growled in her ear.

She squeaked. When had he gotten so close? Her hands obeyed him and flattened against the bed without consulting with her brain.

Valentine lifted the back of the shirt and draped it over her lower back, then hooked his fingers into her panties and drew them slowly down her thighs. Could a guy get a girl off just by undressing her? She was starting to believe it was possible.

He left her panties around her thighs and she stared at the ornate wooden headboard, trying to ignore the way being exposed to him made her feel small and desperate.

"So you think you're going to get out of doing what I want by being a little tease?" He covered her with his body, his groin pressing against her ass. "You can't ask for everything and give nothing."

Her only reply was to shove her ass back against him. Having him almost where she needed him, except for his damned jeans, was making her crazy. Stupid, stubborn man.

"You want to give me what I'm asking for anyway, so I'm not sure what your problem is," she shot back.

Valentine got off of her but held her in position with his hand. "My problem is a little girl who doesn't know her place." He swatted her ass with the flat of his hand, and she hissed in a breath.

"You're just some sort of pervert who likes spanking women." She meant to move away. He wasn't holding her hard, and she could have moved out from under his hand without much effort. Instead, with the second smack, she felt her arms and legs start to shake, and with the third she melted into the bed. Adrenaline sang in her ears and she had to struggle not to arch into his blows.

"Fair enough, but you're a pervert who likes getting spanked." The swats were starting to hurt.

She squirmed under his restraining hand. Was it her body or her brain that was loving this? The blows were getting progressively harder, and although she tried not to make a sound, eventually she couldn't help it.

"You need to understand, Jory, that with me you'll never be in charge. You won't get to choose anything except when to say 'red.'" The accompanying slap shot a blaze of heat across her already abused bottom.

Her toes were curled against the hardwood floor, and the blanket she was lying on was crumpled in her hands. She could feel her hair, caught in his bindings, full of a frigid power that had no way to discharge. She twisted, almost near the limit of what she could bear, but he manhandled her back into place and kept spanking her. "Do you understand me? I only asked you to say one thing for me, but you expect me to take care of your greedy little cunt, and to hell with what I want in exchange, is that it?"

Who did he think he was, talking to her like that? Overwhelmed, angry, she seethed, trying to ignore her wild arousal.

The next slap made her stomp on the floor, and the one after made her involuntarily kick.

"Should you be trying to kick me?" Several hard swats rained down on the back of her thighs.

Jory's awareness had reduced itself to the haze of pain, her throbbing pussy, and a desperation to please him.

"No. I'm sorry." Tears dripped off the end of her nose. She squirmed, horny as fuck, trying remember the magic words he said would get his cock into her. Oh fuck. She was going to combat school in a week and having a guy spank her as though she was a naughty child was making her into a groveling, messy puddle? "I don't remember what you wanted me to say. Please!"

"Close, but not quite." He pulled her upright and stripped her naked.

She was hyperaware of how he'd taken charge of her body, and how she was bare but he wasn't. Cowed, she couldn't look him in the eye, her gaze following his wide chest down to the vee of muscle that led to the waistband of his low-slung jeans. Her burning ass throbbed as if it had grown its own heartbeat.

Valentine grabbed Jory by the jaw and every other thought in her head stuttered to a stop.

"Look at me."

She looked. His black eyes held her captive.

His hand slid down her waist to her hip then grasped one of her sore ass cheeks. She mewled and went up on her toes, and he chuckled.

"Are you going to be a good girl now?" He wiped the tears from her face with his hand.

She nodded.

"The price has gone up."

She pressed her thighs together, wishing her pussy would give her a moment's peace.

"I'll pay it."

"Then you'll have to ask from your knees."

She sank down, startled when he corrected her stance and posture with impersonal hands, and horrified that wetness trickled down her thigh.

The sound of a belt being pulled free from the loops of his jeans made her cringe, but she was ready to take almost anything he wanted to give her. She fantasized about him unzipping his jeans and shoving his cock in her mouth, not that she'd really know what to do, but she was sure she could figure it out. She was frightened by the overwhelming need to have him inside her. In any way he'd allow.

Valentine wrapped the belt around her neck.

Oh god, he was going to kill her. She should fight or something, but she just stared at his beautiful face.

He tightened the leather just enough so she felt it when she swallowed, then latched it in place and grinned down at her.

"I made that hole guessing how big your neck was. It was a good guess."

Before she'd even come over? He'd been sure of her eventually showing up, then, even though she hadn't realized she would. She blinked up at him, suddenly knowing how a dog felt looking up at its owner, waiting for his command. Only wanting to please him.

Where were these thoughts coming from? Lust had usurped her common sense.

"You look so pretty on a leash, Jory." He stroked her hair then crouched down and kissed her. His approval was so thick she could have buttered her toast with it, and for some reason it pleased her deeply.

"Can you ask nicely for what you need now?"

"Please fuck me, Valentine." She squirmed where she knelt, trying not to move out of position, even though she wanted to press her legs together and relieve some of the ache in her pussy.

"Close." The evil, evil bastard just chuckled. "Get on the bed. We'll see if I can help you remember."

"Please." She whimpered as he coaxed her up onto the bed. "I need you inside me. Please."

They stared at each other and for a moment she thought he was going to give in.

26

"Lie back on the bed and we'll see what you need." He guided her up and propped her head on pillows. "Has anyone ever gone down on you?"

"No. But you can't."

The idea of him doing that – of seeing her that up close – made her want to hide. To feel his mouth there, though? She shuddered. Maybe it would be worth the emotional discomfort. Her roommate always talked about how good oral was, and part of her had always felt like a dork for not knowing.

"I can't?"

"No."

He started to laugh, as though she'd surprised him. "Just no? You're not going to say red?"

There was no way she could take any more torture. "Well no, but I...probably won't like it, so you'd be doing it for nothing."

"Okay. Let me try, and if you don't like it, tell me red."

A ridiculous series of sobbing noises came out of her, embarrassing her. Didn't he understand she was already too turned on as it was?

Oh god, the glint in his eye was wicked.

Valentine kissed her, then worked his way down her body, nipping and tasting, making her even more desperate. He moved between her legs and she strained upward at him, her muscles twitching and shivering. She was going to puke, she was so horny. Was that even a thing?

He spread her legs wider and the intimacy of him being down there, looking at her up close, made her struggle for a moment, but he held her down and forced her legs to stay open.

"Shh...let me show you what this is like before you say red, okay?"

She hid her eyes.

"Don't cover your face. I want to see how what I'm doing makes you feel."

The feel of his fingers spreading her labia made her screech. She bucked. He wrapped his arms around her thighs, holding her captive. He kissed her pubic bone, then sucked on the inside of her thigh, marking her there with another big purple hickey. The small pain helped ground her, and she appreciated the fact that he was taking his time. He played around, teasing and nipping, getting close to her slit but avoiding it until she couldn't be shy anymore.

"Please, Valentine!"

"Now?" He chuckled. It was apparent he had no plan to cooperate.

"Yes, now," she moaned. Predictably, he ignored her, and when she tried burying her hands in his hair to direct him, he untangled his arms from her legs and pried her hands free. He glared at her, and slapped the back of each of her offending hands.

"You don't get to choose when. If you try that again, I'll be forced to tie you down. Understand me, little girl?" He slapped her pussy. It stung and turned her on and confused her. She howled, her ass coming up off the bed.

Fuck, that was close. Getting off on being slapped in the privates would have been mortifying.

"I think you might be a masochist," he murmured, with interest. "Maybe we'll explore that more later."

Nooo.

He pinned her again, and with painful slowness he grazed his tongue over the sensitive area around her clit. Jory's muscles froze and her eyes rolled back. Oh fuck…oh fuck…

It was the most pleasurable torture she could possibly imagine. His tongue gave her no peace, flicking and tasting, making her squirm and mewl. If he didn't stop she was going to die, but if he stopped she'd kill him.

Now and again he'd murmur directions at her, to spread her legs farther apart, to play with her nipples, and she cooperated with every demand without hesitation. Every few minutes he'd stop and hold her down while she fought and screamed in frustration, letting her arousal ebb away from an impending orgasm only to start over and bring her to the brink again.

His mouth clamped down on her clit after he'd flicked and teased it until she thought she'd go blind with pleasure. He slid something inside her – a finger? Two? It pressed upward, curled forward, found a spot that made her suffer the most bone-melting pleasure, while the suction from his mouth and slide of his tongue brought her to the very edge.

He stopped again, but this time he didn't hold her down. She screamed at him, senseless, tried to hit him, but he deflected all of her blows as though she was a small, tantruming child.

"Use your words." He grabbed her arm and yanked her over his lap, spanking her twice. "Kneel pretty, like I showed you."

His cold expression made her choke on the flood of insults that threatened to spill out. She hiccupped, and realized she'd been crying for a while. She kneeled on the mattress, every bit of skin she owned wide awake and pleading for more of his attention. The tension in her body, and the flood of power in her that had no way to discharge, made her tears come harder.

"Please use me, Sir," she begged, the words he'd wanted earlier finally popping into her head. She squirmed in place, her words making her feel slutty and desperate.

"Use you? Should I use your mouth? Your ass? Do you want me to make you come?"

She sank deeper into her kneel, spreading her knees as far apart as she could manage. "Please, Sir. Anything you want. Please choose to let me come."

The terrible man chuckled, then turned her around and shoved her face down on the bed. "Stay."

Fuck. What had she just signed up for?

A second later he was on her, spreading her legs. She whimpered into his blanket, not sure what he planned on doing to her. The tip of his cock slipped up and down against her pussy, then he pressed slowly inside her, having to coax his way in despite her wetness. He felt like he was a million sizes too big. Pinning her down with his body, he started to move inside her.

He groaned in her ear.

"You're too big," she complained, the statement sounding sulky even to her own ears.

"I know. Shh. I'll be careful." He fucked her slowly, and her body gradually figured out where to put all of him. He filled every bit of her pussy, making her gasp and moan with each cautious thrust. He cupped the back of her head in one hand, pinned her legs down with his own, and slid a hand beneath her to toy with her clit.

She was trapped, helpless, full, sore – her clit sensitive and aching. He pumped into her, slow, animalistic, rough, his belt half choking her. She squirmed, trying to get away from him and the orgasm that was building again, even though there was no chance of escape. But her orgasm stalled, and she started to scream and fight.

He swore. "What the fuck, Jory? What's wrong?"

"I don't know. It's just frustrating me, and I don't know why." She whimpered. "I can't come."

He pulled out. She rolled over and watched him adjust the condom.

"You don't need that, Sir."

"The pill doesn't protect you from everything, little girl."

"My power won't let you make me sick or get me pregnant."

Valentine stared at her a moment, then stripped the condom off and pinned her face down again. "Fine. Is this what you want?"

He rammed back into her, the viciousness of it stealing her breath. God, yes. This was what her body had been screaming for.

Inside her, she could feel their power touch, twine. Tighten. Fuse.

He cried out, his movements violent and erratic.

A high-pitched keening rippled from her. Valentine yanked the rope from the ends of her hair, setting it free. Her power awoke, gathered, rose. Threatened.

He buried his hand in her hair and growled in her ear. "You tell your power whose bitch you are, Jory." He fucked her into the mattress.

Beneath him, she screamed, her orgasm building, roaring, wild and uncontrolled. Pleasure burst, spilled over. She was lost, a receptacle for his lust, only able to take what he wanted to give her. Her orgasm crested, then built again, using and exhausting her whole body. A string of swears was grunted into her ear, setting off an aftershock that made her shudder. He came inside her, and she was limp, weeping, her body accepting the mastery of his, glorying in his satisfaction.

Fuck.

She was well and truly fucked.

Her mind hummed, so deeply sated she felt drunk with it. The terrible need for him had eased, as though they'd finally done what had been expected of them.

This was crazy. Maybe this one time would be enough and now they could go their separate ways.

But did she really want to give up sex this intense?

"Shit." He rolled off of her then pulled her into his arms. "Are you okay, snowangel?"

"Tired." She was pretty sure her limbs were filled with rocks. Muscular arms tightened around her and Valentine rested his lips gently against her temple. It was an intimate feeling that warmed her inside, as though what they'd done had meant more to him than a quick fuck. But why did she care? Maybe that was just the euphoria talking. "Valentine?"

His own eyelids, which had been drifting closed, flickered back open. "Yeah, baby?"

"I'm into kink."

Valentine nipped her ear, and wound the end of the belt around his hand, pulling her closer. He growled. Heat flashed through her, and she felt his cock stiffening against her thigh.

"That's good, because in a minute I'll need to use you again."

*

A million pieces of her consciousness dipped and wove, swooped. She distracted, blinded, froze. Maybe it wasn't as effective as a flying attack, but not many Atypicals could fly, let alone fly and attack. The other team had broken through their defenses, and she worried at them from behind, trying to give her team leader time to adjust her plan. Summer probably just needed a second to breathe.

Davin flung balls of heat into the heart of her storm, but he was too slow to force her back. Sasha was the linchpin holding the other team together this session. Take her out and they'd beat them in the ensuing chaos. She swept behind Summer, and raised her hand to launch a bolt of ice at Sasha's back.

Jory's hair crackled with the gathering power.

She felt his hands in her hair, braiding it, taming it, putting her at his mercy. He kissed the back of her neck...

"Jory!"

The vision vanished. She blinked, looking around at her current team and realizing it had happened again. A ball of fire hung in front of her eyes, where a sergeant had suspended it.

That would have been...unfortunate.

"Jory, report to medical." Sergeant Eisen was watching her with a peculiar expression.

"I'm sorry. I'm just tired." Her cheeks burned, even though Davin had let his fireball fizzle out. They were all staring.

If this had been actual combat she would have been a liability. Letting her attention wander at the wrong time could cost somebody their life. Pretty soon training would be over, and what had seemed like fun and games for the past few years would be dangerous business. Not that training wasn't dangerous.

But the thoughts that had distracted her? So humiliating.

Sergeant Eisen smiled in what she probably thought was a supportive way, but it just made her look more dangerous. "Go, Jory. Until you get this dealt with, you're a hazard in here."

She nodded, too mortified to stay, anyway.

How was the sergeant supposed to get a good idea of what team she fit in with if she kept spacing out every five minutes? She'd never get chosen for any of the stronger teams if she didn't smarten up.

The hall was quiet, other than the echo of her booted footsteps. The spandex suit itched, as if her every tiny body hair had been forced in the wrong direction when she'd struggled into it. Sure, spandex was flexible and didn't get in the way when they fought. But seriously. As soon as she was done combat school, she'd burn...or melt every spandex uniform she owned.

Just because a girl fought evil didn't mean she had to dress like an escapee from a troupe of '80s jazz dancers, did it?

The few active heroes who'd come to speak to their class had all been wearing a variant of their school uniforms. However, if a girl was going to risk her life to save humanity, she deserved more than one fashion option. Thankfully, the underwear-over-the-tights style of uniform seemed completely passé, and absolutely no one wore a cape.

If Valentine were here, he'd mock her. Then he'd probably drag her off into an empty classroom and do horrible, horrible things to her. Things that made her scream with pleasure, but also shamed her, especially later, when she remembered every vivid detail.

No self-respecting hero-to-be should crawl after a man, begging to suck his cock. At one point he'd made her to do it to get what she needed. She'd been mortified, but too desperate to refuse. A combination of humiliation and desire swept over her when she thought about the things he'd inspired her to do. As much as she hated the effect he had on her, and tried to forget about him, she couldn't get thoughts of him out of her head.

Why couldn't she have an insane attraction to a nice guy, like Aaron in her class? He'd just have sex with her respectfully, like a regular person. No ropes. No commands that made her insides shiver.

The medical unit was a sedate shade of blue, and although it hummed with activity, the efficiency and dull sounds were soothing, especially after the cacophony of the training room. A miserable-looking girl with bad burns on her hand was being treated by someone in a white coat, and was healing faster than any Typical would have believed. Then again, fighting was what the school was about. If they couldn't heal students quickly, no one would ever get enough training to graduate.

Would someone in medical be able to block her intrusive thoughts? But even if it was a possibility, how could she admit she was sexually preoccupied with a pervert?

A tall African American woman, with the most beautiful face Jory had ever seen, stopped in front of her. No lab coat, but she'd made a beeline over. Did she work here?

"Good morning, Jory. Are you hurt?"

"Uh…the sergeant sent me to…talk to someone, I guess?"

The woman smiled kindly, and the effect smiling had on her face was even more stunning. "Okay, that would be me. I'm Dr Gardner. I'm an Atypical psychiatrist."

The term "Atypical psychiatrist" made Jory want to laugh, but she managed to hold it in. What did she do, cheer people up by prescribing them Skittles? That would be pretty atypical for a psychiatrist.

Dr Gardner led her into a room that was comfortable but didn't have a couch for her to lie on, or a big wooden desk. Instead, it had two couches and a coffee table. The lack of formality put Jory at ease, which was probably the point of the design.

"Have a seat."

Jory hesitated. Did where she chose to sit say something about her personality? Would Dr Gardner know all of her secrets from one wrong move? The doctor sat first, and Jory uneasily chose a spot on the other couch.

"So the sergeant who was working with you this morning sent you to see me?"

"Yeah. I keep getting distracted during combat training. During class time too."

The woman nodded as though this was reasonable enough. "Just to establish a baseline, do you have a history of ADD or ADHD? I don't recall."

Jory shrugged. "I've never been tested, but I don't think it's that."

"Ah." The doctor leaned forward slightly, her body language interested and non-judgmental. How did a person even do that with posture? And what was her power? Could she see Jory's thoughts or make people instinctively trust her? She was definitely Atypical. Jory could feel power coming at her in big, comfy waves, like the swells of a duvet on a warm bed.

Jory relaxed in spite of herself, hoping she wouldn't accidentally tell her too much. Was this a test to see if she could hold up under soft forms of interrogation?

"I can feel how suspicious this is making you. What you say to me in this room is confidential. The only thing I disclose when I write in your chart is whether or not I feel you're able to continue training at this time. The details are no one else's business." She smiled kindly. "We understand that this can be a difficult time. For you there's extra stress because you're here training on breaks, but still trying to keep up with your college courses. Plus, identity and relationship issues are almost expected around this time in your life. No subject is off limits here."

This was ridiculous. She was supposed to be in training to be a hero, not talking to a therapist about her guy problems. Weren't there a million other things she should be more concerned about right now? Being obsessed with a man seemed about as mature as being obsessed with a rock band or a brand of shoes. Who ever heard of a hero getting distracted from fighting evil because they wanted to be tied up and treated like a sex toy?

The visual made her shift in her seat.

"Okay." There was no point in lying to the woman. Lying to stay in a school that taught students to fight evil seemed wrong somehow.

"So, you already seem to know what's been distracting you. It's your business whether you want to share that with me or not, but often talking about things does help." Dr Gardner smiled at her sympathetically. "Sometimes it's hard to open up and trust people, but in this situation if you don't deal with the underlying issue, people around you might end up getting hurt."

Jory swallowed and let her gaze sweep the room. Looking directly at Dr Gardner would just make admitting what was happening ten times worse. Her gaze fell on a silver statue in a cabinet otherwise filled with books of the official leather-bound persuasion. The statue vaguely resembled a woman, and Jory wondered whether it held any significance, or if it was just a decoration.

"I don't even know where to start. It all seems kind of ridiculous. I'm a grown woman in university. I'm training to be a hero, but I'm in your office because of a guy." She shook her head and pressed her lips together, staring at the abstract statue and trying not to cry. Could this be any more humiliating? She felt like a fifteen-year-old in the guidance office talking to the counselor about her crush.

Dr Gardner had the decency not to look amused. Instead, she nodded encouragement. "Relationships can be complicated, no matter how old you are. Most people I see need to talk about their relationships. Our interactions and difficulties with other people are basic part of life." She gave an apologetic half shrug as though the complexity of relationships was partially her fault. "So what is it about this guy that you're finding so distracting?"

"First of all, I don't even know how to classify him. He's not my boyfriend, we're not really seeing each other per se, we just…" Jory grimaced and put a hand over her eyes for a second. "I don't know. There's something weird going on between us, and I'm getting the impression that he doesn't understand it either. It's not like normal attraction. Who hasn't seen someone across a crowded room and thought they were attractive? But walking away isn't usually an issue and who cares if you never see them again."

Dr Gardner nodded but didn't offer any words of interruption. Jory plowed on. She had to get this out, but also wasn't ready to tell Dr Gardner everything. There were many, many things that had happened between her and Valentine she didn't plan on telling anyone. Ever. Like the way his ropes snaked up and around her, holding her still so that he could do whatever he wanted…and how much she loved it. How she'd allowed him to dominate her and treat her so callously. The worst part had been leaving the next morning and secretly hoping he'd keep her there whether she liked it or not.

"So you're attracted to this guy can't stop thinking about him? It's not technically a relationship – so are you friends? You've talked to him?"

Oh jeez. "I don't know what we are to one another, but yes, we know each other. I'm not some kind of crazy stalker, if that's what you're wondering. If anything, I think he's been following me."

A small twitch of the doctor's eyebrow led Jory to believe that the woman thought she was paranoid.

"Actually, I know he has, because he told me so. It's kind of a mutual stalking. But neither of us seems to be able to help it. We just suddenly find ourselves together and there's this insane attraction. No matter how much we try to stop ourselves from having sex, we can't stop." Oh God, she'd said it out loud. She hadn't meant to actually use those words with Dr Gardner. Now what was she going to think of her? "It's uncontrollable…like we've been drugged."

Dr Gardner's eyebrows went up, which probably wasn't an expression she'd authorized her face to make. "That is peculiar. And he honestly seems to feel the same way?"

"Yes, I think so. We only spent one night together, but after I left his place, I had to barricade myself in my dorm room so that I didn't go back out looking for him again. Even though I was sore for days. I can't think about anything other than…what I need from him." *What the hell, Jory, can't you keep any of your thoughts personal today?*

"And it's not just regular lust? Is it every guy, or just him?"

"Just him, thank god. One is bad enough."

"Hmmm." Dr Gardner rose from the couch and went to her fancy bookcase, opened one of its glass doors, and pulled out a book that didn't match the others.

"What is that?"

"It's the *Compendium of Atypical Conditions and Diseases*." Dr Gardner smiled kindly. "Sorry. I'm a doctor but we can't remember everything. What you're describing sounds like something I've heard before, but I've never seen it in my practice."

"It's a disease?" Her heart lodged in her throat. Oh great, when she had pictured her life someday being in danger, it hadn't been from a sexual attraction to another Atypical. She'd thought maybe in battle, or preferably in her sleep when she was an old woman, but not this.

"A condition. Nothing dangerous, if I remember correctly, but I'll have to do some reading up on this to make sure. There must be something that we can do to help you with symptoms. Have you been in a lot of discomfort?"

That was putting it mildly. "It makes it really hard to sleep. And even when I do fall asleep I have crazy dreams and wake up...uncomfortable."

Talk about over sharing, but luckily, when Jory looked at the doctor, she was busy leafing through the compendium.

Dr Gardner pursed her lips and shook her head. "I wish I remembered what it was called, but I think I'm going to have to spend some time with this book before I find the right condition. If it's what I'm thinking, it's very rare. I haven't heard anything about it since medical school, and that was a long time ago."

The condition's rarity might have been an interesting fact to the doctor, but it didn't make Jory feel any better.

After a few minutes the doctor closed the book and laid it aside. "There's no point in me making you sit here while I read. I'll keep looking after our session is done and then call you back here when I have more information to give you. Don't worry, though, from what I remember it's something that goes away in time."

"It goes away?"

"From what I remember, but like I said, I have to find the entry for it before I can be sure it's nothing to worry about. For now, deal with the symptoms and try to go about your daily life."

"Do you think there's some sort of treatment available until this goes away? The symptoms are horrible. There'd be nothing more embarrassing than trying to explain it to people, especially the ones on my team."

"It's like any other medical condition. It's not your fault. If anybody gives you a hard time about it, you send them to me. What you have going on here is no one's business but your own, and that of the medical professionals in the facility. Even your sergeants don't need to know if you don't want them to."

That was a relief. Jory had tried to think of how she would tell her sergeant that she couldn't concentrate because she was too horny, but in every scenario when she told her, she immediately died of embarrassment. It was worse than having to tell him she couldn't go out crime fighting because she had her period. There should be a tampon commercial for that.

However, telling people that the reason why she was distracted was 'personal,' wasn't much better. It was the type of thing that would keep her from getting onto one of the good teams.

Shit. She couldn't let whatever this was screw that up for her.

Since she'd been a little girl, she'd wanted to be on one of the high-profile teams, fighting criminals and saving people. At this rate, she was going to end up on one of the beta teams, saving kittens from trees and helping little old ladies cross the street. On a beta team, heroes were more or less one step up from glorified Boy Scouts. Not to disparage Boy Scouts, but with the amount of power she had, she really hoped to be able to do more good than a ten-year-old with a few merit badges.

"Okay. I'll try to think of an excuse that doesn't make me look like a slacker."

"Other than your sexual preoccupation with him, which seems to be causing you distress, is there something else about your interactions with him that are bothering you? You seem uneasy about something."

Uneasy? If the woman had any idea what kinds of perverted things he'd made her do. Made her like. She prayed those perversions had made her hot because of her unreasonable attraction to him. Even the way he walked set her pants on fire. Somehow the situation seemed worse because of the kink. If she'd been the one in charge when they were together, she might have been able to preserve her self-respect.

That wasn't how he rolled. She didn't think it was how she rolled, either.

Unbidden, she remembered his hands buried in her hair as she knelt at his feet, worshipping his cock with her mouth. She was ashamed and confused about the fact that it had gotten her off – like his come was magic orgasm juice.

And it was weird, but their powers seemed to be just as obsessed with each other as their bodies. Every time they had sex, their powers tangled together and it was hard to pull them apart again. Like being Atypically dog-locked.

It was ridiculous. She'd called him Sir, and let him tame her hair. Her hair – and the rest of her – were his bitch. No one would ever respect her again if they found out. Especially if they found out how much she wanted more.

She never wanted to see him again, but sometimes when she let her mind wander, she plotted ways to sneak back and beg him for another orgasm. She could see his smirking face in her mind's eye.

Valentine was a total asshole who spanked her, gave her multiple orgasms and then wanted to cuddle. What the hell was a girl supposed to do with that?

"Jory?" Dr Gardner's voice dragged her mind out of Valentine's bed and back to the office.

"Um… Nothing I feel like discussing right now. I have to sort things out before I share anything else. With anyone." Like the fact that he'd made her a list of words, terms, ideas, and web pages to look through. And how when she'd done the research he'd suggested, some of the pictures had made her desperate for him all over again. There were so many things she'd never even heard of, and now there were so many things she wanted to try.

Things that made her insides wilt with shame but also made her panties scandalously wet.

Chapter Four

The echo of his footsteps as he moved through one of the Spartan marble hallways of his parents' home didn't supply Valentine with the comfort of familiarity.

Growing up, the house hadn't been filled with laughter and the sound of children playing. Instead, he and his brother had been expected to comport themselves like young gentlemen. Rambunctious play had been limited to the grounds, under the watchful eye of whichever nanny hadn't abandoned them yet.

That wasn't to say that Valentine had some sort of horrible childhood where his parents had neglected them. Their parents had been affectionate and generous with their time. There had simply been an expectation that the children would behave like small adults.

The house, though, had never felt like a home. It was too big for a child to feel safe in. If anything, it felt more like an institution or museum.

Instead of going to look for family members as soon as he arrived, Valentine sought out the comfort of his own rooms. The suite he'd been given as soon as he was old enough to be out of the nursery was as big as his current apartment. When he had gone away to school, his things had been left untouched, awaiting his return. He hadn't even bothered to bring a bag from his apartment, since everything he could possibly need was still here.

Except Jory.

He closed the door to his suite behind him, turned on the flat screen, powered up his laptop, paced the floor, decided to take a shower. Abruptly, he changed his mind, and eventually settled for throwing himself on his bed the way he had during his angsty teenage years. He dragged a pillow over his face and groaned into it.

The worst of his need for Jory had passed several days before, but that didn't mean his obsession with her had abated. Instead of being focused on how she felt beneath him and how she screamed for him, for days he'd been obsessing about snowflakes melting on her eyelashes, about her docile expression after the storm had passed from them, and how he'd held her for hours, kissing her and watching her watch him.

When he came out from under the pillow, he felt like a petulant child who'd lost his favorite toy. Making the choice to bring her back to her dorm had been one of the hardest things he'd ever done. Some of the urges that had gone through his mind had been disturbing.

Not only did he know he could have kept her against her will, he doubted it would have been difficult to convince her to stay and ignore her other obligations. He'd tried to play it cool, but when it came to Jory, someone had poured gasoline on his common sense and put a match to it.

Control. He needed to relearn it when it came to her.

When he'd driven her back to her dorm, she'd told him she was flying home for Christmas the next day. He hadn't been thinking clearly. He'd been thinking about taking her again, right there on the hood of his car, or maybe in the stairwell to her room. She hadn't offered him her number, but he hadn't asked, either.

Sometimes playing it cool was a dumbass move.

The look she'd given him had been expectant, but he'd just smiled and kissed her goodbye when she refused to let him walk her up, so he got in his damn car and drove off with no way to contact her until she came back to school after the holiday.

What happened if the crazed desire for her returned before the month was out? What if she found herself a boyfriend while she was away and wanted nothing else to do with him? The latter idea gnawed at him. Maybe she could have this kind of bond with someone else, but the idea of her having her needs met elsewhere made him jealous, and sparked a rage he didn't have any right to.

Their time together had fed his obsession rather than sating it.

For all he knew, to her it was just some fun in bed. Something to be remembered as a good time, but not necessarily repeated.

But the sight of his belt around her neck had made him a desperate man. She needed to wear his collar, before some other man claimed her. He wanted to own her in a way he'd never wanted anything else in his life. As a dominant, in the past, he'd never been interested in any of the new bits of fluff that he came across at clubs. He had only played with experienced submissives and masochists who wouldn't be shocked by his proclivities.

With Jory it was different. Every reaction he won from her was open and honest. No wondering if she was suppressing or exaggerating. No studied porno expressions or false submission. What he saw in her face and her posture was a mirror of what was going on behind her silvery-blue eyes.

And so he was miserable.

After about an hour, there was a knock at his door.

His mother, Emma's, cultured voice came through the door. "Valentine? How long have you been home? Everyone's here. Why didn't you come down?" A twinge of guilt hit him. It wasn't his family's fault that Jory had him turned inside out. He just wasn't sure he was ready to talk to people about anything calm or reasonable.

"Yeah, sorry, Mom. I passed out for a bit after the drive. I'll be down in a sec."

"Okay. It'll be dinnertime in a half hour. I'll let you be until then, but after that you can expect me to follow you around the house talking your ear off for a few hours." A short pause followed as though she considered her next words carefully. "You haven't been calling very often, and I'm always worried about bothering you. I feel like I haven't spoken to you since September."

Valentine winced. Phone calls with his mother were always a little awkward. They hadn't had the best relationship for the past few years, but that had more to do with his behavior toward her during high school than it had with anything she'd done wrong. He hadn't realized that until he'd hit his twenties. He'd never figured out how to make things less uncomfortable between them.

"I know," he said gloomily. "I suck."

"I didn't mean for that to sound like a guilt trip." She sounded upset with herself. "Just ignore me. I'm being clingy. I'll see you downstairs." She made kissing noises at him through the door. Belatedly, he realized he was an ass for not at least opening it to speak to her, but she was already gone by the time he got there.

He wondered for maybe the millionth time in his life whether their relationship would be less strained if either he'd been born Typical or she'd been born Atypical. Even then, there was no guarantee that was their only barrier to communication. Maybe the problem was that he was the oldest and his father's favorite, or maybe it was because he'd actively avoided being controlled by other people even as a child. It was no secret he was a difficult person to like.

Being an asshole came naturally to him, but sometimes it gave him an attack of conscience.

Maybe it was a pipe dream, but for once it would've been nice if they'd ordered pizza and sat around in the living room like a regular family. Instead, unless his parents were out, dinner was a formal affair every night and involved dressing appropriately. He hadn't known other families didn't dress for dinner until he'd stayed over at Dane's the first time, when he was eight.

Despite the dress code, there was something to be said for having meals prepared by someone else, and not eating macaroni and cheese out of a pot. University had been a reality check. Refusing to have a live-in servant had been a good idea, even though his mother had been horrified at the idea of him doing things like cooking and laundry. It had been his first experience with being relatively normal, and although he loved it, sometimes being taken care of was pleasant.

When Valentine went downstairs, his family was already at the table. Pascal, his younger brother, looked just as laid back and well adjusted as always. The family had always thought Pascal would eventually go through a rebellious stage, but the fact that he just hit twenty gave Valentine the impression it was never going to happen. Pascal was Atypical enough to make him interesting, but not Atypical enough to make him useful on a team. A Mundane Atypical. He didn't even have the temperament to be a mad scientist. A slightly eccentric scientist was the best they could hope for. There were Atypicals with completely useless powers, though, so at least Pascal wasn't, say, someone who could turn bread into flour.

"Val, you look like shit." Pascal laughed then grimaced. "You look like you haven't slept in days."

Great now that he'd drawn attention to it, their mother would worry.

"I've been studying a lot. My thesis isn't going to write itself. Some of us didn't take easy subjects like math and chemistry." He chuckled and punched his brother's shoulder, then went around the other side of the table and took his customary chair. "At least with chemistry there are right and wrong answers. With sociology, sometimes the right answer is whatever your professor believes. It's easier to memorize a formula."

Their father smiled indulgently. "It's nice to know my money is getting put to good use."

"You should try to get more sleep, Val," his mother interjected. "Not sleeping isn't healthy."

"I know. I'll try." He sipped at his wine, wishing it was something stronger. Maybe something that could make him forget about how Jory's voice went high and desperate when she begged to come.

Be sane. Be social.

"I figure after this I'll do my doctorate. Then I'll start over in another discipline, so that I can be a perpetual student and I'll never have to get a job." He smiled back at his father, who grimaced.

Dietrich Ott still didn't look a day over thirty-five. If they were out somewhere together, Valentine was often asked if his father was his older brother. Dietrich joked that he was so busy he didn't have time to age. For all Valentine knew, though, one of his father's powers was slowing down his aging process. Maybe he'd have the same luck.

Pascal had taken after their father in intelligence, but his mild manner and amiable personality kept him from being Dietrich's favorite. For some strange reason, the man valued Valentine's brashness and challenging demeanor over Pascal's polite intellect. That was okay, because everyone knew that Pascal was Emma's favorite. If they'd ever had a third child, they would have spent a fortune on the kid's therapy.

"Well, Valentine, that's something we need to discuss while you're here."

Emma cleared her throat. "Dietrich, I thought we decided it would be better if we didn't have this conversation the first night that we had them both back. Can't we just enjoy this time together as a family without making it all about business?" His mother looked crestfallen. "Dinner hasn't even been served yet."

"Why avoid a subject when you can address it head on? If we tiptoe around this, I won't have time to talk to Valentine about the details. I assume that once his team finds out he's home, we won't see him again until he's headed back to the university." Dietrich smiled as though that was exactly the way things should be. He'd always been one to encourage Valentine's friendships with the children of his cohorts, and it just so happened that their powers worked well together. It was amazing how a group could bond when they'd hung out since they were children. Atypicals didn't need combat school when they had connections.

"What's up?" Valentine smiled apologetically at his mother then turned his attention to his father.

"You know we're at the point where we're turning away contracts on a regular basis. There's too much work for my group, and the Bureau has been interfering more and more with mercenary transactions that used to get disregarded."

The Bureau of Atypical Affairs seemed to have a bee in its bonnet about how much money mercenaries made, more than anything. Once in a while they started throwing their weight around, trying to get groups outside of their control to obey their laws, but mercenaries had their own rules that made a hell of a lot more sense – probably because they governed themselves. It was hard following nonsensical rules that Mundane Atypical bureaucrats made up just because they liked feeling important.

"Your group is mature and experienced enough now to take on some of the lower-risk contracts. The idea would be to train you to take over the more complicated jobs eventually, after we start getting too old." His father smiled grimly. "We'd be grooming our children to take over the family business, so to speak."

Valentine suppressed a groan. He'd always known this was the plan, but he'd signed up for his master's degree hoping to avoid it a while longer. As much as he enjoyed working with his team, he wasn't sure he wanted to dedicate his whole life to mercenary work. Sure, it was lucrative, but it didn't feel like his calling. Maybe he was reluctant simply because he knew it was what his father wanted. He'd never had a chance to make his own decisions.

He caught sight of his mother's anxious face. It wasn't time for arguments now. He'd think about it and get back to his father in private. "I'll talk to the others. This isn't a solo decision."

Dietrich nodded, then unfolded his napkin and laid it across his lap. The signal given, food started to pour out of the kitchen, the servers silent, swift and efficient.

Nothing in this house or this family happened without his father's approval.

*

Dane, Jurgen, and Xana splashed around the indoor pool at Xana's parent's house, just like they had as children. Being apart while they attended post-secondary was hard on all of them, but Valentine felt it had helped them grow as people, so they were less dependent on each other.

"And what's wrong with Mr Ott this evening?" Xana asked with excessive decorum, like a character from a British historical film.

Valentine grunted and tossed back the rest of his vodka.

"I tried earlier, Xan." Dane laughed. "If you can get him to talk, I'll give you a gold star."

Jurgen shook his head in mock dismay. "He's having man pain. Leave him alone."

"Man pain?" Xana grinned. "Is that what you get when Dane doesn't use lube?"

Both Dane and Jurgen glanced at the door then glared at her. Their relationship was a secret between the four of them, and they were still afraid of being discovered, even though they'd been committed to each other for years. Poor bastards. This wasn't medieval times. They shouldn't have to hide.

Xana pulled herself out of the pool, the water giving a sheen to her dark skin. She sauntered over to Valentine, the bikini she was wearing showing off her lovely body.

"Eyes in your head, rope geek."

Valentine sighed. He'd bottomed for her when they'd dated for a while, years ago, but two dominants in a relationship with no real submissive always had a hard time working out the kinks in their dynamic. They'd both been baby Doms at that point, and the relationship had been short lived, but it had been experimental and fun. She'd discarded him after a few months, but neither of them had been emotionally invested in a romance. Things between Dane and Jurgen, though, were serious.

"So what's the problem?" She arched a brow. "Either spill it or cheer the fuck up. I didn't invite you over so I could play therapist."

"But you've always been my therapist. You suck at it, but there's comfort in familiarity."

She sat down beside him, her dreads bouncing and shifting like they had a life of their own. What was it with him hooking up with Atypicals with sexy hair?

"That was when we were teenagers, doorknob. Now, spill it. Only a hot piece of ass could put that sorry look on your face."

Valentine shook his head at her and leaned back, the vodka making him warm and relaxed. "It's not what you think."

She cocked a brow. "You have a hard-on for some new girl. How can it not be what I think? Just don't tell me she's Typical."

"No, no. Nothing you'd disapprove of that much. Actually, I think you'd like her."

"Mmm…submissive?" She curled up beside him on the wicker couch.

He nodded. "And sweet, and new, and oh-so curious."

Xana groaned. "You poor bastard. Have you been sleeping at all?"

"Wait. You haven't heard the worst of it."

Dane and Jurgen got out and toweled off, then wandered over to join them.

"It's about time you found someone," Dane said, his approval thick. He was the most practical, level-headed man on the planet, yet still believed in true love. Weirdo.

"Oh fuck, Dane. Ever since you realized the love of your life was right under your nose, you've been trying to get Val and me to hunt for partners. Like we need to hurry the fuck up." Xana shook her head. "Not everyone needs that."

"So, she's hot. What else?" Jurgen cut in, grinning.

"I –" He stalled, not knowing how to explain it and make it understandable. Even in his head it sounded crazy.

"Shit. She has him tongue-tied. I don't think I've ever seen this happen before." Dane chuckled then punched him in the shoulder. "Spill it. You want the gory details of everyone else's love life, so don't expect pity from anyone in this room."

"I don't even know where to start." Valentine ran a hand through his hair. "It's not starting out well. I haven't exactly been behaving like a…gentleman."

Xana rubbed her hands together gleefully. "It's about fucking time."

Valentine sighed. Xana couldn't understand why the others were so careful about conventions when they stood in the way of things they wanted.

"Seriously, Xan? If it was up to you, she would already be tied up in my apartment, just waiting to be shared."

"Don't be ridiculous. If she was tied up in your apartment, why the hell would you be here?" Her smile might have been described as nefarious.

"Just start at the beginning," Jurgen suggested. "And quit dicking around. So you met an Atypical girl. Big deal, we've all had our share."

The more he stalled, the more their minds were jumping to conclusions. "No. You don't understand. Yes, she's fucking perfect, but it's so much worse. Let's put it this way – the first time I saw her on campus, I was in the middle of doing something important. She walked past, and I got…kind of pulled along in her wake. Before I knew what I was doing, I was a goddamn stalker. For days, I followed her all over the place, trying to stay where she wouldn't notice me, tracking her habits and her patterns."

"It sounds like you had her marked as merchandise for retrieval, rather than as a potential girlfriend, or toy." Dane arched a brow at him.

"And that was just the beginning."

"So, are you trying to tell us that it was love at first sight, or some crap like that?" Xana eyed him skeptically.

That would have been easier to deal with.

"No, nothing that romantic." Maybe he shouldn't bother talking about her when he might never see her again, but he had a need to tell someone. "It's more like uncontrollable lust at first sight. There was no getting enough of each other while we were together." Ugh. He was explaining it all wrong. "But it's more than that. I don't know if there's something wrong with me – with us. It's too much. Too intense. She's a sweet vanilla thing, but I've gotten more submission from her than any other woman I've been with." He thought of the way she looked at him. "And I like her. Too much, considering we just met."

Dane whistled. "No wonder you look like shit."

"So if things between you are that intense, how did you end up parting ways?" Jurgen asked, combing his fingers through Dane's long blond hair.

Valentine squeezed the bridge of his nose between his thumb and forefinger, still wondering that himself. "It was for the best. Being together just seems to make the obsession stronger. We'll have to spend time apart on and off until we get this figured out. It'll work out better for both of us that way in the long run."

"In the long run?" Xana looked as though she wasn't sure whether to be stunned or laugh. "You turning into Dane now? You screw this girl a few times, and now she's the future mother of your children?"

In the long run? Where had that come from? Sure, he'd thought about keeping her around for a while so he could figure out what made her so irresistible to him, but he had the feeling if he fucked things up he would live to regret it.

Jurgen got to his feet and held his hands out in front of him. "Wait, wait. I think I remember hearing something about this before." He frowned, his eyes rolling upward as though it would help him access a filing cabinet in his brain. "Can't remember exactly where I heard about it, or I would know how to look it up. Maybe it was in abnormal Atypical psychology, or maybe it was in high school health class." He chuckled. "Yeah, that wasn't at all helpful, was it?"

"Not exactly." Dane teased. "Good thing you're hot."

"Did you try looking it up online, to see if how you're feeling is a thing?" Xana asked.

"No, I turned into a complete fucking idiot this semester. Thanks for the tip." Valentine dumped a glass of ice water on Xana, who jumped on him and made sure to drip thoroughly on his dry clothes.

"I'm glad this semester hasn't done anything to change your naturally sweet nature," Xana chuckled. "You're still a fucking douchebag."

"Get off me, woman. Don't you have a sub to terrorize?"

"Actually, I'm between subs at the moment, but I'm starting to get the impression I'd like to borrow yours." She climbed off him and winked.

Valentine knew she was teasing, probably, but even so, an annoying wave of jealousy flowed through him. "I don't think I'll be sharing this one, so don't count on it."

Dane laughed in disbelief. "You won't even share her with *us*? Not even once?" They were all watching him, incredulous. Normally, they shared everything if one of the others was interested, up to and including their sex partners.

"I – We'll see," he mumbled. Right now, if anyone else laid a hand on Jory, he'd spontaneously combust. Just the thought made him want to mark her as his somehow. "Enough. Life isn't all about sex."

Time to talk business.

They'd been dreaming of the day when they could finally start to work together and get paid for it, but now that the time had possibly come, Valentine wasn't feeling ready for it. It was like giving up every other dream he'd had as a kid. They could have been heroes, if they wanted, or joined the military – there were multiple options for groups like them. The best money was in mercenary work, but was money really supposed to be the biggest motivating factor in his life?

It seemed odd that he would be given his powers just to make him as wealthy as his father. Was he squandering his power? He'd tried talking to the others about it before, but only Dane had even understood him. Not that Dane had the same feelings on the subject. Maybe because they'd always been rich it made it hard for them to think altruistically. For that matter, they'd been raised to think of heroes disdainfully, considering they usually weren't financially compensated anywhere near enough for the work they did.

Only suckers worked for free.

But still, being a popular enough hero team to win the adulation of Typicals held some attraction.

"Let me guess." Dane grinned. "Your father thinks it's time we follow in their footsteps."

"It's about fucking time," Jurgen grumbled. "He was the last hold-out in their whole group."

Xana nodded. "My dad was ready for me to start working three years ago. Then again, I've always been the mature one in the group." She smirked and Val shook his head. Just once he'd like to spank her, but even if he managed it, she'd kill him in his sleep.

"So I take it I'm still the only one who isn't sure, then?" That sucked. That meant he'd have to try to get school done around their merc schedule. As if he needed more stress. And what about the Jory issue? He could barely concentrate on assigned readings at this point. His mind kept drifting to what he'd done to her when they were together, and what he still wanted to do to her.

"We'll try it, and after we've done a few contracts, we'll reassess." Dane shrugged. "Saying yes now doesn't have to be a lifetime commitment."

Then the others were talking excitedly about shopping for equipment, and new fighting leathers. They scheduled practice times and chose locations.

Valentine remained silent. No one seemed to notice.

Chapter Five

Atypical Aphrodisia.

At least it had a name, although knowing it didn't make Jory feel any better. Dr Gardner had provided her with an article to read, and some counseling. Couples who developed Aphrodisia could be expected to stay sexually infatuated with one another anywhere between a few days to several years. Jory hoped theirs was one of the cases where she and Valentine fucked like mad rabbits for one night then got over it. She couldn't let herself wonder what would happen if it was a long-term case. Or worse.

Her plane was crowded, and the man sitting next to her was a creeper who kept reading over her shoulder. Why couldn't they put people a little farther apart? The guy had a bony elbow and kept hogging the armrest. She considered opening some erotica on her Kindle, just to give him something to gawk at, but when it came down to it she was too shy to do anything so bold.

She'd have to get over being shy if she was going to live up to her letter.

Unable to resist, she took the envelope out of her jacket pocket and unfolded the paper within, which was already getting dog eared from the multiple times she'd read it.

An acceptance letter. "Dear Miss Savage, you've been chosen."

Even after her craptastic performance during holiday break, a team had seen her potential.

Her father had been ecstatic about it, and her mother warmly supportive.

Getting chosen was her life's dream. A fucking Alpha team! The letter had a list of the other heroes she'd been matched with, and she'd seen them all fight. They were damn good.

The only problem would be leaving university to go to combat training full time for a while. The university would give her leave – they had to under the law – but it might be hard to get back into her studies later, after a long hiatus.

And what about Valentine?

She'd tried not to think of him too much over the past few weeks. Maybe the out of sight, out of mind approach was working, because her desire for him had faded to a dim ache. Or maybe it was only a matter of time before the symptoms came back.

What would happen if the symptoms came back and she was across the country from him, or they were on different continents? Would she have to call in sick until it passed? Would that be good enough, or would she have to go to the hospital?

Apparently, most afflicted couples stayed in the same city for the duration of their condition, but in their case it just wasn't possible. She refused to give up on her dream because of a man and uncontrollable lust.

No matter how hot he was…and regardless of the orgasms.

The plane landed. There was a delay with disembarking. She waited.

The temperature in the cabin rose. No one else seemed to notice. Flashes of heat shot through her, and she felt faint. She prayed she was getting sick, but then the throb between her legs was there. Nagging. Growing. Unbearable.

No. Jory bit the back of her hand and did her best to breathe.

Don't think about him.

She felt him close by. Maybe even at the airport. Her sudden need for him was about as comfortable as suddenly having her guts tied to someone else's. Except not her guts. And if she didn't find him immediately, she might die – possibly of embarrassment.

She squirmed against the seat, trying to get comfortable, but it made things worse. Mr Creepy sitting beside her seemed to still be asleep, and she draped her jacket over her lap then dropped her purse on top of it for good measure. As casually as she could, she slid her hand down under her jacket, sat still that way casually for a few minutes, trying not to whimper with need. She pressed her fingers between her legs, trying to ease herself, but it was him she needed – some part of him sliding into her. Any part of her.

Her eyes closed and she gritted her teeth. When she looked again, the man in the next seat was awake and watching her.

Don't move.

She let her breathing go shallow. "Stomachache," she told him.

He opened his newspaper and ignored her, and she did her best to pretend everything was fine.

Finally they were given permission to disembark. Thank god she didn't have checked baggage.

She hobbled through the airport, searching for a bathroom that wasn't packed with people. Every second or third man stared at her as if she'd sprayed Pheromone de Horny Girl in their faces.

Her pussy ached and burned, each step making the seam of her panties feel like it was pressing harder on her swollen clit.

The discomfort grew. Too aroused to read the signs and find a bathroom to hide in, she stood in the middle of the hallway, fat tears dripping down her cheeks.

People flowed around her, a small sandbar in a fast-moving river. Some people stared. She should take out her phone and move off to the side, to make it seem as though she was waiting for a flight, but she couldn't move another step. Humiliation burned in her cheeks.

To be so incapacitated by lust? She'd read the information Dr Gardner had given her, but this wasn't like having something physically wrong. Everyone else on earth controlled themselves – why couldn't she?

A man moved toward her and she wondered what to say if he offered to help. How could anyone help her? She pictured being wheeled out to the curb in a wheelchair and cabbing it back to her dorm, but there was no privacy there, and this wasn't the kind of issue you explained to a roommate. Where could she go? She didn't have the money for a hotel, and she was far too ashamed to go to the hospital.

Tears came harder, but they did nothing to calm the storm of lust in her brain or soothe the desperate ache between her legs.

At the last minute, the man went around her. Jory managed to shuffle off to the side of the hall, hiding on a tiny section of blank wall between a snack shop and a side hallway that led to an area marked 'employees only.' She fumbled and fumbled with her pocket, but couldn't figure out how to get into it. Eventually security would notice her and call for help. This was so much worse than the last time.

What if it got worse every time?

She dug her fingernails into her palm, and pressed her forehead against the wall, chewing the inside of her cheek. Anything to distract herself.

If she died from this, what the hell would they put down as her cause of death?

"What are you doing?" a man's quiet, sinister voice said next to her ear. She yelped, surprised, but was ready to beg a stranger to bang her in a back hallway, even knowing that probably wouldn't ease her.

"I don't know," she mumbled, not caring that she probably sounded like a child. She sniffled and stood there, wishing the man would go away. A more rational part of her made her wonder if she was in danger. She was in a bad way, and if this man had bad intentions, she probably wouldn't be able to stop him. Not the way she was feeling.

"I've been waiting for you outside for an hour. What happens to naughty girls that make their dominants wait?" The words made her want to grovel at his feet.

Fuck. Valentine.

She cried out in a mixture of fear, desire, and relief. Only Valentine could ease her, but she was afraid of the things he'd make her do – the price was too high.

"Leave me alone!"

He clamped his big hand over her mouth and growled quietly, quelling her protest with one guttural sound.

"Shh. I can't leave you alone, love. I need to get my cock into you before we both go crazy." He let go of her mouth, and wrapped a hand around her upper arm, then pulled her, stumbling, after him. Only a few paces from where they started, two men moved into their path, and refused to let them pass.

"You need to let her go," one of them said. "I don't think she wants to go anywhere with you." Several more men joined the first two. Apparently chivalry wasn't dead – it had all just ended up at the Felix Municipal Airport.

Crap. Valentine was going to get the shit beat out of him.

"This is my girlfriend. She gets horrible migraines and panics when it happens." The lie was so glib even Jory almost believed him.

"Is that true, miss?" The man was at her elbow, trying to get her to look at him. What could she do? If she said no, they'd probably call the cops. She and Valentine had to sort this out for themselves.

Jory looked at the man, winced, and nodded. "Migraine." The pain she was in probably made it all the more believable.

"Do you want to leave with this guy? Is he really your boyfriend?"

She could almost feel Valentine holding his breath.

"Yes." She forced the word out. "Need to go."

Reluctantly, still looking suspicious, the small group moved out of their way. Valentine led her through the gauntlet, then through the maze of hallways to the parking garage exit. At some point he'd taken her small duffle bag without her noticing.

"Where are you taking me?"

"Probably to my apartment, unless I find somewhere private before then." He unlocked his car and shoved her into the passenger seat. "I could smell you as soon as I walked into the fucking airport. I probably shouldn't be driving right now." His laugh was dark and full of self-mockery.

Valentine pulled onto the main road before she could think clearly enough to speak again.

"How did you know I was here?"

In profile, his face was grim. "I don't know, I just did. I was working on an assignment, and then I knew. I'm guessing as soon as your plane touched down, my Jory GPS got pinged." He shook his head. "I wish I knew what the hell was going on. How are we supposed to get anything done if we spend all of our time in bed together?"

It didn't seem fair. If Valentine was suffering half as much as she was, he was better at hiding it. Days ago, she'd half decided she didn't want to see him again, but now she knew that was going to be impossible.

She whimpered and squirmed in her seat, and she wondered if telling him to drive faster was a bad idea.

"I know it's awful, snowangel, but we'll be there soon."

"Now," she whined petulantly. Alone with him, her hand went back between her legs.

"What do you want me to do? Pull over on the side of the highway and lean you over the hood of the car?"

Jory got a very realistic visual of him doing just that. Helpless, her arms twisted behind her back, his cock thrusting into her, owning her, sating her.

"Fuck. Stop making noises like that or I'll pull over right fucking here."

Was that supposed to be a threat? He reached over and slipped a hand into her panties. She slouched in the seat, tipping her hips to give him easier access. One finger sank into her, bringing a mix of relief and heightened arousal.

"Someone made her panties all wet." He made a sound of disapproval, and she grabbed onto the leather seat, wondering if she was going to leave permanent claw marks. A haze of lust settled over her mind, and she watched him dividing his attention between driving and finger fucking her.

"Are you going to come for me, baby?"

She didn't answer, too lost in sensation to try using words. Cruelly, Valentine withdrew his finger and turned all of his attention back to driving.

Jory's screamed in protest, writhing. She braced her feet against the floor as her hips came up, searching blindly for his hand.

Valentine made a sound of disapproval. "It was a simple question, Jory. I don't ask a lot from you, but when I ask you a direct question, you'd better answer me. Now, are you going to be a good girl?"

"Yes, Valentine," she whimpered.

"Valentine? You can do better than that." His disapproval struck her deeply. "Am I just some guy, or am I more?"

"More! You're more." She sounded hysterical, even to her own ears. "Please, I'm sorry. Sir."

He stared at her for a moment. "You're ready to do anything I want, aren't you?"

'Duh' probably wasn't a smart answer, and no doubt he'd make her regret it if she dared say it to his face. Deciding to go with a safer response, she nodded.

He put his finger to her lips. "Clean the mess you made."

Tentatively, she opened her mouth. How bad could it be? Valentine shoved his finger in, and she latched on, hardly noticing the taste of herself past the pleasure of sucking on him. It was almost as good as being fingered. Like any part of him inside her was good enough.

Valentine's breathing turned ragged, and he pulled into his driveway before she realized where they were. As soon as he threw the car into park, Jory stopped sucking his finger, unbuckled her seatbelt and turned, attacking the top button of his jeans.

"Jory, wait. Just a few more steps and we'll be inside."

"No, now!"

He tapped her face with the flat of his hand, just hard enough to get her attention. She tried to be offended, but she only felt chastened and more aroused.

"You get cock when I say you do, and not a second sooner." Valentine

55

got out of the car and came around to open the door for her. It seemed gentlemanly until he tangled a hand in her hair and dragged her out. Her hands went to her sensitive scalp, trying to lessen the pain he was inflicting, but he ignored her protests and pulled her along into his apartment.

"Shoes off and crawl, girl."

She kicked off her shoes, glad they had no laces. Crawling in a dress was difficult, though, and she tucked the hem into the waistband of her panties to keep it out of the way. He used her hair as a leash, and she crawled after him like an obedient puppy, wondering vaguely where her self-respect had gone.

By the time they got to his bedroom, her knees ached. Small stones had embedded themselves into her skin, but she dared not pause to brush them off.

When he stopped, she stayed on her hands and knees, her gaze averted. The pain of the grit digging into her skin was a welcome diversion.

"You're a distraction."

"I'm sorry, Sir." Hadn't he chosen to show up at the airport? She hadn't called him there.

He paced the floor in front of her, and she could feel the weight of his gaze on the back of her bowed head.

"I was busy. I have other things I have to do." He sounded as helpless as she felt. He was, she supposed. They were both victims.

She remained silent, the throbbing of her pussy not giving a rat's ass about how busy he was. Like he was the only one who had a life?

"What the hell is wrong with us?"

"Atypical Aphrodisia."

His footsteps stilled. "What?"

"That's what it's called."

"Who told you that?"

"A Bureau psychiatrist."

He grunted. "I don't care what the fuck it's called. It's pissing me off."

Damn it, he was stalling. Maybe he was too proud to give in to it.

Another wave hit. Jory collapsed onto her side and pressed a hand between her legs. Her own moans were loud in her ears.

She breathed through the ache. The toe of his boot became her focus, and she longed to kiss it and beg him to ease her. Only he could make this better.

Valentine scooped her up, as though her weight was inconsequential, and dropped her on his bed.

Their gazes met, and Jory felt herself sinking down, down into his coal-black eyes. So dark, with no sclera, and so difficult to read.

"What am I going to do with you?" he muttered.

"Anything, Sir. Please. Anything you want." Her breath caught.

In that moment, it was true. It scared the hell out of her. She barely knew this man, and yet a bond was forming that felt too serious and permanent for what she seemed to mean to him. Maybe because the desire she felt was stronger, the feelings were too. It felt as though their fates were lacing together, knot upon knot. Would she ever get free? Did she want to?

"You should never say that to a sadist." He broke the spell his eyes cast, replacing it with another made by his lips on her own. When she was gasping for breath, he stood, pulling his t-shirt off in the sexy, one-handed guy way. Every muscle in his chest and stomach, the bulges in his arms, all stood out in stark relief. She was tempted to explore every inch with her mouth and tongue, but before she took the time for something like that, she needed the fire in her belly banked.

"What if I was to tie you to my bed and tease you for hours, stopping whenever you got too close to coming? Or worse, if I tied you to my bed and went to sleep?"

She stared at him for a long moment, not sure what he wanted her to say. Rather than respond with words, Jory squirmed out of her sodden panties and rolled into a face down, ass up. It was a position that many dominants seemed to favor, at least according to the internet searches she'd done. She couldn't believe she was shamelessly presenting herself for use and hoping he'd stop talking and fuck her already. She didn't even care if he beat her for being pushy. Anything was better than him standing around and being chatty when she needed cock.

He groaned.

"I should punish you for being presumptuous," he told her, as though he was blaming her for making him weak. "But you're so fucking hot, and I can't really spare the time right now."

Valentine shoved her dress farther up out of his way then ran greedy hands over her body. "I had dreams about you every night we were apart. I think I'm going crazy."

She backed toward him. *Fuck me, please.*

"Are you trying to let me know you need something?"

Please, Sir. Why was he stalling?

"What if I fucked your ass instead of your pussy?"

Jory held her position and waited. He'd given her a safeword, and from what had happened between them last time, she trusted he'd be kind. Or take it slow, at least.

She hoped.

Valentine made a sound of aggravation, and unbuckled his belt. His jeans had barely slid down when he grabbed her thighs and shoved into her pussy so roughly she was crushed into his mattress. Her power rose, and she could feel his respond, surrounding hers, taming it. There was no tenderness, no finesse. He fucked her hard and fast, grunting like an animal, biting her neck, overwhelming her senses. A big hand slid between her legs and rubbed roughly at her clit.

She squealed and wept, each of his thrusts jarring. As much as it hurt, it was ecstasy. She wanted more, wanted him to come inside her, to make the storm in her quiet again. When she came, he did too, but fucked her through a second orgasm, and a third, until he came again.

They collapsed in a panting heap.

"This is so fucking crazy," Valentine mumbled into her hair. "How am I ever going to train you if I can't resist you?"

Jory felt sleep trying to suck her into its depths. "Train me? For what? I'm not your pet."

"Mmm." Valentine chuckled. "We can discuss that later. For now, let's get you cleaned up." He rose from the bed and pulled her into his arms again, then carried her to the bathroom as though she weighed nothing. This carrying thing was working far better for her than crawling on the gritty floor had.

He sat her on the toilet lid and tugged a lock of her hair. The gesture was downright playful, but his eyes hinted at rekindling sexual interest. As he ran water in the tub, he poured in some body wash, which promptly turned into bubbles. The room filled with a manly scent.

"Take a lot of bubble baths, do you?" She snickered.

Valentine sauntered over, menacing her with his naked body. His cock twitched and started to rise again. Jory clenched her legs together, nervous he'd want her again when she was so sore. If he got insistent, she'd offer him her mouth instead.

"You have a problem with men taking baths?" His mouth curled into a smile. "I like baths. Usually I read in them, but tonight I have better company."

She eyed him slyly. "And what do you read, self-help books for budding villains?"

"You think I'm a villain, do you?" Valentine quirked a brow at her. "Watch it with the bratting. You're on thin ice."

What on earth was he talking about? "It's called teasing, Valentine. Look it up. Just because you use me like an inflatable doll doesn't mean I don't have a personality."

"True. And an inflatable doll wouldn't beg for me like you do." His black eyes glittered, but Jory couldn't figure out what he was thinking.

Her cheeks heated and he grabbed her chin.

"You're the sweetest fucking thing." He stared at her for a long while, which only made her blush harder. As he let go of her face, he shook his head. "I don't know how the fates chose to put you in my bed, but I plan to thoroughly enjoy you while you're in it."

"I'm not a pet, Valentine. What I let you do when the Aphrodisia is uncontrolled isn't my fault." She thought about all the times she'd called him Sir today and acted like his whore, and had to look away. "It's not very nice for you to take advantage like you do."

"You have a safeword." His mouth quirked at the corner again and his eyes narrowed. "I may not be a villain, but never claimed to be a nice man."

He turned off the water and put her in the tub. Rather than leave her in peace, he got in behind her, then leaned her back against his chest.

Jory leaned against him, stiff and uncertain. She'd never bathed with a guy before, and she had a feeling it wouldn't stay sweet and cuddly for long. Especially not with the way his dick was prodding her in the back.

"I have friends coming by in about an hour," Valentine announced. "My team. They want to meet you."

Panic set in and Jory tried to struggle free, but he held her in place with his arms and legs.

"Do you want me to freeze this bathtub over so they'll need an ice auger to find your dick? Let me go!"

"Shh. They'll like you. They're just curious," he said in her ear. The rumble started a slow burn low in her belly. "It's not a big deal."

"It is a big deal. What if we have to...while they're here? I can't do that! And you can't treat me like you do, if there's other people around. It's not dignified."

He was petting her like a skittish animal, making soothing noises.

"Maybe this is nothing to you, but I just got accepted onto an alpha team at combat school. I can't have my reputation ruined because of the things you make me do."

Valentine's hand slid between her legs, and although she meant to ward him off, she found herself spreading her thighs to give him easier access.

"Oh, I *make* you do those things, do I?" The ironic smirk in his voice made her shudder. "Poor little submissive. I can tell how unwilling you are." He moved his fingers a few inches away from where he'd been making her sore parts feel good, and she whimpered and her hips followed his retreating hand. "What I do to you, I do because you like it. Actually, I'd say you love it."

"I don't," she frowned. "I just can't help it."

"You can't blame it all on the Aphrodisia. The truth is you're a freaky little pervert, Jory. The Aphrodisia just forces you to admit it."

She wanted to argue, to tell him she couldn't be held accountable for what she did when she was hot for him. The problem was she couldn't reconcile that with the fact that when she'd felt normal again at combat school, she'd spent quality time in the shower reliving the memories of the things he'd made her do. The Aphrodisia was an excuse for her to do things she didn't want to admit aroused her. Maybe he'd presented her with ideas she hadn't been familiar with, but so far she'd secretly loved almost everything he'd done.

When she didn't respond, he didn't force an answer out of her, which she appreciated. She snuggled into him, enjoying the heat and closeness, until she felt herself drifting off to sleep.

Jory woke to Valentine washing her, and she had no idea how long she'd been out. Had he warmed the water? She tried to take over, but he was insistent and she gave in, enjoying the way he touched her – possessively, tenderly, as though she was his and precious to him. It was so different compared to how he usually expressed his dominance over her.

"Do you promise you won't treat me like a whore when they're here?"

"I promise I won't make you do anything you don't want to do. You have a safeword. Besides, all three of them are into kink and we've known each other a very long time. Nothing we could do would shock them." He chuckled. "If anything, they might shock you."

He rinsed her hair then started to wash himself. She scooted to the other end of the tub and watched him while he watched her.

"Is watching a man wash that interesting?"

She felt her cheeks burning again, along with other parts of her. "I've never watched anyone else wash themselves. It's very...intimate."

He reached for a towel and folded it, making a cushion on the ledge that surrounded the tub. "Belly down."

"But..." She didn't want to. But what was he planning to do? If she safeworded, she might never find out.

"Now." His voice was soft, but his gaze was as hard as his dick. Did being horny for so long make him lightheaded? And why did he have so much more self-control than she did? Why wasn't he the one dropping to the floor and begging to be eased?

"But I don't want to." She whimpered.

"I didn't ask what you wanted. I gave you an order. Do you need a punishment to remind you who's in charge here?"

"You don't actually own me," she grumbled.

"Yet."

She shivered at the finality in his tone. Valentine was so fucking sure of himself that he was convincing her he was right. She'd read things on the Internet about sexual submission, but some of the stories there horrified her. What if it was a slippery slope, and she ended up with no free will, or he put her life at risk? Was he was using her desire to brainwash her?

Her hesitation must have lasted too long, because he pushed her into position.

"What are you doing?"

"Inspecting what's mine." His breath on the cheek of her ass made her clench up.

Could this be any more humiliating?

He ran a finger along her labia, spread them, toggled her clit until she was squirming and gasping.

"Hmm. I didn't wash here yet." He touched the divide of her ass and she jerked, startled, her heart stuttering as her breath caught.

Ignoring her squeaked protest, he soaped her there, then moved lower until his slick fingers swirled over her anus with an alarming attention to detail. She tried to squirm away, but he held her in place. The feel of his warm hand on her lower back overrode her objections, and so even though it was humiliating, she submitted to his touch. He was far more thorough than he needed to be, and by the time he rinsed her off, she was disgusted with herself for the heat burning in her belly.

"That needed to be clean for company?" she mumbled into her hands.

He kissed one of her ass cheeks then bit. She squealed and squirmed, her pussy throbbing. More kisses trailed over her bottom and she tried to slide away from him, but he dug his fingers into her hips.

"Stay."

His mouth inched closer to the cleft of her ass and the strange sensation made her whine, her blush extending to prickle her entire body.

"No, Sir, no!"

Something warm brushed against her anus and she dangled over the edge of the tub, her mouth hanging open at the sensation and the shock of what he was doing. Every sensitive nerve ending tingled, wide awake. He ghosted his fingers over the globes of her ass, as he licked her, sending shivers chasing each other up her back and into her hairline.

Her whispered protests were punctuated by wails and moans as he held her down and explored her with his tongue. She tried to be disgusted, but it felt too good.

When he got out of the bath and pulled her out, she couldn't meet his gaze. She couldn't believe she'd allowed him to do something so…perverted.

He toweled her off like she was unable to take care of herself.

"Go wait on my bed. Kneel there with your hands behind your head."

She blinked at him. Was he kidding? She needed sex now, not when he got around to her. Desperation flooded through her. She had to convince him to show some mercy.

"But Sir, I need you." Reluctantly, she knelt at his feet and clung to his leg. Once on her knees, the position reinforced her feelings of submission, dragging her further into that headspace. She squirmed and pressed her forehead to his thigh.

"Go now, or the next thing to kiss your ass will be my cane." It was always so hard to guess what he was thinking behind those creepy eyes of his, but she doubted he was bluffing.

The cane didn't sound fun. She'd seen cane marks on girls in pictures, and was pretty sure that kind of pain was anything but hot. A little spanking was one thing, but more? She shivered and rose to her feet, but Valentine grabbed her arm to stop her.

"I said go. I didn't say walk." They had a stare down, but it only took a breathless second before she knew she'd lost. Jory sank to her hands and knees and crawled back to his bed, ashamed that she was obeying him without argument, but even more ashamed that her freshly washed body was already slick with desire.

Nothing like having a major girl hard-on for Mr Wrong.

Once she'd clambered up onto his bed, she brushed the grit off her hands and knees. She knelt the way he'd asked, putting her body on display like a shameless whore. *His* shameless whore.

Part of her was mortified, but being treated like his property was wildly addictive. The swing between being handled like his treasured possession and being ordered around like a dog was messing with her head. For every smack or caress he bestowed upon her, she got hungrier for more. She wanted to believe it was about the orgasms, but there was some deeper need in her that he was answering.

In the dim light of the room, she waited, listening. Every passing moment made her more aware of the soreness between her legs, the ache and throb of new bruises, the heaviness in her breasts and stinging itch of her nipples. She shifted in place, silently begging him to hurry.

She imagined him standing around in the bathroom, maybe watching her from the mirror, wasting time, amused by her discomfort. When her arms went numb from holding her position, and her legs trembled, tears pricked her eyes. She blinked them back. It was bad enough she was weak enough to want this. She could at least take her debasement with dignity. The reading she'd done said that submission took strength, but she hadn't understood what that meant at the time.

Then Valentine was there in the doorway, his black hair unruly. The man was a beautiful demon. He'd dressed in a pair of old jeans, his belt riding low on his hips, but instead of mocking her or ignoring her, he was watching her as though she was the focus of his world.

"Good girl."

The quiet words ran straight to her core, more satisfying than any dean's list or combat school commendation. Why did it matter so much to her that he was pleased? And why was she so damned excited to see him, as though she was madly in love and they'd been apart for weeks?

He strolled to the bed, his air of serene command filling the room.

"Did you say you were offered a spot on an alpha team?" His expression was neutral, but his words seemed loaded with a latent disapproval.

"Yes," she smiled again, thinking of the letter in her pocket.

"Where are you going to be based?"

"No one's told me yet." Her smile fell away as his lack of expression sent her into a mental scramble. "Sir."

His silence held disapproval.

"I – I didn't think to ask you first," she blurted. Was she supposed to? They barely knew each other, but a pang of guilt rose anyway. "I didn't have your number. It's been a dream of mine since I was a little girl, and when the letter came, I emailed them immediately to accept." She paused, not knowing what to say. Would she have asked his opinion if he'd given her his phone number? Why would she? She wouldn't give up on her life's work because of a few mind-blowing orgasms.

"Of course you accepted." He waved his hand dismissively, the magnanimous lord and master. "I enjoy our time together, but our relationship is new, and we haven't discussed how much control you're willing to part with. You were under no obligation to discuss it with me."

Relationship? Is that what this was?

Damn right she was under no obligation. So why did she feel guilty?

"So you want to be a famous hero?" There was a hint of scorn in his tone, and she frowned.

"I guess guys like you are too cool to want that sort of thing," she chided, "but protecting people, helping them, has always been what I wanted to do. Maybe it makes me a dork, but I think doing good and making a difference in the world is worth having to wear the spandex."

His slow smile was infuriating. "So you want to do what? Save the world from maniacal supervillains? There are very few of those running around, just so you know. I'd hate for you to be disappointed. Sure, there's a megalomaniac once in a while, but mostly it's just one team against another. The only difference is heroes do charity work for the state, while mercenaries are well paid by private entities."

Jory let her hands drop from behind her head to her lap. There was no way she was sitting like that all night, and her arms were tingling. "You're going to be a *mercenary*?" She raised her brows in condescension.

When people were born with gifts, they had a responsibility to use them to make the world a better place. Her parents had hammered that home ever since she was small. What kind of Atypical would use their power just to make money?

"It's a matter of perspective." He moved her hands to the back of her head again, and patted them as though that would make them stick there. "The only thing that makes you a hero is that you're fighting for the idiots in power, instead of the idiots who want power, who will pay me well to do the same things you do. That doesn't make you a saint. It also doesn't make me a sinner."

"No, the depraved things you do to me takes care of that," she shot back. And yet, she was still in position.

He chuckled then kissed her. His tongue tried to access her mouth, but she was annoyed and pressed her lips tightly together. In response, he grabbed a handful of her hair and when she gasped, his mouth and tongue coaxed her into reciprocating. He pulled back just far enough to lie on his side and look up at her. With gentle touches, he explored her body, making her arch toward him for more.

"Don't be a sheep, Jory. Here you do what I tell you to because that's what we do, but when you're out in the world you need to think for yourself. Think critically. You don't want to be used as an unthinking tool. Just because someone is in a position of power over you, doesn't mean they're good."

She sighed and rolled her eyes, "Yes, absolute power, blah, blah. I'm not stupid."

"Well." He shrugged, as though that was up for debate. "I'm not sure about that. You did come back here."

"You kidnapped me from the airport!" she objected, tempted to swat him, but not game to find out what would happen if she tried it.

He leaned in and bit her thigh, which made her moan. "No. I just picked you up – unexpectedly. Do you want to see what real kidnapping is like?" His dark eyes seemed to go darker, if that was at all possible.

"No, Sir?"

"I'm more than willing to keep you as my captive for a few weeks, but playing with no safeword this early in our…acquaintance…wouldn't be safe or sane, even if it was consensual." He shook his head. "Quit putting such terrible ideas in my head."

This time she did smack him. Just on the arm, but Valentine rose on his knees over her, and glared.

"Now that was a very bad idea, little girl." He hauled her over his lap, facing upward.

Crap. What was he going to do?

"Sir, I didn't mean to," she squeaked. Trying to run from him would probably be a bad idea, but it did cross her mind. "I wasn't thinking."

"Here we are having a discussion about the importance of thinking before you act." His disapproval made her cover her face with her hands. That, and she was reluctant to find out what he would do.

"I'm sorry, Sir."

"I wonder how sorry you'll be when I'm done." His hand stroked the front of her thigh, and all of the muscles there quivered in response.

She groaned, the heat between her legs growing with his threat. "I'll be good. I'll be a good girl now, Sir."

"You need to learn to be respectful." He pinned her to his lap with a hand on her belly.

A chime rang out through the room and Valentine's raised and threatening hand stalled in midair.

"Fuck."

He dumped her facedown on the mattress, and swatted her ass.

"Quit being so distracting! You were supposed to be getting dressed." He threw a clean t-shirt at her.

She yanked it on as he headed for the stairs down to the door.

"Valentine? I need pants!"

He turned to look at her from the top of the stairs. "You don't need them. That shirt is as long as the skirt you were wearing when we met."

What? Jory yanked at the hem of the shirt then ran to her carry-on, which she spotted across the room. There was no way she was meeting people with no pants on.

"You may get a brush for your hair, but you may not put on more clothing." He walked down the stairs and she stared after him. She had a safeword, and had the urge to shout it down the stairs at him. Had he forgotten that?

Jory opened her bag, then grabbed her brush and tugged out a pair of jeans, and some clean panties. Lord knew she couldn't put on the ones that had been so thoroughly dampened, even if she had any clue where they'd ended up. She ran for the bathroom and slammed the door behind her.

Carefully, she brushed out her hair, wincing every time she found a knot. Her avalanche of a mane looked even more frenzied than usual. Great. There wasn't much she could do without her stuff. When she looked in the vanity, all she found was a straight razor, shaving cream, soap, and his toothbrush. Damn. The cupboard under the sink had cleaning products. If she was staying with a girl, she'd have had a huge stash of hair products, but apparently the sexy unruliness of Valentine's hair was all natural.

She picked up her jeans and panties and stared at them, wishing they'd give her some advice. What would he do if she wore them despite his orders?

The door creaked open and the monster himself looked in.

"Are you hiding in here, snowangel?" His gaze drifted down to her bare legs and the muscle in his jaw twitched.

Jory lowered her gaze. "I can't go out there like this, Sir." She pulled and pulled, but the shirt barely covered her bottom. If she sat or leaned over, everything would be on display. He'd said her skirt at the club had been this short, but he'd been exaggerating. If only she was the kind of girl who could cry on cue, she'd have him running to find her a parka to go with her jeans.

Valentine sighed regretfully. "I suppose you can wear pants. Just this once." He entered the bathroom, but left the door ajar. She couldn't see anyone peeking in.

Without a word, Valentine helped her step into her panties and drew them up her legs, then helped her with her jeans. Thank goodness they weren't too tight, or he would have had a hell of a time trying to shimmy her into them.

He buttoned and zipped up her jeans, then patted her ass as though it was his property.

"Just like that?" She laughed, relieved. "I thought you'd say no, or that there'd be consequences."

"Hm. I hadn't thought of that." His grin became dangerous. "When they leave I'm going to fuck your ass."

"But... That's not fair!"

He shrugged and steered her toward the door to the rest of the apartment. "Well, maybe I will and maybe I won't. I was thinking of doing it anyway, and now we can pretend it's because you're disobedient."

Chapter Six

Jory stared at him, her silver blue eyes wide and nervous.

Messing with her was far too much fun. He had no intention of fucking her ass tonight, but the apprehension in her expression said she obviously believed his threat. Without another word on the subject, he led her into the main room, eager to show off how tousled and sweet she was.

Jurgen and Dane rose from the sofa and smiled at his introduction, shaking Jory's hand as though they were gentlemen. They'd been born wealthy, as his whole team had, but none of them acted well bred very often. Xana's eyes narrowed and Valentine felt Jory step partially behind him.

"She's fucking adorable." Xana watched Jory self-consciously hiding, and Valentine wrapped a protective arm around the girl. Maybe she was only a few years younger than they were, but she was so fragile and ethereal he had the urge to guard her, even from his rambunctious friends.

Xana held out her hand to have Jory shake it, and when she did, she pulled Jory out from the safety of his draped arm.

"Aren't you a pretty little thing," Xana held her at arms' length, then made her turn, lifting the back of the t-shirt so she could check out her ass. Shocked and defenseless, Jory let her do it. "Why is she so…distracting?"

"Apparently, one of the Bureau doctors thinks she and I have something called Atypical Aphrodisia. I think it gives her pheromones a boost. Between that and her natural submissiveness, she'd be hard for any dominant to ignore."

How was she going to be on an alpha hero team when she couldn't handle the advances of one horny dominant? He could imagine a mercenary hitting on her during a battle, and Jory losing all of her concentration and control.

Her powers were more than strong and useful enough to be offered a position on an alpha team, but the idea of her being put in harm's way made him feel sick to his stomach.

As soon as Xana let her go again, Jory ducked back behind Valentine. He could have sworn she held her breath until Xana sat down.

They shot the shit for about an hour, then ordered pizza. Valentine had chosen to sit in the big armchair, and Jory alternated between sitting on the arm of the chair and on the floor at his feet. He wanted her in his lap, but she refused the one time he offered, and he wasn't going to force the issue. At least not today.

The girl was trying not to stare at Jurgen, who sat at Dane's feet, serving him drinks and getting him pizza when he asked, but he could almost feel her curiosity. Their system of hand signals reminded Valentine of how much Jory still had to learn.

"Did you take a look at the file?" Apparently Xana couldn't handle waiting anymore, but she cast an uncertain glance at Jory. Talking about work in front of strangers was a bad idea.

"I did," Valentine replied. "It looks pretty basic. Get in, get out."

At Valentine's feet, Jory's posture went from relaxed to alert, and he stroked her hair. She leaned into his knee, like a blissful cat.

"So we're accepting it, then?" Dane asked.

"I don't see why we shouldn't." At first Valentine thought Jory was being nosy, but then there was a subtle squirm. Shit. He felt it too. A few more minutes and things were going to get intense. Why the hell had he invited his team over when his girl was basically in heat? When the possibility of needing to have sex in front of them had crossed his mind, it hadn't seemed like a big deal. They fucked each other or in front of each other all the time. But with Jory, it was different. She was so sweet and shy it would embarrass the hell out of her.

"Valentine?" she whispered, gazing up at him. Her voice held a hint of desperation.

"What's the matter, girl?"

The word made her eyes widen, and her lips part. Would she beg in front of the others? Should he send them out for a while, or just drag his horny little girl into the bathroom?

"Sir, I…need you." She whimpered and squirmed in place. From one breath to the next, Valentine went from mildly aroused to ready to use her, but there was no reason to let her know that.

"What do you need?"

Jory kissed his knee and butted her head against him, apparently too shy to say what she needed aloud.

He turned his attention back to his friends, who were watching their interaction with interest and amusement.

"This doesn't seem anywhere near as bad as you said." Dane was grinning and playing with Jurgen's hair.

"Wait for it," he replied, gritting his teeth as the tide of lust rose within him. They were visiting to discuss the contract, but also partially as observers. His team needed to know what he was dealing with. What if this happened during a contract? A battle? Not having control over himself was disgraceful.

For another few minutes he attempted to engage his friends in a rational conversation, but soon Jory's low moans and the desperate grip of her fingers on his pant leg became impossibly distracting. She clung to him, breathing slowly as though controlling pain. The answering throb in his own body threatened to undo him.

"Shiiit," Jurgen said under his breath.

"Val, can you hear me?" Xana was on her feet and standing next to him, but he didn't remember seeing her move.

"We have to find something to fix this. We can't fight if he's like this." The voices droned on, retreated. Footsteps faded. They were alone.

"Please," her whisper in the empty room became his life's focus, his only concern. Time, ambition, everything that should have mattered, became inconsequential when compared with the glow of her pale eyes, the fumbling of her hands with his belt. Her mouth closed over him and she grunted in gratified pleasure. His fingers dug into the arms of his chair, and he felt his power surge forward to engulf her.

*

She lay bound at his feet, his ropes writhing on her body. The knot he'd tied over her clit pressed, shifted, made her gasp and cry out. She mewled and begged for him.

What day was it?

When was the last time they'd eaten?

At that thought, his stomach rumbled. The girl had already been too thin, and for days they'd been starving, too distracted to make food or eat. Their last meal had been sandwiches, hastily made and half eaten before he'd thrown her onto the counter and plunged into her again. When had that been? It seemed like years ago, or perhaps another life.

Jory wept and he went to the kitchen and gulped down two glasses of water before returning with one for her. He propped her in his arms and coaxed her into drinking, although he'd poured so much come down her throat during their time together that maybe she was less hungry and dehydrated than he was.

"Please, Sir!" she begged. "I need you."

"I can't, love. I need to stop." His body hurt as though he'd been running a marathon, which he had, in a sense. So many parts of him were chafed and sore – something he hadn't thought possible. But if he untied her, if she somehow managed to chew through her restraints, she would be on him again. Even now, the unholy lust rose within him, pleased to see her trapped and at his mercy.

The delicious curve of her ass caught his gaze, and he allowed himself to look, but only look. He couldn't take. Not while they were like this. It seemed like ages ago that he'd made the threat to fuck her there. He couldn't trust himself to be gentle in this frame of mind, and she hadn't been used that way before.

He closed his eyes, exhausted, knowing he needed to take her at least once more before they could sleep.

*

Her whispers crept into his ear, working their way inside him, deeper than he thought words could reach. His shoulder was still damp from her tears and their combined sweat, but his arms knew her so well now that when she was out of them he felt bereft.

"I love you, Sir." The words were desperate and helpless, and he wondered if she'd feel the same if he hadn't been deep inside her for most of the past week. Only a week. He'd had to check his phone to find out for sure. Messages were accumulating, but nothing and no one else mattered. She was the sum of his days.

He called a length of hemp string from the drawer in the low table next to his bed. It slithered up the mattress and over Jory's shoulder, then wove and undulated, arranging itself into a delicate lace pattern, before wrapping itself around her neck. It had been years since he'd tried to make anything beautiful with his power, other than using it for rope bondage. The lace collar was a useless thing – just a token.

Sealing the ends of the rope together with a brush of his finger, Valentine fought the urge to bite every inch of her skin. Nothing would mark her as his thoroughly enough to satisfy him.

*

His girl crawled to him, half crazed, begging. He walked backward, his perpetually hard cock pointing at her, luring her to him. She was crying, distressed.

"Come on, pretty baby. I'll give you what you need." He led her into the kitchen and pointed at a chair. "Sit."

Tears trailed down her cheeks, but she pressed her forehead to the top of his feet then climbed into the chair.

"You have to eat before you get more."

"I don't need food, Sir. I only need you."

Yet, she obediently ate what he put in front of her while he stroked her hair. He had to coax her to hurry, knowing it wouldn't be long before she couldn't do anything except be a receptacle for his cock.

She did everything he asked without question now. It was terrifying. There was never any hint of disobedience in her behavior or even her body language. They were like drugs to each other, and he wondered what would happen when they came down from the high.

*

He woke to her pulling away from him in the dim light. Automatically he reached for her, grabbing her wrist before she rose from the bed.

"Where are you going, girl?"

Jory's eyes were round, confused, and she looked around as though she didn't know where she was.

"I – I have to pee." In the time they'd been trapped in his apartment she'd become painfully thin, and her skin had gone from pale to translucent. She slid off the bed and steadied herself, her legs wobbling beneath her like a new fawn.

Standing? She hadn't stood in his presence for days. The raw calluses on her knees were an indication of where she'd spent most of her time. If she was standing up and lucid, maybe the Aphrodisia was passing. The madness had lasted so long he'd wondered if it would ever ebb again. He'd had visions of them forgetting to pay their rent or go to work, and ending up homeless and fucking in a park. Or possibly dying of dehydration or starvation.

He slid out of bed and went to her, wrapping his arm around her shoulders. She flinched away from him, but accepted his help rather than complain.

Every step she took was shaky, and he kicked himself for not taking better care of her. Not that his condition was much better.

Ignoring her objections that she could manage on her own, he lowered her onto the toilet, then turned away and drew her a bath. He helped her into the bath, feeling terrible about the way her ribs showed under her flesh, and although he wanted to crawl into the steaming tub with her, he thought maybe it was time she had some privacy. Now that the fevered feeling had passed, there were things that had transpired between them that made him feel guilty. If she was rethinking those same things, they had a lot to discuss.

With the Aphrodisia, the line between consensual and nonconsensual had become blurred. Even he hadn't had a lot of choice. He'd never taken a woman against her will, but was it really her will when she wanted him just as badly? They'd fucked so hard and so often that he wondered if he'd damaged her.

As an acknowledgement of where things stood between them, he brought her fresh clothes. He'd kept her naked for days, although she hadn't asked to be dressed. Clothes would have gotten in the way.

He helped her from the tub when she was done, dressed her, and turned the television on for her while he went for a shower. Every bit of him smelled of her, and although the scent had driven him mad only yesterday, today it made him wistful. A girl like Jory, would never settle for being his submissive twenty-four seven. She had passionate plans for her future that didn't involve serving him on her knees.

One night while she'd been sleeping, he'd looked up Atypical Aphrodisia, and read with relief that it usually went away after two or three cycles. Briefly, he'd been ecstatic, but that had been days ago, and a lifetime had passed in the interim.

Jory the submissive was his without question, but free Jory would be a fool to stay.

Chapter Seven

The silence between them was awkward and painful. It reminded her of movies where the girl woke up after a bender and had to make small talk with a guy she didn't remember sleeping with. Except in her case, she remembered every moment in gruesome detail.

How many times had she begged for him, like some slutty little whore? How many times had he pushed her down on a piece of furniture, or taken her mouth? It was a miracle he hadn't tried anal with her, considering she would have agreed to anything he wanted. He'd treated her like his property, and she struggled to convince herself that she hadn't liked it, and that it wasn't okay. Instead, the memory made her want him again.

In the kitchen, she'd stared at her reflection in the kettle, stroking the rope collar around her neck and struggling between the urge to cut it off, or keep it on and treasure it forever. He'd claimed her over and over again, and she'd wanted all of it and more.

Now, completely conditioned, every time he entered the room she was in, she had to fight not to fall to her knees. She had to forget how right everything was in her world when she pressed her lips to the top of his feet. Inwardly, she groveled to him. Outwardly, she tried to remain cold and aloof. As a modern woman and someone who was becoming a hero, the feelings he inspired in her were dangerous. They needed to stop.

She zipped up her bag, realizing that other than her toothbrush, she hadn't used anything in it for almost two weeks.

They'd discovered it was January twentieth. She was supposed to have gone to the school the week before, packed her things, and given notice to her professors. As it was, it was going to seem as though she was running away from school, rather than running toward combat training.

"You're going?" His voice was soft behind her, but her first instinct was to crawl to him and beg to be held. She managed not to.

He didn't seem surprised.

"Yeah, I have to give notice at school and pack my stuff at the dorm. I'm supposed to be back at combat school the day after tomorrow. It's been…" She searched for an appropriate term. "…enlightening."

His chuckle was hollow and ironic. "Yes. It has been for me, too."

When she stood, he stepped into her personal space. Inside, she quavered, her knees threatening to buckle under the strain of separating from him. She had to get away now, before she lost the last of her will to free herself. His arms went around her, and although she tried to hold herself rigidly away, she couldn't help but melt against him.

"Can I give you a hand with anything?"

It was so tempting, considering how much work she had to do, but she couldn't chance having him around. She didn't want him in her space. People would see how they were together. They'd know.

"Thanks, but I don't think that's a good idea."

Valentine pulled back first, steadying her by the elbow before he let her go. He handed her a set of keys.

"What are these for?"

"The car. You'll have an easier time doing all that with a vehicle."

She tried to hand them back, but he wouldn't accept them. "Maybe you don't understand. I'm leaving in a couple of days. I don't have time to bring it back to you." *And I can't see you again. It's too much temptation.*

He seemed to hear the words she didn't say, and only smiled at her with what looked like regret. "Keep it. I'll get another one."

Talking to him after that was like talking to a stone wall. He hadn't just checked out, he'd completely shut himself off.

She thought of leaving the keys in the foyer, but the idea of disobeying him, of disappointing him that way, was more than she could handle.

Leaving him without explicit permission was hard enough.

*

Summer was watching her. Jory tried to think back to what she'd done in the past few minutes to have her roommate stare at her that way. Had she been talking to herself?

"What?"

The blond girl shrugged. Sharing a room with her team's alpha was turning out to be difficult. Everything she did and everything she didn't do was under scrutiny. Jory got the impression that although the other team members had voted her in, Summer wasn't sure she was the right choice.

"I don't know. You tell me."

"Tell you what, Summer?" Jory sighed inwardly, wishing the girl would leave her alone so she could focus on reading the tactical manual they were supposed to memorize. Hundreds of pages of the most boring combat advice on the planet stretched out in front of her.

What if the teams they fought read the manual? Wouldn't deviating from standard procedure be safer and more effective? She'd tried to ask in class, but Sergeant Oleg had shut her down before she had time to engage in a meaningful discussion about it. The message was clear. This was combat training, not question period.

She'd sat at her desk in her scratchy blue uniform, imagining Valentine laughing his ass off at them. *You're smarter than this, Jory. Don't be a sheep.* That was when she realized that she had a constant Valentine commentary running in her head. What would he think, what would he say? And at night, what would he do?

"You were different at break. Since you came back, you've been challenging me, and all of the sergeants, to the point of being hostile. Did something happen that you want to talk about?" Summer smiled with what looked like false sympathy. What was it about her intonation that always made her sound so condescending and fake? The implied disrespect was grating. "Joining a team is an adjustment for anyone, so if it's that, I understand."

I spent almost two weeks on my knees. I'm still half in love with the man who was using me, and I don't know what to do with that. The idea of admitting it out loud to another student was out of the question. She doubted she could even tell Dr Gardner, much less an insincere bitch like Summer.

"Sorry, I…"

Summer grimaced and rolled her eyes in self-mockery. "I don't want to come off too strong, but as the team lead, I have to think about what's good for the whole team. If you need some counseling or something, we can get that arranged."

"No, I…"

"I just want to have the best team out there, you know?" It was as if

Summer couldn't even hear her. Had Jory suddenly developed the power to mute herself, like a television?

"Yes. I…"

"If your eye isn't on the prize, Rime, just let me know." The use of her hero name in casual conversation was still jarring and felt strange. "There's no shame in switching to a beta team if you can't hack it. You might even be a team lead there."

How could she sound like such a stereotypical, hair-flipping mean girl at their age? Didn't that end with high school? She was going to have to shut this shithead down before things got out of hand. There was no way she was going to accept being treated like this for the next twenty years.

"Alright…back the fuck up, Summer. First of all, you being our team lead has nothing to do with me being weak or sucking. You're good at organizing people, and your family has money, but I can hand you your ass, power to power or hand to hand. Just because you're team lead does *not* mean I'm your bitch, so let's just make that clear right now."

"I –"

"Shut it. Second of all, I've wanted this longer than you have. If I'm a little distracted, it's because I have a lot of shit going on. I got nine hundred and fifty eight on the entrance exam. What did you get?" Out of a possible score of a thousand, that was pretty damn good. They only needed six hundred and fifty to get in, and even then some people were rumored to bribe their way past that requirement.

Summer stared at her in shock, like a beach bunny whose favorite sunning spot had been usurped. Perky nose, long blond hair, overly white teeth and tanned complexion, Summer's given name should have been Summer. As it was, there was no question her hero name had been well chosen, even if it was anything but badass.

"Rime, that's not an acceptable way to address your leader."

"You may be team lead, but I didn't vote for you."

"Do you think any of the alpha teams will keep you, if you get a reputation for mouthing off to your superiors?"

Oh, like this bitch was her superior in any way? Jory could imagine the disdain Valentine would have for this girl. With Summer at the helm of Jory's hero team, Valentine's mercenary team would eat them alive.

"Like I give a shit? I can always go rogue."

The girl's mouth hung open but her eyes darted around as though she was looking for backup. Hadn't anyone ever put this annoying bitch in her place? There was no way she could have gotten this far in life and been this exasperating, without someone calling her out on it. Or was she too beautiful and wealthy to get criticized? Was she just a spoiled lapdog whose main talents were looking pretty and not messing on the floor?

"I'm starting to think this won't be a good fit, Rime." She flipped her hair. *Oh my God, she actually flipped her hair at me.*

"Maybe they can find a team with a bad attitude to take you on."

Fuck this. It was fifth grade gym class all over again. That shit didn't belong here.

Jory clenched her fists, trying to control the surge of power that had collected in her palms. Ice gathered, sharp and vicious, ready to launch at her slightest inclination.

"I agree. I'll ask for reassignment." It was no big loss, really. She'd only been with her new team for a few days, and she already thought two of them were asshats. It hadn't boded well for the future. Teams often stayed together until they got too old to work, and having to deal with them for most of her life was a daunting thought. Could she trust someone like Summer to watch her back? Not bloody likely.

"Don't worry," Summer said blithely. "I'll save you the trouble." She breezed out of the room and Jory paced with impotent fury. Bitches like that didn't belong in hero uniforms. What was the Bureau setting loose on society? Was having someone who was attractive on camera worth the fucking drama?

They'd find Jory a team. She was too powerful to go to the betas.

However, she wasn't too moral to feel a small bit of satisfaction when she froze Summer's bed and her Egyptian cotton sheets into a solid block of ice.

*

Going home again was always a strange feeling. She didn't have a permanent address, other than the bungalow on Kimberly Court, but after having been away so much, she felt like a visitor. Her parents, Leah and Eric, were excited to have her home for the weekend, but being treated like a child was awkward, to say the least.

She sat through Friday night's dinner, happy to have a home-cooked meal, but less pleased about the interrogation.

"But I just don't get it, Jory. You've always had a lot of friends, so why does this Summer girl not like you?" Her mother's concerned frown made

Jory feel bad for yet again shattering her delusion of having a popular daughter.

Her mom had always been part of the in-crowd, and when it came to Jory, she had a hard time not seeing her through the lens of what she should have been, rather than what she actually was.

Jory had to stop herself from rolling her eyes. Other than her best friend Amy from down the street, she hadn't exactly been sought out for friendships. Being an Atypical at a Typical school and living in a Typical neighborhood wasn't an easy way to make friends. If she'd been good at something useful but safe, she might have had a chance at living a Typical life with Typical friends, but being able to use cold as a weapon made her scary and a freak.

As for Summer, Jory had no idea what the bitch's problem was with her.

"We're just not compatible, Mom. It's okay, though. Sergeant Oleg and Sergeant Eisen are looking for another team for me."

Her mother's eyes widened with worry. "Another alpha team, I hope? It would be awful if you missed out on your dream because you had an argument with one girl."

"If they can't find me a team, I can always work solo."

Both of her parents made sounds of disapproval. "The Board of Atypical Affairs frowns on that, Jory," her father said. "Working solo would pretty much mean you'd have to go rogue, unless you got special dispensation."

"I don't care. All I know is that if Summer is an example of the talent the Board is hiring, they need new scouting agents."

Leah sighed. "That's how jobs are, honey. You don't get to choose who you work with most of the time in life, so you have to learn how to deal with difficult people." Her mother had a penchant for self-help books that she worked hard at applying to every situation. She meant well, but the advice could be annoying. "Maybe the two of you have different communication styles. You should do one of those personality inventories and post your communication style where your teammates can refer to it."

For a long moment Jory stared at her mother in disbelief. Did she think heroes had cubicles? Morning huddles?

"Anyway, I'm sure that'll all work out fine. Just keep an open mind." Her father put his last forkful of mashed potatoes in his mouth and laid his napkin aside. "Speaking of open minds, the MacDonalds who moved in next door have an Atypical son too. He's home for the weekend, so we set up a time for the two of you to hang out tomorrow. Maybe you'll hit it off."

They set up a fucking play date for her? Seriously?

"Dad, you do realize that I'm not six, right?"

"Oh Jory, they're new to the neighborhood. There's no need to be standoffish with people." Jory's mom patted her arm. "See if you can pick up my casserole dish while you're there. I brought a welcome to the neighborhood meal over to them two weeks ago and his mother still has my CorningWare."

Her mother stood and started to clear away the dishes, and her dad went to run water in the sink. Doing the dishes was usually a family affair, but she'd had enough togetherness time for the night.

Jory slunk to her room, shutting the door behind her. With a vague hope, she pulled her phone out of her bag, but there were no new messages. Day after day she found herself checking, hoping Valentine would say something, but he never did. If he thought of her at all, it was probably just to remember how pathetic and weak she was. How she'd begged him to fuck her any way he wanted.

That had been weeks ago. He probably had some hot new chick in his bed, and that idea was like a kick in the chest.

For her, there had been more to their time together than sex. That was the part that stung. She'd told him she loved him, and it hadn't been a lie. It had been way too soon to say it out loud, but the feelings were there. Obviously he hadn't felt anything for her, but he was in her head now, and she couldn't get him out.

In bed, he'd been demanding and uncompromising, but he'd also taken such sweet care of her. And the conversations they'd had about everything when they could think straight – even the nature of good and evil – had blown her worldview out of the water.

He really believed nobody was strictly one or the other. It was something she should have thought about more rationally by her age, but the Atypical training programs had more or less brainwashed her into thinking she was on the side of righteousness if she did what they told her to. But Valentine had pointed out that the victors wrote the history books, and just because someone was in power, didn't mean they were right. Maybe he was a little subversive, but people following blindly led to abuses of power. Everyone thought they were on the right side. Even people who perpetrated evil justified their actions in their own minds. An unobjective mind was a dangerous thing.

Of course, thinking about Valentine would make her think of abuses of power. She sat on her bed and leaned back against her headboard, her fingers exploring the ridges of her collar. She should have taken it off before coming home, considering Mom had quizzed her about it. At no time in her life had Jory ever been fond of jewelry, but she just couldn't bring herself to take it off. There were no knots holding it in place. She'd have to murder it with scissors to remove it. The thing almost seemed like a living creature, since she'd seen it weave itself. It was as if Valentine had made a pet for her, and brought it to life around her throat.

Tendrils of his power still clung to the collar, and every time she touched it she could almost feel the way their powers intertwined when he was inside her. It was almost spiritual – at least to her – and made her feel deeply connected to him and less alone in the world. Valentine had seen her in her weakest moments and yet he still gave the impression he respected her…when he wasn't making her beg for his cock.

Feeling sorry for herself got boring. While her parents were busy watching television, Jory went down the street, hoping Amy was around.

It was funny how her life was so different now, and yet the sidewalk cracks she'd stepped over to go visit her best friend as a kid were all in the same spots. When they'd met, their relationship had been based on a mutual love of Pokémon – neither of them willing to admit their dreams of becoming Pokémon trainers would never be fulfilled. A decade and a half later, Jory still thought it would have been a better vocation than anything real – even better than being a hero.

Jory rang the bell of the A-frame house, glad Amy's dad had salted the stairs. Maybe she could control the cold, but that didn't mean she didn't wipe out on icy steps on occasion.

Amy came to the door, her short brown curls bobbing enthusiastically around her face. When she saw Jory she nearly ripped the door off its hinges.

"Where the hell have you been, woman?" she whispered harshly, casting a glance back over her shoulder. "You haven't answered a motherfucking text for weeks!"

Jory grimaced. "Long story."

Instead of inviting her in, Amy put on her coat.

"Jory's here. We're going for a walk!" she called. Without waiting for her parents to reply, Amy shut the door behind herself and dragged Jory down the sidewalk.

When they were a few houses away, Amy finally stopped pulling and slowed to a normal walking pace.

"Spill it. Why are you so skinny, and what's with the dark circles and the necklace?" Amy's sharp gaze was still assessing her. No secret would be left unexposed.

"It's been a rough month."

Amy stopped and arched her brow at her. "That's the lamest answer in the history of answers. Do you seriously think I'll let you get away with that shit? I don't care if you're on some sort of top secret Atypical mission, you're not hiding anything from me, capiche?"

"Aye-aye, captain."

They glanced around when they got to the next street then ducked into the forest behind their subdivision. The wooded area wasn't a secret, but old habits were hard to break, even though Amy's pesky little brother, Zach, had gone away to college now.

When there were enough trees between them and the road, they slowed to a stroll. The cold air was already numbing Jory's cheeks and nose, but she was happy that after everything else that had transpired, she still had this. She and Amy were the kind of friends where they might not see each other for ages, but they'd always pick up where they'd left off.

"Okay, you first," Jory prompted.

Amy laughed. "Way to deflect, doorknob. You do realize you're not putting me off indefinitely."

"Yeah, yeah. After I tell you what I've been up to, we won't be talking about much else. I want to know what's going on with you, too."

Her best friend sighed and rolled her sweet brown eyes. "Hmm. Let's see. A whole lot of nothing." She pulled a silly face that never failed to make Jory laugh. "I'm volunteering at Shining Tree Elementary and hoping I'll get a position there when someone has the decency to retire. I've been on a few dates with boring-assed men and watched an obscene amount of Netflix. You know, the usual."

"The volunteering part is different," Jory said with enthusiasm. "It's a step forward. Better than sitting around waiting for something to happen. I still say you should apply for jobs in bigger cities. If you're willing to relocate..."

"My parents would be so disappointed." Amy smiled ruefully. "Like I'm not enough of a disappointment already."

"Shut up. You are not." Jory punched Amy's shoulder then hugged her when the girl laid her head on Jory's shoulder.

"My life is so fucking boring. Save me from my boring life, Rime!"

"You know there's no point in having a secret hero name to keep my family safe if you keep dropping it everywhere. Hence the *secret* part."

Amy shrugged then winked. "I'll be more careful when you're famous. For now no one cares about your lame-assed hero name."

The squeak of the snow under their boots distracted Jory temporarily, along with the jeweled glint of snow crystals in the glare of the setting sun.

"Seriously, though. You look unhappy." Amy brushed the dusting of snow off a fallen log, sat down then patted the spot beside her.

Jory sat, even though she felt more like pacing.

"I'm not unhappy," she replied automatically. Was she unhappy? Not really. It was more that she was restless. It made her lie awake at night and question all the things she'd worked toward.

Amy's eyebrows were up, and Jory knew she was waiting impatiently for the rest of the story. Her eagerness, though, made her look fanatical.

"Oh my god, you *are* bored."

"You have no idea. I've been playing with my Tamagotchi and I've kept it alive for almost two months."

A laugh burst from Jory's lips at the unexpected visual. She'd totally forgotten about their brief Tamagotchi obsession. She had no idea where hers even was and had a moment of guilt about being a bad Tamagotchi owner.

"You're officially responsible enough to be a mother."

"Just need a sperm donor and I'm all set."

Jory winced. "Don't remind me. My parents have set me up on a blind date with their new next-door neighbor's son. Am I too old to run away from home?"

Chickadees flitted through the trees, and the wind picked up. Amy tucked her face farther into her scarf and groaned. "Are you serious? Let me guess, he's Atypical."

"You know it. Like being Atypical is the only thing that matters when it comes to dating? I'm more worried about finding a better team to join."

"You had a team? You left it? Crap on a cracker, woman, you can't keep me in the dark like this!" She smacked her arm.

She gave Amy a one-shouldered shrug. "The alpha was a stupid bitch and she hated me. It's no big loss."

"Give me a name. I'll curb stomp her."

"Down girl. Besides, I have other things going on right now that are a lot more serious."

Her friend snorted, drawing in the snow with the toe of her boot. "More important than your life's work? I find that hard to believe. Just don't say it's about a guy and I won't have to disown you."

Stuck, Jory fell silent.

Amy turned suspicious eyes to her. "Jory Savage. You are going to tell me everything. You are going to start at the beginning and if you leave out any of the details, I'll skin you alive."

How much should she tell? How much could Amy even begin to understand, and how much could Jory bear to recount?

"He's handsome, rich, and maybe dangerous. At least for me. I might be in love with him, but if I never see him again it'll be too soon."

"Seriously, Jory? I'm not interested in your Hiddleston infatuation. I thought you were talking about an actual guy."

"Oh, he's real." Her hand went to her neck to reassure herself that their time together hadn't been a dream. Or a nightmare?

"And he not only knows you exist, but he gave you a necklace?"

"It's not a necklace," she mumbled, the words almost disappearing in a gust that made them yank their hoods on. "It's a collar."

She could feel Amy watching her, but there was no way she could look her in the eye. Her blush was so ferocious that it felt like it might give her a sunburn.

"Oh my god, you've barely had sex before. He dragged you into *that*?"

"I wasn't dragged," she said, ashamed of her weakness for him, but not willing to betray Valentine by making it sound as though she'd been forced. "He would have stopped if I told him to."

"Shit." Amy breathed. "Is it whips and chains like you see on TV? And those black masks with the zipper where your mouth goes?"

That had been so far from what Valentine was into that Jory rolled her eyes. "No, I don't think those are his kinks. But who knows, maybe he started me out slow because I didn't have experience." Crap, if that was true, she couldn't imagine what else he could convince her to let him do. Not that they were going to see each other again. "We're over now, though."

Amy draped an arm around her shoulders and gave her a squeeze. "Just make sure that when you're his full-time sex slave, he lets you text me once in a while."

"Shut up."

"Even if you just text me screams so I know you're okay."

"You're the worst friend ever. I just told you it's finished. I never want to see him again."

Amy looked at her skeptically. "If that's true, why are you still wearing that?" She pointed at Jory's collar.

For a moment Jory wondered if the collar was listening, and she had the urge to cover its nonexistent ears.

"It's complicated."

*

Inviting Amy on her blind date with the neighbor's son had been a stroke of genius, except that Jory was starting to feel like a third wheel.

Amy and Talbot hit it off in about five seconds flat, and the way she hung off of him while they were skating, as though she had no idea how to skate, was almost embarrassing. As they sat on the outdoor benches, taking their skates off and wiping the snow from their blades, Talbot was hinting that they should go to the coffee shop to warm up.

Enough was enough.

"I think I pulled something," she said, giving Amy a *don't worry about it* look. "I've got to head home, but you two go on without me."

They insisted on walking her home, so she was forced to hobble to keep up the façade.

Amy walked her to the door, while Talbot started his car to warm it up.

"Call me later," Jory whispered to Amy.

"Don't wait up!" Amy whispered back.

Jory went inside, and excitedly told her parents about her budding wedding plans for Amy and Talbot. It wasn't exactly what they'd wanted to hear, but they were satisfied enough with things to let her go to her room and shut the door without any more fuss.

The sexual tension between Amy and Talbot had been pretty intense. It made her miss Valentine worse than she already did.

When she was safe in her room, she got undressed and lay in bed wearing only her panties and collar, the touch of the smooth, cool sheets on her bare skin making her close her eyes and think of how Valentine's strong hands felt when he touched her. Maybe the Aphrodisia was gone, but she craved him. She tried to imagine what he might be doing, but it was hard to guess when they'd spent most of their time in bed – a bed that would hardly be empty of company for long. She stomped down the jealousy that came with that thought.

It was for the best anyway. Valentine was sexy, perfect, and worldly. Smarter than she could ever hope to be. Older. And he was rich. His friends were cool and self-possessed, and hanging out with them made her feel like the poster child for Sunday school. No one would ever describe her as sexy.

She'd captured his attention briefly, because of the Aphrodisia. It was time she admitted to herself that it hadn't meant anything to him, other than an inconvenience.

Miserable, she wrapped her arms around her pillow and laid her head on it, pretending it was his chest, although it was too soft to satisfy her. She could almost feel his fingers running possessively through her hair. Maybe tomorrow she'd text him to see if he wanted anything to do with her. Or if he even remembered her name.

Sleep came slowly, and every dream was more vivid and erotic than the last.

She woke in darkness, twisted in her sheets. For a panicked moment she thought the Aphrodisia was back, but as she squirmed in futile frustration, she realized it was just the result of her dreams. She pressed a hand between her legs, but no matter how she touched herself the ache there wouldn't ease. She reached for her phone and clung to it, and on a whim scrolled through her contacts, finding Valentine's number at the very end. She wished she'd been brave enough to take his picture.

She stared at the contact. A message in the middle of the night would look desperate, but if there was any definition of desperate, it was her staring at her phone, not able to come.

Fuck it.

Jory jammed the button then realized her phone was dialing him instead of opening a text screen.

Idiot.

She hung up fast then pressed the phone to her bare chest, willing the call not to have gone through.

Shit, shit, shit.

The traitorous phone buzzed against her breast. Jory slapped a hand over her eyes. The phone buzzed a second time.

Please let it be Amy, just getting in.

She looked at the phone screen. Of course it wasn't Amy.

Would he believe she butt-dialed him?

She hit answer.

"Hello?"

"Did you just hang up on me, snowangel?"

His words went straight from her ear to her pussy. A whimper escaped her.

"What's the matter, little girl?"

The rumble of his voice made her squirm. She'd woken him but he didn't sound the least bit annoyed. And he'd used a pet name. She imagined him warm and sexy, his hair tousled.

"I had a dream about you."

"Is that so?" There was a hint of amusement in his voice, and her embarrassment made her hotter.

"And I tried to come…but it didn't work. I need you, Sir."

He groaned. "Where are you?" She could hear him rummaging around.

"Far." Her heart raced. He'd consider a booty call? She was ashamed of how excited that made her, but it was more than she'd expected. "I'm at my parents' house in Shining Tree."

"Mmm…that's a four-hour drive. I could be there by seven. I have to head back here right after, though."

He'd drive eight hours round trip just to put his dick in her? That was so fucking hot. Her face heated. Apparently he hadn't forgotten about her after all. But four hours?

She whined. "Can't you fix it from there? I can't wait that long."

"You're killing me," he muttered, as though to himself. "This is the first time you tried to masturbate since you were with me?"

Oh jeez. Her cheeks burned. That wasn't the kind of word she was used to throwing around. "Yes."

"Yes, what?" he growled.

"Yes, Sir," she whispered, suddenly realizing her parents might hear.

A satisfied chuckle came from the other end of the line. "And do you know why that is, girl?"

God, why was he so hot and such an asshole? The man had no self-esteem issues, that was for damn sure. "No, Sir. Why?"

"Because you can't come without my permission."

His words were starting to fuck with her head. Of course she could come without his permission. She just… She shook her head in disbelief.

"That's not true."

"Go ahead and try it, then," he said, sounding amused. "I'm going back to sleep." The line went dead.

Oh, hell no. She'd show him.

Jory grabbed her laptop off the floor and flipped it open, then Googled a porn site. She didn't usually let herself watch, but porn often got her off fast, and she had a man to prove wrong.

Self-conscious but determined, she scrolled through the free clips. She tried two or three but gave up after a few minutes because they weren't working for her. Her brain kept wandering back to the hot and embarrassing way Valentine spoke to her, the way he handled her, and realized her fantasies had shifted. Watching a guy go down on a girl wasn't enough anymore.

With trembling fingers, she typed in BDSM porn. The first site she went to was insisting she had to register first, so she got the hell out. The second site had free clips, but the stuff it featured had her staring at the screen, aghast. Was he going to do these sorts of things to her if she went running back to him?

Painful-looking bondage, fucking machines, girls getting peed on – she was too vanilla for anything she could find. After a few harrowing moments, she closed the site and cleared her browser history for good measure, then peered around her room to make sure her parents hadn't installed spy cameras while she was away at school. A BDSM porn site with training wheels would have been nice, but it was taking too long to find one. She needed relief now.

She loved the way Valentine did things, but there didn't seem to be porn about dominant men who weren't too freaky for her. A guy who knew exactly where to put his hands and what tone of voice to use…

All the thoughts she'd pushed away for the past few weeks came streaming back when she let them, like a graphic, intense porn reel, complete with remembered sensations. Some of it was blurry, since she'd spent a lot of her time with him in a kind of haze, but in a minute flat she was on the brink of coming. She was so close, but she couldn't make herself go over. She swore then pictured the first time Valentine had told her to come. The timbre of his voice, the intent way he'd watched her…

Nothing.

Motherfucker.

She tried and tried for at least a half hour, until her hand and clit hurt as much as her pride.

Desperate, she grabbed the phone. Her teeth tugged at her lip, and she thought about trying to go to sleep but couldn't imagine it working.

It was a mind fuck. He hadn't trained her to come only on command. She would have remembered something like that, right? Was that sort of thing even possible?

She screwed her eyes shut and thought back, remembering him commanding her to come every time, but she would have come anyway, right? So it was just a hot command. No weird brainwashing shit. Just a sexy, bossy man with a dirty mouth.

But damn it, she was starting to believe him.

Sheepishly, she let her thumb hover over the green phone icon under his name. He'd be pissed if she called back.

So what? That's what he got for fucking with her.

Brazenly, she punched the button.

The phone rang once before he picked up.

"Jory, my dear, what seems to be the problem?" He didn't sound groggy this time. Had he been waiting? Had he known it wouldn't work?

All of her bravado dissipated with one question asked in his sexy voice.

She pressed her fingers between her legs again. "Valentine?" she whimpered.

"Yes, girl? Are you touching yourself?"

"Uh huh." Why had she just admitted something so mortifying? Could she have no secrets from this man?

"You can't come," he rumbled, "can you." It wasn't a question. He knew.

"No, Sir." Her voice had gone up a few octaves, and because she had to whisper she sounded ridiculous and small.

"Why are you calling? You said you didn't need me." His voice was mocking, and Jory wished she were the kind of girl who could faint when she was this ashamed. Instead, she was just more turned on.

"Sir, I need you," she whispered in desperation. "Please help me."

"Come for me, Jory." Fuck. Instead of being commanding, the words were coaxing. Dirty. He was turning her into a pervert. "Pinch that little clit of yours. Use your nails to make it hurt. Come on, baby, let me hear you come for me."

A squeal escaped, and her hips came up off the bed. She dragged her pillow over her face and screamed into it. The orgasm went on for far too long, and she started to cry. She missed him. She shouldn't miss him, but she did, and now he'd fucked with her brain, and made her dependent on him.

She put the phone back to her ear, surprised when she sobbed and didn't care that he'd heard it.

"All done? Good girl." He sounded more relaxed now too, and she felt lethargy sneak up and ambush her.

"Thank you, Sir." She hesitated, afraid to ask. "But why can't you just give me permission to come whenever I need to?"

"What's wrong with calling me?" His voice sounded sleepy again too, and she wished she was curled up with him, tasting his skin and sniffing his sexy guy smell when he wasn't paying attention.

"Because I don't want to call every time I…do that. You're going to think I'm a pervert."

"You are a pervert, Jory. Just think of all of the things you let me do to you…that you beg me for."

She didn't want to discuss that at the moment. That had been Aphrodisia, desperation, and a hot guy who knew how to sweet-talk her, not her own perversion.

"I'm vanilla – so vanilla that I'm barely even ice cream," she mumbled at him. "And besides, I'm not independently wealthy. I can't pay to call you all the time. I'm going to run out of minutes."

He snorted. "Give me the bill the next time I see you. I'll get you a new phone too. Yours is ancient."

"What? No! It's bad enough I still have your car."

His laugh was delighted. "You're so adorable when you're haughty. You'll take the fucking phone like you took the fucking car, and you'll tell me if you run short of money for anything. Gas, car repair, food, shoes. Whatever you want. You're going to tell me, and if you don't, there'll be hell to pay."

She sputtered. "But…I…that's not right!"

"What's not right? The fact that I'm trying to take care of my girl long distance, or the fact that I let her leave in the first place?"

"I'm not—" she whispered.

"Oh, but you are." His voice was sinister and determined. "You're mine, and you're my responsibility. I've let you off-leash to pursue your dream of being a hero, but at some point I will snap my fingers and you will crawl back to me. Whether it's for a day, or a week, you'll crawl back, and you'll obey."

"No I won't! And I'm not for sale!"

"I'm not buying you, silly girl. It's my responsibility to take care of you, and it's your place to let me. As far as you coming when I call you, that will be because you want to, not because you feel like you owe me. You don't."

Jory let the warmth of that sink into her. Right then she just wanted to sleep, and to feel that maybe a little part of his black soul loved her back.

"Yes, Sir."

"Are you feeling floaty right now?"

"Yes."

His voice husked an almost soundless laugh. "Go to sleep, princess. We'll talk about this another time."

Sleep started to claim her, until she heard his voice.

"Jory," he commanded.

"Yes, Sir?"

"Thank you for calling me tonight. It pleased me."

Jory grimaced at herself as she tried to think of something to say in return. "Um, it pleased me too?" She winced and draped her arm over her eyes. Why was she such a dork?

"So I heard." He chuckled as he ended the call.

Chapter Eight

Valentine was filthy.

He swept his sweat-damp hair out of his eyes, and glanced around the clearing, wondering how the rest of his team was fairing. The target had been secured, and was on the ground, at his feet. Was it safe to go looking for Xana, at least, or should he stay put?

He strained to hear details of what was going on. There were still rapid footfalls in the surrounding forest, and blasts of power, but it was hard to tell what was from his group and what was from the Atypicals hired as guards. At least no heroes had turned up to complicate matters. They seemed to be everywhere lately.

Glancing down at the crate, Valentine struggled with the feeling that no matter how much they were getting paid for this, the stupid box wasn't worth risking his friends' safety.

Why was it that as soon as an Atypical showed power in certain areas, their fates were decided for them? He'd yet to meet a kid who could throw a bolt of power whose parents didn't expect them to have some sort of career in combat. What if the kid wanted to be an accountant or a mechanic? They didn't choose to have the abilities they were born with, but once their talents manifested, their life choices narrowed considerably.

Wind cooled the sweat on his neck. Waiting was killing him.

A branch cracked nearby, and Jurgen wandered out of the woods, with Dane at his heels. Valentine's heart sank.

"Where's Xa – Squall?" Hard to remember to use team names when he was worried, but there was no knowing who was listening.

The two blonds shrugged.

"I thought she was with you, Rigg," Dane said, looking around as though Xana would appear on cue.

Valentine grimaced. "She took off while I was fighting the ogre-looking guy. One of you stay with the crate, and one of you come with me."

A hand gesture from Dane made Jurgen stay. He was seething, still not happy with how their D/s was starting to leak over into their work. Dane was always trying to protect him, even though Jurgen was able to fuck with people's gravity, and all of them were extensively trained in melee fighting.

In a way, Valentine was glad that his relationship with Xana had ended years before they'd started working. He couldn't imagine accepting the humiliation of having his Dom tell him what to do in a work context. Submitting had never been a natural role for him. He'd loved Xana enough to submit to her, but he really wasn't switch material.

The forest had fallen quiet, and the slanting sunset cast strange shadows through snow-heavy tree limbs. The ground's white blanket was churned up in places, and a chaotic collection of footprints in different sizes looped around trees, disappearing, reappearing, mixed with slush and clods of dirt.

He stood and listened, hoping to hear something that would at least give him a direction to work with.

In the distance, he heard a cough, and with silent steps he tracked it.

Xana. She was leaning against a tree, spitting blood on the ground.

Fuck.

He got to her only moments before Dane.

"Squall – you okay?"

Xana snorted. "That guy had a fist like a hammer. I think my molar is loose. The rest is just a split lip."

Valentine breathed a sigh of relief. "You can't go fucking off like that," he whispered angrily. "You might be our team lead, but that doesn't make you invincible."

Dane left Valentine to take care of her and scouted the area for lingering enemies.

"I think they're gone," Xana murmured. "The redhead gave a whistle and they hightailed it out of here. At least they were other mercs. Money only buys so much zealotry."

Not like heroes. Heroes were motivated by their convictions more than money. It made them more dangerous, but also put them in more danger. What was he thinking, allowing Jory to get mixed up with those fanatics? A vision of her lying in the trees, alone, bleeding out, made his insides twist. He felt sick. Had he done the right thing by letting her go, even though he couldn't protect her from so far away?

Valentine led Xana out of the forest, but only after she absolutely refused to be transported by his ropes. Why were women so stubborn?

They got back to the others, and headed back down the road to their truck. The chalet-style cottage still smoldered, which was unfortunate. When they'd arrived, it had been lovely sitting there in the midst of the newly fallen snow. Like the cover of a Christmas CD. Now it looked like the set of a horror movie.

"Should we check to see what's in the crate?" Xana asked.

"We looked. The items that were on the retrieval order are all there. It looks like they were going to deliver them to one buyer," Jurgen assured her.

Dane helped Valentine load the crate into the back of the truck then got in the back with it, in case they were followed or attacked from behind.

"What is that shit, anyway?" Jurgen asked.

"We don't get paid to ask questions," Valentine reminded him. "It's probably better that we don't know."

They were words he automatically parroted, but they were his father's beliefs, not his own. He'd found himself repeating them under his breath lately, but it had been easier to think that way when the work had been theoretical. Jobs like this, when they didn't know what they were retrieving, sometimes made it hard to fall asleep later.

There was no guarantee their actions wouldn't hurt innocent people, and that bothered him. Using the excuse that he was just the hired help seemed to work for his father and the older team, but he doubted that bullshit would fly with someone like Jory. She'd never said much about him becoming a mercenary, but for some reason the fact that she was aiming to become a hero made him feel unworthy of her.

Before her, he'd only known Typicals, mercs, and Mundane Atypicals. He'd been raised to think of heroes as a joke.

Jory and her passion for good were no joke.

Xana glanced over at him with a brow raised, but turned her attention back to the road. "Your father might believe that, but we need to figure out what our limits are. Far be it from me to be the fucking moral compass in this group, but just because we're taking paying jobs now doesn't mean we have to abandon our ethics."

"Holy shit. Did *she* just say ethics?" Jurgen chuckled and she glared at him in the rearview mirror.

"Oh, like you're one to talk. You weren't complaining about my ethics when Dane and I double teamed you the other day," Xana shot back.

"Enough." Valentine sighed. If the three of them were sleeping together again, it complicated things. They tended to argue more, for example. "Not until we make the drop, okay? We need to focus on the job."

The two of them fell into a sullen silence. He thumbed the bulge of phone in his pocket. It had been hours since he'd checked it. Had Jory sent anything? She texted him at least once a day, lately, but he seldom replied. Maybe it was the wrong way of doing things, but he was hoping if he didn't respond to text messages, she'd call again.

Her call from two weeks ago still replayed in his head when he lay awake at night. Aside from being hot, it had meant something that she'd called him for help. Thinking of the details of the call while on a job was probably a bad idea, though, considering it was one of the most distracting memories he owned.

"We should discuss our limits later tonight, after the drop, then," Jurgen suggested. "I don't want to go too far down a rabbit hole and discover there's no way out."

Valentine watched out the windows, waiting for trouble, but there didn't seem to be a high speed chase looming in their future. "Fine, but I'm not staying up drinking or anything. I'm still going upstate tomorrow morning."

"You do realize that puts you over the line of creepy, straight into disturbed, right?" Xana laughed mirthlessly.

"I know. I just have to check, then things will go back to normal." No. He had to check so he didn't go crazy.

Jurgen snorted, but Xana just stared at the road.

*

A hotel room would have served Valentine's purposes, except for the lack of privacy. As it was, it had only taken a few hours online to search for and buy the converted coach house in the country, and have everything changed into his name the same week. Early Friday he drove out in his pickup, and arrived at the real estate office four hours later. It was amazing how fast people moved when you threw money at them. No mortgage crap to deal with. No sitting in offices or waiting for appointments.

He collected the keys from the agent then went alone to the house. Considering he'd bought it after only seeing it online, he was pleased that it was clean and well maintained. A few more calls, and an obscene amount of money later, his orders were prioritized, and furniture and food were delivered.

For the first time in his life, he owned a house. He stood in the living room and looked around, awed by his own lunacy.

What the hell was he doing?

He spent a few hours rearranging things and wandering the grounds while he tried to talk himself into going home. But where was home, exactly?

His apartment by the college was decent, but it was too far from the rest of his team to make sense. Now there was no point in keeping it, either, since he'd quit his job as a TA and had switched to online courses. Jory was gone. He had no reason to be there anymore.

Staying with his parents put him closer to his team, but being under their roof was uncomfortable. What he should have done was get a place near there – maybe bought a house with the others to start off with, so they'd have a base of operation. Meeting in the poolroom at Xana's parents' house was awkward.

Instead, here he was.

She hadn't even asked him to visit, even though he'd offered, and yet he'd brought things to a whole new level of obsession. Other than the one desperate phone call, she didn't give the impression she needed him at all, other than to send him occasional blasé texts. Why would she? Jory had her shit together. She knew what she wanted out of life, and it had nothing to do with him.

He just had to see that she was all right then he'd sell this stupid house and go look for an apartment near his team.

He'd see she was all right then vacate the house for now, and keep it just in case.

He'd see she was all right then invite her for dinner.

He'd kidnap her out of her bed and keep her in the damn house. Forever. Naked except for her collar.

Although Evil Valentine was promptly told to shut up, the other Valentines had to concede that the villain had a point. She made him crazy and didn't seem to notice. It hardly seemed fair.

Frustrated by his own indecision, he got in the truck and drove into town, not sure where his obsession would lead him.

Prescott, the city that hosted the training center, thrived because of it. Even the older downtown section had been revamped. Atypicals walked along the main roads, peeking into quaint, restored shops and chatting with each other on the sidewalks. It had the surreal air of a movie set. As he looked for somewhere to get coffee, he felt the pull of her behind his ribs. She was close.

He parked quickly and barely had the presence of mind to put money in the meter. The pull led him a block away, to an old, distinguished building with columns and ivy, and stone steps leading up to double doors. Library? Why would she be at a library? Maybe no one had told her the Internet delivered books to a person's house.

As he pushed open a heavy wooden door, he was greeted by the smell of old books. Even though he always thought he preferred technology, there was a comfortable and satisfying feeling that came with the scent. The young woman at the front desk smiled a welcome, and he absently smiled back, but the closer he got to Jory the less in control he felt.

His internal Jory location system was insistently urging him to seek her out, but he slowed his steps. It was ridiculous that he was there in the first place. Not knowing what else to do, he found a spot tucked away upstairs where he could sit. He picked up the novel someone had left on the seat and began to read.

Maybe just seeing her from afar would satisfy his longing.

The feel of her moving along the stacks, beelining to him as though they'd arranged to meet there, made his pulse quicken. Soft footsteps sounded, and the tension in his body became almost unbearable. So many weeks they'd been apart.

The steps slowed, and a wide-eyed Jory peeked around the corner of the bookcase. Her pale cheeks bloomed pink. A tension he'd been carrying eased. She was okay.

"Valentine?" Her voice quavered.

"Yes, girl?"

Jory's eyes shut and she clutched at the bookcase. Even in this dark corner, her beauty lit the shadow. His memories of her didn't compare to the real thing.

"What…what are you doing here?"

He gave a half-shrug, trying to seem calm. He was anything but calm. It might have helped if he'd decided what to say beforehand.

In frustration, he snapped his fingers and pointed to the spot in front of his feet. She whimpered, and glanced around, but there was no one in sight. Clumsily, she knelt before him, as though she didn't want to but couldn't help herself. With her head bowed and her shoulders rolled inward, she looked completely miserable.

He shouldn't have come.

With gentle fingers he nudged her chin upward, until she met his gaze. Almost without thinking, his hand shifted to her neck.

She still wore his collar.

The apology he meant to make evaporated.

Valentine froze, staring into her eyes and feeling the pulse in her throat stutter to sync with his own. "Do I need an excuse to check on my property?"

She sighed and leaned into his hand, as though his grip there was exactly what she wanted.

Her head tilted to the side, and he leaned in and bit the flesh she exposed for him. Quietly, she cried out, and Valentine's dick stirred in response.

"No, Sir. You don't need an excuse."

Perhaps it was juvenile, but he admired the purpling mark his bite left. The collar would never be enough evidence of his ownership.

He claimed her mouth with his own, and felt their powers straining for each other, but he reined his in. Deliberately, he broke the kiss first, enjoying the way she leaned toward him for more.

"This is a public place, love," he chided.

"But I need you," she whispered.

"Is that so? And yet you haven't called me in weeks." He raised a brow at her and she melted into a little puddle of girl.

"I know. I've been trying to forget about you," she admitted. "Between training and studying, I almost managed."

He chuckled. "Liar. You lie awake at night thinking about me."

She didn't answer. Her hands crept up his thighs toward his zipper. He grabbed her wrists and her whimper set his teeth on edge.

"Please, Sir."

"Public sex isn't very hero-like behavior."

A desperate smile trembled at her lips. "No kids are allowed up here, and hardly anyone is here today. Please, Sir. I'll be so, so quiet."

Valentine glanced around casually. There was no one in sight, but that didn't mean things would stay that way.

Without warning, he yanked her up into his lap, facing away from him, and shoved her leggings down. She gasped in surprise, as though she hadn't really thought he'd do it, but didn't protest when he unfastened his jeans and pressed into her. He gritted his teeth to keep from groaning aloud, but it didn't stop her whimpers. Her body was ready for him, welcomed him, clenched around him, daring him to lose control. With one hand he held both wrists behind her back. Slowly, he fucked her, delighting in every tiny tortured sound that escaped her, his heart hammering as he kept watch for staff and other patrons. Her ass was a perfect white canvas, and he longed to take his belt to her. She was so fucking gorgeous.

Being inside her made everything clear again.

She struggled against his hold, wriggling on his cock as he pumped his cock into her. Her tight pussy clutched at him, quivering. She tensed, whining softly, waiting for permission. The elation of having this control over her was heady.

"Are you going to come for me, snowangel?" he breathed the words into her ear.

Jory's breath caught, and her body froze, his words giving her the permission he could feel her body waiting for.

She fought against his grip as she came, and he held her in place with both arms wrapped around her, letting her frenetic movements bring him to the edge. He waited, reveling in the feel of her fighting her own pleasure, letting her use his cock to get herself off. Just as her orgasm started to wane, he bit down on her earlobe. His girl squealed and he clamped a hand over her mouth as she came again, squeezing his cock so tightly that it forced his own orgasm. He grunted, his noise muffled by her hair as he spilled into her, hoping to hell it wasn't so loud that people came to investigate.

The way she whimpered into his hand stiffened his cock again before he'd even gone soft.

"Shh, baby girl. We have to go." He pulled out and urged her up, then chuckled at her grimace when he fixed her clothes for her. Rezipping his jeans as quietly as possible, he glanced around.

Heeled shoes clicked nearby, and Valentine wondered if they'd had a voyeur.

Jory's cheeks were flushed, her pale hair wild. She was more lovely than ever.

"Whenever you see people do things like this on TV, they never talk about not being able to clean up afterward," she whispered. "If you were any kind of gentleman, you'd offer me your handkerchief or something."

"The only person I know who carries a handkerchief is my grandfather, and whether he's lent it to my grandmother for this sort of thing isn't something I want to think about."

She giggled – an uncharacteristic sound for her – and covered her face with her hands. She sniffled, and Valentine rose and slipped an arm around her shoulders. Quickly, she led him past oblivious readers and studiers, to the table where she collected her coat and backpack. They left the building, and made their way down the street to the truck. By the time he buckled her in, she'd dissolved into quiet sobs. In moments they were headed down the main road, and Valentine cranked the heat. He hadn't thought about the logistics of doing aftercare in public.

As he drove, he rubbed her knee and stroked her hair, touching her any way he could manage. The size of the truck made it harder to reach her, and for the first time in his life he regretted not owning an Austin Mini.

The drive wasn't that long, but struggling between whether to get home or pull over made it feel endless.

"Where are you taking me?" she asked as they left the city limits.

"Not far. I should have asked if you had plans for today, but the truth is I don't care."

Jory lifted her chin, showing a willfulness she never kept long around him. "If you're expecting me to safeword a drive, forget it. I'll save that for more important things."

He smiled at her sidelong. "I have a place nearby where we can go and talk."

"Talk?" She wiped her face with the back of her coat sleeve. "We don't seem to be very big on talking."

The girl had a point. She seemed to have pulled herself together, so he figured she might be able to handle being teased. "Hey, the library wasn't my idea." He chuckled. "Not that I'm complaining."

"I couldn't wait," she whispered, leaning her head against the car window. "I had to have you inside me right away." She went quiet for a few minutes before speaking again. "You were right, I am a pervert. I don't think I can blame it on the Aphrodisia anymore."

Valentine stared out the window at the snowy landscape. They'd made it far enough outside of the city that there were only occasional houses, with white smoke spiraling up from their chimneys like thread binding them to the pale sky. The sunlight was weak – someone needed to spoon feed it and coddle it back to its former brilliance. For weeks there had been weather like this – no sun, no light. Being away from Jory made the winter cold and desolate. Without her eyelashes to melt it, snow held no magic.

"This isn't impossible. I'm not going to show up on your missions and drag you off by the hair." Although the idea of dragging her away from danger and off somewhere to amuse him was, admittedly, an interesting one. "The only people who know about our dynamic are on my team, and they'd never out us."

"Oh, and how can you be sure about that? What would stop them? I'm nothing to them." Her tone was challenging, and his initial instinct was to pull over and deal with her attitude, but he could feel the anxiety under the words. Just like being a mercenary, being a hero partially relied on a person's reputation. Unfortunately, submissives still got little respect outside of BDSM circles, as though being strong enough to put themselves at someone else's mercy made them inherently weak. People who thought that had obviously never tried it, but the stigma remained.

"They're kinksters too, as you saw. They'd never out another kinkster. It's considered worse than just bad manners, Jory. And they're loyal to me. Very loyal."

She exhaled shakily. How long had she been worrying about that? Probably since she'd met them.

He turned off on the unnamed side road, then onto his long driveway, pleased that a fresh layer of snow had blanketed the place and made it pretty for her.

Jory peered through the windshield at it, eyes round. "Wow – what a beautiful old house. Does it belong to a friend of yours?"

With the truck parked, he got out and went around to the passenger side to help her down. Confession time. "It's mine. I took possession of it this morning."

Her brows knit. "I didn't know you had any connection to this area."

Valentine smiled down at her, and twirled a finger into a lock of hair near her face, then gave it a playful tug.

"Wealthy men don't take their stalking lightly."

Chapter Nine

The fathomless black of his eyes lured her in, and trapped her in their depths. A thrill of fear cut with pure lust buzzed through her. Stalking was only disturbing if the victim was unwilling. With him, it was sinister in a way that made her want to run so he'd chase her. It held the heart-pounding terror of a game nearly out of control, but ultimately safe.

She trusted him even though sometimes it seemed like he wanted her to think she shouldn't. Maybe he didn't trust himself. It was possible this man was capable of true evil, but not when it came to her. He'd honor her safeword, even if he didn't really want to.

His smile was feral.

Wouldn't he?

Why would a man like Valentine think she was worth all of this? No one else seemed to notice her.

"Did you just say this is your house?"

"Yes. I just moved in."

"And you bought it to make it easier to stalk me?" She lifted a brow at him teasingly.

His chuckle was as dark as his gaze and even though her pussy was sore, she felt herself responding to him. It was the kind of chuckle that implied he was going to chain her in his basement and alternate between making her scream in agony and making her come so hard she fainted.

If only she could have this and have a future as a hero too. But no one would respect her if they found out what she let him do – and how much she loved and craved it.

She'd tried to convince herself no one would find out, but there was too much danger that they would. This was the sort of thing scandals were made of. If her new team achieved any kind of celebrity status, the details of her personal life wouldn't be private for long. She couldn't imagine being able to live with her family finding out, let alone having it splashed all over the news. How could she ever look people in the eye?

"We can't be together, Valentine. Not long term. This…situation…isn't good for my career."

His eyes narrowed and he backed her against the closed truck door. With gentle fingers he peeled back the collar of her coat and tunic top, baring her neck and shoulder. He nipped her there, then sucked long and slow, his mouth and tongue doing things that made her toes dig into the soles of her shoes.

A cold hand slipped down the front of her leggings, and she squealed as two frozen fingers worked their way into her heated core. His icy thumb rubbed over her clit. Jory leaned her head back against the truck window, the chill of his hand making her squirm, helpless, wanting desperately to get away, but afraid he'd let her go if she tried. Valentine pulled his fingers out of her suddenly, because he was a complete bastard. He walked away toward the house, turning back to smirk at her.

She followed like a toy on a pull cord.

What the hell was he planning?

When she stepped inside the house, it felt as if she'd been transported to a different time. It was very old, and made her think of long, sweeping dresses and characters from Jane Austen novels. There were modern amenities, she saw, as they passed the kitchen, but they were disguised among things that seemed original to the house. Stone and plaster were everywhere, and exposed wooden beams. Was love at first sight with a building possible?

"Do you like it?"

"Yes! It's beautiful! Did you see it first, or did you buy it sight unseen?"

"There were pictures online, but they didn't really do it justice." He led her into a living room with a ridiculously huge window seat. She almost fainted. Could she bribe him to let her read books at his place? "Look." He gestured out the window. There were the ruins of a huge, old house.

"What is that?"

"This is the coach house for that grand house. It rotted and fell in after it was abandoned a few decades ago. I haven't had time to look around there much yet. Behind that are overgrown gardens that look like a winter jungle right now. I'm going to have my work cut out for me if I decide to keep the place."

"If?" Jory asked. "Why would you buy it just to sell it again?"

He unzipped her winter coat and slid it down off her shoulders, then took it away with him into the foyer. She followed him and kicked off her boots when she saw the puddles they were leaving on the wood floor.

"I don't honestly know. I bought it on a whim, and thought I'd keep it while you were training here, so we could see each other away from prying eyes." He pulled her into his arms and kissed her once, then let her go. "If you want to end things, though, you could use it for whatever you want until you're done here. I'll sell it later."

She snorted. "You're crazy. You already lent me a car I can't drive. You're not lending me a house too."

"What do you mean you can't drive the car?" He frowned. "I saw you drive it."

"I can't drive that thing around. It's worth a zillion dollars. I don't come from that kind of money and I'll never make that much. What am I supposed to tell people? That I have a rich…um…sugar daddy?" Even saying the words made her uncomfortable. She shook her head, thinking of how embarrassing it had been renting a safe garage to keep the car in until she could figure out how to return it to him without hurting his feelings.

"I wouldn't mind if you told people." He winked and she felt herself flush. "But I understand why you want our situation to be discreet. I'll sell the car and get you something less suspicious-looking."

"No, you won't. That's ridiculous."

"Did I ask you for your opinion?" He hooked a finger under her collar and hauled her to him. "And you're lucky the house is still a bit cold, or I'd punish you for not being naked in my presence."

"You didn't make me crawl into the house, either, Sir. You're slipping." She smiled sweetly, and wasn't surprised when he tangled a hand in her hair. Her nipples immediately hardened in response.

"If you want pain from me, all you have to do is ask," he growled. "I'm sure I can accommodate you without the bratting."

She blinked at him, afraid to tell him how much that idea excited her. What if he went further than she could handle? What if he introduced her to all sorts of horrible, perverted things that she ended up loving, and then couldn't get off without?

The way he looked at her implied that he saw everything she hadn't said. "Maybe we'll talk about that later, when it's warmer in here." He went to the stone fireplace that graced one wall and built a fire in it as though he'd done so many times before. In no time one was blazing, and the chill started to fade from the room.

Valentine joined her on the window seat, pulled her into his arms and brushed her cheek with his lips. She relaxed against him, not too proud to steal his body heat even though she didn't need it. The warmth still felt nice. "So what have you been up to while I've been at combat training?"

He sighed. "My father decided that I'd been wasting time at school long enough. He's letting me finish my master's online, but he and his group have started arranging extra contracts and giving us the work that's straightforward."

She could feel him tense where her back rested against him.

"You don't sound very happy. Is it that he pulled you out of school? Or have you not liked the contracts?" The thought of Valentine dressed in leather and looking mean in some sort of clandestine situation was hotter than it should have been. Heroes weren't supposed to lust after mercenaries. They were self-serving troublemakers, and often ended up on the wrong side of the law.

"The money's good." He gestured around the room, as though his recent work had paid for it. "Maybe it would be different if my team was a bunch of people I'd just met. But as it is, I spend a lot of my time worrying about the others getting hurt. They're good fighters, but money doesn't feel like a good enough reason to put my friends in harm's way."

"You've known them for a long time?" Lying in his arms gave her the calmest feeling she'd had in weeks. Tension she hadn't known she was carrying started to loosen and dissipate.

"Yeah, we were raised together. I'd say we were like family, but the fact that we've slept together makes that sound bad." He chuckled, and Jory had to push away a jealousy she had no right to. It was none of her business, but she'd seen the way Xana looked at him. Even if he wasn't in love with her, his team leader still had feelings for him.

Jory was also envious that he had a team he could rely on, that he'd known forever. As it was, the new team she'd been assigned to seemed nice, but they were strangers. Her new roommate, Seraphina, seemed to have her head screwed on straight, at least.

Although she was curious and wanted to ask him for more details about the missions he'd been on, she wasn't sure how much was appropriate to ask. With the other Atypicals at training school there were no real secrets about who had been on what mission and why.

Did mercenaries know the purpose behind all of their contracts? Did they only get told what they had to know? Were they told where their work fit into their employers' bigger plans?

In various classes at combat school they'd been learning about world politics, both official and unofficial. At any point they might be asked to help with missions to keep people safe from international threats, or home-grown criminal elements, and they had to have a rudimentary understanding of how things were connected.

Who taught that sort of thing to mercenaries? Was there some sort of mercenary training school? If there was, why hadn't she ever heard of it? Maybe they were homeschooled or something.

It was probably safer to stick to personal information for the time being. She didn't want to sound like a spy for the Bureau of Atypical Affairs.

Shit, what had they been talking about? Oh, his team.

"So…you've slept with all of them, even Dane and Jurgen?" She was waiting for him to laugh and shake his head, and say she'd misunderstood. Instead his smile was enigmatic.

"Yes. Like I said, we've known each other for a long time, and we've gone through several different…relationship configurations together. They'd all be interested in me sharing you with them, but I've put them off. At least for now." He paused. "Does it bother you that I'm bisexual?"

Bisexual?

Oh…my.

The thought of Valentine making out with his handsome teammates made the chill room suddenly warm. But the idea of the lot of them sharing her stalled before anyone even had the chance to get naked in her head. It wasn't something she was ready for, and doubted she ever would be.

"No, it doesn't bother me at all."

"Good. Some girls have a hard time dealing with the fact that I got my first blowjob from Jurgen."

Was there a fan or something in the room that she could use? She thought of sexy blond Jurgen going to his knees, Valentine's hand tangling painfully in his hair…

She whistled under her breath. Maybe talking about personal things hadn't been as safe as she'd thought.

Think about something else, Jory. Think about…uh…work.

"Your team hasn't been doing jobs that are too dangerous though, has it?" She wrapped a protective hand around the top of his calf, as though it would save him from the bad guys she imagined him fighting for whatever they fought for.

"We've only done a few jobs so far." He patted her shoulder. "Nothing to worry about."

She had the urge to strip him down and check for new scars, but figured he'd probably take that the wrong way.

"Remember that you always have the option to say no. It's just money."

"I suppose you don't figure there's any reason for me to risk myself, if it's just for money," he growled. "Although you may not think my work is as important as yours, I do take it seriously. Incomplete contracts don't look good."

Oops. Had she hurt his ego?

"I didn't mean it like that, but if it's not a matter of life and death, at least walking away might be a little more possible."

"We were discussing that the other day. With mercenaries you only get as much loyalty as you pay for." He laughed humorlessly. "But our performance reflects on our parents' team. Basically, they're vouching for us. If we fuck up too badly it makes them look bad too."

"I can see that, and I'm sure if you have a string of unfinished contracts, it'll make it harder to get new business."

"Yes, exactly."

Jory rolled onto her side and gazed up at him. He didn't look annoyed, thank goodness.

Valentine traced her lips with his fingertip. "You don't have to tiptoe around the subject of my work. Your opinion about my lack of morality isn't exactly a secret."

She frowned at him and sighed. "I don't think you're immoral." Maybe he was a little immoral, but she wasn't about to say so, considering she liked it.

"Why don't we talk about something less sensitive for now, like your work. What's new with you?"

"They assigned me to a different team a couple of days ago. The first group they assigned me to was annoying, and I had a few choice words with the team leader, Summer. I just moved into my new room. My roommate, Seraphina, is on my team, and she seems really nice."

"It's a team of four?"

"Yup. Me, Seraphina, and two guys. It seems like a much better fit so far." She kissed his neck and he pressed his cheek to the top of her head. The affection warmed her to her toes. "It's funny. The team-matching process is very high school. Those days seem like ancient history to me, but I guess it forms the basis of how some people interact indefinitely."

He squeezed her as if in apology for the state of the human race. She couldn't help but snuggle into him as though she hadn't been trying to put him out of her mind for weeks. It had been self-preservation. Truthfully, she'd thought he'd taken her call in the middle of the night out of politeness. Afterward, she'd focused hard on all of the humiliations he'd inflicted on her, and how he'd used her, and she'd purposefully pushed aside memories of moments like this when he held her and kissed her and they talked. It had been easier to think of him as a user rather than try to figure out how he actually felt.

"It sounds like the first group was immature and you're better off getting away from them now, while you can. It must be hard to get to know a team as an adult. For us, we know all of each other's little quirks and triggers. All the history. You have to learn everything about your team from scratch."

"My last group was very...perky. That means they'll probably get a lot of airtime on news reports and things like that – their own comic books, cereal, maybe even a cartoon. There is a lure to that sort of life. You get to be a role model, but that isn't the reason why I wanted to become a hero."

"No." Valentine laughed. "You definitely aren't that type."

"Lord, I hope not. There are enough of those types hanging around the world already and from what I've seen of them in real life, they're basically beta teams with good hair." She traced a finger down the inseam of his blue jeans, by his knee, then tried not to laugh when he twitched away, ticklish. "Did you know, sometimes they give teams like that credit for jobs that other teams actually did the work on? It's ridiculous. Like only popular people are capable of doing good in the world?"

Valentine sighed and she could have sworn he put his nose to her hair and smelled her. "Those groups are just PR campaigns for Atypicals, really. Before Atypicals started doing marketing, and the Typicals were still afraid, life was harder for people like us. So really, as silly as they are, there is a place for trophy teams in the scheme of things."

"I think the whole thing insults the intelligence of Typical people. Just because they're Typical doesn't mean they're gullible."

"I hear what you're saying, love, but you also have to remember that you're smarter than the average person, Typical or Atypical. Most people prefer not to have to think very hard."

Jory rolled her eyes. "If Typicals are ignorant of the facts, it's because we encourage them to be."

"True, but that keeps us safer. Think about your Atypical history. I kind of enjoy the fact that nobody is trying to lock me up or exterminate me. The government stays out of my business, and no one is telling me who I am or am not allowed to sleep with."

"Oh?" Jory said carefully. "And do you…sleep with a lot of people?"

"Only you since I met you." Valentine chuckled. "Considering how things are between us, do you seriously think I could settle for anything less?"

Fish for information and you shall receive. His words were so sincere, and he wasn't a liar, but it was so hard to believe that he'd settle for her – average, boring, careful Jory – instead of hooking up with some hot, rich, mercenary girl. He had to have a string of those lined up outside his house. Well, maybe the lineup was at his apartment, since she hadn't seen any women in the front yard when they'd come in.

When she didn't say anything, he patted her arm. "So, what's in your backpack? It looks full even though you didn't check out any books."

"I wasn't there for books," she said. "I was just there to do some research."

"Were you researching how to drive men crazy?" he asked with mock irritation. "Take it from me, you don't need extra credit in that subject. However, I would like to have a word with your ethics committee."

She snorted. Like she knew the first thing about how to lure a guy? "It's just some notes and my uniform. They want us wearing it when we can so we get used to it before we actually start fighting in the field. They're not comfortable."

"Interesting. So they get you to work for next to no money, and give you uncomfortable uniforms. Are you sure you haven't joined some sort of religious order? Next they'll be ordering you to engage in self-flagellation."

"Meh, I have people for that."

"Oh, do you?"

"I'm sure I could convince you to beat me." Beneath her, he went very still. Shit. Her and her big mouth.

"I might even make you like it." His words hung between them like an electrical current. If anyone moved or said the wrong thing, this pleasant conversation could explode.

His fingers slipped into her hair and dragged along her scalp. Jory full-body shivered.

"Show me your uniform," he commanded.

Bossy.

"It's silly," she replied, glad the dangerous moment seemed to have passed. For now. "At least our colors aren't too bad, though. The costume for the last team was too flashy for me. Like spandex isn't bad enough without adding Technicolor and competing patterns."

He coaxed her up and she went to her backpack. The costume slipped along her fingers, as she yanked it out, just wanting to get his derision over with. She brandished it at him, the bodysuit's fabric bouncing in her nervous grip.

"Black and red? Very goth." The corner of his mouth twitched, but he was polite enough not to laugh out loud.

"Yeah, nothing says badass like spandex. We're like an eighties metal band. I almost have the right hair for it, too, except I don't need to backcomb or hairspray mine."

"Put it on."

"Now?"

"The now was implied."

"But…" She didn't want to. It was her uniform. It was going to be hard enough to take herself seriously without having memories of him defiling her while wearing the thing.

"Obey now or there will be consequences." The crease between his brows said he was serious, even though his voice had actually gotten quieter.

Oh fuck. The consequences sounded exciting, but she wasn't brave enough to test that theory.

"Can I get changed in the bathroom, Sir? Believe me when I tell you there is nothing sexy about watching someone trying to wiggle into a spandex bodysuit." She looked at him hopefully and he waved a hand.

She ducked out of the room before he could change his mind, stripping fast in the bathroom she'd spotted down the hall, and trying to wipe away some of the mess he'd made in her at the library. Putting the suit on was a feat of athletics that left her breathless. If nothing else, it would be a good warm-up for combat situations.

When she got back to the living room, self-conscious, she was surprised to find Valentine still sitting in the huge window seat, but now wearing black leather.

Hot fucking damn.

With the way he looked, Jory was reminded again how much less cool uniforms were for heroes. The male heroes at combat school were so clean cut compared to Valentine. Come to think of it, it probably had a lot to do with his presence and aura too. Absolutely nothing about Valentine suggested he was harmless.

He sat there, smiling at her, with the air of a man who enjoyed what he was seeing. "That uniform is…very distracting. I can see why they dress you up that way."

She moved closer to him and he stood. The leather he wore creaked slightly, and smelled divine.

"It's not supposed to be distracting." She pressed her lips together in disapproval. "It's aerodynamic and lightweight."

"It doesn't leave anything to the imagination, that's for sure. If I fought you while you were wearing that you'd win, but it would be cheating."

She laughed, and flushed. "If you're that easily distracted, it's a wonder you ever complete any of your contracts."

His gaze wandered over her like she was every bit as distracting as he'd claimed. "Cold?" He was close enough to touch her now and he reached out a hand and trailed gentle fingers over the peak of her breast. "Or is keying cars with your nipples one of your powers?"

"Wouldn't you like to know?"

"Yes, yes I would." He smiled slowly, and her belly fluttered in response. "I guess if I'm going to pierce your nipples, we'll have to figure out how to hide the telltale bumps it will leave."

"Pierce my…hell no." She moved away from the fire, suddenly feeling overly warm.

"I guess I could pierce your clit hood instead. Eventually they'll make you remove my collar, and I have to make sure you're marked as mine."

"Oh?" She cocked her head at him, and his eyes flashed with a dominance he was holding back. "I'm yours, am I? To the extent that you need to mark me?"

He traced the spots on her neck and shoulder where he'd bitten her, and she could almost still feel the marks throb.

"I thought it would be more pleasant for you than me having to pin you down every day to leave bites and hickeys on you, but suit yourself."

Time to change the subject. "We'll talk, stalker boy. So where did you pull those leathers from? I know you weren't wearing them under your other clothes. I checked." She winked, and he chuckled.

"No, I had them in the truck. Apparently they're easier to get into than your uniform is."

"I had to clean myself up, too. Someone left a mess in my underwear."

"You're blaming me for that? Most of that come was yours."

The blush she'd been trying to hold off roared up her neck to set her cheeks on fire. That whole library thing had been so unlike her. For a moment, she covered her eyes with a trembling hand, ashamed. He'd made her come so hard.

"You were dripping down my cock and all over my balls before I even came," he said darkly, close enough now that his chest was right in front of her nose. "And here I'd thought you might not be happy to see me."

"Stop, please," she begged. "I don't want to talk about that." She leaned her forehead against his jacket, inhaling the mixture of man and leather, his breast pocket's zipper digging into her skin.

"There's nothing shameful about wanting your dominant, girl. It's in your job description."

She punched his chest playfully and used the momentum to step away from him. "Why did you bring your leathers, anyway? Just to show me how much cooler the dark side is?"

"No, but you should get some leathers, too. They provide more protection than your uniform, as interesting as it is." He frowned at her spandex, looking concerned. "I thought we should spar for a few minutes. I want to see what you can do."

"Why?"

Valentine's eyes narrowed. "You haven't had any missions yet. I have. I've also had years of training. After what I've seen in the field, I'm worried about you. If you're going to be fighting alongside a bunch of strangers, you need to know how to take care of yourself when I'm not there."

She walked away and perched on the arm of the sofa. "You're not my father, Valentine. What are you going to do – forbid me to fight if I don't spar well enough to satisfy you? I hate to have to break this to you, but there are qualified people overseeing that sort of thing at the school. I don't need you to be a backseat driver in my training."

A harsh sound escaped him. "You're so sweet, Jory. You don't know how bad things can get. Hell, I don't even know how bad things can get yet. But what I do know is that if you don't show me you can fight well enough to satisfy me, I'm going to keep you here until I decide you're ready."

"You and what army?" she growled.

"I don't need an army. You'll do what I tell you, when I tell you. I'm *allowing* you to continue your training, but you'd better remember that I'm your dominant, little bitch, and you answer to me. When we're together, you will remember your place."

Jory felt her teeth grinding in response to her frustration. He was unbearably sexy, but sometimes he was also insufferable.

"I've read enough about submission to know that what I submit to is up to me. You can huff and puff all you want, big bad wolf, but you don't have any power over me that I don't give you." They stared at each other and the stubborn set of Valentine's jaw led her to believe she might be in trouble.

"Then show me you can handle yourself, and there won't be a problem." He shrugged, but his gaze was anything but casual.

"Fine. We'll spar. And when I kick your ass, you have to agree to submit to *me* for the rest of the day."

He chuckled. "And what are you planning to do to me if I submit to you, smartypants?"

Jory chewed on her lip and tried out a dommy eyebrow arch. "That's for me to know and you to regret later."

His chuckle implied he wasn't intimidated by her expression. "So what do I get if I win?"

"You're not going to win. I suppose for the sake of argument we should agree on something now. What do you want?" she asked cautiously. If he was going to ask her to give up training or something crazy, she wouldn't agree to that. He thought he was hot shit, but her power was probably more useful than his. Probably.

"If I win, you stay here with me until Sunday night."

"Like, have a sleepover? Are we going to do each other's nails, too?"

"Oh, I'll be nailing you. Don't you worry your pretty little head about that."

Pig. "What? No pillow fights?"

"Those are negotiable. I may give you a pillow to bite while I fuck your ass."

She did her best to keep her sudden anxiety out of her expression. Anal wasn't a hard limit, and he'd been trying to brainwash her into thinking she could like it, but if she lost their little competition, maybe he wouldn't care if she liked it or not.

"Hmm." She arched a brow at him, trying to appear worldly and tough. Maybe she wasn't sexually experienced, but she did have the damn Internet. "There's a thought. Maybe I'll let you have a pillow to bite when I win. I hope you're into pegging."

He chuckled low, a sound that made the little hairs stand up on the back of her neck.

"Shall we?" He led her outside, and she was glad the sun had come out. That was one thing she'd wondered about with their uniforms – was exertion supposed to keep them warm? It wasn't a huge issue for her, considering she didn't usually feel cold unless she wanted to, but even in his leathers Valentine must have been feeling the chill in the air today.

Between the house and the garden was a wide cleared area where the snow had been removed. Jory was glad that the one practical part of her uniform – the knee-high boots – were also somewhat waterproof.

They squared off against each other, and Valentine looked her up and down as though he'd rather eat her than fight her.

"So how do we decide when the fight is over? First blood? Or is this to the death?" She tried to snicker at the serious look on his face, but he was so damn…serious.

A stone of dread dropped into her belly.

Chapter Ten

The house had a perfectly good basement to lock her up in. The idea was sounding more attractive all the time. Except how would he keep her safe when he had to go away on a contract? Money paid for silence, but he didn't have the first clue where to find a servant or two who wouldn't balk at the idea of taking care of someone who was being forcibly confined.

Movies always made that sort of thing seem easy to sort out.

For her part, Jory seemed to be completely oblivious to the thoughts running through his head. That was probably for the best.

She stretched, loosening up, her flexibility and grace unintentionally making him crazy to be inside her again. The uniform left nothing to the imagination and he was glad his leather pants were thick enough to restrain his erection. Sure, he'd seen hot heroes on TV before, but Jory in spandex sent his imagination into overdrive. Being around her, or even thinking about her, charged him with restless sexual energy.

Except when he was thinking of holding her, and the way she laughed at his stupid jokes. Those thoughts were very different.

"Aren't you going to warm up? Fighting without warming up first isn't good for your body. This line of work is hard enough on us already. Heroes never stay young for long."

"Maybe you should try being a mercenary, then. We tend to last longer. Maybe because we have a healthier dose of self-preservation. Or maybe it's all the scotch." Her concern for him was adorable, as though he was the one who needed babysitting.

"I don't think I've ever seen you drink."

"Drinking and BDSM don't mix. Every time you've seen me, I've had my sights set on playing with someone." He leaned against the wooden fence that ran the perimeter of the property and smiled suggestively.

"Do you really consider what we do together 'playing'?"

"No. Definitely not. It's just a euphemism some people use, but I definitely don't think our dynamic is a game. I haven't been more serious about anything in my life."

The blush that bloomed across her cheeks in response was fascinating.

Her gaze drifted to the side, as though she couldn't look directly at him. Was he coming off too creepy? Something about her brought that out in him, but luckily she didn't seem to mind.

"And that's why this is necessary." He smiled, pretending he was civilized. "If I'm going to allow you to put my property in danger, I'm damn well going to make sure you know how to kick ass."

"Has anyone ever told you you're an overbearing dickwad?"

"Maybe you misunderstood. This is supposed to be a sparring match – physical, not verbal. I already know how clever your tongue is."

She glanced surreptitiously at his bulge, then away again.

Don't even start thinking of using her mouth, or you're going to lose.

From the hook behind the house, he summoned a coil of rope that slithered obediently to him. Jory stared at it, hypnotized. She already knew what he could do, so it shouldn't have surprised her at all. Her reaction didn't fill him with confidence about her ability to handle herself in unknown situations.

"Hey!" He clapped his hands. "Pay attention. I'm not going to take it easy on you just because you're mine."

"I don't need your paternalistic bullshit, Valentine."

"I come with complimentary paternalistic bullshit. It's a package deal."

"There's no 'opt out' button?"

"There may be, but I doubt you could find it." He was like this with everyone he loved. If she was hoping he'd back off and let her get her head blown off with dignity, she was going to have to live with disappointment.

She glared at him. "Just so we're clear, when I'm in this uniform, you're not allowed to use my attraction to you as a weapon. Hard limit. No groping, either."

Valentine stifled a groan. Of course he'd fantasized about defiling her while she was in uniform. Maybe he'd eventually convince her to budge on that one.

"Fine. If you want to play dirty, then I'm not wearing my leathers when I fuck you later, either." It was a gamble, but her face fell.

"Well… Maybe it's okay to grope me a little if we're alone and sparring, but not if we ever fight each other in the field. Something like that would kill my reputation. You have to promise me."

Fight her in the field? The muscles in his neck were tense and he could feel a headache coming on. It had never occurred to him that they might have to fight each other. Was there a way for Atypicals in this line of work to get lists of which rivals were being used for missions so they could decline jobs? Could he claim conflict of interest? He and Jory couldn't be the only couple in the position where one was a mercenary and the other was a hero, right?

"I'll never fight you in the field," he admitted.

"If I'm there, I won't be able to walk away, if walking away is the wrong thing to do. Are you allowed to just leave if someone paid you to be there?"

They stared at each other for a long moment. The wind picked up and whipped crystals of snow around her, as though they were bees worshipping their queen. Although she didn't need it, he had the urge to wrap her in something warm. She was so small it would only take a second for her to freeze solid in this weather, even though from a rational standpoint he knew she was fine.

"I'm a free man. No one can make me blindly follow orders, and no one can pay me enough to hurt you. At least, not like that."

"So what? You'll wait on the sidelines while we kick the rest of your team's ass? I don't think you'll stand by and watch."

She had a point, but he didn't have to like it. "You let me worry about that, if and when it comes up. Now quit stalling."

"I'm ready."

"Then attack me."

"Heroes don't start fights." She shrugged. "If you're not going to fight me, I'm going to go take a nap."

She took two steps toward the house and his rope tangled around her ankles then caught her as she tripped.

For a moment she struggled, and he bound her more tightly.

As she laid a hand along a section of rope, it turned white. The whiteness engulfed length of it, but the rope didn't break. Valentine struggled to get it to move, but although the cold, stiff fibers were less biddable than normal, he still had control.

Cautiously, he approached her, wondering if she had to touch things to use her power on them. If so, she was quite literally fucked.

"So that's it?" He smirked, trying to goad her into doing more if she was able.

"Fuck." Jory struggled frantically as he stepped closer, trying to untangle herself from ropes that could almost anticipate what she was going to do next.

Perhaps part of him was trying not to gloat, but a larger part of him was terrified for her. Why would they let a girl with so few defenses engage in such a dangerous line of work?

Maybe the Bureau was getting soft in its old age, or careless. There weren't presently any big campaigns, so there was no reason for them to be desperate for heroes. Someone needed to tell the girl this wasn't the line of work for her.

Showing her would probably be more effective.

Valentine drew a throwing knife from one of the hidden sheaths in his leathers and walked toward Jory, showing her one of his most dangerous smiles. She watched him approach, her breathing shallow and erratic, her breasts heaving in their thin covering.

The knife probably should have stayed sheathed.

Evil lurked within him, trying to slip its leash. There were parts of his mind Jory was better off not knowing about. The parts that fantasized about keeping her, hurting her. No consent and no safeword. She was afraid, but she wasn't screaming yet. And how he ached to hear her scream.

Uncertainty flickered behind her eyes.

He poked the creature back into its mind cage. He had to keep it under control.

"Look at what I caught in my net. What a pretty thing." He twirled the knife in his hand, the steel catching the light. "Tell me, little pet – do you like knives?" At the very least, he wanted to slice the uniform from the writhing girl. He wouldn't cut her without her permission. He was almost sure.

Her eyes showed fear, and his heart threatened to punch its way out of his chest.

Calm down.

Fun. Just fun. Nothing that crosses the line.

Valentine reached toward her with his empty hand, and a blast of cold air hit him full in the face, knocking him a step back.

He laughed. "Well, that was adorable."

"That was a warning shot, asshole. Let me go or I'll be forced to hurt you."

Had her fear been fake? Or had she forgotten what she could do?

Valentine grabbed the front of her uniform and brought his knife up to slice it. Her hand opened and hail pelted him backward. It stung, but as soon as the accompanying wind stopped, he ran toward her again. She'd used her right hand so he ducked the left and around behind her. He grabbed her hair and she gasped. He could feel the power in her mind groping for his own – they were so in tune now it was almost automatic. Without guilt he let it happen just as he saw the beginnings of an ice storm leaving her hand. Interrupted, the launched shards of ice lost momentum and bounced harmlessly off his leather. There was no doubt that if he hadn't let their powers join those would have hurt like hell.

The power within her greeted his happily, and let his wrap it tight.

Jory was swearing and trying to struggle free, but this time she really was helpless.

"I should've known better," she grumbled. "I had the advantage over you earlier but I didn't take it. This is just supposed to be sparring, though, and if I would've poked a bunch of holes in you it wouldn't have been very sportsmanlike." She turned her head slightly to the side, trying to see what he was doing. She probably wouldn't have liked the lecherous look on his face.

"Your scruples mean nothing to me, except that knowing you have them gives me an advantage. In a fight it makes you weak. Before you start whining about not wanting to hurt me because we're together, think about this – what if I'd been an old man attacking you, or a pregnant woman, or someone who looks like child? Your scruples will mean very little if you're dead."

"Yeah I know that, asshole, but we were sparring. You weren't about to kill me. I know the difference between a game and real life. Do you?"

"What if this wasn't a game to me? What if it was a trick?"

"You needed to use a trick to get me where you wanted me? Bullshit. You've had me where you wanted me before without resorting to trickery. Now get the fuck out of my head."

Invisible fingers pried at his power, but she was fighting herself too. Her power didn't want his to go.

"Part of fighting is using all of your opponent's available weaknesses. If you don't want me in there, you're going to have to train your mind not let me in." He let go of her hair and moved to stand before her. Desire prevailed. He pressed the flat of the blade against her bare skin, and slid it along her collarbone. It drifted lower, over the poke of her nipple. She whimpered, and he became aware of how painfully hard he was. Down her belly he guided the steel, and Jory sucked in a breath. He spun the blade in his hand, cradling the underside of the handle so that the blade's tip was facing him.

"What am I going to do with you, pretty hero? So many things I could do. Some of them you might even like." He pressed the knife handle between her thighs, rubbing it back and forth until it parted her labia even through the suit. He tilted the knife and put pressure on her clit.

Jory groaned. Her head fell back, and she ground against the metal handle, as though it was a dick she was desperate for. The scent of her desire was subtle and maddening. A wave of uncontrollable lust swept over him, and he sheathed his knife and let his ropes fall to her feet.

He reached to steady her.

A boot hit him in the jaw, snapping his head back. He fell flat out, and for a moment he lay there stunned. She kicked him in the side then loomed over him and threw a punch at his face.

Recovering, he shunted her blow aside and her fist connected with the ground. Valentine shoved her away and flipped onto his feet.

The little fucking bitch.

Horny and angry, he had to admit she'd beaten him at his own game. Just because he currently had control over her power, didn't mean he controlled the rest of her.

They circled each other. Jory's eyes were gleaming, but it seemed more like anger than excitement. He thought she'd taunt him for his stupidity, but apparently she was above such childish things.

He tried to get in close, but she was better at hand to hand than he'd expected, and was wickedly strong. They fought long and hard, with neither gaining the upper hand. When they were both dirty, scraped and sweating, he finally managed to get her to the ground, face down.

"Okay." He grunted. "Maybe you're not as helpless as I thought." His balls ached where her fist had grazed him, and he struggled to keep discomfort out of his voice.

She screamed in frustration and tried to buck him off, but he forced her arms higher up behind her back, bit her neck, and allowed himself the pleasure of grinding against her ass. He was lucky the hellion hadn't taken his eye out the first time he laid a hand on her. Things might have had a very different outcome if it hadn't been for the Aphrodisia.

He summoned several small pieces of rope to him, and they slid over obediently, if a little stiffly, and he made quick work of tying her wrists and ankles together. When bound, Jory stopped struggling and lay passively over his shoulder as he carried her into the house.

"So, are we still sparring, or are you just being creepy?"

"I'm always creepy. There doesn't need to be a special occasion."

"Touché. Now put me the fuck down."

Valentine threw her onto the sofa.

"Good boy. Now untie me." At first he thought she was joking, but her expression said otherwise.

"No." They stared at each other a long moment, but she didn't safeword. He yanked down the neckline of her uniform, and her breasts sprang free. With the fabric supporting them, the small swell of them was shoved unnaturally high, as though they were being offered up to him.

"I'm not sure where you got the impression you get to make rules around here, but you don't. Just so you're aware."

"It was worth a try."

Valentine needed a minute to gear down his adrenaline and testosterone before he got more aggressive with her than he meant to. Without explaining anything, he went to the bathroom and washed the grime from his hands and face. The banality of the activity helped him to find some calm, and he centered himself as he walked back into the great room. The glare she focused on him had a different flavor when he returned. Was this still part of the sparring match? He'd thought it was over, but now he wasn't sure.

He unzipped his leather jacket, and draped it over the back of a chair, the weight of the sheathed knives clattering against each other. The black fitted t-shirt he wore underneath came off next. When he approached her again, in only leather pants and boots, all of the fight had gone out of her.

Her tongue shyly swiped at her bottom lip, and she was staring at his chest, or perhaps at something slightly lower. His abs? Hips?

In the silence of the nearly empty house, he stood and watched her devouring him with her eyes, then had to force himself not to laugh when she realized she was busted.

"You're allowed to look at me, girl, unless I tell you otherwise. There's no need to be shy."

She reddened and averted her gaze. He sat on the couch beside her, but she didn't deign to look at him.

"You're filthy," he observed. "Are heroes even allowed to get dirty?"

"You're the one who made me dirty," she said, but the gaze she turned to him was sardonic, as though she wasn't talking about literal dirt at all.

"I know. Isn't it fun?"

Jory's response was simply to stick her tongue out at him. He grinned at her, and took rough hold of one of her exposed breasts. Her gasp was delicious.

He tugged gently at her nipple. She squeaked and tried to squirm away, but her wordless objection, when he ignored it, soon turned into a sigh. She pushed against his hand as though she was seeking crueler attention.

Experimentally, he took her nipple between thumb and forefinger then gradually increased the pressure of his pinch until her eyes went wide. Her mewl turned into a cry.

"Ow! Ow, stop!" She squirmed where she lay, but thrust her breasts out, begging for more, no matter what her mouth was saying. She *would* have to be a masochist. Like he wasn't obsessed with her enough already.

"I don't think you want me to stop."

Silence was her response.

When he released her nipple, she sagged in relief, but he had no intention of leaving her alone. He rubbed a gentle thumb over the peak, back and forth, until the rough pad built friction between them. Jory cringed back and he caught the nub between his fingers again, squeezing gently, then too hard, then brushing it with his fingertips, then crushing it until she screamed for him. He leaned down and swept over it with his lips. The girl was squirming and crying out now, and it was hard not to let himself take her.

"What's wrong, snowangel?"

"It h-hurts."

"And do you like it?"

She whimpered and her hip butted against his side in a silent plea. "No?"

"Poor baby," he crooned. "Then you'll probably hate this." He took her nipple in his mouth and sucked, her cry of pleasure torturing him. When her moans became more desperate, he closed his teeth over it and nipped. She squealed and arched up further into his mouth. More? He grabbed her shoulders to hold her still, then bit down.

"Fuck! Fuck!" Her screams were half pain, half pleasure.

Precome pooled against the inside of his pants. He was going to have to hose them off.

Gradually, he relaxed his bite then worried at her nipple with his teeth and lips. Jory gave a desperate hiccup of a cry and her muscles seized.

"Are you going to come for me?" he whispered against her flesh.

Immediately she came, the sound more beautiful to his ears than any other.

When she was done, she full-body shivered. He gave the tip of her poor, abused breast one last kiss and chuckled as she flinched away. Maybe she was done, but he sure as hell wasn't. He untied her long enough to yank her uniform off, then hogtied her before she recovered enough to give him a hard time.

"Oh god," she complained, "My poor nipple is going to fall off. Why are you so mean?"

"Because hearing you scream does this to me." He unzipped his pants and released his suffering cock, stroking it in his hand so close to her face that she went cross-eyed. "Besides, did you get to come?"

"Yes, Sir," she whispered, staring at his cock with avid eyes.

"Then don't complain. I could just torture you and leave you wanting. The Aphrodisia is nothing compared to how hard up I could make you."

She blinked up at him then nodded.

"Now thank me for allowing you to come."

Without hesitation, she replied, "Thank you for letting me come, Sir."

She was such a good girl when she wasn't trying to claw his eyes out.

"Open your mouth."

Her pale eyes shone and she clamped her mouth shut.

"So you want to do this the hard way, brat?" Valentine pressed on her chin and wedged his cock in her mouth. Her small noises of distress were almost too much, both because she was complaining but not safewording, and because every sound she uttered made her mouth vibrate.

He grabbed the back of her hair and fucked her mouth. The way she gagged and struggled to breathe made it hotter, especially since her mouth still worked desperately to please him. Out of curiosity, he groped between her legs and found that she'd soaked through her adorable panties. Turtles this time. Cartoon turtle panties under her uniform? Just the idea almost set him off. There was something so very dirty about making a good girl enjoy bad things.

Tears from gagging tracked down her cheeks, but he wasn't at all sorry.

Loving how helpless she was, he slid his hand down the front of her little panties. Her clit was stiff and he pinched it between cruel fingers. She choked and whined, her pale brows knit, then she came for him again, long and sulky, as though getting off on his hand wasn't good enough for her. Spoiled. With one hand he pressed her head against the couch, while he jacked off into her mouth. He came in hot spurts on her tongue.

"Swallow." He forced her mouth shut. She hadn't looked like she was going to do otherwise, but watching her obey the order made it even better.

With a thought, his ropes fell away from her. Indentations from his rope marred the smooth texture of her skin in red patterns of indentation. He massaged the marks, then pulled her into his lap. She fit so well there, as though they were designed to sit together that way. With her head tucked into the curve of his neck, he gave up trying to push away the feelings of warmth and protectiveness she inspired in him. They were what they were.

"Who's my little bitch?" he murmured.

"I am, Sir," Jory whispered in his ear. She planted a kiss there and he suppressed a shiver. If she believed she was his bitch, that was all that mattered, but sometimes he wondered if it wasn't the other way around.

For a few minutes she was so quiet, her breathing so even, that he thought she'd fallen asleep. They both needed a bath, but it could wait.

"Sir?"

So not asleep, just very relaxed.

"Yes?"

"Who won?"

He smiled into her hair. "I'm not sure. You're tougher than you look."

Jory made a pleased sound then started to laugh. "I guess that means I'll have to shop for a strap-on."

Valentine swatted her ass and she squeaked. "If I so much as find a strap-on in your browser history, I'll beat you, then invite my team over to see how you like being shared. Think you could handle having four people touching you? Or fucking you? Three men, three holes, and Xana wouldn't hesitate to lick anything that wasn't being used. Or was."

She moaned an objection then pressed her forehead against his. "I'll be good, Sir."

"You always are."

Chapter Eleven

They'd been nicknamed Team Halloween because of the color scheme of their uniforms, but none of them gave a shit. The black and red spandex was more dignified and ten times less dorky than the garish multi-patterned uniform she'd had when she was on the team before this. Jory's new team also wasn't comprised of asshats.

She struggled into her uniform, doing an undignified dance to get various parts of her anatomy to sit properly in the stretchy fabric. Luckily, all of the ground-in mud from her sparring session with Valentine had washed out.

Seraphina and Vance were warming up, but Arigh had paused to look at Jory. "You ready?"

Finding out his name wasn't actually spelled 'awry,' like it sounded, had been a bit of a shock.

Jory forced a smile, and did a half-hearted stretch. Several of her muscles protested. It had been a long, sex-filled, and enlightening weekend, but now she had to get her head in the game. She was just happy Valentine had forgotten about trying anal. Or he'd just been messing with her. Again.

"Yeah, just thinking."

Arigh grinned down at her. Between his long dark hair, dark skin, and dazzling smile, she almost wished she was single. Honestly, her whole team was drop dead gorgeous, and if she hadn't already been addicted to Valentine, she would have had a hard time deciding which of the guys to have a secret crush on...not that they'd notice her when she was standing next to Seraphina. Compared to her three teammates Jory felt plain and washed out. Seraphina joked that they were the United Nations team, with a Latina, an African American, a Mongolian American, and Jory, whose ancestors had been from England.

"Nervous?"

She shrugged. "Not so much nervous as psyched."

Arigh clapped her on the shoulder. "We're going to kick ass."

He was a good team leader, but he really needed to quit being so hot. It was distracting. Jory had heard that Atypicals found other Atypicals much more attractive than Typicals did, but that awareness didn't help her any.

As first missions went, this one seemed fairly basic. They were just supposed to provide extra muscle to another, more experienced team.

They were summoned to their transport moments later, and Jory was surprised to find they'd be traveling in an unmarked passenger van. From what Valentine had told her, mercenaries traveled in black SUVs, not in white rental vans like high school debate teams.

Valentine had given her carte blanche to talk about work, but maybe it was a bad idea. Every time they discussed things, it was a reminder that being good literally didn't pay – at least not well – and it also made heroes seem kind of dorky to her.

The older team rode up front, and mostly ignored them, which didn't seem very charitable, but suited Jory just fine. This was the real deal. The last thing she wanted was to have the more experienced team giving them last-minute lectures on the rules.

She scratched at her shoulder underneath her spandex and caught Seraphina grinning at her.

"Why are you the only one not bitching about these getups?" Jory asked, grimacing.

"I spent way too many years in gymnastics to worry about spandex." Seraphina laughed. "I think Vance is about ready to claw his skin off, though."

"It gives me a new respect for gymnasts everywhere," Vance grumbled.

"You girls think you've got it bad? Try being a guy. The cup we have to wear under the uniform, so it doesn't look like were smuggling plums, isn't exactly comfortable." Arigh shifted, as though the issue was first and foremost in his mind.

"You know, a friend of mine is on a team that wears fighting leathers. They seem to be a lot more comfortable, and a lot more practical." She floated the idea out there, and stared out the window, afraid to look at their expressions. Suggesting a team wear something other than the assigned uniform was *almost* heresy, although she'd heard of a few teams who'd abandoned their colors for other types of clothing. Some teams liked to be more anonymous than Bureau supplied uniforms allowed for.

Seraphina made an incredulous noise that had Jory staring even more fixedly out the window. "And do you hang out with mercenaries often?"

"The Bureau doesn't have any rules saying it's not allowed." Jory tried to keep the resentment out of her voice, but the more she learned, the more this hero thing seemed to be a whole lot of rules, a whole lot of freedom given up, without much payoff. She'd chosen to be a hero so that she could help people, not so that she could be treated like a child for the rest of her life. She could only hope that once they had more experience, the rule mongers would disappear, and they'd be allowed to have some independent thought.

"Touchy, touchy." Seraphina teased.

Jory rolled her eyes.

"I'm guessing from the casual way you mentioned that, that you're dating one of them." Seraphina winked at her, and Jory could feel blood flowing like lava to her cheeks.

"If she is, there's nothing wrong with that," Vance said. "I don't understand why the Bureau has a problem with it. I know they told us when we were in school that it was a bad idea, but there aren't any laws against it."

Arigh nodded at Vance. "It's none of the Bureau's fucking business, as far as I'm concerned. And if you guys are down with the idea, I'd like to look into leather. I swear to god fighting in this shit is eventually going to make me turn mercenary. Why should mercs be the only ones who get to be comfortable?"

Seraphina nudged Jory's arm. "I'm sorry. Now I feel like a bitch. I didn't actually think you were dating one. I was just trying to be funny." Seraphina gave a half shrug and an apologetic smile. "The Bureau shouldn't be allowed to dictate who we have relationships with. I'm not sure whether or not I'll like leather, but I'm willing to give it a try. If worse comes to worse, black spandex still matches black leather, right? And we could get our uniforms done in the same colors as these ones so we don't look like were thumbing our noses at the Bureau too much."

One of the older men turned back to look over the seat at them. "Leather? Leather is what mercenaries wear. If you change to leather, how are other teams supposed to know you're heroes?"

"Because we'd be fighting against the same people?" Vance replied, with mild sarcasm.

"How often do we work with teams who don't know us, anyway?" Arigh asked. "We usually go out in the same transport."

The man frowned. "It just isn't done."

The van pulled off the highway onto a side road, and Jory's heart sped up. The wardrobe discussion had been a good distraction, but it was time to work. If she fucked up now, no matter what they were wearing, someone on her team would pay the price.

The weight of that responsibility settled on her, and she remembered Valentine's haunted expression when he'd said the same thing. When your team was made up of people you loved, that burden and fear had to be so much worse.

Seraphina grabbed her hand and squeezed. She leaned over and whispered in Jory's ear. "I'm scared shitless. If I fuck this up, I'm really sorry."

Vance slapped Seraphina on the back and gave her a sexy smile. Jory was starting to think Vance had the hots for their female teammate. Who wouldn't? "We'll kick ass, Seraphina. And if we screw up, the senior team will help us figure it out."

Jory nodded in agreement. "We're new. No one expects us to be perfect."

They poured out of the van and trailed the other team up a stinking, garbage-strewn alley. The guy who'd spoken to them in the van jimmied the door of a derelict warehouse on the right, and Jory struggled to steady her breathing. Her anxiety was barely under control, and she was worried the others would see her leaking power. It was a waste of useful energy, but sometimes it was unavoidable.

Inside, they fanned out, each team staying in the formation the combat school taught. If they always used the same formations, though, wouldn't it be easy for enemies to guess how they'd respond to each scenario? It didn't make sense. Wasn't being a predictable opponent bad if you wanted to win? She'd have to talk to the others about that later. The sergeants had never allowed her to open the subject for discussion, but maybe her teammates would be more open-minded.

The building was filled with an eerie, unnatural silence, as though it were full of people making a concerted effort to be quiet. From time to time, a hero's boot scuffed the concrete floor, but they were stealthier than she'd expected.

High overhead Jory heard a soft cry. She gestured toward it, hoping she hadn't misread the direction. The groups split off into twos, heading for the stairs, but the leader of the other group indicated that Seraphina and Vance needed to stay on the main floor. It sucked that they might miss the action, but leaving them behind made her nervous too. If the kidnappers got past the rest of them, Seraphina and Vance would be all alone. Of course they'd practiced in pairs, but had it been enough?

Jory and Arigh crept up their assigned set of stairs, boots quietly ringing on the metal grate. Some Typical mercenaries carried guns, Valentine had told her. Why hadn't they been trained for that? Sure, Atypicals were expected to be firearm-free, but not training for the possibility was stupid.

A commotion broke out above them, and they bolted up the rest of the stairs. Jory kept her hands up and ready to blast the bad guys.

No. Not bad guys. Mercenaries.

Believing everyone on the other side was a bad guy was lazy thinking. Although the Bureau taught there was a huge division between good and evil Atypicals, most seemed to fall somewhere in between. Just because the Bureau signed a fighter's paycheck didn't make that fighter's decisions automatically good. The decisions people made in life, and their motivations, were never simple.

It was strange how she'd never questioned any of that before Valentine came along. Valentine certainly wasn't evil, and his teammates seemed like decent people.

In Atypical history, they'd learned all about hero missions where teams had done things such as kidnap political leaders. Hero hands were just as dirty as mercenary ones. The excuse was that the people who'd been targeted for kidnapping by heroes had been evil, but who measured that? What type of scale did they use? Didn't everyone get the right to a trial? People were apprehended, but why didn't they hear about what happened to them afterward?

As they rounded the corner to the second floor, an airborne chair grazed her ear and slammed into the wall behind her. Eight mercenaries against the heroes' four. Jory and Arigh moved in, drawing opponents off of the two heroes who were outnumbered.

The heavy man Jory faced off with was significantly older than her, and she assumed more experienced. He threw a punch at her even though he was too far away to connect. No time to dodge. She expected an elemental force, or jolt of power to hit her, but his meaty fist connected with her jaw. She skidded backward across the floor, landing in a heap a few feet away. What the shit? How the hell had he done that? It was as though his arm had extended, just long enough to hit her.

Hopefully he wasn't impervious to cold.

He ran toward her, and she leaped to her feet with speed borne of fear. The adrenaline that zinged through her didn't let her feel what he'd done to her face. Talk about failing to take initiative. She'd just stood there like an idiot, and let him hit her.

It was all so much faster when it wasn't practice anymore and no one was fucking around. Jory threw her hands up in front of her, and ice shards whistled through the air toward him. He dodged aside, and she wove an icy nimbus around her, hoping to give him a blurred target. Flying fists whizzed past her head, but failed to connect. She allowed an ice dagger to form in her hand, and slashed out at him. There was a satisfying grunt. Something barreled into her side, and she was knocked away from her fog, her knife spinning out of her hand and clattering away. A younger man jumped on her, and wrestled her to the ground. The shaggy black hair and smell of leather was all too familiar. Valentine? Shit!

She struggled beneath him, horrified at the way her body was trying to respond. Wrestling and the scent of leather meant sexy danger in her animal brain. He pinned her arms over her head. Jory fought off her daze, realizing her first instinct had been to spread her legs for him. His face was so close to hers now she could feel his breath on her cheek.

Not Valentine.

"Aren't you a pretty little thing? Girls like you should be in a man's bed, not playing hero."

Jory widened her eyes and blinked at him like an innocent bystander. His grip went slack. Idiot.

Being underestimated because she was a girl had never worked before. She let her eyes go dreamy, and when he let go of one of her arms to grope for her breast, she nailed him with an arctic blast.

He fell back, clutching the side of his face and howling. Self-righteous anger filled her, pushing aside the remorse that tried to takeover.

How dare he touch Valentine's property?

What the fuck? Where the hell had that thought come from?

The older man had recovered, and watched her with narrowed eyes, as though she'd won the privilege of being considered dangerous. She rose to her feet, ready.

So she was small and female. She was a stranger, and they were wrong to assume the size of her power matched the size of her body.

Stupid sexist assholes.

Jory dodged a fist that narrowly missed her stomach, but the move had put her off balance. Flailing, she collided with the tall, muscular woman fighting Arigh.

She bounced off the woman and hit the floor hard, then rolled up again, trying to concentrate enough to hit the older man with anything more effective than a snowball.

As she dodged under a grab, she threw down sleet and froze the patch of ground between them into an ice rink. With his next step, his foot slid out from under him. He tried to catch himself but went down, grabbing a handful of her hair and yanking her down with him.

She kneed him in the belly as she fell, and air hissed out of him like deflating tire. Kneeing him had been an accident, but it worked.

Before he could recover, she threw a palm heel strike at his nose and he howled, a fountain of blood spraying from it. He clutched his face, and curled onto his side. A touch on her shoulder made her spin, ready for the next attacker

Arigh held his hands up to ward her off.

"Down, killer." He grinned at her, his dark eyes flashing. "We got the hostage out safe. All the mercs are down."

Jory looked around. Eight mercenaries were on the floor, and she couldn't help but check to make sure none of them looked familiar. They didn't.

"You took out two of them," he said, sounding impressed. He pulled her toward the stairs. "And now we get the fuck out of Dodge."

They ran down the stairs and past Seraphina and Vance, who followed them through the alley.

The older team had already bundled the woman they'd rescued into the van. Their driver sped off while Jory, gasping for breath, was still trying to buckle in.

*

"You're seriously disappearing for the weekend *again*?" Seraphina complained amicably as Jory stuffed clothes into a duffle bag. "And how, pray tell, are we supposed to be Elizabeth and Charlotte if you keep ditching me for your bad boy?"

"Sorry, Mr Darcy is waiting and he's been texting me impatiently for over an hour." Jory tossed her toothbrush into the bag. "Give my regards to Mr Collins."

Seraphina laughed. "I wish you were single. Vance and Arigh are both trying to get into my pants. I need a wingwoman."

"Sleep with the one you like the most. It's not like the other one will be single long. They're both hot."

Seraphina stretched out on her bed, a small night table the only thing separating it from Jory's. "Therein lies the problem, my dear Lizzie," she intoned with a bad British accent. "Both of them are handsome men of good character, and I cannot choose between them."

"Then don't." Jory shrugged and threw her bag onto her shoulder. It connected with a few of her bruises, but not hard enough to make her wince. "They might think it's fun to share you."

"Oh…my…" She grimaced. "Have sex with both of them at the same time? They'd never agree. Besides, I couldn't handle that."

"Suit yourself, but if you don't even ask if they're interested, I may never speak to you again." Jory flashed her a wicked smile and headed out the door, not waiting for a response.

Valentine was getting impatient. It was hard not to run down the hall and across the lawn to meet him, but she managed to achieve a more or less sedate pace. The last thing he needed was to know how excited she was to see him. The week apart had lasted forever.

He was out front with the motor running. At least the truck made him less conspicuous than his sports car. The music blaring from the speakers throbbed through her as she approached, even though the windows were closed. It was loud, guttural, and nasty-sexy, leaving very little doubt as to what the listener was thinking about. Luckily, no one was standing around gawking, or she might have lost the nerve to get in.

She opened the truck door and shut it fast once she was in her seat. Maybe it wasn't very badass, but she had the urge to hide her face until they were off the premises.

Valentine shut off the stereo and turned a lazy smile toward her. "I didn't like not talking to you all week, girl. For the next two days you're all mine." He hooked a finger into her collar and pulled her close, then kissed her until she didn't care who might be watching. He could fuck her on the hood of the truck right here if he wanted to.

"I missed you, too, Sir. Weren't you out of town all week anyway, though?"

"I was," he conceded. "Between missing you and having to watch my teammates get it on, though, I was feeling…inconvenienced. Any chance I can convince you to live out the rest of your days as my concubine and give up all of this hero business?"

"Concubine? Would you keep me naked?"

"Hell, I'd do that this weekend if we were staying home." He sighed.

Jory glanced down at her bag where she'd stuffed it at her feet. She hadn't brought much, thinking they'd be spending most of the weekend in bed.

"Where are we going?"

"We're going to take a drive, then go shopping. Then I'm going to fuck you all night, and part of tomorrow. Tomorrow night, we go to a party." His glance was enigmatic, but for a moment he was the old, mysterious Valentine again. Jory hadn't realized how comfortable she'd gotten around him until she'd seen that expression.

"Do I get more details, or are you worried that telling me will ruin your surprise?"

He slapped the button to turn the stereo back on, and the growls of the lead singer and whispered little-girl voice of the female lead were apparently her answer.

"What is this?" she asked, poking a finger at the stereo.

"Music. Don't you listen to music in your dreary little school?"

"Only if the headmaster lets us, otherwise we get punished for our naughty behavior." She fluttered her eyelashes at him and his grin became more of a leer.

"Hot."

"You would think that."

"So is that a fantasy of yours, Miss Savage? Do you need a headmaster to discipline you?"

"I'll play almost any game you want, if you promise me orgasms," she said lightly.

His inky-black eyes became hooded, and he stared at the road.

Jory leaned back in the seat and let the music flow through her. If he wanted to be quiet and enigmatic, she could play too.

Valentine drove past the turn off to his house and kept going. The warmth of the truck cab and his silence lulled her, and she started to drift into sleep.

"Kink Monsters."

She blinked at him. "Pardon me?"

"You asked the name of the band. They're the Kink Monsters."

"Oookay." She settled back against the seat and closed her eyes again.

"They're pretty big right now, for a metal band. I'm surprised you haven't heard of them."

"I don't really follow new music. I'd rather read."

He clutched his heart like she'd wounded him. "You don't listen to music? Blasphemy! And how did I not know this?"

"Most music is loud and irritating. Like men." She ran a hand through her hair to tame down a few locks that were tickling her face. "Besides, what's the point of listening to sex music if we don't even get to have sex? I've been waiting all week."

"You'll get cock when I say you'll get cock," he growled.

Silently, she shifted in her seat. He was always hot, but when he was irritable he was irresistible.

"How was your week?" If she didn't change the subject, she was going to end up trying to give him road head. The console between them was substantial, but if she unbuckled and shifted toward the dash…

"Two jobs, no incidents. Watched my teammates screw like three-peckered goats every night."

"You weren't tempted to join in?" she asked, trying to sound casual.

"So I could fuck someone else while thinking about you? That wouldn't be fair to anyone involved. Besides, doesn't that go against our agreement?"

"You've been with them for a long time. I might be okay with sharing you with them, but only if you like me more." She desperately wanted him to tell her it would never happen, but his lips quirked in a smile.

"Why are you offering? Do you want to watch?"

What?

She frowned at him and he laughed.

"No?"

Jory turned away from him and gazed out the window. Maybe the idea that he'd been with other men in the past was hot, but the idea of him touching anyone but her now made her want to cry. She wanted to be cool and worldly like Xana, but the truth was she didn't think she had it in her to share him. Not like that. Was it something he wanted?

"Whatever pleases you, Sir." It hurt to say the words, but the truth was if he wanted them there was nothing she could do about it, other than leave him. That wouldn't fix anything. She'd rather share than lose him entirely.

She sucked on her bottom lip and tried to stay in control.

"Hey," he said, his hand closing over hers. "You shouldn't tell me you're okay with things if you're not. You're my submissive, but that doesn't mean I don't care about your feelings. You brought this up. I might be okay with letting my teammates touch you, but I'm not interested in anyone else. That's over and done with. My teammates are better as my friends rather than my lovers."

The way he smiled at her melted a tightness that had been forming in her belly. He did care about her, even though he did some things to her that were humiliating. It was hard to believe he could make her crawl to him, yet still respect her, but she got the feeling he really did. Wait...had he just said he'd be okay with letting his friends touch her?

"Is watching something you're interested in?" he asked.

"What do you mean?"

"We're going to a BDSM club with my teammates tomorrow night. There'll be people doing all sorts of things. Dane, Jurgen, and Xana will probably play together, and you'll be able to watch, if you want to."

She stared at him. This whole idea was a loaded question.

"I don't want anyone else," she said simply.

"But you'll watch it if I want you to." It wasn't a question. He knew the answer.

Pleasing him was starting to mean more to her than she would have thought possible. The list of things she'd submit to for him had already grown exponentially since their first time together.

"But you'll never share me with anyone, right?" What did this all mean? Was he already getting bored of her?

"I might let people I chose touch you, but not fuck you. I don't think I could handle that."

"I...uh..."

"I doubt it would be this weekend. You have time to think about it."

The idea of letting Jurgen and Dane touch her – even at Valentine's direction – scared her. Could she handle being the center of attention like that? None of them seemed to think sharing was a big deal.

Was she being a chicken, considering she'd just teased Seraphina about asking Vance and Arigh to share?

"Maybe I'd be okay with watching this weekend, but if I get turned on by it, will you be upset?"

He patted her hand. "No, but I might be tempted to get you off."

"In front of other people?" she whispered, looking around as though someone might overhear.

"We'll talk about your limits."

She thought about him sharing her, and wondered why he'd want to. Weren't guys supposed to be possessive if they liked a girl? If he liked her so much, why did he want to hand her around?

"Would you really want other men to touch me?"

"No, not other men. Just my team, and only if and when I said it was okay." He smiled wryly. "It might seem weird to you, but I've always shared with them, so to me it's normal. Having more than one person touching you can be overwhelming and mind blowing. I love blowing your mind, if you hadn't noticed."

It all sounded a bit too wild for her, but for him she might try it. Maybe. Eventually. Possibly next year. Too bad drinking beforehand would be out of the question.

"I had a dream about it the other night," he admitted, his voice low and husky. "I love hearing you scream."

She shuddered, getting aroused by his arousal, but not sure if it was wrong to even be considering such a thing. What would people think of her if they found out?

The view out of the windshield was dull and muddy, which suited her mood. Most of the snow had melted over the past week. Not long until spring. A month?

"How were the past few days for you?" he asked, drawing her out of her thoughts again, which had turned to the added possibilities presented by the idea of outdoor sex with the warmer weather approaching. Outdoor sex with Valentine, and *only* Valentine.

"Uh…okay. We went on our first mission."

"The fighting went well? You didn't get hurt?"

"A few bruises – nothing serious." She remembered the huge dark bruise that had covered a third of her face by the time they got back to the school. Most of the marks had been healed by her abilities over the past few days, and only a few small spots on her ribs remained. "It was freaky, but this guy jumped me and pinned me to the ground and I was sure he was you. You'd never grope me like that during a fight, though. Not in front of other people."

Jory caught her breath and held it as the truck swerved onto the gravel shoulder and slid to an abrupt halt.

"What the fuck did you just say? Someone groped you?"

Her breath whooshed out of her. Crazy man. She rolled her eyes. "It was nothing. He told me I was pretty and tried to grab my...chest."

Valentine's jaw set in a grim line. "He looked like me? And the job was in the area, here?"

Jory didn't answer him.

"Tell me."

She made a sound of disgust and rolled her eyes again. "Yes. You do realize I've had worse things happen to me at school dances, and at my job at the burger place. At least this asshole wasn't my boss."

"Unacceptable," he growled. "We're there to do the job, not sexually assault people. I don't care if we're not heroes, there are rules." His mouth set in an angry line. "I'm sorry he did that to you. Are you okay? It won't happen again."

A thrill of fear stole down her spine, tinged by a dreadful excitement. Valentine's implied threat to the man made her feel oddly loved. His disgust for what had been done to her meant he wasn't one of the sexist assholes – at least not where their jobs were concerned.

"Don't intervene," she objected. "If my boyfriend steps in to save me from the big, bad mercenaries, that doesn't earn me any respect. It makes me a joke. The fact that I gave him a frostbitten ear and broke his teammate's nose should be good enough."

Valentine crowed. "My badass little bitch." He grinned, looking impressed, and she tried not to act smug.

He considered her for a moment then nodded. "Okay. I'll stay out of it for now. If it happens again, though, I'm kicking his ass – whoever he is. That type of behavior is just bad form. We can't go around acting like animals. Mercenaries are supposed to be more controlled and neutral than heroes and the crackpots who lean toward evil. And we all work with women – I'm surprised his teammate didn't beat the crap out of him and save you the trouble."

He kissed her, then pulled back onto the road. For a while they discussed lighter topics, then fell into companionable silence. Jory dozed off to the band on the stereo screaming their dark ecstasy and making her think of terrible, naughty things.

*

She could roll in that smell.

Valentine led her through the pleasantly lit shop, and she inhaled until it felt like her lungs would burst.

So much leather.

Pants, jackets, corsets, boots – it was enough to make a girl drool. Most of it was black, but there were dashes of red and hints of blue. Unable to resist, she stroked her fingers over a few of the pieces as they passed. She would have preferred to slow down and browse, but Sir was on a mission.

Jory trotted along behind him like a well-trained dog, and she could feel the satisfaction it gave him. He hadn't told her to do it. Some things just felt natural with him, even though the idea of a woman walking a respectful distance behind her man would have met with her scorn only months ago. Here, where no one knew her, she could express her submission in subtle, public ways. It felt right and natural, and it turned her on.

As they got nearer to the back wall, the merchandise became more interesting. Crops, canes, straitjackets, harnesses and restraints.

Oh…

"Valentine, where the hell have you been, you evil bastard?" the man behind the counter drawled. He was tall and had glasses, a goatee, and a long blond ponytail. As they approached, he came around to thump Valentine's shoulder as though they'd known each other for years.

Valentine only smirked in response, and the man's gaze lit on Jory. "Ahhh…and it all becomes clear."

"Derek, this is my submissive, Jory."

Jory's stomach sank into her shoes. For the first time in her life she was too embarrassed to blush. Announcing it to a complete stranger? So humiliating.

"New to the lifestyle?" Derek asked Valentine. The man gave her a sympathetic smile.

"It's safe here," Valentine assured her, and pulled her into the curve of his arm. "I wouldn't tell someone I didn't trust implicitly."

Derek nodded in reassurance. "I'm a submissive, too. My Domme, Olivia, and I own the place. She's just in the back measuring someone."

Jory could only imagine for what.

"I'm looking to dress her for a private club party tomorrow night. She doesn't own anything appropriate yet. I also want to have her measured for fighting leathers. Spandex won't do enough to keep her safe."

The man nodded again, as though it wasn't an odd request. "How naked do you want her for the party?"

Jory's mouth dropped open, and she turned her gaze to Valentine.

He glanced at her, then away, as though her opinion didn't matter.

"A harness, a collar, a leash. Maybe a skirt, if she can convince me she deserves one."

Where the hell did he think she was going dressed like that?

Derek showed Valentine the section with harnesses that would fit her. Valentine chose one with a lot of rings, which looked the same as the others, as far as Jory could see. Next, they were shown row upon row of collars in glass cases, in more colors and with more embellishments than she could have imagined. Valentine walked back and forth in front of the cases, his expression intent. After a few minutes, Derek went to help other customers and left Valentine with the cabinet key.

"A little pink one with a kitten bell?" His dark eyes sparkled with amusement. "Or maybe you need a posture collar to remember to stand straight even when you're feeling shy?"

He gazed down into her eyes and all of her embarrassment and discomfort dissolved. Small hairs on the back of her neck rose, and she shivered.

"Whichever you like best, Sir." At one point she might have cared about how things looked on her, but in this world, with him, the only thing that mattered was whether he liked it. The idea of being mostly naked in public at this party didn't make her happy, but if that's what Valentine wanted, that's what Valentine would get. Knowing him, he'd convince her it was what she wanted too, soon enough.

He turned back to the cases, and stopped near the very end.

"These are new." He crouched down, looking intently through the glass. "You trust me to pick something?"

"Yes, Sir."

He went around the back of the display, unlocked it, and reached deep inside. The collar he emerged with was made of ice blue leather with pearlized white borders, and was embellished with snowflakes. It also had a small O-ring front and center. Although it was very sturdy looking, the quality of the craftsmanship somehow made it seem feminine.

Derek walked back up as Valentine turned the collar over in his hands. "Ah, I was just coming back to point that one out, in case you hadn't seen it. It doesn't fit the usual black studded collar motif, but my mistress got the idea for this one and had to see whether she could make it the way it looked in her head. I thought it might suit her." He inclined his head to Jory.

"It's like it was made for her," Valentine murmured. "It couldn't be more perfect."

As Derek showed him the lead that had been made to go with it, Jory caught sight of the boutique price tag that dangled from the collar. She considered complaining about the cost, and had to remind herself that he'd just bought a house for them to hang out in, and he'd more or less given her an expensive car. In that context, a handmade collar that cost a few thousand dollars should have been the least of her worries. But seriously, what the hell was it made of? Unicorn hide?

Derek's Domme, Olivia, became free just as Valentine finished piling all sorts of unfamiliar objects on the counter near the ancient cash register. She led them into the back, and stood Jory on a low platform.

"You chose the snowflake collar! I can't tell you how happy I am about that. It took weeks to make, and I wasn't sure whether the right person would ever come along for it. Not many submissives could wear it without being overshadowed." She pulled out a measuring tape and started taking down Jory's measurements. "She's tiny, but with all this glorious hair, and her bone structure, she'll be wearing it, rather than it wearing her. In fact, if you were as poor as a church mouse, Valentine, I would have insisted you take it free of charge. I hated seeing it sitting in that case, but it had to go to the right person."

"Lucky for you I can afford to pay for it." Valentine grinned. "If you run this place as a not-for-profit, how are you going to pay the bills?"

She swatted Valentine's shoulder. "Do we look like the shop's about go under? We're the only place in the area that sells quality stuff."

"I know. Why do you think we're here?" Valentine chuckled. "Some of it I can make myself, but I'll never reach your level of artistry."

Olivia finished taking Jory's measurements then wrote down a description of the uniform color scheme.

"I'll be sending you measurements for three more sets of leathers too. Same pattern."

"What?" Jory said, frowning. "That's ridiculous."

"You'll be shy about wearing yours if everybody else is wearing spandex. When your whole team is outfitted with leathers, you won't have an excuse not to wear yours."

If a collar was so expensive, she could only imagine how much fighting leathers would cost in a place like this. She shook her head in dismay.

Olivia smiled at Jory sympathetically. "You can complain all you want, but Valentine will do whatever he wants, just like he always does. Fucking dominants." She shook her head with mock disapproval.

"Fucking dominants," Valentine echoed in amusement. "But if you wanted to get your way in life, Jory, you shouldn't have started stalking me."

"There were extenuating circumstances, and you know it," Jory said defensively. "Besides, it was a mutual stalking, and you started it."

The Domme snorted. "Shall I get you a tawse and a chair?" she asked Valentine.

"No, thank you. She's new, and I like her a little mouthy, at least for now. Besides, I think beating her in a public place might be too much for Little Miss Vanilla to handle."

Jory stared at Valentine, suddenly less interested in sassing him in public. Would he really do things like punish her in front of witnesses once they'd been together awhile? She was aghast, and wildly turned on.

"Vanilla? With her body language?" She looked Jory over more carefully, making her feel like she was up for auction. "I don't see any vanilla in there. Inexperience perhaps, but she's thoroughly yours."

Chapter Twelve

Dancing and drinking in a Typical bar wasn't how he'd pictured the evening unfolding. However, the harassing texts had started as soon as they'd left the shop, as though they'd been spotted.

YOU PROMISED TO HANG OUT WITH US THIS WEEKEND. NO HIDING.

WE KNOW YOU'RE ALREADY HERE. ANSWER YOUR PHONE, COCKSUCKER.

HOW ARE WE GOING TO GET TO KNOW HER IF YOU KEEP HIDING HER?

Sometimes having three best friends was a pain in the ass, especially when his entire plan for tonight was to check into the hotel and see how many ways he could fuck his girl before they passed out from exhaustion.

Bastards.

So instead, his Friday night had turned into drinking beer with Xana and Dane while they watched Jurgen dance with Jory, whom they'd managed to get very, very drunk. There was something to be said for a girl who could still dance and look sexy in her condition.

As they danced, although they never touched, their attraction to each other was obvious. Other than the fact that they were both submissive, in a lot of ways easy going Jurgen would have been a better match for her. Even so, Valentine wasn't about to hand her over.

"I think Jurgen might be falling in love," Xana mused. She put her beer bottle to her lips and tipped it back, draining it. She motioned to their server to bring her another. "They're pretty together."

Valentine smiled to himself. A submissive falling for a submissive was generally an unsatisfying experience, from what he'd heard. It made sense, considering how tempestuous dating Xana, another dominant, had been for him. Maybe Jurgen was enthralled with his submissive, but if he ever managed to convince Valentine to share her, both Jurgen and Jory would walk away from the experience frustrated.

"Honestly, I can't imagine how anyone wouldn't want her." Xana smiled slyly. "She's sweet, hot, and innocent. I liked her last time, but I like her even more now. You *sure* you don't want to share?" She was teasing, but he knew if he said yes, she wouldn't refuse.

Even if Jory was interested in playing with multiple people, though, he didn't think his friends deserved the ass kicking he'd want to give them.

He thought of Xana running her hands over Jory's naked body, and how Jory would probably respond, then pushed the thought away, annoyed that it was turning him on.

"I don't think that would be a good idea," he grumbled. "I know we're used to sharing everything, but with her I just can't. I think it would kill me."

"From the look on your face I think it would be more likely to kill us." The gleam in her eyes meant she was teasing, but Valentine hoped she wasn't secretly hurt. "Come on, Val, not even me? I don't even have a dick. That means I'm not really competition, right?"

"Nice try, Xana. The answer is still no. I think I trust *you* less with her than I would trust her with Dane or Jurgen. She and Jurgen would just frustrate each other, and Dane… I think Dane is too in love with Jurgen to be interested in anyone else for long."

The implication of his statement hung between them, and Valentine winced, feeling like a shithead.

Xana sighed. "I'm not stupid, Valentine. I know the guys love me, and want me around, but it's not the same as it is between them. I'm a BFF with benefits. It's not serious relationship love. They'd take a bullet for me, but neither of them would marry me." She barked a laugh. "Which is fine, because I wouldn't marry them, either. It would be like marrying you. Fuck around, yes. Not interested in making it permanent." She ran the tip of her finger over a swirl in the wooden tabletop. "I couldn't be that serious with any of you. We've known each other too long – we all know too much about each other, and too much of each other's pasts. It might work for Dane and Jurgen, but I like a little mystique when I'm dating someone."

"Eventually you'll find someone." It was a platitude, but he couldn't think of anything else to say.

"You might think this is weird, but I've been realizing more and more lately that I'm happiest when I'm single. If I have needs, I know where to get them met, but having someone underfoot twenty-four seven, having a needy little sub who wants my full attention – it's too much for me. Maybe someone will change my mind someday, but right now I need my space. Hell, I couldn't even manage having a plant."

"Didn't you just get a plant? Like two weeks ago?"

She leaned her head companionably on his shoulder. "Taking care of things is a nuisance. Even worse if you can't take off spur of the moment and not bother coming home for a few weeks." She sat up again and arched a brow at him. "Quit looking at me like that. The plant is safe at Bachelor Central."

Bachelor Central was their euphemism for Dane and Jurgen's apartment. As far as their families were aware, Dane and Jurgen were roommates. Not the most creative ruse in the world, but it was surprisingly effective. The two of them were always complaining about how their mothers wanted to set them up on blind dates with girls they approved of. Their families assumed they were just immature and wanted their freedom. There was ongoing speculation about which one of them would marry Xana.

Dane came back from the washroom and folded onto the bench beside them. He watched Jurgen and Jory dancing and rolled his eyes.

"So are you going to let Jurgen sleep with her so he can find out firsthand why it'll never work?"

"I considered it," Valentine said, trying to soften the response that wanted to come out. "But that would involve Hell freezing over."

"You're a hard man." Dane leaned his head back on the wall and kept watching the dancers. "I like how she moves."

Xana nodded. "We'd even let you sleep with Jurgen, as payment."

"So what's the plan? You convince me to give Jurgen permission, and then you to try to sneak in on the deal?"

"Did I not let you try out the Camaro I got for my sixteenth birthday?" Xana reminded him.

"And didn't you sleep with the love of my life before I did?" Dane added. "Man, you owe me."

Even though he'd entertained the idea of sharing her with them, the anger he felt burning in his chest as they harmlessly teased him gave him the final answer to the question.

"Do you remember what I said to you the first time you met her? The answer stands. It's not going to happen. She's mine. No matter what argument you present I won't be changing my mind." *Mine, mine, mine, mine.* A jealous storm raged in him and he had to fight down the urge to stomp over to where she danced with Jurgen and drag her off. Jurgen wasn't even touching her, but they were getting along far too well.

"Will you look at that?" Dane grinned. "He's actually *jealous*. Of Jurgen! Maybe I should go retrieve my submissive before Valentine castrates him."

"Jeez, Val, you know none of us would touch her without your permission. We're not assholes and we're not vanilla. We know the rules."

"I know, I know. You know I trust all of you. It's just that… Sometimes I don't even know how to explain it to myself. I don't see her all week, and I know she's with her team, working. I try to be okay with that because she's a smart girl and gifted." He rubbed a hand over his face. "I don't expect her to sit around my house waiting to serve me, but at the same time I resent every second we can't be together. I'm not happy with just a day or two here and there, but in this line of work this is probably all we'll ever have." He sighed, and chugged the rest of his beer, realizing his legs and face were a little numb, and that maybe he was starting to over share.

"I really want to make fun of you for that, but I think you just convinced me to feel sorry for you." Xana handed him the beer the waitress dropped off in front of her and ordered another.

"You poor bastard. There is no pain worse than being madly in love with your submissive." Dane brandished his bottle of beer in a salute to Valentine. "Don't you remember me warning you never to do it when I fell in love with Jurgen? But no, you had to be stubborn and try it for yourself."

"It's her fault." Valentine nodded in Jory's direction, trying to keep a straight face.

"Of course." Dane winked at him. Jory and Jurgen were making their way back over to the table, both of them giving their dominants eager looks. "I thought the three of us agreed that everything is always the submissive's fault."

Xana nodded. "Absolutely."

Jory slid onto Val's lap without asking for permission. The driving beat of the dance music and the warm scent of her skin gave him too many indecent ideas. She took the beer out of his hand, and took a sip before passing it back. The sight of her lips on the bottle stiffened his cock. He put his hand on her thigh, maybe a little too close to her pussy to be appropriate. Her body swayed a little, and she planted a sloppy kiss almost on his mouth.

Why had they agreed to drink tonight? Now he'd have to wait to play with her until at least tomorrow. Damn it.

She wrapped her arms around his neck, and kissed him again, more aggressively.

"Do you need a smack down, snowangel?" He took firm hold of her waist and she shifted in his lap, rocking subtly against his erection.

She leaned over and put her mouth next to his ear, but either forgot to whisper or didn't care who heard. "I'm sure you can figure out how to fuck me and show me who's boss without breaking any of the 'no kink while drunk' rules. You won't tie me up, and I won't try to give you an icy blowjob. Deal?" She ground against his dick.

"And that's our cue to leave." Xana laughed. "We need to get out of here before we're arrested for public indecency.

Valentine glanced over and the guys were making out. Dane was sliding his hand into the front of Jurgen's jeans.

Xana shook her head. "I can't take you people anywhere."

*

The sound of his ringtone woke him. His limbs felt like wet sandbags and they didn't want to obey his commands. Phone. Jory needed him.

He pushed a heavy thing off his arm, staggered to where his phone flashed, and stubbed his toe on something that shouldn't have been there.

It took two swipes to get the phone to pick up. "What's wrong?" he croaked, his adrenaline ramping up. The darker shadows that lurked in the stillness seemed to be in the wrong places. Where the fuck was he?

"Valentine. The team we hired to cover for you for the weekend had to back out. Your team needs to come in and assist." His father's voice was terse and commanding. It set Valentine's teeth on edge.

He looked around again, realizing where he was. Hotel room. Jory.

Still a little drunk.

"I took the weekend off for a reason. Call someone else. We're out of town."

"All of you? How long will it take you to get back here?"

Stubborn old goat. "We'll be back Monday." He groped his way to the bathroom and shut the door behind him before flipping on the light and the fan to deaden the noise, although Jory was so drunk he doubted a phone call would wake her. "You know we said no to that job for a reason."

"Your concerns are unfounded. My group and I vetted this job. There's no reason for your team to refuse to do it." Dietrich's voice was harsh. He never liked it when Valentine disagreed with him, but he knew that if he didn't, his father would have little respect for him. In this case, it was a necessity rather than a show of independence.

"None of us is interested in pulling a target out of bed and delivering them to a third party. How do you know the third party will behave honorably?" Valentine shook his head in disgust.

"If you want to start getting all moral about every job you take, your team will never be successful. You don't make money by asking too many questions."

He'd tried to be okay with not asking questions, especially since that rule had been drilled into him from the time he was small. However, his team wasn't comfortable with doing what they were paid to do without thinking about consequences. It was easier not to worry about the ramifications of their actions when they were contracted to retrieve or transport *things*. Stealing a man from his family and not knowing if he was going to be tortured or executed wasn't something they could be okay with.

"We're not responsible for what happens after the target is safely delivered. Policing other Atypicals isn't our job. We're not heroes, Valentine, and we're not paid to be."

"Maybe we're not heroes, but I refuse to be complicit in villainy." He sat on the edge of the tub, which still smelled like the bath he and Jory had taken together before bed, after she'd complained endearingly about how sore he'd made her.

"Complicit in *villainy*?" his father mocked. "Melodramatic, even for you, Valentine. Lofty morals will only make you poor. I didn't spend long hours building our clientele and reputation up just for the good of my team. This was supposed to be my legacy for you and your brother – although Pascal will never amount to much now. Don't let that Typical school of yours ruin you for real life. Only sheep live their lives by other people's morality."

"So you want me to think critically except when it comes to your orders? You should be happy you didn't raise a toady."

The line was silent for an uncomfortable length of time.

"You're a toady either way, son. I just expect your first loyalty to be to me, rather than to your new whore."

The call ended. Valentine stared at his phone, wondering why his father knowing about Jory made him feel uncomfortable. She was a chink in his armor, but that shouldn't matter when it came to his own father. Surely, as Machiavellian as the man was, he wouldn't use her or her safety against him?

No matter what happened, he refused to be intimidated into evil.

But…

He thought of how small and fragile Jory was beneath him, and how much she trusted him to keep her safe from his own twisted urges. He wanted to be her shield, not the reason she had a target painted on her back.

If his father or his job ever caused her harm, he'd never forgive himself.

*

The girl clung to her coat, knuckles white.

"It's okay, baby. I know everyone here. It's safe." Maybe this had been a mistake, but ever since he'd claimed her, he'd longed to show her off. Friends and acquaintances looked over at them curiously, but were kind enough not to rush over.

Jory whined quietly, then unbuttoned her coat, her reluctance making his dick hard. Why was making her do things she didn't want to do so arousing?

The act of helping her out of her coat might have seemed gentlemanly, but wasn't. He handed it off to a waiting servant then had to coax her out from behind him.

Although he'd dressed her himself, he got distracted again by the way her firm, high breasts stuck boldly out of the ice blue leather chest harness. He'd covered her nipples with X's of electrical tape for now, but the scanty coverings would be coming off as soon as she relaxed a little. She'd pleaded for both that and the blue leather skirt, and he'd been helpless to refuse her.

It was a good thing he'd put a collar on her, or he'd be staving drooling Doms off her all night. Maybe it was silly, but the idea of her neck being bare made him uneasy. How did vanilla men handle their women walking around looking unclaimed? A ring wasn't a bold enough symbol – hell, even a collar was too subtle, as far as he was concerned. Keeping her leashed twenty-four seven might have been enough to satisfy him, but he doubted she'd submit to that.

Tonight he had the luxury of leashing her. The smoothness of the leather in his hand was reassuring as he attached it to her collar with a gratifying click. He led her into the busy private club, acting nonchalant, but feeling conflicted.

He was eager to show her off, but didn't want to look like a kid with a new puppy. To make matters worse, he didn't want anyone to look at her or talk to her, and he wanted to drag her into the back and bury himself inside her sweet body.

There were darker things he wanted, too, like to steal her from her life and lock her away. To keep her as his groveling little submissive, as though she was made for nothing more than obeying his commands and yielding to his mouth, his hands, his cock. She couldn't know how fanatical and dangerous she made him feel, and that she should run from him before he lost control and did something they both regretted.

Worse yet, she couldn't find out he was in love with her.

He'd paused not far past the room's threshold. She was at his elbow, staring up at him with those innocent eyes of hers. When they'd sparred, he'd seen the other side of her, but most of the time there was no sign of the cold calculation she was capable of. Instead, she only showed him the unwavering regard and trust that seemed completely natural to her. She made him want to deserve such reverence, but he was painfully aware she was deluding herself.

She deserved a good man, but he wasn't good enough to tell her that he wasn't one.

He watched her reactions to the club, enjoying her range of expressions.

The first time Valentine's team had been invited to Prospero's, they'd been surprised about the upscale Gothic décor. The place looked like Dracula had been the main investor, but in this case Dracula was an Atypical named Prospero, who had a fascination with the time period. From the outside, the place looked like any other generic, uninspired office building. The sign out front marked it as Janarius and Son Document Storage, and Prospero Janarius was the son in question. His dearly departed father might have been surprised at what his son had decided to do with the second floor of one of their many enterprises, but then again, knowing Prospero, perhaps not.

Prospero turned up almost immediately, as though he'd been waiting for them. Valentine liked Prospero, and had even thought of him as a friend until he saw the way the bastard eyed Jory. Tonight the other dominant was gallingly charming, with his flashing smile, pierced nipples and tight leather pants. Did Jory like men with ponytails?

"Valentine, good to see you, my friend." Prospero clasped his hand in greeting. "So what – your team finally sees action and you forget about us?

Or maybe you've had a more pleasant distraction?"

There was no way around the introduction. "Prospero, this is my new submissive." Valentine stepped between them. He didn't so much as want him to touch her hand.

"What? Not even her name? My fantasies of her won't be complete without at least a name."

Valentine had brought women to the club before, but Prospero had never been more than vaguely polite to them. Although his interest in Jory might have been flattering to a dominant who wanted to curry favor with the man, Valentine just wanted to curb stomp his face.

"My girl's name is none of your concern." Valentine bared his teeth in what might have passed for a smile, but only to an imbecile. "But thank you for complimenting my taste."

Valentine led Jory away, not missing the apologetic expression she gave the man. He choked up on her leash, but forced his jaw to unclench. For a moment he thought of ordering her to keep her eyes on the floor, which was something he never did with his submissives, but Prospero's interest in her wasn't her fault.

Several friends nodded to him as they made their way through the dimly lit space. Valentine acknowledged them, but didn't stop until he'd reached the couches where his team lounged. The three of them stared at Jory as though she was in danger of being thoroughly licked.

He motioned for her to kneel on the floor mat beside Jurgen, and he took a space on a sofa in front of her. None of his teammates bothered to hide the fact they were checking her out.

In the room, there was a hum of interest in her that Valentine could feel all along his Dom synapses. His whole team had wanted her the first time they'd met her, but now, seeing her like this, he could almost taste their desire in the air. Strangers and acquaintances wanting her made him jealous, but when his team checked her out he didn't feel threatened anymore. Not after last night. Watching her dance with Jurgen had turned him on, even though he hadn't admitted it to himself at the time. And when things had almost turned into an orgy right at the bar?

"Miss anything?" Valentine asked. He tried not to think about what could have happened after the bar if they hadn't all been drunk.

"Jules beat his sub for a while," Xana replied, dragging her gaze away from Jory. "Stella is getting passed around between four of the guys. It's been about a half hour and she's starting to get desperate." Valentine's gaze followed the flick of her finger. The submissive was begging any of the men involved in the teasing to fuck her, but they were ignoring her pleas and looking amused.

"Do you see that, girl?" Valentine gripped Jory's chin and turned her head in the direction of the scene. When she caught sight of what was going on, she looked horrified and slightly aroused. Her lips parted. When she tried to stop watching, he didn't let her. After only a few minutes, her hips shifted, as though she wanted to squirm but was aware she was being observed. Valentine let go of her face, but crouched beside her and whispered, "Do you feel sorry for her, or do you envy her?"

Jory stared at a spot on the floor, as though she was a prisoner of war being interrogated.

"Answer now or I'll ask Jurgen to spank you."

Jory and Jurgen, kneeling almost thigh to thigh on the mat, glanced at each other, then straight ahead again.

"He wouldn't," she whispered.

"Wouldn't I?" Jurgen asked. Apparently Jory was making Jurgen a little switchy after all. No one could resist the poor little thing.

She wilted, caught Valentine's expression out of the corner of her eye and knelt prettily again. She had to be doing research on D/s during the week to be so perfect. No one was this intuitive. The thought pleased him. Research meant she was doing her best to be a good girl for him.

"I feel sorry for her *and* envy her, Sir."

His team was far too attentive to the conversation, like a pack of voracious wolves, probably wondering if he was going to share even though he'd said he wouldn't. If he didn't keep careful control of them, this party would turn into a Little Red Riding Hood buffet.

"I'm going to go introduce Jory to a few people," he said to Xana. "Keep these idiots in line."

"I always do." She smirked.

As usual, the club was getting more crowded as the hour grew late. Even with Jory's leash in his grip he wasn't satisfied that she looked taken enough. By the time they walked up to the first group of people he knew, he was holding her hand too.

"How on earth did you land this one, Valentine?" Brock asked, his faint English accent barely discernible over the din of the crowd. A broad smile spread across the mercenary's face as he looked Jory over. "Chloroform?"

Valentine grinned. "You don't give me enough credit, Brock. Aphrodisiacs are so much less barbaric. Why club a girl over the head and drag her off by the hair, when you can convince her to follow you willingly?" The conversation was treading perilously close to the truth, but he had no intention of telling Brock that. Maybe his relationship with Jory had started off in an odd way, but it had turned into so much more than sex.

Brock and his team had been friends with Valentine and his team since middle school. It was strange how many of the mercenaries in their generation seemed to be into BDSM. The joke was they'd all been inhaling leather fumes for too long. It was a bit creepy that Brock's sister, Brontë, was on his team and hung out with him at the club, but there was no incestuous vibe there, just a mutual respect.

"Obviously she's Atypical, but I don't remember meeting her before. What team is she on?" Brock asked.

Valentine wondered if Jory felt offended by the fact that no one was addressing her directly. He probably should have explained things were more formal here, and that dominants would never address someone else's submissive without permission. Oh well. She was a smart girl. She'd figure it out.

He smiled, not knowing the most tactful way of skirting around this issue. "She's not a mercenary."

Brock and Brontë came to completely different conclusions – he could see it on their faces. Brock assumed Jory was a Mundane Atypical, but Brontë's eyes widened and she looked Jory over as if she was trying to memorize her. *Shit*. Maybe he should have put Jory in a half mask. Too late now.

In this world there were strict rules about not outing each other, but how did that work when a mercenary was bringing in a submissive hero? Did that change the rules? He hoped like hell that it didn't. The damage had been done, but he was going to have to learn to think of every eventuality if he was going keep her safe.

He cut the conversation short, hoping that Brontë would forget all about her, yet knew Jory was far too striking to forget about. They were a good team, though, and decent people, so he hoped they'd make the right decision if Brontë shared her suspicions with Brock. For that matter, it might never come up. That team tended to take work overseas a lot, so the chances of them accepting a job that pitted them against an American hero team was unlikely.

They made the rounds, saying hi to a few more people, but not staying long enough to answer questions. When they got back to Xana and the guys, the others were deep in conversation. The three of them looked over at Jory with an intensity that suggested that giving them time to calm down had done the opposite.

Valentine unclipped the leash from Jory's collar, and motioned for her to kneel on the mat beside Jurgen.

"Dane, the look in your eye isn't giving me the impression I should leave you unattended with my submissive."

"Why, were you planning to?" His wolfish grin was less than comforting. "I promise we'll take real good care of her."

There may have been an episode from several years ago where Dane had left Jurgen in Valentine's keeping, and there had been a slight misunderstanding. Apparently the phrase 'taking care of someone' could be misinterpreted. Dane hadn't been that surprised or upset, but sometimes he liked to remind Valentine that a debt was owed.

"Have you fucked her ass yet?" Dane asked him, ignoring the girl's gasp.

"No."

"DP is out, then," Xana said. "I don't care how much prep work you do with her here, she won't be ready for that."

Jory's brow furrowed, and she crawled to him and laid her head in his lap. The action put him further into Dom space. He stroked her hair and her back, and he wished he could curve his body around hers and shelter her from these people, even though he'd brought her here to experience being around other kinksters.

"Slow the hell down. You're freaking her out."

Jurgen snorted. "Called it. Him threatening to have me spank her was a joke."

It hadn't actually been a joke, they were just going too fast for the poor little thing. The more he thought about introducing her to group play, the more interesting the idea of shocking her appealed to him – but he wouldn't allow it to go as far as sex. Probably not ever. She hadn't said playing with other people was a hard limit, so he'd ask her and see what she thought. Her reaction to what was being done to the girl across the room had helped seal the deal.

"Oh well." Xana shrugged and smiled unpleasantly at the top of Jurgen's bowed head. "If we're not allowed to play with her, we'll just have to torture you instead."

If Jurgen swore under his breath, they were all kind enough to pretend they hadn't heard it. His mouth had a habit of getting him in trouble.

"What do you think, Jory? Should I torture you and let them watch, at least?" He'd start with that. She seemed turned on by the idea of public play, but wasn't sure how ready she was.

Her response was to bow lower until her forehead touched the floor between his boots. She waited there for him to choose what to do.

Jory's submission was addictive. Every new foothold Valentine gained in her mind made him euphoric. Her abject submission gave him a bigger shot of adrenaline than skydiving or fighting ever had.

He couldn't imagine the feeling ever getting old.

"Up." He nudged the girl with the toe of his boot.

Jory rose gracefully to her feet, but her gaze stayed on the floor.

"I'm going to tie you up and torture you while they watch."

"W-why?" She bit her lip. "Wouldn't you rather watch what's happening over there?" She motioned over her shoulder to the scene she'd been watching before. "I'm not pretty like that Stella girl."

He frowned at her. "Quit insulting my property or I'll punish you here and now." How had she gotten to this point in her life without realizing how hot she was? It was odd, but charming.

Complete obedience smoothed her face. "Yes, Sir."

Valentine removed her skirt, leaving her in only the blue thong and her harness. She wasn't wearing little girl panties tonight.

She grimaced and tensed, but he stroked her until she relaxed. He was stalling, waiting for the faintest hint of her safeword, but it was not forthcoming.

When he thought she was calm enough, he unzipped the duffle bag that held his rope. As though it had been eagerly awaiting the opportunity, it snaked out and slid up Jory's body. The sensual way it caressed her skin made her shake – or maybe it was the feeling of being bound and at his mercy, or the knowledge that most of the people in the room were watching him tying her.

"Are you cold?" he asked.

"No, Sir."

"Are you wondering what the rules are?"

"They are whatever you decide they are, Sir."

Xana whistled. Having a submissive this new not trying to control a scene was a surprise.

His rope spiraled around her, threading through the harness she wore, suspending her upright in his web, inches from the ground. She was a work of art. Experimentally, she tugged at her bonds, then sighed and relaxed into the suspension when she'd confirmed she was completely immobilized.

Valentine smiled apologetically and gently peeled back the electrical tape that clung to her skin. She didn't object to the loss of her last bit of modesty – the thong she wore was so small it didn't leave much to the imagination. Her pink nipples were peaked, and her breaths came deep but shaky.

When her pale blue gaze locked onto his, full of trust and adoration, he paused. What had he ever done to deserve this from her? She was like a dog with a cruel master, who didn't understand she deserved to be treated better. She kept coming back, and submitting to his rough treatment.

Maybe someday she'd run from him, but tonight she wasn't going anywhere.

Tonight she was his.

Chapter Thirteen

She hadn't thought she would ever want this. She was submitting to it for him, right?

Lies.

There was no point in trying to fool herself. Her belly housed a tight ball of lust. Being defiled in front of an audience had never been one of her fantasies, but now, with the hungry eyes of so many strangers upon them, adrenaline sang through her.

Rather than think about her traitorous body's arousal, she focused on what the people around them were doing. With Valentine's teammates so close, she noticed again how big Dane and Jurgen were. Xana wasn't much smaller. Compared to her they were all giants.

They milled around as though they were trying to choose the best vantage point. All three watched her with hard, ravenous gazes that made her insides feel weak. She wasn't stupid. If Valentine gave the word, they'd be on her. The look in Xana's eyes was particularly wicked. Women had never interested her, but Xana was dangerous and hot. She got the impression the female mercenary had the potential to be more of a sadist than Valentine.

The room had fallen almost silent, and she was glad she couldn't turn to see why. She hoped there was a really interesting scene happening elsewhere, and that everyone wasn't staring at her naked ass. Damned thong. Mortification crept up the back of her neck. Exposed and on display, embarrassed and aroused by her own embarrassment, she forced herself to focus on Valentine.

"Yes, they're looking at you, Jory. All of them. They either want to be you or they want to be inside you," he growled from somewhere right behind her ear. "But you're mine, and only mine, do you understand?" He wrapped his arms around her and pinched at her nipples, sending electricity zinging to her pussy. While she wriggled and whined, he ran his hands over her possessively. "I decide what happens tonight."

Valentine crushed Jory's nipples almost flat between his rough fingers. The burst of pain made her cry out.

Shame welled within her to have her own weakness exposed in front of Xana, a woman who would never submit to such a thing, let alone be excited by it.

He grabbed her jaw, and she flinched.

"Stop that." His lips were set in a firm, disapproving line that made her anxious to please him. But what had she done wrong?

"Stop what?"

He brought his face so close to hers, that for a moment it seemed as though he'd kiss her. Jory held her breath, shaking. She hadn't even trembled so much on her way to her first battle. His disapproval shouldn't be so intimidating.

"I can see what's going on in that head of yours." He brushed her wild hair back from her face. "You're allowed to enjoy this. There's no shame in submission. Without submissives there can be no dominants. If I didn't deeply respect you, you wouldn't be wearing my collar. We've discussed this, remember? No one here thinks less of you because of what you're into."

Maybe they'd discussed it before, but she harbored an abiding fear that he secretly laughed at her. How could he not think of her as a joke, considering what she let him do? But no one around them was laughing. Maybe his words were truer than she'd thought. It made sense, in a way. Without people like her being able to enjoy what a dominant did, a dominant's life would be full of frustration. However, just because it made sense didn't mean her existential crisis about the subject would permanently disappear.

"Life's too short to be ashamed of the way your brain is wired. That's especially true in our line of work," he continued. "We all deserve to have our needs met. It may seem like one side gets more respect than the other, but anyone who lives this life knows the strength it takes to submit one's will to the desires of another."

He dug in his back pocket and pulled out a length of black fabric.

"We're going to play a little game."

"A game?"

"I'm going to blindfold you. Will that freak you out?"

"No, Sir." A blindfold wasn't a big deal, right?

"Good."

He tied the blindfold around her eyes, the soft material draping over the contours of her face, so that she couldn't even peek through the bottom.

Thoughts whirled, but before she could sort them out, he kissed the side of her neck below the collar then sucked there until it hurt. She whimpered and shifted, trying to dislodge him, but he sank his teeth into her and made her yelp in pain before letting go. Her skin was hyperaware of every sensation, even the stir of air around her. His hands stroked over her belly and sides, the tops of her thighs, the contours of her ass. As he neared her pussy, she arched toward him, but there was no way he was going to make this easy.

"So, the game is: I'm going to let my friends touch your pretty body, and you have to try not to come."

"What?" She gasped. Flames of shock and arousal licked through her body. Fear pricked along her armpits and groin. "But you said it wouldn't be this weekend."

"I changed my mind." His voice was cool. "Tormenting you will be entertaining. I won't let them fuck you, or use your mouth, but anything else is fair game."

"But...I've never done anything with a girl before." Oh jeez – was that her only hesitation? Really? Her heart beat crazily.

"I know."

Xana groaned, then chuckled, low and throaty. "Hell, she would have to say that out loud."

Jory worried at her lip in consternation. The garden path Valentine led her down was getting steep.

"I'll give you a few minutes to decide. 'No' is an acceptable answer."

She hung there, her arms and legs spread as though she was tied to one of the padded crosses she'd seen on the other side of the room, knowing Valentine wasn't far, feeling the gazes of strangers upon her. Nearby she could hear the hushed rumbling voices of men having a private discussion. Was it Valentine talking to his friends, or people she didn't know speculating about what would happen – or were they discussing what they'd do to her themselves if Valentine let them?

If his teammates weren't allowed to have sex with her, maybe it would be okay. She wasn't sure if the blindfold made it better or worse. Not seeing might make her feel less guilty, but then she'd also feel less in control.

She could say no. He wouldn't be angry, but what if this was a test to see if she was loyal enough to refuse to let other people touch her? Would he play that kind of mind game?

No. Valentine wouldn't test her like that.

"Sir?"

"Yes, pretty girl?" He was closer than she'd thought.

"I want you to choose."

"You're willing, but don't want to do it if it will upset me," he observed. His touch on her cheek made her twitch. It was hard not being able to anticipate when she was going to feel something.

"Yes, Sir."

"What a good girl you are." His words full of approval. Although patronizing, the sentiment warmed her and bolstered her resolve. "Don't forget your safeword."

Fuck.

Someone's breath stirred the small hairs by her ear.

A feather-light finger trailed from between her shoulder blades, down her spine, to the cleft of her ass. Who was it? She tried to arch away, but the slight movement the ropes allowed for brought her to fingers that brushed over her nipples so lightly at first she thought she'd imagined it.

Touches ghosted randomly around her body. She clenched her jaw, trying not to respond, knowing they couldn't keep this up forever.

So many fingers everywhere, leaving tickling trails on her skin. It overwhelmed her, making her wish she could see and anticipate. The sensations they gave were random and disorganized, constantly catching her by surprise.

All too soon their teasing knocked aside her self-control. She mewled and strained after them, but the most she got from it was the occasional pinch or gentle slap.

"Please," she said in a small voice.

"Patience." Her dominant's voice was hard, and she melted at the command it held.

A mouth tasted the back of her neck. Valentine, obviously. But then something warm and wet flicked over her nipple, and a mouth closed over her other nipple, sucking and tugging. Her brain tried to explain away the sensations as something else, but there was no mistaking it.

He'd never said anything about them using their mouths!

He hadn't said they wouldn't, either.

Now it was too late to object – she couldn't ask them to stop. She didn't have that much willpower.

Hands slid over her boldly now, mouths suckling, biting, tasting. Their bodies were close – hot, bare skin brushed against her own. Murmurs of desire filled the air around her. What if he changed his mind and let them do more? The temperature in the room seemed to rise along with the volcano roiling in her pussy.

One of them explored her with nips and bites – her neck to her breasts, her belly, her thighs, her ass – sometimes light and threatening, sometimes too damn hard. She twitched and jerked, her body a puppet, feeling and reacting. The hurt was soothed away with kisses and licks, soft touches. Her nipples ached and itched. Her own breathy noises deafened her. The scrape of rope on her skin, holding her still to suffer for them… If only someone would touch her clit, she'd get off so hard.

"Please, Sir," her voice was more of a croak. "Please let me come."

A man swore.

"Be careful or I'll fuck you in front of all these people."

"Yes, Sir. Please," she begged, too frenzied to care who would be watching. "I need it."

"You don't need it. You want it," he growled. "Your greedy little cunt has to wait."

She moaned, his words adding fuel to the fire between her legs. The tiny underwear she wore dug into her, sodden and distracting.

Around them, the crowd was dead silent.

A hand buried in her hair and she shivered.

"You want me to fuck you in front of all these strangers?" he mocked. "Your body was made for my cock. You don't care who watches as long as you get what you need."

Valentine's voice held most of her attention, but the others drew it away again. She tried to focus on him, but someone was sucking on the inside of her thigh, and someone else bit the sweet spot between her shoulder and neck.

Her breath came in a series of shallow gasps and low moans.

"Please, Sir," she pleaded.

"Please what?"

"Please use me. Please? I'm sorry." A sob escaped.

"Sorry? For what?"

"I'm sorry," she repeated. "I'm sorry I'm a bad girl. I'm sorry. Please use me." The words came out in an uncontrolled tumble. "Please, Sir – I'll do anything. Just please let me come."

She only realized what she'd said after it had all come out of her mouth. It was so quiet in the room that everyone had to have had heard it. What had he turned her into? She squeezed her eyes tighter, not that she could see a thing.

"There's no reason to rush this," he chided. "Have patience."

Rush? Hadn't it been hours? Trapped behind the dark cloth, time moved differently.

Kisses moved downward, hovering above her pubic bone, straying no lower. A cool breath brushed over her pussy, through her damp panties.

Gasping, desperate moans poured from her mouth. She strained and wriggled, trying to get that mouth where she needed it, but it refused to cooperate.

"Please! Please, I can't take anymore."

"My poor girl." Valentine comforted her sarcastically. Fingers dug into her hips. A hard cock wedged against the cleft of her ass. "I wonder if these nice people would like to watch you lose your anal virginity?"

A visual of him shoving roughly into her ass, stretching her and hurting her while everyone gawked, was both terrifying and arousing. She sobbed, and the tear that leaked out from under the blindfold was licked from her cheek. The callousness of the gesture almost made her come.

"I'm yours," she said simply, hoping he'd choose to do something else. Something that didn't scare her. Her body was wound tight enough to snap.

"I know, snowangel, but I won't do it here and now. Probably."

Anxiety gripped her, but she was so desperate to come that she probably wouldn't safeword anything he chose to do anyway.

"You're lucky he's protecting you," a deep male voice rumbled in her ear. "Would you like it if we filled your pussy and your sweet, virgin ass?" Was it Dane? Jurgen? Speaking low and rough, it was hard to tell which.

Her breasts were pushed together and her nipples were bitten painfully over and over until she screamed. Her thong was pushed aside and a finger explored her wetness then circled her clit, which throbbed in time with the horrible cramp of need in her belly.

The pressure inside her grew, ached, pulsed.

Fuck.

She was going to come so hard. She felt a scream building in the back of her throat.

All of the touches stopped.

Nooo. No.

She arched her neck and listened hard, desperate to find anyone to help her.

A scream tore from her, a terrible, mournful cry. Part of her wanted to fight, but it was no use. She hung limply in her bonds and let the tears come. They mostly absorbed into her blindfold, making it just as damp as her thong.

The ropes adjusted. Were they letting her go? No such luck. She was tipped onto her back, still held spread-eagled.

"You don't really want to get away from us, do you, Jory?" Valentine asked mildly, as though he could read her thoughts. One of her nipples was twisted painfully as the other was bitten hard. She screamed again, and her body turned the pain into a debasing, desperate pleasure. "Do you think you deserve to come?"

She panted and whimpered at him, not sure what the right answer was.

Hands yanked at the delicate fabric of her panties, and the tiny strap that held them together on each side snapped. The garment was peeled from where it had dug into her, the exposed dampness cooled. Other than her harness and collar, she was naked.

His ropes tugged her legs wider apart then pulled her knees back until they touched her chest.

"So pretty. So open and helpless." His voice rumbled with thick satisfaction. He ran a hand from her ass to her upper thigh then worked two fingers inside her slick pussy. "Why are you so wet, princess?" His thumb pressed down on her clit, vibrating gently.

Her pussy clenched and ached...so close to coming. A hand gripped her hair and someone was nipping her earlobe. Her nipples were being flicked and suckled. The pressure built, her body stiffened.

They stopped.

She struggled and wailed. "Please, someone help me!"

Hands stroked her. Understanding voices murmured in compassion, but no one helped.

Just as she calmed, a tongue over her clit, making her breath catch.

Pleasure flooded through her. The mouth fastened down, sucking rhythmically until her whole body tensed and arched again, teetering on the edge.

Oh god, they were going to stop again. She knew it.

She was going to die. She had to come. He had to let her this time.

All sensation stopped, other than the feel of the ropes on her skin and a multitude of hands holding her still while she struggled. So many cruel hands doing nothing to ease her.

No! She couldn't take anymore. Not another second.

"Please, Sir!" She could feel him in her mind, curbing her power and holding it hostage. She was trapped in every possible way. What was the point of fighting? It didn't get her anywhere.

Her tears stopped. She meant to keep begging, but she couldn't find the words. She was need, but if he didn't want her to come, she would suffer. Fighting to come wasn't her place. It was for him to choose. Her body was his. Her torment was his.

She drifted. Valentine's face centered in her mind, his smile at once cruel and loving. She wanted to give him everything. She was his toy and it was her place to be used or broken, at his whim.

"Come back, snowangel," he commanded.

She struggled through the haze, trying to figure out where she'd left herself.

"It's no fun torturing you if you're that far into subspace."

He bit her shoulder and she shrieked. Her body shook like she was freezing. Awake. No more drifting.

"I-I'm sorry."

Valentine chuckled. "Are you?" She heard the click of the belt buckle. He must have unfastened his belt. Her heart leapt – would he fuck her now? "Would you like me to make you sorrier?"

"What do you mean?"

There was the sound of a belt being pulled free, making her brain short circuit.

"I'm going to hurt you now."

"Yes, Sir." The tears started again, and she wasn't sure why. They trailed hotly down her cheeks, over the drying, itching tracks of their predecessors.

They were wiped away, and someone made soothing noises. Lips pressed against her own, and she tasted herself on them, but then they were gone.

The ropes straightened her legs upward. The first stroke of the belt landed with a crack on the front of her thigh, painting her skin with pain. She screamed. Someone groaned and kissed her mouth again, as fingers tugged her clit. A stroke landed on her other thigh. Burning, aching. Every touch hurt. Every blow was erotic. Sensations mixed and muddled in her mind.

Her breath was coming hard and fast, and she scrabbled to hang onto control. Before she'd just wanted to come, but now she was trying to claw her way back from the precipice, not sure she was allowed.

"I'm going to come, Sir. Please," she begged quietly, her own words making her desperation worse. Another stinging stroke landed on her thigh and she could feel the mark pulse on her skin. The blows were moving higher each time, closer to her pussy. She knew what he was working toward, but needed something there – would accept anything. He played with her again, teasing and hurting. She writhed. This had to be a specific circle in hell. "Sir, I'm going to come. Please, I can't stop."

"You want to come?" he growled.

"Please." The smell of arousal wasn't all hers. Around her came the sound of shaky breaths. Bare skin and jean-covered erections rubbed against her.

"They want you so bad. I should let them have you." Valentine's voice was husky, barely in control.

"No, Sir. I want you."

"Only because you know they can't make you come."

"Valentine, please! I love you. Please make this stop!"

Would he finally fuck her? Jory's insides cramped and twisted. She needed him to make this agony end.

A belt blow caught her between the legs. Pain exploded. She screamed. Her clit felt as if it would burst.

"Oh, your poor little clit," he said regretfully. "I'm going to hit you there one more time, and you're going to come for me, aren't you princess?"

"No," she cried. Her safeword hovered in her brain, but if this was what he really wanted, she'd take it for him. Maybe she could change his mind. "It hurts too much. Don't hurt my pussy, I'll be good."

"Fuck," Dane rasped.

"Good girls say 'Yes, Sir,'" Valentine reminded her.

"Nooo." She struggled to back away, but the rope held her still, chaffing her skin.

"Bad girl." He leaned down and planted a kiss on her clit. She thrust her hips at him, hopeful. He'd been bluffing? Even he couldn't be that cruel.

The belt came down with a *snap*.

Her mouth hung open. She couldn't process the pain. Her body went taut and the pent-up orgasm released with a violence that was more agony than pleasure. His iron-hard cock plunged into her. Her body tried to refuse his sudden invasion, but he thrust harder, farther. Between their bodies, he stroked her brutalized clit. Violent thrusts followed long pauses, over and over, making her keen high in her throat. Her entire body felt weak and hot.

"That's right, my sweet little bitch. Come for me again."

"No!" she screamed.

The orgasm was determined to obey him, even though she hurt. Helpless and breathless she fought it, but it claimed her anyway, making her eyes roll back. She shrieked incoherently. Valentine's strokes became erratic. His vicious fingers dug into her thighs. He grunted as he emptied into her, his body and mind claiming all of her as his own

He collapsed onto her, his warmth delicious against her skin. She felt him stretch upward, and he tugged at the knot of the blindfold. A few strands of hair had tangled into it and were yanked free as the cloth fell away. She blinked up at him, her vision fuzzy.

Exhausted, spent, she drifted in and out of awareness. In her head, she could feel his power curled around hers, shielding them both. He rose and his ropes set her down on her feet. He swept her into his arms just as they let her go.

His black eyes burned into hers, intense and possessive.

He kissed her. "Shh, don't cry. You're such a good girl for me." It was only a few steps to the couch. When he sank down, he kept her on his lap, his arms wrapped tight and protective, around her shaking body. At some point he'd rezipped his jeans, and the denim was rough against her bottom, and growing wet from the come leaking from her body.

Only a pace or two away Xana and Dane watched them, their avid gazes eating her alive. She was too exhausted to be ashamed. Only Jurgen's face held any sympathy, but his eyes, too, were hot. Sympathy only went so far. They'd stripped him at some point. Dane's hand had a painful-looking grip around Jurgen's cock. The tip glistened with precome. She couldn't bring herself to look past Valentine's friends to the strangers who still crowded nearby.

Valentine pulled a blanket out of a bag next to them and enveloped her in the soft folds. He whispered sweet things to her and she snuggled into him. Euphoric lethargy crept over her. Valentine held her as though she was a fragile and precious doll. The feelings she had for him eclipsed love – went entirely past it and into some other realm where his every breath was more important than her own. The emotions were too big. They hurt. She let herself drift, hoping some of that frantic adoration would dull so she could relax again.

A gasp drew her attention. Xana shoved Jurgen down onto his back and skewered herself abruptly on his cock. He swore in surprise then moaned. Dane straddled his sub's head and shoved his cock into his mouth, muffling his cries of pleasure.

Buzzing and thoughtless, she lay in Valentine's arms, numb. Watching.

*

Seraphina was awake. Jory knew she was, but neither of them spoke. The girl had gotten back to their dorm room even later than Jory had, sneaking in as though she had no desire to talk to anyone. Jory had pretended to be asleep, her body still aching even though they'd left the club close to twenty-four hours before. There'd been more sex since, and her body needed time to recover.

She could feel the other girl lying there in tense silence.

"Rough weekend?" Jory finally asked, too wrapped up in her own thoughts to care about the answer, but knowing it was polite to open that door. She liked Seraphina, and if she wanted this team to work, she needed to make an effort.

The long pause that ensued led Jory to believe that maybe she'd been mistaken, and that Seraphina was actually asleep.

"Remind me never to follow your advice," the girl said finally, the rueful-sounding sigh taking the sting out of her words.

Jory stared at the dark ceiling, trying to remember when she'd ever given Seraphina advice at all. In training? She was good at what she did and didn't need Jory giving her pointers. Obviously it had been something recent, otherwise she would have been more specific.

"Were you in a fight or something?" It had been a long weekend, and if she was going to follow the conversation, Seraphina was going to need to speak slowly and use small words.

She laughed bitterly. "If only it was something that harmless. Don't you remember what you said to me when you were leaving on Friday? I know you said it off the cuff, but then I thought 'Hey that sounds fun, maybe I'll give it a try.' Sometimes I think I need to have my head examined." She shifted on her bed, and grunted in discomfort.

Jory was rewinding their last conversation in her head. She'd told her to have a good weekend, there was something about having fun deciding which one to flirt with, but then Jory had asked her why pick between them if she didn't have to.

Whoa.

"Shit, you convinced them to have a threesome?"

"I didn't even need to use my abilities to charm them into it. It just kind of happened."

Jory wasn't sure what to say. Should she apologize? She hadn't actually thought Seraphina was going to listen to her. It had been a joke.

Seraphina sighed. "There are moments in my life that seem so right and so good at the time, but then when I think about them in retrospect I have to shake my head."

If anyone knew what Sera was talking about, it was Jory. Every time she thought about how hard she'd begged to come in front of a roomful of strangers she wished she could erase her memory. But then, all the hot stuff that had happened would disappear too.

"The guys were very respectful and we had a lot of fun, but how will I be able to fight alongside them, remembering what we did together? I keep feeling like I should feel cheap and used, but it was my choice to do it at the time. I don't regret it. I like both of them a lot, but what if people find out? Will anyone respect me if they find out I was with them both at the same time?" She groaned, and must have covered her face with her hands because her next words came out muffled. "Do *you* even respect me?"

Scenes from her weekend with Valentine and his team replayed in her mind. She was the one who'd put the idea to try both guys in Seraphina's head, so she kind of owed her some personal disclosure – but Sera was almost a stranger. Then again, she'd trusted Jory with very private information, so it almost obligated Jory to out herself. She pressed a hand to her forehead, willing herself not to say too much.

"Of course I respect you."

Seraphina snorted. "You have to say that. What else can you really say to my face?"

"Sera, think about it. Do you think Vance and Arigh are lying awake and feeling weird about it? If they're not in their room talking about how awesome you are, they're probably thinking about you and whacking off."

The girl shrieked a laugh, which she smothered fast. "Oh my god, Jory!"

Jory's face heated, and she was glad it was dark. It was easier to sound nonchalant when Sera couldn't see her face. "It's true. Why should guys get to enjoy sex guilt free, while we have to second guess everything we do? We're modern women, not Puritans. If everyone involved is a consenting adult, there's nothing wrong with anything we choose to do."

They were quiet for a moment. Jory struggled with the urge to blurt out what happened to her at the club. Or even what her relationship was like with Valentine. Compared to any of that, there wasn't much Sera could have done to shock her.

"I-I've done things," Jory stammered. "I—"

"Oh, sweetness," Seraphina laughed. "I'm sure you have, but getting to second base with a guy in the backseat of your mom's car isn't a big deal compared to what I'm into. Do you even know what a safeword is?"

Jory frowned, not sure whether to tell Sera off or laugh. Why did everyone think she was so innocent? Annoyed and defensive, she blurted, "I'm a submissive. Considering who I'm with, I'm lucky I even get a safeword." As soon as the words were out, she wished she could reel them back in. What a stupid thing to get prideful about. Now she'd seriously over shared.

Way to fit in, Jory. Way to make friends.

Seraphina's mattress springs protested, and her shadowed outline sat up in bed.

"Well fuuuuuck me," the girl drawled. "Not as naïve as you look, hey? I never would have guessed. I hope you don't mind gory details, because you're about to get an earful."

Chapter Fourteen

They'd switched vehicles at the assigned location. It was a simple enough job. Drive to the drop-off point, and be alert for "the fucking Bureau pricks who seem to be everywhere lately," as his father put it. Maybe in their line of work it didn't pay to be too curious, but the mystery of what was in the back of the temperature-controlled truck had Valentine's stomach roiling.

The silence in the truck cab was loud in his ears. Xana had wanted more details about what they were transporting, but their team had been told to mind their own business. Now they were avoiding each other's eyes.

Surely their parents wouldn't hire them on to do anything involving human trafficking or anything else horrific? Valentine had always known that his father was basically a rich thug, but it wasn't until his team had started taking orders from his father's team that he'd done any sort of soul-searching with regards to what the old man's limits were. Or what his own limits were, for that matter. It had taken one girl to make him question everything.

What right did he have to lecture Jory about the dangers of being a sheep, when he was asking questions about jobs, not getting answers, then doing the jobs anyway? Whether or not a contract would put his team in danger wasn't a high enough bar to set when it came to deciding which jobs to reject. They'd said yes again, but it had become clear that if they wanted to live with themselves, they'd have to set up shop on their own and stop letting the older team be their team's manager.

The way thing were now, the pervasiveness of smaller evils could creep in where no one was watching. Maybe Valentine wasn't the most scrupulous person, but the idea of blindly following orders for the promise of cash was only one short step from evil, depending on the job. Willful ignorance didn't make him innocent.

A man who didn't take responsibility for his own actions – a man who didn't make his own decisions – wasn't good enough to speak to someone like Jory, let alone be her dominant.

"That's it. Pull over."

Dane eased over onto the shoulder without hesitation, as though he'd been hoping someone would give the order. None of them were bad people. Not yet.

"Stay here with Jurgen. Xana, come with me." Leadership of the group had passed between him and Xana so often over the years, he sometimes forgot which one of them was in charge. So did she, depending on the day. She seemed glad to follow his lead on this one.

They said nothing as they walked to the back of the truck. At this point, it was impossible to know when they were being listened to or watched, or how much was a test. The old bastards were sneaky.

He checked the door for booby traps, and when he found none he picked the simple padlock with the picks in his boot. When he opened the door to the cargo area, they found it held a large metal crate.

"It could be almost anything," Xana whispered as she toed the box. It didn't move when she nudged it, as though it was heavy and full.

Valentine examined it, but the lock on this was complicated and coded. He had no clue how to pick anything so advanced. Smashing it might be an option, but rather than finding out anything important, it might just make them look guilty when they got to the drop point. Getting a reputation as a group that tried to steal valuables wasn't going to help them at all.

"There are no air holes, at least," Xana said with a brightness that sounded almost brittle.

Valentine held a finger to his lips and pointed around the ceiling. There was just as much of a chance that the cargo area was bugged. They both stared at the crate. Valentine crouched next to it and listened, but didn't hear anything, although the passing traffic could cover something faint.

"Money, gems, electronics, weapons – it could be anything," she hissed.

"Electronics, some sort of germ warfare, something living – the cargo area is climate controlled. I doubt they'd worry about that for anything else," he whispered back.

"Ice cream?" Xana asked slyly.

He snorted. "If there was ice cream in there, you'd have figured out a way in by now."

"True." She peeked out the door. "We should get moving. That box doesn't look any more suspicious than our other deliveries. Maybe it's just an overly cautious client."

They shrugged at each other and edged out the back door. Valentine locked it again, hoping they hadn't left telltale marks anywhere.

Once they were back on the road, the tension in the cab eased. They were still quiet, but it was companionable rather than anxious. If they hadn't had to stay alert, it would have been nice to turn on the radio, but the distraction wouldn't have been very professional.

"I want ice cream now." Xana sighed.

"Later." Jurgen snorted. "It's not time to think about your stomach."

"Ice cream is for your mouth, not your stomach." She shook her head in mock disbelief. "Have I taught you nothing?"

"Well," Jurgen considered. "You did teach me that thing he likes you to do with your tongue." He and Xana high-fived, and Dane frowned at them. It was usually Xana and Dane teasing Jurgen, and he never liked it when the tables were turned on him.

"I saw you use it on him at the club last week." Xana laughed. "We should teach it to Rigg's sweet little thing."

Valentine glared and gestured to his ear, then pointed around again, reminding them about possible listening devices. They'd agreed it would be best not to talk about Jory in unsecure locations, but leave it to Xana to bring her up.

"What? That kid is capable of a lot more than you give her credit for. She's not Typical or a child. She can protect herself." Xana and Valentine narrowed their eyes at each other. Just because one of his teammates thought his girl was badass, didn't mean it was acceptable to put her in harm's way.

Dane started to pull off the road again, and for a moment Valentine thought it was because his friend knew he wanted to yank Xana out of the truck and lecture her, but then he realized they were at the drop point. Not long now. After this they'd go back to the spot where they'd parked the SUV, switch vehicles, then go home. He just wanted to head to his new house and work on the place. The other three could go get ice cream without him.

Fuck this shit. He just wanted to see Jory.

The dilapidated roadside diner crouched in its nest of cracked pavement, creepy and deserted. Maybe they were the first ones there, but Valentine didn't count on it. Dane pulled around behind the building to see a freshly painted utility van waiting. When Dane parked beside the van, four older men in leather emerged from it. Run-of-the-mill mercs doing a run-of-the-mill contract, from the looks of them.

Valentine and his friends got out of the truck. Maybe he was getting paranoid in his old age, but something about this job stank.

"You have any issues?" the team leader asked Xana.

"Nothing at our end."

Valentine's team stood back as the strangers unlocked the cargo door with a key they must have arranged with Dietrich. Two of them entered and grabbed the handles of the crate, then carried it to just behind the van and set it on the ground.

"That's it then," the team leader said with a nod. The rest of the arrangements had been made through the senior team, so there was no payment or paperwork outstanding. Contract complete.

He was trying to be easy with this, but something wasn't sitting right with Valentine. The stance of the men near the crate was too casual, as though they were still nervous about something, even though the transaction was basically finished. They hadn't moved the crate into their van.

Xana, Jurgen, and Dane moved toward the cab of the truck after Valentine secured and relocked their own cargo door, and he followed them reluctantly. When he glanced back, the other team leader smiled politely at him. All four stood around as though they were in no hurry. Odd.

Dane turned onto the two-lane highway then pulled off again at the side road almost next door. Without a word they all got out of the truck.

"That whole transaction reeked." Xana frowned.

"Something is indeed rotten in the state of Denmark," Jurgen agreed.

They ran back through the woods that separated the side road from the diner. As they neared the back parking lot, they slowed their steps, and focused on moving quietly. The utility truck was still parked. They crept closer, until they were at an angle and could see two of the men looking down into the now open crate, while the other two kept watch. One of the men near the crate gave a nod and without hesitation the other drew a gun from a side holster under his jacket and shot into the box. The sound of the shot rang in Valentine's ears like an accusation.

Horrified, he scrambled forward, but the others tackled him to the ground. A branch snapped under him, alerting the guards. They trotted over to peer into the woods. Adrenaline pounded through his body, making him sure he could throw his team off of his back like an angry giant. But what would he do? Bullets weren't something they had experience defending against, and even if they attacked these men and won, what would they do with them? Kill them? Drop them off at the nearest police station bound hand and foot, with a note pinned to their shirts?

They were mercenaries, not vigilantes, and not heroes. There was no way to report illegal activity they objected to, if they, themselves, were on the shady side of the law.

He and Xana had stopped to check the crate, but had given up when confronted with a lock they couldn't pick. They'd all felt there was something wrong, but they'd finished the job anyway.

He'd delivered someone to their execution.

The other team was careless and seemed to be in a hurry, so they didn't look very far into the woods. Two loaded the crate into the back of their van and the older team left without a backward glance.

For all the good it would do them, Valentine memorized the license plate. The truck and the plate would disappear, but he couldn't think of anything else to do.

Slowly, the others rose, swearing and muttering to each other. Jurgen punched a tree several times, bloodying his knuckles before Dane wrapped his arms around him to make him stop. Valentine lay still in the cold, damp leaf mold, angry, betrayed, and sickened by his own inaction.

There had been something wrong from the beginning of this job. All of them had felt it. It was serious enough to make them pull over to check things out, but they'd given up too easily. None of them had wanted to believe the older team would set them up for something like this. Even if his father denied knowing what was in the crate, Valentine would never know whether he was telling the truth.

"But there weren't any air holes." Xana was sitting with her back braced against a tree. "Maybe it was an item they had to destroy. Maybe it wasn't a person." There was always the chance that someone could get killed on a job, in a fight, but this kind of dirty business was usually left to Typicals. Even when Atypical mercs held a hostage, killing people wasn't part of the plan. If it was done after they left, they didn't know about it. But Valentine had been very specific – his team was interested in fighting and moving shit, not dealing in people. Their limits had not been respected. Or had they been set up for this to get their hands dirty, as some sort of blackmail to force them into future dirty work?

"Do you think our parents know?" Dane was sitting now too, holding Jurgen in his arms. Both of them were pale. Dane was shaking. "Maybe they do. Fuck, maybe they do this shit all the time."

Jurgen made a sound of self-derision. "We knew they did things like this. We've known since we were little kids. I remember having that conversation when we were still in grade school. We turned a blind eye to the obvious because it was easier not to think about it. I never felt like we had a choice other than to follow in their footsteps." He swallowed noisily and when he went on his voice was hoarse. "But that's all bullshit. We're not stupid. We knew we had other choices."

They sat in the relative silence of the woods, listening to birds and chipmunks crashing through the underbrush. The smell of damp rotting leaves was strong in Valentine's nose, but even though he was getting cold, sitting there together was better than the stark reality of getting back in the truck and dealing with whatever came next.

Weak sunlight filtered through the trees, casting shadowy lacework on his friends' faces and clothes. Sometimes he wished they could ditch all the crappy adult shit they had to deal with and go back to the past when they built tree forts, fought imaginary enemies, and talked about how cool it would be when they were grownups and could live together and have sleepovers every night.

He loved these people even more than he loved his own family. They *were* his family. They got him the way no one else did, except maybe for Jory. Now she knew him in ways even they didn't.

Just thinking her name filled him with guilt. She'd never get mixed up in something so stupid – so passively evil. How could they have trusted the other team to arrange jobs for them when they had a track record of being less than ethical? Trusting that they'd respect their limits had been idiotic.

"We can't stay here forever," Xana said. "We need to decide what the hell we're doing. We have another job scheduled for tomorrow, and the last I checked, that one was sounding sketchy too."

Dane scrubbed the palm of his hand across his forehead. "Screw that. I'm not letting them vet jobs for me anymore. I like cash just as much as the next guy, but I also have to be able to live with myself. What if the guy had kids?"

"Fuck. It could've been woman or kid. We have no way to know. We don't even know if their family's going to be notified, or if the person's just going to disappear." Valentine broke a stick and threw it. It turned end over end and landed with a small crunch a few feet away.

"Screw work." Jurgen threw up his hands. "How can I go to my parents' house and look my mother in the eye knowing that she sent me to do this? I know they started treating us like adults when we were still in high school, but you'd think that as parents, they'd want to be proud of us for something other than having money." His voice was thick and shook with rage. "I can't take money to do jobs like this. Knowing that my entire childhood was funded with blood money... Every scrap of food I put in my mouth, every t-shirt I wore, might have come at the expense of someone else's life." Dane tried to hold him, but Jurgen pulled away and got to his feet. "I don't know about the rest of you, but I'm never setting foot in that house again."

Valentine's feelings echoed everything Jurgen had said. He'd been thinking about how nice it would be to just move into the house he bought to be close to Jory, but it was too far away from his team.

Xana and Dane were nodding.

"I'm not going home," Xana growled. "I don't care if I have to live in my fucking car."

"Like we'd let you live in your car," Dane replied. "You could move into our apartment, but I think we need something bigger if there'll be three of us living there."

"Make that four. I might not be there all the time because I have my place by Jory, but when I'm in town I don't want to stay with my parents, either. Dietrich and I were already having differences of opinion on this subject, and apparently he thought he could ignore my limits. After all the conversations I had with him about this, I can't believe he'd do this to us."

The mood was grim as they trekked back to the truck. Someone was dead. They were involved, even if they hadn't actually known, and hadn't pulled the trigger. How could they atone for that?

His team didn't really have a plan, but Valentine took some comfort in knowing that they were still on the same page. None of his best friends had secretly turned evil while he was busy getting laid.

*

The meeting hadn't gone the way Valentine had hoped. In his mind, there was going to be a grand gesture, a throwing down of the gauntlet, where Dietrich and his team either admitted they'd been evil all along, or that they had also been duped.

Instead, there'd been a long, drawn-out discussion about how Valentine's team was welcome to be young and idealistic, but that the older team would be there to bail them out when they lost their naïveté and got hungry.

Then the entire meeting had gotten derailed by Jurgen's spontaneous decision to out himself and his relationship with Dane, who'd wanted to come out for the past couple of years.

Havoc ensued, and Valentine's group had ended up walking out.

There had been no victory, and no satisfaction. Cutting the apron strings had been overdue, but there had been no dignity involved.

His friends were determined to move on and forget about trying to save their familial relationships for now.

As much time as they spent together over the years, Valentine hoped that all four of them living together wouldn't ruin their dynamic. The four-unit apartment building they bought meant they'd have their own space, plus an apartment to use as their meeting area, but there was still a danger of discovering their childhood dream of having a clubhouse with electricity and cable might not work out. There'd already been disagreements on important matters, like that it was lame to call their meeting space their headquarters or command center, and that Xana refused to let Dane post a sign on the front door saying "No Typicals Allowed."

Under the joking and high spirits, Valentine could sense the anger and guilt. The people they should have been able to trust had betrayed them. They, themselves, had done something they couldn't undo.

"What are you working on?"

Valentine hadn't heard Xana come in, but none of them had been closing their apartment doors. At least not yet. They'd only moved in a few days before, and he assumed that eventually they'd want more time alone.

He glanced at the document on his laptop, then back at Xana. "My term paper for social psychology."

"We have no jobs scheduled for the weekend. Why don't you work on it then?"

"Jory." He smiled, eager to spend a quiet weekend with her at their house after all the crap that had been going on. The weekend he and Jory had spent with his team had been fun, but he wanted a whole weekend to lie around in bed with her and talk. He was sure sex would happen too, but they'd been so busy for the past few weeks he felt as if they hadn't really spoken.

"Between work and keeping a submissive, why are you bothering with your master's?" Xana pulled out a chair and turned it around, then straddled it and sat. She leaned on the chair back, her eyes tired. "I can't imagine doing more than work right now. Even doing laundry seems like a pointless time-suck."

He shrugged. "I don't know. I guess stopping feels too much like giving up."

Xana went to his fridge. "Want a beer?"

"Sure."

She threw him one. This coming into his apartment without permission and drinking his beer before noon was setting a bad precedent.

"For all my father blustered about us never getting work, we already have three jobs set up for next week, and one's out of town." She shrugged and took a swig of her beer. "It seems like they just want us to do everything they did, in the same order, like they have the perfect recipe for life, you know?" She pushed her dreadlocks behind her shoulders. "Sometimes I envy Mundane Atypicals like your brother – or even Typicals. Choosing your life's path based on what you're good at and what you're interested in, instead of based on what abilities you've ended up with, seems like a more satisfying way to live. It's like going through life on a sports scholarship, instead of just college. You know?"

Valentine cracked open his beer and drank some. It was too early for beer, but this conversation was dragging him back into the morose thoughts he'd been trying to throw off since the shooting.

"Pascal is so laid back that even if he could throw fireballs he'd probably never be a fighter." He leaned back in his chair. "It's funny how we're doing exactly what we always thought we wanted to do as kids, but we're still not happy with it."

"We're not doing what we always wanted to do. Originally you wanted to be a gorilla."

"Hey, the news said guerilla fighters were coming down from the mountains and attacking people. I thought being part of evolution would be epic. When I found out guerillas weren't gorillas and revolution was different from evolution, I changed my mind."

She was laughing at him. "Yeah, but then you decided you wanted to be a priest. We're not even Catholic."

"Those kinds of details are irrelevant when you're seven. Plus, I didn't know about sex, let alone that priests weren't supposed to have it. Look who's talking, though. You're the one who wanted to be a teacher if you couldn't be a fighter. You hate kids."

Xana chugged the rest of her bottle and went back to the fridge. "I didn't really want to be a teacher, I just wanted to be like my nana. She's a tough bitch."

"You succeeded on that count."

She sat with a fresh beer and drew a random pattern in the condensation her last one had left on the table. How it had time to drip at all was a mystery. The woman could drink him under the table.

"So were you just lonely and bored, tired of watching Dane and Jurgen make sappy faces at each other, or just single-handedly trying to derail my master's degree?" he asked, taking another swallow of beer. What he wanted right then was coffee and maybe some eggs and toast, but that would involve getting up.

"No, I was just thinking. As a friend, I think this needs to be said."

"Let me guess, you don't like my new truck."

"I would've bought a Dodge, actually, but that's not why I'm here."

He chuckled and shook his head. Leave it to Xana to start what sounded like a serious conversation with a jab at his taste in vehicles. If it hadn't been that, she would have complained about the beer.

"This beer is disgusting too," she added. "If you want company, you really should buy the good stuff." The 'good stuff' being the brand she preferred, of course.

"If it's so disgusting, why are you on your second one?"

"I have to go fast so I don't taste it."

"That's what she said."

"Speaking of which…" She smiled grimly and put her beer bottle carefully down on the table, as though if she set it in the wrong spot the entire dinette set might explode.

He might explode if she said anything bad about Jory.

"What about her?" he grumbled.

"Down boy," she patted his arm, and grimaced sympathetically. "I told you before that I like her. There's no need to bite my head off. Actually, I like her a lot. To the point where if you ever get tired of her, I'd appreciate it if you let me know first."

He waited for her to laugh, and when she didn't he could feel the subtle growl in his chest wanting to make itself heard.

"Oh, come on. You can't be mad at me for that." She snorted at him and rolled her eyes. "A dominant would have to have an aversion to girls not to fall half in love with her the first time they spoke to her. Prospero called me the day after we were there to ask if you two were serious. Like the collar she was wearing, or the fact that you stood on her all night wasn't a big enough indication."

Valentine shoved himself to his feet, and paced the room. "Fucking Prospero. That was pretty fucking ballsy. I should kick his sweet-talking, rich boy ass." An impotent rage filled him, and he wondered if killing the man would be overreacting.

"Like Jory has eyes for anyone else but you, maggot. She's completely yours, in case you missed that. It would be about as likely as Jurgen leaving Dane for him. Not going to happen."

He grabbed the back of his chair and gripped it hard enough that the wood creaked. "If you think that, why are you bringing up Prospero? Or your own interest, for that matter?"

"She really hasn't been with a woman?"

"Xana." He frowned in warning.

"What? I'm not allowed to have an innocent little corruption fantasy about her?"

"No." The growl he'd been trying to suppress got out. "Are you going to tell me what this is about, or are you just here to torment a jealous man?"

"That wasn't why I came, either, but since I was here, it was too fun to pass up."

Valentine drained the rest of his beer and thought about getting another. There was a good reason why he and Xana hadn't lasted long as a couple. Aside from the fact that submitting to her was one of the hardest things he'd ever done in a relationship, her sadistic interpersonal habits got fucking irritating.

She smiled impishly at him for a long while, and all he could do was wait and hope she got bored of teasing him. Eventually she sighed.

"You're no fun today. You need to get laid."

He inclined his head. She had a point, but that was something he just needed to have some patience with.

"I know you're keeping her as twenty-four seven as you can, and freeing her to do her work when she needs to go, but any Atypical can see the power that comes off of her. The only reason you're not a Valentinesicle is because the Aphrodisia lets you in to control her power when you're together."

Valentine nodded. It wasn't like any of this was news to him. "I think it started off as her being surprised, but she's into kink now, so she doesn't kill me. What's your point?"

"You told me before that she didn't go to Atypical school, right?"

"No, just a few rounds of combat training, and some independent experimentation." He laid his beer bottle on its side and nudged it until it spun on the table. The sound reminded him of playing Spin the Bottle with Xana, Jurgen, and Dane when they were fourteen. The game had escalated quickly.

Xana smiled at him, probably remembering the same thing.

"So she's still figuring out what her powers can do," Xana said, absently sticking her finger into the mouth of his bottle and snagging it away from him. "If you keep her power bound too often, you might stunt her as an Atypical. She could end up never learning everything she can do, and that could come with a steep cost."

"She's away from me all week," he said, trying to keep the desperation out of his voice. "On weekends, I just help her control her power while I'm toying with her or using her, or else she'll lose control and accidentally freeze my dick off. Not my kink."

"Getting her killed shouldn't be your kink, either. If you keep subjugating her power to yours, she could stop learning. If she never learns her powers well, and she gets seriously hurt because of it, you'll suffer too. Possibly worse than getting your dick frozen off." She leaned her chin on the back of the chair. "I know she's hot and she loves what you two have together, but she's not a toy or a pet. She's a hero now, and you can't expect her to just pretend she's one during the week. It's got to be a full-time thing, with full-time access to her unimpeded power."

"She's fine."

"What if she dies?"

The scene from the parking lot replayed in his mind, except this time the person in the crate was Jory. A dreadful, icy sickness trickled from his scalp and down his neck and spine. He struggled to keep his hands flat on the table when he desperately wanted to punch Xana out.

"What the fuck, Xana?" His voice sounded panicked even to his own ears. "You don't just say things like that. Take it back."

"Oh my god. Are we five?"

"Take it the back, or get the fuck out of my apartment!" He was on his feet then and pointing at the door, as though she might have forgotten the way out. "That was over the line."

Xana stood and shook her head in exasperation. "This is serious business, Val, and I only said it to remind you this isn't a game. You take your D/s relationship seriously, but sometimes I think you're still playing at your work. We knew this was a life-and-death business, even before the reminder we just got." She closed her eyes. "If you want what's best for her, you have to stop monopolizing her time when she should be training. She didn't have the advantages we had of training from the time we were young and knowing our team like the back of our hand. Her team is a group of strangers, and she's almost a stranger to her power, at least where combat is concerned."

What? Hadn't he done his damnedest to stay out of Jory's hair where her career was concerned? He'd never tried to derail her from her dream of being a hero. It wasn't a joke to him. If anything, he took her career more seriously than he took his own. But the truth was that even knowing what she could do, he still looked at Jory and saw someone soft and sweet. Maybe she didn't need his protection, but he still felt compelled to protect her. She was his woman – his responsibility.

Part of him argued that she was a smart girl, a gifted girl. She didn't need a man to protect her or guide her. But he was also her dominant. Being overprotective was inevitable. Or at least that's how he felt about her.

He shoved his hands in his pockets. "You really think I'm holding her back? That I'm putting her in danger?"

"I can't say for sure. All I know is that what you have with her is very different than how things are between Dane and Jurgen. I just want you to keep it in mind when you have her under your thumb. Damaging her as a hero isn't what you mean to do – I know that, but she needs space. She also needs to bond with her new team, and that won't happen if she's spending all of her free time in your bed."

There was nothing sane about the way he felt about Jory, but if what Xana had said was true, he had a responsibility to make sure he backed off enough to let her grow. He didn't want to. Was needing to keep her close such an evil thing?

He loved her. Damn. He did.

Doing what was best for her was more important than what he wanted.

"Fine. Fine," he grumbled, feeling sick to his stomach. "But if I give her space and she wanders off on me, things are going to get ugly."

Chapter Fifteen

"This is how it's always going to be now, isn't it? Until we're old, I mean." Amy shoved Jory's arm affectionately. "Remember when we used to say we'd buy a side-by-side duplex and live there forever with our husbands and million kids? Now I'm lucky if I see you every few months."

They lay on the floor of the pretty bedroom in Amy's new apartment, scrolling through the movie listings for that evening. Jory hadn't seen or even heard of any of them. Her life didn't allow for those sorts of amusements anymore. She didn't even have much downtime to see Valentine, not that he was an amusement. He was more of a compulsion, even without the Aphrodisia shoving them together.

"You're just as busy as I am now. I can't believe you finally got your own classroom!" She grinned at her friend, excited that her dreams were coming to fruition. Even getting out of her parents' house had been a dream come true – if only to give her some privacy for once in her life. Amy's parents had never treated her like an adult. Maybe this would make the difference. "Did your Tamagotchi survive the transition?"

Amy shook her head, shame-faced. "Between work and Talbot, I forgot about it. How am I ever going to be a good mother?"

"Kids scream at you until you feed them. You'll be fine." She took a sip of her freshly opened Pepsi, which was so fizzy it made her eyes water. "Hang on, now. Are you needing to know how to be a good mother *imminently*? Did Talbot MacDonald get you in a…*family way*?"

"Why Miss Savage," Amy said, "I'm not that kind of young lady. I most definitely am not *increasing*, although I have to admit I finally got my own place just so Talbot and I could screw like bunnies." Amy smiled to herself. Her one crooked eyetooth made Jory want to cry.

Amy's smiles had always been one of her favorite things, and she missed her like crazy. She never seemed to have the chance to call anymore. To her chagrin, she'd turned into one of those friends who was too busy to keep outside relationships once she had a boyfriend. Amy had work and Talbot, but at least she still made an effort to text Jory a few times a day. It made Jory feel like a shithead.

Admittedly, hero work was grueling. They kept long hours, and didn't get to sleep much, between missions and training. It was probably for the best that her and Valentine were apart during the week, just so she wasn't tempted to forgo more sleep.

"Talbot has been staying over on weekends, and he's been teasing me saying he's moving in one day while I'm at work. I think he just likes my cooking, personally." Amy winked at her and Jory rolled her eyes.

"Sure, you keep telling your parents that, and I'll plead ignorance when they call and ask me what Mr MacDonald's intentions are in regards to their pure, virginal daughter."

"Yeah, I can't cook worth shit. Little known fact, but the way to a man's heart is actually though his dick. Blowjobs make them forget you burn water."

Jory snorted. "Blowjobs seem to be a universal lure. I'm sure there are guys who aren't into them, but I haven't met any."

"Yes, you with your vast dating experience." Amy laughed. "And you know what I love? The fact that the man knows how to enthusiastically reciprocate. He's lucky I let him up for air. I may have calluses from his tongue." She rolled onto her back and stared dreamily at her ceiling.

"Classy."

Amy snorted. "If you wanted a classy best friend, you should have thought about that in grade school. Besides, I'm not the one wearing a collar." She winked.

Jory smacked her then put a self-conscious hand to her throat. She'd almost forgotten that Valentine had put the knotted rope collar back on her.

The levity left Amy's face, and she sighed. "It's so awesome, though. I know I joke around about the sex, but even better than all that. He's a good man. We just clicked so instantly, and so thoroughly. Thank God your mother set you up with him. To think that the man of my dreams was living down the street and I had no idea. Jory – I think he's going to ask me to marry him."

"You're crazy. You barely know each other."

Amy shifted closer and laid her head on Jory's stomach. "You barely know Valentine and I'm guessing he does more dangerous things with you than put a ring on your finger. My peril isn't that perilous."

True. It wasn't like they couldn't go to counseling if there was an issue, or get a divorce if things were unfixable. At least Talbot was a Mundane Atypical with a talent for cake decorating. Jory pictured them getting married and buying a sweet little house and having sweet little babies. Tears pricked her eyes. That was a life she'd probably never have, no matter how much she and Amy had talked about it as kids. Even if Jory and the Big Bad Wolf split up eventually, she'd never have a placid, suburban life.

Why was she bemoaning the loss of a childhood fantasy when she was finally getting the hero's life she wanted? Maybe because she could see how happy Amy was, and how confident. Amy would never have to worry about Talbot sliding into the darker realms of cake making, or worry about him being dead if he was late for dinner. A man who made cakes could only cause a woman to question her dress size, not her relationship to good and evil. Unless, perhaps, he made a particularly evil fondant.

When Amy nudged her arm, Jory was picturing Talbot rolling out nefarious icing while laughing manically.

"Now spill it. You need to tell me all the nasty, naughty things you've been doing with Valentine. If I get scared, I'll cover my virgin ears."

*

At least the Mustang Cobra was less unlikely for her to own than the Audi R8 Spyder Valentine had originally given her.

Jory had been notified that the man from the dealership had dropped off the keys at reception, and she'd walked through the parking lot pressing the button on the key fob to find the car that was apparently now hers. She never would have picked that shade of blue, but then she realized it matched the collar he'd bought her to wear at the club. It must have been custom. Was the car color supposed to be a sly reminder of the collar, or did he just like blue?

After glancing around to make sure no one was paying much attention to her, she slid behind the steering wheel. The interior smelled like leather – another not-so-subtle reminder of who owned her. A hot blush crept over her cheeks, and she pressed a hand between her legs. He'd mock her if she masturbated in the car he'd bought her. Creepy bastard probably had cameras installed in the vehicle. Was he watching her? And if he was, why did the idea make her hotter?

It wasn't fair that he'd gotten her addicted to his cock, then disappeared on her.

Unable to resist, she opened the glove compartment and flipped open the folder. The ownership was there. It said Jory Savage.

She turned the key in the ignition, wondering why she was disappointed the car wasn't in his name. Maybe part of her had wanted the car to belong to him like she did. It would have made it dirtier somehow.

Lord, the man was turning her into the world's weirdest pervert.

She took it around the block once, then parked out front and ran up to her room to grab her bag, her heart beating an eager staccato. The weekend. Finally.

The previous weekend Valentine had begged off their arranged meeting at the last minute, saying he had to work. The tone of his voice had seemed suspicious, but he hadn't been in the mood to chat. For that matter, he'd barely texted her back during the past few days.

She missed him, but it had freed up time for her team to practice, and take an extra, short mission – there had been plenty of those lately, with the crackdown on some mercenary activities and the growing animosity between the mercenaries and the Bureau. The extra practice sessions had done her good, and she could feel her power getting stronger. She was learning the way she fit in with the rest of her team – both in practice and socially.

The time apart from Valentine had made her realize she hadn't been bonding with her team the way she was supposed to. She'd either been absent or distracted while the other three were getting closer to each other. People had noticed her mind hadn't been on her work, and for the first time she realized that they noticed. It wasn't very professional.

How did other heroes find balance between their team bonds, improving their skills, and starting or maintaining a relationship with a significant other? She was so far behind the Atypicals who'd combat trained their whole lives. Why had she ever thought being a hero was a good idea? Her power was strong and useful, but her attention was too divided, and she had so much time to make up for.

But going without Valentine for two weeks had been too much. She ached to see him but was embarrassed by how much more she needed him than he seemed to need her. It was making her anxious, and her mind was straying to all sorts of scenarios.

If he was getting bored of her, she didn't know what she would do. She'd spent too much of the second week wondering if he could be so cruel – to bind her completely to him then withdraw his affection. All day today she'd been half waiting for him to cancel on her again, but then the car had shown up. It meant he wasn't done with her.

Or was it a parting gift?

It wasn't okay that it mattered so much to her. She was a fucking hero, not a sappy idiot who didn't have anything better to do in life than wait around hoping for a man's attention. Right?

In her room she checked her phone again. No point in driving out to the house if he was going to cancel.

"I wish you weren't going this weekend." Seraphina stood in the doorway to their room, grimacing at her. "You're coming back here Sunday night?"

Jory nodded. "Yeah, I'll pack the rest of my shit then, and I'll be at the new house bright and early on Monday." It was hard to believe that they were moving out of the training school. They'd had the option of moving into the barracks, but most heroes agreed that the best teams lived together away from Bureau housing to form a tighter bond.

"Okay. It would be more fun if you were moving with us this weekend, though. The guys are going to get all domineering about where things go, and I'll have to try to manage their bossy asses all on my own."

She raised her brows at Seraphina. "Oh, like you don't like it when they're bossy? I've seen the look on your face when they pin you between them. You don't seem to mind one bit."

Seraphina bit her lip. "Maybe I don't, but I'm going to have to choose between them eventually." She sighed. "It's going to suck."

"Why? If the three of you are happy, there's no reason to end things."

Seraphina threw herself onto her bed. A half-full duffle bag tipped over and threatened to spill clothes onto her, but she righted it. Most of the stuff in their room belonged to Seraphina, who teased Jory regularly about her disinterest in clothing. "Can you imagine if my father finds out I'm having sex with one of them, let alone both? One I may be able to bring home to visit, even though there'll be hell to pay, but then which do I bring? Who gets left out?"

"Aren't you getting ahead of yourself? It's only been what – four weeks since you started seeing them? If things end up getting serious, just tell your family. It's your life, Sera."

"Like you're out to your family about Valentine and what you two are into?"

"Shaddup."

Seraphina laughed then shut her eyes. A more tender smile curved her mouth, as if she had a private thought that was sweet but not something she could share, or maybe explain. "They're both so beautiful and kind, even if they're both pigheaded. It's funny that they get along so well."

Whenever the three of them were together, it was magic to watch. In the beginning it had only been some not-so-innocent fun together, but it had quickly turned into a relationship. Who knew if it was going to work, but they all seemed professional enough not to fuck up the team if things between them ended, at least. She thought of Valentine's team and wondered if relationships between teammates were more common than people let on. It would make sense.

"We're heroes. It's not exactly a safe line of work. Why deny yourself pleasure or love when you don't know what could happen tomorrow?" Jory said, feeling the echo of Valentine's words.

Seraphina stared into space for a while then turned to Jory with a devious gleam in her eye. It was the look that meant she was up to something, and it made men completely lust-crazed. "You know...if things between you and Valentine crash and burn, you're welcome to join the three of us. I wouldn't kick you out of bed for eating corn flakes."

Stunned, all Jory could do was blink.

"It's fine if you're not into girls. I'll even just share the guys with you if you want." She chuckled evilly. "Although I can't promise not to perv on you a little. You're hot."

Until Valentine had claimed her, no one had paid Jory a second glance. Getting this kind of attention was still weird. It must have been something about him rubbing off on her. How did actual hot girls like Sera and Xana deal with this all the time? It was so awkward.

"Um, I'm not allowed to play with other people," she said shyly, feeling like an idiot for not knowing how to respond. "I'll...keep that in mind if he decides to uncollar me." Hopefully that would be good enough not to hurt the other girl's feelings. She watched Seraphina's pretty face and for a moment wondered what sex with her teammates would be like. Would it be vanilla? She didn't know much about vanilla sex.

Seraphina swung her legs over the edge of the bed and put her feet on the floor. "Wow – you *are* pretty hardcore into the D/s." She got up and moved closer to Jory. "It's a shame you're not interested in us. Arigh and Vance both have serious hard-ons for you. So do I." Sera sank into a crouch, until their faces were level. Up close, the girl was even more beautiful. "You look so afraid of me. Have you ever kissed a girl?"

"No." At least, she didn't think she had. The blindfold at Prospero's had left her with questions about what she'd done and with whom.

"Do you want to?"

Jory stared at Sera's soft mouth for a moment then looked away, her cheeks hot. "I'm not allowed."

Her chuckle was seductive, and the way she narrowed her eyes made Jory swallow hard. "You keep hiding behind that collar, beautiful. We'll see how long that lasts."

With a peck on the cheek and a swirl of her skirt, Seraphina was gone from the room, leaving a hint of alluring scent in her wake.

*

The cheerful green of new leaves gave the coach house a completely different feel than the stark winter landscape had the first time Valentine had brought her there. The house's foundation was adorned with a row of bright yellow tulips that had stubbornly pushed their way out of the thawed earth.

With her mood exuberant, Jory stepped from the comfort of her car, the strains of The Kink Monsters' newest release still thrumming in her head. It was strange how music that used to creep her out now instantly turned her on. Her mind linked the driving beat and disturbing lyrics with Valentine.

She closed the car door, still humming to herself. Something barreled into the back of her, crushing her against the vehicle.

"Stupid girl. Are you ever safe – even here?"

His voice was low and gravelly, the way it got when he was both irritated and wanted her in a bad away.

Fuck, it had been so long. She ground her ass against him, taunting him, hoping he lost control and fucked her on the spot.

"You are never safe," he repeated. "Never. Your work will piss people off because you're good at it. Never let your guard down, woman."

She tipped her head to the side, giving him access to her neck. Sharp teeth closed over the delicate flesh there, and she yelped then melted against the cool metal of the car.

"Thank you for the present, Sir. I love it."

He grunted an answer she didn't understand then manhandled her until she was bent over the hood.

The man had the best ideas.

"I'm sorry I wasn't more careful," she said in false contrition. He was getting so paranoid about her safety lately.

His response was to yank up the back of her dress and slide her panties down.

"Ducks?" He groaned. "Motherfucking ducky underwear?"

"Do you like duckies, Sir?" She hid a grin against the smooth paint.

Something cold slipped up and down against her anus. She gasped but stayed still. Leisurely, he pressed and twisted the thing until her body started to open to it. Wide, wider, it spread her. It burned, and her body protested, but she was too shocked to complain past a few desperate sounds.

Finally her bottom closed over a narrower part, and the relief made her sag against the car. The damn plug felt huge.

"Why?" she whimpered. She meant to ask why today, and why in the damn driveway, but the answer was obvious. He was Valentine. He didn't need a reason for being a dick, other than that he felt like it.

"Because today I'm going to fuck your ass, little Jory."

He always threatened to, but maybe the buttplug meant he was serious this time.

"Is this my punishment for not being careful?"

He pulled her panties back up and patted her on the base of the plug, making it vibrate disturbingly within her. She was glad he didn't check to see how wet being treated like that had made her, but her face burned with humiliation anyway.

"No. I just don't want to waste time I could be buried in your ass, so I thought I'd greet you with my present. Do you like buttplugs?"

"No, Sir. Not if that's what you shoved in there," she said, annoyed it came out more as a whine than the grumble she'd intended. The thing felt as big as a soda can.

"Good." Valentine traced a finger along the leg hole of her panties. "Whimper about it whenever you like. Your whimpers make my dick hard." He took a firm grip of her hair, and dragged her toward the house. "I do like your duckies, by the way, Ms Savage."

"You'd better be nicer to me or you won't see my duckies again today," she warned, her heart thudding loudly in her ears as she wondered what he'd do with that statement.

With a growl, he stripped her coat, dress, and bra off of her, leaving her shivering on his doorstep in just her panties. She crossed her arms over her chest and looked back toward the road, suddenly worried someone might spot her.

"I'll see whatever I want to see, whenever I want to see it."

"Yes, Sir."

A black leather collar appeared from his pocket, and he fastened it around her neck. He reached down and grabbed a chain off the ground.

"And here I was annoyed the last owners left their dog chain behind." He clipped the thing onto her collar. When he let go, the cold links fell against her skin, feeling like brands. Cold didn't usually bother her much, but this whole idea was chilling.

With a stern gesture, he signaled for her to kneel on the doorstep in the position he favored.

"Stay." He walked into the house and the door clicked shut behind him.

She stayed.

For several breathless moments she panicked about who might see her, then realized he'd placed her so that the car and the trees both shielded her nakedness from any possible passersby. The road was low-traffic and rural. For someone to see her, they'd have to be invited to the house, or checking the water meter. Or delivering pizza.

He wouldn't do that to her, would he?

His team had already seen her naked, but there was something even more humiliating about being tied outside like a dog.

As her pulse started to calm, the throb of her ass around the plug matched the throb in her neck where he'd bitten her. Her nipples hardened against the cold. She sank into her position, letting her body relax.

Sir wants me here. Sir will take care of me.

Part of her mind stayed alert in case he tried to sneak up on her again, but most of her thoughts trailed off to focus on him. Had she disappointed him somehow? Could she have been more pleasing? He hadn't greeted her with a kiss. Did that mean something?

By the time the door creaked open again, she was empty of every thought except wanting to make him happy. Wordlessly, he stood in front of her, as though he waited for something. She longed to kiss the toe of his boot and beg for forgiveness.

How did he do this to her? She had a decent amount of self-respect, but it blew away as soon as she saw him, or heard his voice. Had this degree of submission always been inside of her, waiting to be tapped, or was he the only one who could have found it?

"Good girl," he rumbled. "You stayed, and you didn't ask why."

She forced herself not to move, but his words brought her pleasure deeper than any orgasm.

"I think you're in a better place now." He tapped her forehead then cupped her cheek. She leaned into it like the loyal dog she'd just worried about being. Euphoric adoration welled in her chest. God, she was so desperately in love with him. She'd do anything he asked.

Her dominant unclipped the chain from her collar. "Inside."

She crawled in, grit digging into her skin, every movement making the thing he'd put inside her shift in weird ways. Hyperaware that he was walking behind her and getting an eyeful, she tried to move gracefully. When he swatted the plug in her ass she yelped and moved faster.

"Do you like what I've done with the place?"

From her hands and knees she looked up at the transformed living room. The cozy window seat arrangement was the same, but the rest of the room now held a freestanding wooden cross, a padded bench, and several other things that made the place look like Prospero's club. Everything was right out in the open. Weren't things like this supposed to be hidden in downstairs dungeons, rather than in the same room as the sofa and the television? Was this going to be life with Valentine – never even trying to pass as normal? She didn't want to be out about their kink to everyone.

She imagined trying to host a dinner party for her parents, or Amy and Talbot, with their guests politely trying not to let their gazes drift to the shackles dangling from the O-ring in the ceiling.

"So how about that Presidential Address?"

"Fascinating!"

"Could you pass me that a bowl of pretzels next to the lube?"

She bowed her head. "It's...nice."

"Kneel up." When she did as he asked, he lifted her chin and met her gaze. "What are you thinking about? You look unhappy."

Although her first instinct was to lie to spare his feelings, he *was* always telling her to be honest with him.

"We're never going to have a normal life, are we? No Christmas parties or family barbecues, or vanilla friends visiting. If we stay together, we're never going to have children?"

"*If* we stay together?" He sounded confused. "To me our relationship is as permanent as relationships get. These things are easy enough to relocate downstairs, into a locked room, if that's what you want." He shrugged, but his expression was odd. "I just thought you'd like to see the sun when you're with me, and not be hidden away downstairs like something I'm ashamed of."

"You're not ashamed of being with someone so weak? With someone so…" She tried to think of a word that wouldn't make him angry, but couldn't think of anything else. "Easy."

He sighed, then sat on the floor beside her and pulled her into his arms. When her ass met his leg she squeaked at the sensation of the plug shifting and tried to scramble off of him, but he held her there. "You're not weak, and you're not easy. You're mine and you do what I tell you to. Understand?"

"Yes, Sir."

"And as for children, I'll put a baby in your belly when I choose to put one there."

A blush chased its way all over her body. It was such a crude thing for him to say, so why did it make her hot for him? No question about what *she* wanted, or when *she* was ready. Apparently, it was his decision. As though her body would just agree and get pregnant immediately if that was what he wanted. He did remember that her power kept her from getting pregnant, right?

"I control your power when we're together. It will do what I want." He kissed her and she could feel his power touch hers and convince it to submit. It was more than willing.

"I would safeword that!"

"Would you? Somehow I don't think you would." He kissed her again, then again, and all of her objections melted away. The thought of growing a piece of him inside of her was profound. She'd thought of having children, but not of what it would be like to have her genetics fuse with someone else's to create a whole different being. What kind of power would their child have? Would he love the child even if he or she was a Mundane Atypical?

His power stroked hers, stoking her arousal.

"Get out of my head!" She tried to struggle out of his arms, and faster than she could have imagined, he shoved her face down on the floor. He pinned her there and spread her legs with his own, then ground against the buttplug. She hadn't been eager for the day he'd take her ass, but it was less scary than his other train of thought had been.

"You like me in your head." He chuckled against the nape of her neck.

She groaned and tried to press back against him, but he rose and urged her up.

"What are you doing?" She let her steps lag, but his grip on her arm was firm.

"Stand there and take off your panties. Bend at the waist. Give me a show."

"But…" she started to object.

"Now. I'm going to beat you for a while. You probably don't want to piss me off first."

Crap. "Yes, Sir."

She did as she was told, feeling like an idiot, but trying to do it seductively. Other than when her toes got caught on her panties as she took them off, he didn't laugh. Polite of him, considering she knew she'd never make it as a dancer. If anything, he seemed to get off on how awkward and foolish she felt.

After what seemed like an eternity he spoke. "Very nice. Now, belly down on the spanking bench." If he hadn't pointed, she might not have figured out which piece of furniture he meant.

With a sigh she lowered herself onto it. He fastened leather cuffs around her wrists and ankles and attached them to the contraption so that she couldn't get up. Although she tugged at them, they didn't budge.

"Are these really necessary?"

"Yes. I want you to feel as trapped as you make me feel."

She cringed at his words. He was in a mood today and she still had no idea why.

The rattle of his belt buckle and the slip of leather from his belt loops made her insides clench. "Are you angry at me, Sir?"

"No," he grumbled, as though grumbling didn't indicate annoyance. "I'm just in a position I don't want to be in, and I'm at a loss."

"What do you mean?" The belt painted her ass with white-hot fire, once, twice. She squealed and yanked harder at her restraints.

Valentine made a noise that sounded vaguely like a purr and slid a finger up inside of her. When she was gasping, he stopped and backed from her again.

"Please, enough, Sir?"

"I'm not done. Do you want me to stop when I don't feel like I'm done – when you haven't met my needs?"

"No, Sir," she replied honestly. Would it be so awful for her to wish what he needed was a blowjob instead?

He grunted then beat the back of her thighs. She managed to hold her tongue for that, but when he landed multiple blows on the insides of her thighs she screamed. Pain layered over pain, with little time to breathe or process the sensation.

Two weeks of nothing – barely even talking to her, and then this?

Was he angry? Did he hate her? She started to cry, tears blurring her vision then dripping down her cheeks and nose and chin, pooling on the smooth leather under her face. What had she done wrong? What position did he not want to be in?

Maybe he regretted collaring someone so green, and he was tired of holding himself back. Was he going to turn into the kind of dominant who wasn't happy until he drew blood?

The word 'red' played on repeat in her mind until she let go of her desperation to control what was happening. Did she trust him or didn't she? He wouldn't kill her. If this was what he wanted, she'd taken worse at the hands of men who didn't love her. Her work was about taking pain from strangers. Giving this to the man she loved wasn't too much to bear.

When it finally stopped she was sweating and limp. Low whimpers shook her where she lay, each breath accompanied by a pitiful sound she had no control over. Dimly, she felt his hands running over her, making the welts sting worse. He whispered depraved things in her ear, but she didn't understand the words. Exhaustion crept over her and she laid her head in the wet mess her tears had left on the leather. She shivered, but wasn't sure why.

Her dominant kissed the backs of her thighs, crooning to her as though she was a wounded animal. Fingers toyed with the plug in her ass then withdrew it. Desire radiated through his power to hers, and against all reason her beaten body responded to him.

"Did that belting make you horny, princess?"

"No, Sir." She sniffled, but his inquisitive fingers were calling her a liar. The stripes he'd left all over the back of her burned and throbbed. For some morbid reason she wanted to look at herself in a mirror. The welts and bruising were going to be spectacular. "I can feel you in my head, making me want you. It's not fair."

"There is no 'fair.' My ownership of you doesn't end with your body."

He fucked her with the plug until the sweat on her skin warmed again. It was impossible to forget how close he was because she could feel his warm breath on her bottom. What did she look like from his vantage point? Undoubtedly pornographic. She shut her eyes as though she could pretend none of this was happening. When he wiggled the plug out of her, he chuckled.

"This isn't going to be easy for you. Your little hole just clamped up tight again." He *tsked*, implying she was being difficult on purpose. A bottle of lube appeared magically out of some hiding spot, and he smeared some on her. With two fingers, he pried her bottom hole back open.

"I'm getting impatient to be in here. Are you going to give me a hard time?"

"No, Sir." She ground her teeth as he worked on making room for himself. "I'm trying to be good."

"Fuck," he breathed, more to himself than to her. "You really don't want me in here, do you?" He sounded delighted.

"No, Sir."

His interest got louder in her head.

"You have a safeword, if you need to use it," he reminded her. Before Jory had the chance to reply, he withdrew his fingers, wriggling them in ways that made her breath catch and her eyes roll back. Then it was the wide head of his cock pressed against her instead. She sucked in a breath and held it. "Breathe, baby."

Jory's mouth hung open in shock as he broached her. The huge thing burned like a brand as he coaxed her anus to accommodate his girth – wider, wider until her eyes felt like they were going to pop out of her head. He groaned and braced himself with his palm on her mid-back. The tickle of a finger on her spine almost made her squirm, but fear held her still.

"Fuck, you've got such a perfect ass." Mercifully, he pulled out for a moment, but he only added lube before trying again. Slowly, her body was forced to accept his. "Relax."

Jory tried to obey, but it was all she could do to lie still and try not to cry. His grunted breaths and swears were sexy as he entered her, but it burned and ached and made her legs tremble. She stared out the window, hoping this first part was the worst of it. Valentine was well endowed, but he felt ten times bigger than usual. She whimpered, trying her best to hold perfectly still as he filled her inch by agonizing inch.

"Shh, you're being such a good girl." His voice was tense. "I'm almost all the way in."

Almost? There was nowhere left to put any more. Her internal organs had to have migrated out of his way into other parts of her body. She was pretty sure her spleen was in her armpit.

She felt lightheaded, and wondered morosely whether he'd stop if she passed out or threw up. It would probably just turn him on.

It hurt, but she breathed through it, impaled and humiliated. Some women apparently liked this, but she had no idea why. She felt bad for poor Jurgen, who got used like this all the time, although maybe it was different for men. At least he was bigger than she was. Maybe it was better after the first few times. Maybe she wouldn't be as scared.

When Valentine finally stilled, he was so far up inside her she could swear she was choking on him.

"Do you like having my cock buried up your tight little ass?" he growled.

She opened her eyes to slits, ready to slam them shut again if he moved. Feeling stretched and invaded, she waited for things to get worse. Valentine lowered himself down over her until his chest was against her back. The weird sensation covered every inch of her skin with goose bumps. If he didn't move it was bearable, and with his body blanketing hers she had to admit they were as close as two people could get. She felt thoroughly claimed.

"All of you is mine now," he murmured in her ear. "Every inch of you. Finally."

She shivered then moaned when he started to kiss the back of her neck under her hair.

"Do you like being mine, snowangel?"

"You're mean," she complained quietly. "And your dick is too big."

He chuckled, which made his cock twitch and jump in unpleasant ways.

"Don't laugh! You're moving. Just stay still!"

"But I don't want to stay still," he rumbled. He pressed his hips tighter against her ass, adding pressure that made him feel inches bigger. The relief when he pulled back again was enormous. Slowly, he started to rock his hips, barely moving within her. The knot of arousal in her lower belly pulled taut again, and she dug her fingers into the bench's leather.

No, she didn't want to like this. She bit her lip and frowned, trying to focus on the discomfort, but that part of it was easing.

"See, it's not so bad, is it?"

She wanted to tell him that it was awful and that he was a jerk for making her try it, but the clamor in her body and her head were too loud to put words together. The way it felt to him mixed with the overwhelming way it felt to her. She felt owned, degraded, excited, ashamed.

Her whole body began to throb, her pussy dreadfully empty, her clit ignored and aching. God, she couldn't come like this. If she came, she'd have no excuse to beg him never to do it again. Her self-esteem couldn't handle this kind of use – not regularly, not if he forced her to like it.

Damn him, he was patient, pausing to tease her and force her need for release higher. He changed rhythm and sensation to bring her to the edge and keep her there for ages. She found herself pushing back against him in frustration, needing to feel him deep inside her even though she'd never admit it.

"You don't want to like this, but you can't hide from me." He thrust into her harder, making her cry out. "You're forcing your body not to react, but I can feel how hard you're trying not to come."

Jory bit down on her arm, desperate for a distraction. He stilled inside her, and when she thought he'd finally lose control, he thrust back in with a lazy roll of his hips.

"Can you feel it from my side – how tight you are? How hot?" His tense words made those feelings in her head impossible to ignore. It was like getting a stereo feed of sexual arousal that she couldn't shut out. "Can you feel how your ass is quivering around my cock, making me crazy?"

She could feel all of it, and it came with an awareness that he was at the limit of his control, struggling not to come as his dick throbbed deep inside her.

They balanced on the very edge of orgasm, both of them too stubborn to give in. Jory's breath came in short gasps as she tried to stay in control and ignore his clever torture of her clit. He bit her shoulder and she shuddered under him, the last vestiges of control slipping through her fingers.

"Please no," she squealed. "Please, Sir. I don't want to."

"Yes," he hissed in her ear. "That's my good girl. You need to come for me."

"No...no."

"Come on, sweetheart. I want to feel your tight little ass clamp down on my cock." He wrapped an arm around her hips and drove himself deeper. "Now."

Helpless to refuse, her body obeyed. She struggled in her bonds, trying to scramble away from the assault of sensation as the orgasm screwed every muscle tight. The initial spasm held fast, as though time had frozen her mid-orgasm. Pleasure rushed through her, tempered by the burn of his thick cock thrusting into her tender backside. She screamed and wept, unable to bear the intensity, but her tears just seemed to excite him.

Another, bigger orgasm built as he fucked her with longer strokes. It ached, but every nerve in her body was alert and begging to be eased. The tension in her belly and the emptiness of her pussy as he thrust into her made her feel used and dirty, fucking with her head while he played with her clit. His cock felt like an iron bar in her ass, the punishment for letting him defile her that way.

"What's the matter, baby, does it hurt?"

"I don't like it!"

"If you don't like it, why do you keep coming?"

It was true. Her body was out of control, rippling and contracting around him, ignoring her twinges and exhaustion, coming even though she just wanted to stop. Their powers wound around each other, mingling and triggering more orgasmic sensations in her mind.

"Fuck!" He thrust into her savagely one last time and froze, then growled several more foul words as she felt his cock spasming inside her. He came long and hard before collapsing on top of her, crushing her against the bench.

Jory lay dazed under his body, drifting on the sleepy aftermath of her adrenaline high. Between the beating and the ass fucking she was more sore than she'd ever been in her life. At least, more intimately sore. The warmth of him on top of her was the only thing that kept her from flying apart.

To her dismay, his dick stayed hard even though he was panting for breath. He withdrew slowly, and for a moment she was worried he would thrust back into her again. There was no way she could manage the pain if he wanted to take her again.

Self-conscious, she wanted to swipe at the wetness that seemed to cover her entire face, but she was still cuffed in place. She needed a shower that scoured off a layer of skin. He was courteous enough not to pull out abruptly, but the sensation of him withdrawing from her body and mind made her shudder.

Come dribbled down the back of her leg and also down the inside of her thigh, bringing her back to reality.

Oh god – she felt so filthy.

Used.

She waited for him to release her, but it was taking forever. He must be standing over her, gloating. She'd let him defile her so thoroughly.

Why did she let him do such horrible things to her? She was supposed to be a hero, for the love of god. Her descent into this level of degradation may have been gradual, but she'd slid so far into the gutter.

The dog chain kept flashing through her mind. The cold of it against her skin. The sound of it clinking against itself in the still spring air.

She'd allowed herself to be chained outside like a fucking dog. Hadn't even tried to stop him. Why hadn't she stopped him?

Then he'd hurt her and humiliated her, filled her ass with come. She'd allowed it.

Who let people do this to them? Who got off on it?

She was never going to have a normal life. A husband. Children. She probably shouldn't – shouldn't even see her family or Amy. They were so pure and good. She was so fucked up. Her entire life was about fighting and fucking. Following orders. Not thinking for herself. All that was left of her was a collection of base animal instincts.

She buried her face against her upper arm, wishing she would die of shame and get it over with.

Tears started again, and Valentine unbuckled her and gathered her to him. He carried her to the couch and lay down, pulling her on top of him. Jory tried to rise, but he held her there.

"I need – I need to go shower." She wiped her nose with the back of her hand, hating the way her voice wobbled, but there was no helping it. "I need to go shower now." All she wanted was somewhere quiet where she could curl up and sob. Alone.

"We'll shower when I say it's time to. Right now I need you here," he replied calmly, wrapping his arms more firmly around her. "You don't need to go running around right now. You need to be held. You need to be with me."

A storm of emotion was coming, and he was being unreasonable. She struggled. "Let me go! You got what you wanted, now leave me alone!"

He held her in place as though she were a tantruming child. "Hey, hey.

Shh. You need to be with me right now," he repeated firmly.

Without another lucid thought, Jory fought him, scratching, punching, kicking, hating him for the casual way he caught her wrists and pinned her legs with his own. She fought and screamed and called him names, but he just made soothing noises and waited calmly for her to finish. When she'd exhausted herself the sobbing started in earnest. It didn't stop for a long while.

She felt hollow and exhausted. Even if he never told anyone else – even if he didn't laugh about this behind her back with the rest of his team – the two of them would always know. There was no going back from today. No way to regain her self-respect.

Valentine had proven she was his little submissive whore, and she'd submit to anything to please him. Even if it destroyed her.

Chapter Sixteen

Hell.

She was a mess. There was a wild look in her pale eyes, as though she'd gladly chew off her arm to get away from him. He'd never seen sub drop so bad.

The scratches she'd left on him still stung, especially the ones on his face. She'd caught him off guard, but his pride was nothing compared to whatever was going on with her. He didn't know what to do. Even after a nap and a bath she was still completely freaked out.

He'd lured her into his lap again, and turned on a movie while he tried to feed her ice cream she didn't want. Neither the blanket nor his body heat was doing the trick. He'd told her he loved her and she'd responded in kind, but her responses seemed to be on autopilot.

Guilt ate at him. She wouldn't talk about it, so he didn't know when it was that he'd gone too far. Or was it just something that had clicked wrong in her head? It was easier to blame himself. Overstepping and breaking trust were easier to fix than making her unbalanced.

If he could call Xana or Dane, maybe one of them would know what to do.

By the twelve-hour mark he was considering the idea of bringing her to the crisis center at the hospital, but he didn't know if they'd understand what happened any better than he did, especially if they were vanilla.

She slept a few hours, but he was too uptight to sleep. He lay in bed and held her, but even then she had pulled away a little, as though he disgusted her but she was too polite to say so.

When she woke, he cooked bacon and eggs, keeping an eye on her as she sat at the table staring out the window at the small creatures stirring in the backyard.

"This isn't your fault." Her voice, small and tired, echoed eerily in the kitchen. For a moment he wondered if he imagined the words. When he turned, her gaze was on him – not on his eyes, but on his chest. It was a start.

He went back to cooking, not wanting to spook her. Maybe talking to him would be easier for her if he wasn't staring.

"No? I'm having a hard time believing that."

She sighed, and when he glanced back at her, she had laid her head on the kitchen table. "I let things go too far."

He let that statement hang there, unchallenged. Did she mean what he'd done the day before, or their entire relationship? He was afraid to ask.

There were times when even dominants didn't know what to say.

They ate in silence. From an objective standpoint, Valentine knew the food tasted good, but it was like ash in his mouth.

After she'd taken a few bites, she lapsed into stillness again.

"I'm going home," she said simply, getting to her feet.

"Let me drive you?" The desperate feeling in his gut told him not to let her go, but she seemed determined. Holding her captive wouldn't fix this, although letting her leave made him itch with every fiber of his being. He had the feeling if she left, she'd never come back.

"No."

There was a short hunt for her keys.

"Call me when you get home?"

She didn't reply.

Without a word, she found her shoes, put them on, and stepped out into the overcast morning. She paused, and he saw her take a step back from the dog chain coiled beside the door. Out of context it had no power, but she seemed frightened of it.

Was it about that? Using it had been a whim of the moment. That whim may have ruined the best thing that had ever happened to him.

Lost, he followed her out. He held the car door open for her, but she didn't acknowledge the gesture or him. She got in and closed the door, started the car, and drove away without looking back.

He watched her go. Clods of mud flew up from her tires as she left the driveway.

For a long while he stared at the road, willing her to come back. He reached out with his power, trying to feel some trace of her, but she was already too far away.

It started to rain.

Wet and cold, he paced the driveway, not sure if he could face going back in. If he'd had a lighter in his pocket he would have burned the place to the ground.

He ripped every cheerful yellow tulip from the flowerbed before he went back inside.

*

Her team looked badass. In black and red fighting leathers, the four of them slipped through the darkening forest, part of a larger force whose aim was to reclaim the briefcase his own team had been hired to protect.

He could see that Xana, Jurgen, and Dane had noticed Jory and were hyper aware of her every move, even though she didn't know they were there yet.

"She's looking good. Strong," Dane murmured, clapping him on the shoulder.

There was no question about that. Jory ran through the forest, as nimble as if she was born to it, her luminous white hair streaming out behind her like a goddess's.

Valentine, on the other hand, knew he looked like hell. Unshaven, tired, pale, with dark circles under his eyes, he resembled a man recently released from solitary confinement. It had taken weeks for them to convince him to come out and work. He still didn't feel like working, and this was their second job in two days.

The rest of the force they were working with had relaxed, considering the fact that the briefcase had been picked up a half-hour before. The only reason they stood guard was as a diversion. The longer the heroes thought the mercenary groups were protecting something, the more time the transport had to get away.

They fell silent as Brontë and her brother Brock moved near. Their group surveyed the oncoming heroes as well. It was a relatively large force, and the mercenaries were outnumbered. Whatever had been in the briefcase had been important. Valentine hoped it wasn't something that would create more evil in the world.

Or he would have hoped that at one time, and now just did out of habit.

Jory had made him think about good and evil. It was a hard habit to break.

"Isn't that your submissive?" Brontë asked, her gaze fastened on Jory.

"Not anymore. That's done." It was the first time he'd said it aloud. Saying the words hurt like hell. It felt more final, somehow.

She hadn't answered any of his calls or texts since she'd left their place almost four weeks before. The one time Valentine had gone to her new house, Seraphina had claimed she wasn't home, even though he'd caught a glimpse of her peeking out of an upstairs window. Just because they hadn't spoken didn't mean anything. The ending of a relationship didn't always have to be a conversation.

"Oh. I'm sorry to hear that." Her mouth turned down in sympathy. "The two of you seemed happy together."

He gritted his teeth, wishing she'd skipped the platitude, but Brontë was always carefully polite.

Even though he kept trying to put Jory out of his head, it wasn't working. It was just his luck she'd end up on the opposing force when his emotional wounds were still open and raw.

Brontë and her team fell back to guard a different section of fence, doing a good job of looking like there were still things in their possession that needed defending. On the other side, Jory flowed toward them, looking more like an approaching storm than a woman. How could he ever have worried she was too fragile for this?

As the heroes reached the open area before the fence, a volley of attacks drove them back. Bolts of electricity, streaks of fire, and high-winded storms slammed into them. A gust knocked Jory flat, and even though Valentine tried not to care, his first instinct was to climb the fence and defend her. Screw the job. That was his woman out there – even if she didn't want to be his anymore. Maybe she could turn off her feelings, but he wasn't wired that way.

Xana gripped his shoulder to hold him back, shaking her head. "You can't. She's a hero – this is what she does. She's given you a pretty clear message that she wants you out of her life. Interfering isn't going to get you any brownie points."

As he watched, Jory scrambled to her feet. She took a step forward then froze in place. Valentine wondered what she'd spotted then realized she was fighting to move forward, but her body wasn't obeying her. Frustrated and angry, she cast around until her eyes lit on him. The glare she sent his way would have melted stone.

Confused, he looked around for the source of her entrapment. From along the fence Brock caught his eye and inclined his head. *Shit.* The man thought he was doing Valentine a favor by protecting her, but he was just making things worse. Jory looked like she thought Valentine had put him up to it. He looked back at her, and saw a bolt of sizzling light bounce off of her. Apparently Brock was shielding her too.

Another wave came, and with it more volleys. He tried to tell Brock to stop protecting her, but by the time he could hear him over the din, the fight was finished.

When she was freed, Jory looked Valentine in the eye, and spat on the ground at her feet before walking back into the forest.

*

"She stopped using the car."

Dane and Jurgen were in the midst of weighing a contract, trying to decide whether the amount that was being offered was worth their time, but work was about as interesting to Valentine as eating was lately.

Xana rolled her eyes, and went back to trying to price out what the expenses would be, considering there would be out-of-town travel and they needed somewhere to stay that was more private than a hotel.

"It was easier when the older team figured this part out. Maybe a few jobs they threw our way were sketchy, but at least I didn't have to play accountant. Can't we hire your brother to do this?"

When he didn't answer Xana's question, she looked up and glared at him. "Have you been going over there, or did you hire someone to do it for you?"

Everyone stopped to frown at him. He didn't give a shit. "She said she liked the car. Was she lying? Or is she just too good to use something I gave her now?"

"And we're firmly back in weirdo stalker territory." Xana sighed heavily.

"I think you need medication," Dane said, sounding sincere rather than judgmental.

"Or counseling. Or both," Jurgen agreed. "If you don't stop, you're going to end up in jail."

"Counseling? Jail?" Valentine rubbed his forehead. "She was mine and it wasn't my choice to end things. You'll forgive me if I'm having trouble moving on. I still feel responsible for her."

Dane sighed. "She doesn't need a babysitter. I know it's hard, but you're an adult, she's an adult. You need to move on."

The desperation clawed at him again. It was the same one that made it impossible for him to sleep. Maybe he *was* losing it, but he didn't belong to the kind of family where he could just go to the doctor and ask for some pills. Showing weakness wasn't an option.

The others had been trying to convince him to go to the club, to play with someone else and try to forget about her. They'd even tried convincing him to play with Jurgen. Valentine was afraid if he did beat someone he wouldn't be able to stop.

"I understand that," Xana said reasonably. "Even though you've had other submissives, I think this is the first time you ever really fell in love. This is your first serious break-up, really. Most people go through this in high school. The first time it happens, it feels like the world is ending."

Even though he understood what she meant, Valentine couldn't help but feel that she was implying he was immature and spoiled. Considering his background, he'd worked hard to avoid being that guy, so the observation felt like an accusation, and it stung. Coming from Xana, though, it meant little. She was the one who'd told him that she was happier single. She'd never been really in love with anyone, so it was easy for her to dismiss how he felt.

"You'd be more understanding if it was Dane having a hard time getting over Jurgen. Maybe Jory and I haven't been together as long, but we've gone through things together that nobody else can understand. There's a bond between us that's stretched thin but still isn't broken. Feeling it is bad enough. I have to keep checking on her to make sure she's okay, but every time I do it makes it worse for me."

"So you think this is some sort of 'one true mate' bullshit, like werewolves? You do know werewolves don't exist, right?" Xana said derisively.

Valentine ignored her sarcasm. "No one knows what Atypical Aphrodisia really is. There's a chance that's it, exactly."

"Or it might just give you extra incentive to fuck a hot girl," Xana shot back, nonplussed.

Jurgen brow furrowed with concern. "I know your first instinct is to blow everything off Xana," he said. "But what he's dealing with almost seems like an addiction. I think we need to cut him some slack."

She glared at him. "We all care about what's happening to him, but we can't enable him. The fact also remains that while he's going through his girl problems, we're starting to get a name for being an unreliable team. If we want to keep making the kind of money we're accustomed to, we can't let that happen."

They all knew it, but the difference was that Valentine didn't care anymore. They'd probably be better off ditching him.

Dane squeezed his shoulder. "Let us finish going through this. You know we won't sign up for anything that you would disagree with. Go have a nap or something." He urged Valentine up, and out of the room. It was probably best for him to leave now, before he tried to strangle Xana. It might make him feel better in the moment, but there was a chance he'd regret it.

He climbed the stairs to his room, exhausted even though he hadn't done anything today other than stare at the television. What had he watched? The day before he'd apparently watched the Home Shopping Network for three hours before Jurgen finally turned the channel out of pity.

His apartment door closed behind him and he leaned against it, staring into the gloom. He was glad the others had stopped opening the curtains for him. Automatically, he stripped out of his clothes, and headed to the drawer in his bedside table. He'd tried to stop himself the first few times, but now that he'd crossed that line again, he couldn't seem to stop.

The little pocketknife was still there, where he'd left it, but a folded piece of paper was tucked into the place where the blade went into the handle. Angered at the invasion of his privacy, he unfolded the note, determined to kick the ass of whoever had left it. In Jurgen's tidy handwriting were the words: WE LOVE YOU. PLEASE STOP.

Desperation choked him. He crumpled the note, and threw it across the room. Then, in a fit of embarrassed rage, he sent the pocketknife after it. He rubbed a hand over the scabbed cuts on his thighs and chest, wondering how the little bastard had known. It had been years since he'd done it last, and from what he knew, Jurgen had never told the others he did it.

He needed something to take the edge off. He didn't trust himself to beat someone. For a week he'd drank too much, but had stopped before it became a problem. The only thing he had left was this.

When they were teenagers, Jurgen had given him a journal and told him that writing out his feelings would be healthier than cutting himself. At the time he'd thought it was a ridiculous idea. Now he'd try anything if he thought it would help, but he didn't think there were words that could explain the rage and self-loathing he had to live with.

He found pen and paper, and sat down at the kitchen table. He stared at the fresh page, but the words in his mind were stupid and pale.

The knife was back in his hand before he'd made a mark on the paper.

Chapter Seventeen

Jory stowed her gear in the back of the SUV, politely trying to ignore the way Vance and Arigh kept cornering Seraphina and groping her. The girl had stopped protesting that they were going to be late, and was now complaining that she needed to come before they headed out.

At that moment, just inside the doorway of their house, Seraphina was pinned to the wall, with Vance grinding against her ass as Arigh gripped her hair and growled nasty threats in her ear. Jory tried not to listen, and tried even harder not to let it turn her on, but the way they toyed with Sera reminded her too much of Valentine.

Stubbornly, she pushed thoughts of him away, even though her hand went to her neck to feel for the collar she no longer wore. It had gotten familiar to her. That was all.

"Jory! A little help here?" Seraphina was laughing as the men dragged her into the living room. "If you don't keep one of them busy I'll be limping into the fight. Don't we have a no DP before combat rule?"

"I don't know. Do we?" Arigh's deep chuckle was enough to make a girl's neck hair stand on end.

Vance bit her shoulder. "I think we put that to a vote and our little girl here got outvoted."

"How is that even fair?" she grumbled. "I'll always get outvoted. Come on, Jory. Fuck one of them for me. It might save my life."

Chuckling, Jory shut the hatch of the SUV, then walked the three steps back into the house and shut the door behind her. They wouldn't be leaving now until this was over.

"No DP. Last time she was so sore it slowed her down," Jory lectured, managing to get past the living room without peeking. The three of them were so hot together, and so open, that it was hard not to perv on them sometimes. It didn't help that they could be found unexpectedly fucking almost anywhere at any given time, and liked when she watched.

"You should come sit on my lap, Jory. We can watch these two fuck and talk about what you like," Arigh said slyly. "I promise I won't even touch you."

"If I sat on your lap you wouldn't touch me? Who taught you how to treat a woman?" Jory sniffed as she marched herself up the stairs. All three of them were persistent flirts. It was fun and funny, but they were polite and had never laid a hand on her.

Arigh poked his head around the corner, his dark eyes narrowed. "Give me the word, baby."

"The word is 'go fuck your sub and quit looking at my ass.'"

"How could I not check out that ass? I'm only human."

"Jory Savage, your ass is fiiine!" Sera yelled from the living room. Her words ended in a choking noise that made Jory curious to see what they were doing to her, but she resisted the temptation to go back down to see.

Her room smelled like cookies and flowers. They'd stayed up late last night baking more cookies than was technically responsible, the four of them laughing and joking and eating too much raw dough. It was the perfect ending to a day spent watching a Monty Python marathon. Sometimes it was hard to believe that her life hadn't always revolved around these silly, sweet sex maniacs.

It wasn't long until Sera's muffled cries of pleasure had Jory shifting where she sat, wishing she could join them and find some pleasure in life instead of having to hide. Until she had the nerve to call Valentine and end things officially, though, she couldn't even distract herself from memories of him by having sex with other people. He would have moved on by now, she was sure, but that didn't absolve her of responsibility. She was the one who'd cut contact with no explanation.

She lay back on her bed, staring at the crimson roses on her desk. Sadly, they weren't from Valentine, even though it was better they weren't. Xana had brought them by, saying they were from Prospero, the BDSM club owner, but the way Xana looked her over said that they could just as easily have been from her. Jory managed not to ask after Valentine, even though his name had silently hung between them.

So many people seemed to want her lately, but why was a mystery. She just wanted to be a hero. Or she had. Maybe some people could manage D/s relationships and still function, but for her the submission had run too deep. Seraphina submitted to Vance and Arigh because she enjoyed it in the bedroom, or whatever room they were using. For Jory it was different.

Kneeling at Valentine's feet hadn't just been about fun. It had become everything to her.

She closed her eyes and her thoughts drifted to crawling to him, begging for him. But it wasn't even about the sex. Even pressing her face against his leg, with his hand possessively in her hair, had brought joyful tears to her eyes. Being owned by him had been all-consuming and blissful, but when she took a step back and thought about it, she realized that part of her had started to overshadow the rest of her life. She wasn't submissive by half-measure. She had started to resent every moment that her former life's dream had kept her from her place at his feet. It wasn't healthy. Every time they were together provided her with yet another example of how much she was willing to debase herself to be owned by him.

He didn't even have to ask. She'd wanted to give him everything.

She tried to fool herself into thinking she could sleep with her teammates, but the truth was, she didn't want anyone else. Even if they could figure out how to keep her powers at bay, or get her off, the deep emotional connection she'd had with Valentine wasn't something she could replicate with just anyone. Possibly with no one else, ever again.

Cape or collar. She couldn't have both. Not with the way they were together. Her self-respect wouldn't let her give up her own dreams, no matter how deep her connection to him was. No matter how hollow she felt without him. Even though she never stopped thinking about him and it sometimes felt like she couldn't breathe.

Some people could handle the depth of their submission and still stay focused on their other goals. With him she'd been horribly tempted to give up every goal she'd had for herself, every thought, even though he'd never asked it of her.

She was too obsessed. Too weak when it came to Valentine. It wasn't right.

The plan was to stay away from him, at least until the strongest of her feelings faded.

Seeing him unexpectedly at the contract a few weeks ago had been like a slap. Trapped by one of his friends' powers, she'd stared at him, trying to hate him but wanting him even more fiercely. The power had held her still, shielded, out of the way, as safe and useless as if she'd stayed home.

Was that what he'd actually wanted from her? That she throw away all of her powers and skills? To content herself with being no more than his little sex toy? He'd always said he wouldn't stand in the way of her career, but at that battle he hadn't told his friends to let her go. They hadn't done it to anyone else, only her. Afterward, her team and their allies in the battle had asked her why, and she'd been too ashamed to tell them the truth. She'd shrugged and told them she didn't know.

And she was so much stronger now. She could feel power pulsing through her every minute of the day, as though all the time her power had been subjugated to his had stifled it. Now it was almost too big to contain.

Yes, ending things had been the right decision.

She'd been freaked out in the moment, about all of it – the dog chain, the talk about babies, feeling as though the only thing that really mattered was being what he wanted. None of them had been truly awful, in retrospect. She'd been running on too little sleep, had been away from him too long and was too keyed up to see him. Maybe he'd been too excited to see her too, and more callous than he'd meant to be.

She'd calmed down since then, but it had been for the best. Sometimes a girl couldn't have everything she wanted in life. Their relationship had been too overwhelming and peculiar to fit into the future she wanted. If she never felt that kind of obsessive adoration or lust again with anyone else, she'd willingly pay that price to be a hero. Her mind had to be on her work, not on a man. She'd chosen her path and she refused to regret it.

He had to be better off without her too.

She focused on the way his friends had interfered with her work, clinging to the insult and humiliation to stop herself from answering Valentine's texts. She reveled in the feeling of her newly expanded power, fortifying herself with it. Hopefully when she saw him again, she wouldn't be so weak.

When Seraphina had screamed her way through a second orgasm, Jory checked her phone. They were only a half hour late leaving, which wasn't bad since they weren't needed until later in the evening.

Jory thumped down the stairs, yawning, wishing she'd taken a nap. It seemed like she never slept lately.

Arigh came out of the living room zipping up his jeans. Vance followed, pulling on his t-shirt. Both of them looked well satisfied and pleased with themselves.

"Did you jerks leave her in one piece?"

"We only spit roasted her." Vance's smile was slow and sexy. "We're not unreasonable."

Jory chuckled and cast a glance into the living room. Sera lay on the couch, looking dazed, her clothing having been pulled back into place, although it didn't look like she'd done that part herself.

Jory clapped her hands loudly. "Sera! Come on, time to go. You can sleep on the way."

The girl groaned and swung her feet gingerly to the floor. "I'll meet you out there. I have a sudden urge to brush my teeth."

"Okay, but no shower or we won't get there on time."

"Ugh. They're going to change my hero name to Spooge Collector."

"Spooge Collector…Divine…it's all semantics, really." Jory smirked. She clapped her hands sharply. "Go now or you're going to have to settle for a stick of gum."

"Yes, mistress." Seraphina headed up the stairs, but not before she'd tossed her hair at Jory and had given her a wink.

*

Even with all of the physical training they did, Jory's legs were cramping up. They'd crouched in the same place for so long, she was seriously thinking about just sitting down.

Where the hell was the other team?

A chill wind blew through the alley, feeling unseasonably cold for summer. It didn't bother her much, but she worried that if her teammates stiffened, it might slow them down if they needed to fight.

Without exchanging a word, she knew they were all thinking the same thing. Were they in the wrong place? At least two hours had passed.

Jory's team was supposed guard the other team while they retrieved the target. They hadn't seen a soul.

This was where their assignment had told them to be, and Jory kept going back and forth between thinking the mission had been canceled, or that the action had started somewhere else. Either way, there wasn't much they could do except wait. No one had ever told them if there was a standard amount of time they should hang around before leaving the site they'd been sent to, so they were going to have to wing it.

Eventually, Arigh got to his feet and stretched. "I don't know what's happening, but there's no point sitting here for another hour. We might as well go make contact and find out what the hell is going on."

"You don't think a couple of us should stay here, to keep an eye on things?" Jory kept thinking something was going to happen, and abandoning their post felt wrong. She was the cautious one of the group, though, so there was a chance she was being irrational.

Vance shrugged. "I guess a couple of us could stay here to keep an eye out. Make sure you're careful coming and going. You go, Rime. Take Divine with you." He came out of his crouch and sat, leaning against the wall.

She rose and stretched, staying in the shadows. The muscles in her thighs and calves screeched in silent protest. Even her back ached. Divine tapped her arm and led her down the narrow alley. Trash and suspicious puddles made it difficult to move quietly, but they did their best. There was no saying when or where the opposing force might appear. Dropping their guard at any point during a mission was tantamount to suicide.

Even though the guys were more than competent, leaving them behind gave Jory the willies. Working with people in close quarters for long periods of time meant they became either friends or enemies quickly. Living with them, too, meant that after only a few months, they'd become some of the best friends Jory had ever had. Only Amy was closer. Knowing them so well made it possible to guess what they were thinking a lot of the time, which meant that missions went smoother because they could anticipate each other's reactions. The downside to that was that in a fight, even though she knew they were all very capable, she worried like Valentine said he did about his own team.

They got back to the van without seeing so much as a stray cat. Having no form of electronic communication on them during missions was inconvenient, but at least it kept them from getting discovered or having their every move tracked that way. It did mean, though, that on odd occasions, they needed to make their way back to transport to check in.

Jory had just put in the call, sitting in the dark of the van, when another van pulled up under the streetlight half a block away.

"That must be the other team," Sera said, pointing. "Wonder what the hell took them so long."

The Bureau receptionist had Jory on hold, and was checking to see who management on call was.

"I'm going to go talk to them," Sera said as they watched four figures in spandex exit the vehicle. "I'll tell them where the guys are and be right back."

"Just wait, Divine," Jory said anxiously. "Just wait and I'll go with you."

"It'll just take a second. Look, two of them went into the alley, but the other two are standing around looking confused. They must know they're late. I bet they got the wrong directions – or we did and they're just coming to find us. I'll be right over there. I'm sick of sitting in that stinking laneway. If we get this sorted out, we can go back to the safe house. We can spend the rest of the night watching a movie and sleeping. I'm so fucking tired."

Jory thought about hanging up to go with her, but the receptionist picked up at the other end of the line.

"Where are you now?" the woman asked.

Seraphina leaned over and kissed Jory's cheek before she opened the door and got out. She closed it quietly behind her and Jory watched as she walked toward the other van.

"We're in Ridgemont," Jory told the receptionist. "By the building we were told to stake out. Twenty-four Melvin Lane? I know it's only been two hours, but from what we understood things were supposed to go down fast. The other team just showed up now. We're just wondering if we were given misinformation. There's no point in us sitting here if we're in the wrong place, you know?" She gave a friendly laugh trying to make sure she didn't sound like she was accusing their superiors of being incompetent, but she was unhappy about Sera leaving alone.

Jory could see now that it was her ex-team, led by Summer. Ugh, dumb bitch. At least Sera hadn't gone alone to talk to strangers.

The secretary put her through to Department Head Fontaine, who asked her the same questions again. She held his proverbial hand and walked him through things again, slumping back into her seat. The man was in no hurry.

"Is there a sunshine team there?" Fontaine sounded lost. "The roster I've got in front of me says it should be Samuels and her team there."

"Yes, it's Summer's team."

"Did they say who assigned them?"

"No, Sir. They may have told Divine, but they arrived just as I was placing this call. I'll have to ask them and get back to you."

"No, no. Just wait. Sorry. I'm not sure which is worse, the fact that they expect us to learn this new planning program overnight, or the fact that the mail system is glitching. This isn't even my portfolio, but Sanderson's gone for the night. It's bad form to wake someone up when they're not on call." He laughed a fake managerial laugh that set Jory's teeth on edge.

When she'd dreamed of being a hero, thoughts of red tape and bureaucratic bullshit had never been part of it. She gave a fake chuckle, knowing she was more likely to get timely cooperation from the man if she played the game. So much fakeness in the Bureau. It didn't seem right. Weren't people theoretically devoted to doing good works supposed to be good people? Did mercenaries have to put up with this insincere bullshit?

She waited, then waited longer. Seraphina and the rest of the other team talked for a few minutes then wandered up Melvin Lane, leaving Jory alone, watching an occasional piece of garbage or old leaf scoot across the road. For a full five minutes she wondered if Fontaine had fallen asleep.

"Here!" he exclaimed triumphantly. "Found it! It says here you were supposed to be at that location... I'm guessing we were given bad intel, or the other party changed their plans. They might have chosen a different drop point and a different time." He sighed. "Oh well. You win some, you lose some."

Such a waste of time. In the darkness, Jory rolled her eyes. "Should I tell the others the mission is called off for now, then?"

"Yeah, go ahead. I don't think it was that critical anyway," his voice trailed off, and Jory could hear more clicking. At least their training sergeants hadn't seemed this incompetent. The people at the Bureau offices seemed out of touch with what was happening on the streets. They were probably just doing time until they were eligible to retire. If there was ever a real emergency, she'd have to remember to handle it on her own and just tell them about it later instead of asking for authorization. She'd ask for forgiveness if she stepped on toes. Who had this kind of time when serious decisions needed to be made?

They hung up, exchanging pleasantries that made her impatient. After a brief scan of the street, she left the van, and headed toward the shadows of Melvin Lane.

Where was everyone? It was so quiet.

A piercing whistle tore at her ears. Light stole her vision. Concussed. The ground fell away. Was she flying?

Wall, pavement, sky flashed past. She tried to relax her muscles for impact. Her body was a bullet.

The ground rose to meet her. She hit. Rolled over and over. Skidded.

Stopped. Wetness was in her eyes. Her head ached. She lay stunned, heart hammering in her ears. The pavement scalded her cheek. So hot. Acrid smoke filled her nostrils. Sounds came to her as though the traveled through wads of cotton.

Wiping her streaming eyes, she struggled to her feet.

Fire. The buildings were burning.

Seraphina, Arigh, Vance – she had to find them. Her leg gave out under her. It bent all wrong. Bile rose and she gagged.

On quivering arms, she dragged herself toward the lane. Smoke undulated from its mouth, clogging her nose and making her eyes leak. A steady trickle of blood kept blinding her. She struggled to the corner building, pulling herself up on the wall before collapsing again. Her leg screamed at her. Shortness of breath suggested broken ribs. But her team – her friends were in there.

Oh god – there was so much smoke. Orange light licked toward her. Overwhelming heat. What was burning? The asphalt? Was that possible?

Through the waves of flame she could see a metal dumpster liquefying, dripping to the ground. Here and there large burning clumps littered the ground. There was the smell of roasted pork and burnt hair.

No one called out. Nothing moved except sinuous blue and orange flame.

"Fuck." The man's voice came from behind her.

She dodged to the side, scrambling for the dagger in her sheath, but it was gone. Lost. Pain. This was no time to faint.

Ten or more mercenaries stood in the street their team van was parked on. They hadn't been there moments before. A woman stepped toward her, hands outstretched, ready to hit her with power. She looked down at Jory's leg, and Jory's gaze followed. Her own dagger stuck out of the back of her thigh like she'd sheathed it there.

"My team," she told them, pointing. Maybe they'd help. Atypicals didn't kill other Atypicals except by accident. There was a code.

"Finish her," an older man growled at the woman. "The Bureau has to learn once and for all. They have to stop sending children to dick around in our business."

The woman nodded and braced.

But it went against all of the laws Atypicals abided by. These were mercenaries, not villains. Murder went against the code.

Jory closed her eyes and felt surreptitiously for the small knife that was part of her belt buckle. Maybe she could take one of these bastards out with her.

"No," an older man said.

Her eyes flew open. The speaker had moved between her and the woman, shielding Jory with his body.

"Not this one."

There was a flash.

Jory's head exploded into a million pieces.

Chapter Eighteen

As Valentine's eyes adjusted to the gloom, he tried to calm himself and stop the ringing in his ears. When he dreamed of Jory, this was always how he woke – a nasty, sweaty mess. It was as if his brain couldn't handle dreams of her and took it out on his body, waking him so that he could get the full effect of his own suffering.

He dug around in his mind, trying to remember what the dream had been about so that he could weed it out and toss it away. He had a vague recollection of running from hippos, or riding them. There may have been zombies. Like every other time, the theme had been Jory in danger.

Jory was a self-rescuing girl who wanted him to leave her alone, but his dreams didn't care about that.

A thumbnail of a moon hung alone in the sky, illuminating the clouds that wreathed it. He crawled out of bed and went to the window, hanging onto the casing and leaning his forehead against the pane. If the weather was good, he'd go up on the roof later and work on replacing the shingles, but for now there was only pacing and sitting and waiting for the sun to rise.

The flight to and from the out-of-town contract they'd taken three days previous had left him with a crick in his neck that kept giving him headaches. There were painkillers in the house, but he was afraid to let himself open the cabinet. Avoiding temptation was best. It would never be his preferred way of ending things, though, being far too clean and subtle. If he ever did it, he'd make sure to leave a mess for someone to clean up.

His life was messy. His death should be too.

Now that the initial crisis had passed, he could admit to himself that he could live without her. His self-destructive urges had shifted to a penchant for poking at his emotional wound. Spending his weekends alone at their house was a prime example. When he was there he didn't have friends hanging around, perpetually trying to cheer him up. He didn't want to be cheerful. There was no law saying he had to be cheerful. If he wanted to wallow in self-loathing, that was his own damn business.

He tried to go back to bed, but he couldn't settle between the clammy sheets.

Cranky and out of sorts, he stripped the bed and remade it with clean linens, then showered. The soothing properties of the hot water lasted only until he toweled off. Maybe it was the dream, but he was even more on edge than usual, as though he'd had a pot of coffee before bed. He prowled the house uneasily, trying to pinpoint what was wrong.

Again he was drawn to the window, gazing out, pacing before it, staring. He slid it open, the night air unexpectedly chill, considering how hot the day before had been. Goose bumps rose on his flesh and he shivered, more awake than he'd been in weeks.

Something was coming. It made his innards clench and twist.

He felt between the mattress and box spring for his knife, and drew it.

Staring out the window at the quiet yard, he finally had to admit maybe he did need help.

Like a stone sentry, he waited, patient, wondering if people who went mad felt it coming on like this.

From between the trees that lined the drive came a light. Premonitions weren't one of his powers, but a non-descript rental SUV crunched over the gravel and stopped at his front door.

Who the hell knew where he was? Was this dipshit lost?

If it was some sort of attack, they weren't being stealthy.

He went downstairs, knife still in hand. As he reached the bottom of the stairway, the door swung open. A large figure paused on the threshold, but didn't enter. Valentine switched on the hall lamp.

His father stood there, looking grim.

"How did you find me?" He slammed the knife down on the hall table. His father wasn't exactly an enemy.

The older man glowered. "Do you honestly think you have any secrets from me?" He turned to look behind him at the SUV then scanned the lawn and the surrounding trees, as though he didn't trust they weren't being watched.

"What do you want?"

"I don't want anything," his father spat. "Just don't say I never do anything for you. This is going to bite me in the ass." He turned and went back to the vehicle, Valentine following in confusion. Apparently he'd come alone. The passenger seat was empty, and there was no one in the rear seats, either. Dietrich went around to the cargo area.

What the hell was his father doing showing up at his door at four in the morning?

The rear hatch creaked open and he gestured for Valentine to look.

When he peered into the back of the vehicle, the dim overhead light revealed a lumpy blanket.

"They were going to kill her. I didn't know what else to do." Dietrich gave an uncharacteristic half-shrug and pulled the blanket back with two fingers.

Jory's pale face shone in the darkness. Valentine's heart froze then stuttered back to life. Her eyes were closed.

"She's alive?" he asked anxiously.

"No, I brought you a fucking corpse," his father grumbled. "Of course she's alive." He gestured at the girl. "Take her. I'm getting too old for this shit."

"But where is her team? Why is she unconscious?"

"Their job went bad," Dietrich said vaguely. "There are people who are getting annoyed about heroes interfering too much, and they decided to make examples of the two teams that were dogging them tonight. The others are dead, but I arranged to get her out."

Holy shit…*holy shit*. Her entire team was dead?

Oh god, she could have died with them.

Mercenaries had killed them? Intentionally? It went against all of the codes between Atypicals.

Valentine grabbed for her and dragged her to him, his distress making him rougher than he probably should have been.

"A sleep was put on her. I think her leg is broken, and she's probably got other wounds. She landed on her own knife at one point, I think. We bandaged that wound, but it'll need stitching." His father shut the hatch and walked to the driver's side and slid behind the wheel, slamming the door. Without another word he drove away.

Shaking, Valentine carried Jory's dead weight into the house then kicked the front door closed behind him.

*

He stripped her, cleaned her, set her leg, and waited for her own healing to kick in. Waited for her to open her eyes and spit on him.

Unconscious, with the covers tucked up under her chin, Jory seemed even younger than usual. He'd memorized her, but his gaze never left her for long.

He sat in a chair next to the bed, keeping watch, as though the people who'd butchered her team would show up on his doorstep to kill her.

Maybe they would. In a world that had gone this crazy, anything was possible.

Mercenaries killing off heroes in cold blood. He would never have believed it, but Dietrich had no reason to lie. And what had he been doing at that massacre, or had he made arrangements to get her out from afar? Valentine had been so shocked he couldn't even recall if his father had been wearing fighting leathers when he'd dropped Jory on his doorstep.

The Bureau would retaliate – the mercenaries involved had to know that. It was bad enough the Bureau always looked down their noses at non-heroes, but now every Atypical who didn't work for the government would be suspect.

Jory stirred, and a sob escaped her. Her eyes didn't open. Taking her to the hospital was too dangerous, not knowing who might be targeting her, but what if she needed more medical attention than he could give her? What if she didn't wake up? If she did wake, how was he going to explain why she was here? The truth sounded too strange to believe.

His father must have been watching out for her. Valentine hadn't realized he knew what she looked like. As much as his father's shady dealings disgusted him, saving Jory put Valentine forever in his debt.

She could have died. Even if she'd escaped the fight on her own, she might have bled out without his father's people there to bind her up.

Did she even know her team was gone?

He thought about the only time he'd talked to Seraphina, at the door of their team's house. She'd been a pretty girl, with dark flashing eyes and a big attitude where he was concerned, as her friend's ex. She'd been protective of Jory, trying to run him off even though he towered over her. The group's men had stood further back, letting her deal with Valentine, but glaring at him. They weren't just her work friends. They cared about her.

Jory had already been talking of them fondly before she'd left him. It would stand to reason her relationship with them had only gotten stronger with Valentine out of the way. Those poor kids. What a waste. And now Jory was alone again.

They'd better not send her back to that other team – what had the bitch's name been? Summer. That hadn't been a good fit. Hopefully the Bureau would pull its head out of its ass long enough to realize that. Jory might be too upset over losing her friends to stand up for herself.

Valentine checked the stab wound in her leg again around noon, pleased to see that not only had it stopped bleeding, it was partially healed. It would be several days before the wound was gone entirely, but it was much more efficient than Typical healing would be. Unable to resist, he slid his hand under the sheet.

He uncovered her hand and laced their fingers together. Already, he anticipated the huge amount of survivor's guilt she'd have. It wasn't fair. Why would a mercenary team think it was okay to do this to a bunch of kids?

The feel of her small fingers in his suffused him with warmth. She was here. Safe. They were together. It was temporary, but her proximity lit him from within.

Even though it couldn't last.

*

It was almost dark before Jory stirred. She grimaced and shook her head, as though she were rousing from a nightmare. There was a grunt of pain and she stilled.

Dread washed over him, leaving him chilled and making his legs feel numb. He didn't want to have to tell her what had happened. Hadn't he caused her enough pain already?

Valentine released her hand and laid it beside her on the blanket before she could object to his over familiarity, although he couldn't resist stroking the back of her fingers with his own. Her eyelids opened to slits. She blinked a few times, then looked around, her eyes widening.

"What?" she said, as though she didn't know which question to start with.

"You were wounded in a fight, but you're healing. I cleaned you up after my father dropped you off here."

"Bring me home." Her eyes were panicked, the pale blue seeming even more translucent in the light of the bedside lamp.

"Later. Right now you need to stay with me."

"I can't be with you. I can't be here." Jory struggled to get out of bed, but he pressed her gently back against the pillow. Plaintive furrows etched their way across her brow.

"Shh. You're okay. When it's safe I'll take you somewhere else, if you want – to your parents or Amy. Your leg is broken, but I set it. It's healing." He brushed a thumb over her lips, wishing he dared to kiss her, but it would comfort him more than her. She eyed him skittishly.

"Take me home. My team will take care of me. They…they…"

Empathetic pain strained under his ribs as he watched the memories return to her.

"They burned," she whispered. "There was so much fire." She shuddered and struggled up to sit again. Tentatively, Valentine wrapped his arms around her.

"All of them?"

"Vance, Arigh. I was supposed to be with them but they sent us to call the Bureau. I told Sera not to go back without me. Why didn't she wait?" She was whispering. The horror and sorrow in her eyes was more devastating than crying. Tremors began. She shook and shook until her teeth rattled. She was sobbing, but still no tears came. "I don't know what went wrong."

He pulled her tight again. At first she was rigid, but gradually her muscles slackened and she flowed against him like water. If he'd messed up everything else between them, at least she was letting him give her comfort.

For almost an hour she was incoherent, dealing with whatever was going on in her mind. She said little, shuddering, teeth chattering, muttering to herself at times, but still too far in shock to cry. Under her breath she started to repeat a question, but he couldn't figure out what she was saying.

"What happened?" she asked hollowly. "Why them?"

"It wasn't an accident," he replied, hoping the truth wouldn't make the ordeal worse for her. He wanted to keep her lucid by getting her to engage, but he wasn't sure what he should say. "It was a warning to the Bureau to make heroes back off mercenary business. There was a time when certain transactions were overlooked, but they've been cracking down."

"Murder?" She pushed away and gazed up at him in bewilderment. "But the laws – the code…there'll be a trial, at least. Maybe a war." Her fingers dug into his arm with bruising strength. "They didn't deserve that from anyone. They're good people. And Summer and her team were with them. All of them were new from this year."

In the stillness of the house there was only the sound of their breathing.

Her hair still smelled of smoke. Hopefully the scent wouldn't bring it all back to her. At least he'd managed to wipe away the smudges and dirt from her skin. Her burns had been superficial – she'd been lucky considering what could have happened.

A thick and unmanageable protectiveness twisted at him. If this was only the first of a wave of attacks, or if it was the start of an Atypical war, she was going to be in terrible danger until it was over. She was good, but so inexperienced, and new to her power. And now she had no team. He thought of her going out on missions alone, or with a team she didn't know at all. In this social climate, slotting her into a new team would be as safe as throwing her into a volcano. It made him sick.

"We'll have to wait and see." He held her tighter, trying to still her shaking frame. "It's not time to worry about that now."

"I have to call the Bureau and tell them I'm alive. Can I borrow your phone?"

He balked. If she called in now, they'd want to pick her up. She'd be whisked away for observation and they'd sequester her. Being trapped with strangers was the last thing she needed.

"If you call, you know they'll expect to retrieve you immediately," he said, trying to keep his tone neutral and reasonable. They couldn't protect her like he could. Other mercenaries wouldn't mess with her if she stayed his, under his roof. Mercenaries didn't mess with each other's families. "I can keep you safe. I don't trust that they can."

"Let me call them, Valentine."

His real name on her lips was jarring, as though she'd moved one step further away from where they used to be. Now he was simply Valentine, not Sir. His own name made him feel like he was being flayed alive, but he managed not to flinch.

For a long moment he stared at her, then got his phone from the dresser. When he handed it to her, she caught his hand between hers.

"I can't stay." She pulled him close and kissed the corner of his mouth, as though he was family, then released him. "We have to talk, but not now. I can't now."

He nodded, leaving her alone to call the people who would take her away.

*

The statewide funeral was televised on all the networks.

Valentine had been there, unable to get close to Jory. Security around her was tight. She was a tiny figure in the distance, dressed in her fighting leathers, but he felt better being present even though he couldn't talk to her. She didn't even know he was there.

Journalists later accused her of committing a wardrobe gaffe. Wearing leather supposedly made it look as though she was aligning herself with mercenaries. They said it was a slap in the face of her dead teammates, even though the pictures of them that flashed during news reports showed them in leathers too.

Her old ones had been destroyed, between the attack and the first aid afterward. Valentine had ordered more and sent them to the team's home address, even though he knew she wasn't staying there. Somehow she'd gotten them. He was glad she'd accepted his gift.

Mercenaries had killed her team, almost killed her, and the only thing the media seemed to give a shit about was her fucking wardrobe. When it came to the heroes who'd died, the news seemed to think the biggest part of the tragedy was that they'd died so young, while they were still so attractive. Nothing about how they'd sacrificed their lives to serving the community, or that they'd been good people.

The in memoriams that dominated news reports often focused on Summer's team. Jory's got second billing, even in death. It made him rail at the television, all alone in his empty house.

When Valentine had been a child, he'd been envious about the attention heroes got from the public, compared to the disdain given to mercenaries. But now that he loved a hero, he saw how shallow and transitory all the consideration they got from the media was. They were just as happy showing heroes behaving badly or having a bad hair day as they were to thank them for their work and sacrifice. They were celebrities and were treated as such. The anonymity of mercenary life now seemed like a blessing. At least he could walk down the street without cameras following him.

The political climate for mercenaries was hellish, though, in the wake of the deaths. They were all being painted as evil, rather than the usual 'greedy and immoral.' Since no one had come forward to claim responsibility, several mercenary teams were under investigation. His father had told him the attack was the result of mercenaries trying to make a statement, but with no spokesperson explaining what that statement had been, it just looked like dangerous, violent people had committed dangerous, violent acts. There was a senate committee discussing more stringent policing of Atypical affairs.

Seven heroes lost. Nothing like it had ever happened before – not even by accident – not in the fifty-three years Atypicals had been out of hiding.

He'd watched the news for weeks, hungry for a glimpse of Jory, but soon the stories moved on to other issues and other people.

As things settled, Valentine waited for her. He checked his phone a million times a day. She didn't call.

He built a wooden box for her collar, so that he didn't have to look at it, but the box felt like a coffin – a symbol. Jory leaving was a withdrawal of consent. Their relationship was dead. The 'we have to talk' line, followed by weeks of silence said everything that needed to be said.

His team had given up on him for now, and were doing jobs without him. He worried about their safety, but couldn't bring himself to leave the house in case she came back. Even though he knew she never would.

He tried to keep busy.

His soul couldn't breathe.

No matter how well he tended it, the garden he planted in the yard withered and died.

Epilogue

People said they didn't want her to be alone, but she couldn't be anywhere else but their house right now. She lay in bed with her eyes closed against the ugliness of her reality, almost able to hear her friends' laughter and banter, their grunts of pleasure, their planning and their jokes. Instead there was only silence couched in the crisp, judgmental ticking of the kitchen wall clock.

The deep, quiet gloom swallowed her for hours. Sometimes it kept her for days. She let it, welcomed it, needed nothing other than the space to be still while her ribcage was cracked open, and her heart was ripped from her with each replayed memory. She studied the pictures on her phone, terrified she'd forget the way Sera wrinkled her nose when she laughed, or the way Arigh's eyes would gleam when he talked about cars, or how Vance grinned when he read them lines from whatever novel he was into.

She forgot to eat some days, forgot to sleep. Forgot there was a sky outside of the house she'd shared with them. Her parents came, and Amy, but they felt like intruders even though they meant to help.

The hospital had kept her until they needed space. The doctors had declared the pills were making her better, but once she got home she forgot what day it was and whether she'd taken them. So instead the pills sat silently on the kitchen counter, pitying her, next to Seraphina's ridiculously huge cereal bowl and the coffee mug Arigh had used the day they'd gone. Vance's novel still sat on the hallway table, bookmarked with the ticket stub for the Marilyn Manson concert the four of them had gone to together.

Slowly, boxes with their names on them were piling up in the foyer as she packed their things. Once she was finished she'd sell the house and give the money to their families. She couldn't live forever with the ghosts of her team and what they could have had.

Sometimes, she wondered how much worse things would have been for her if she'd been sleeping with them. It was a chance she'd never get back, and left her with guilt to carry with her forever.

Guilt to add to the guilt of living. Guilt about doing nothing with her life while they rotted in the ground.

*

The room smelled of antiseptic and chemically simulated lilac.

Dr Gardner looked up from her files with the same compassionate expression that had persuaded Jory, word by word, to confide her every secret. If it hadn't been for her, Jory wasn't sure she would have gotten through the past few months.

Now the woman knew so much that the only person who knew more about Jory was Jory.

On her way to the office, she saw the grounds had been dusted with crystals of gleaming white. It was early for snow, but nature didn't seem to care about what humans expected. The smell of winter brought back memories that went hand in hand with the familiar feeling of desperation.

"Jory, you don't look so good. Nightmares again?"

Jory shook her head, grateful that most of those had ended. The odor of smoke or cooked ham still sent her into panic mode, but at least she didn't wake screaming anymore. Dreams had started again, but they were different – less tragic and more sinister.

"I need help."

Dr Gardner stared blankly at her for a moment. "What can I do to help? Is it the new team they introduced you to?" She closed the file in front of her, probably to make sure Jory felt she had her full attention.

"That team isn't going to work. I don't know if any team will." Jory shrugged, not caring. Getting added to a team, like a rogue bit of clay expected to enhance an existing sculpture, was impossible. She'd never be more than a clay wart on a team that already knew each other and worked well together. Besides, the illusion of being able to serve good while working for the Bureau had faded. They did small good works, but were so caught up in politics and red tape that real good rarely got done. Rogues existed, she knew, but what she didn't know was how it worked.

Pursuing rogue work wasn't why she was here. Her issue now was far more pressing.

"I need the Bureau to hide me," she said evenly, proud of how much of the anxiety she'd hidden from her voice. "It's the least they can do."

"Hide you? Is someone threatening you?" Dr Gardner rose from behind her new desk and walked around it to sit in the chair next to Jory. If the doctor got too close, Jory feared she'd drop to her knees and cling to the woman's hand, begging her to take pity.

Trembling, Jory fished her phone out of her jacket pocket and called up the text she'd received only minutes before she'd fled to the office.

IT'S COMING. DON'T BOTHER TRYING TO RUN.

The words brought a fresh storm of panic even though she'd read the message at least a hundred times.

"I don't understand," Dr Gardner said, passing the phone back to Jory. Her hand closed over it convulsively, as though it could save her.

"It's the Aphrodisia," Jory whispered. "It's starting again."

The doctor smiled reassuringly and squeezed Jory's hand. "You've survived it before. Just rest for a few days until it passes. You'll be okay."

Jory shook her head. No one knew what it was like – what it did to her. She wouldn't be okay. Nothing would be okay again if they didn't hide her.

Now.

"You don't understand," she whispered. "Valentine is coming for me."

Part Two
VILLAIN

Chapter One

The knife on his entryway table beckoned to him, but if Valentine stabbed his best friends he might regret it later. Why the fuck were the pushy bastards in his house?

"Look at you." Xana frowned and shook her head at Valentine, her expression more disapproving schoolteacher than badass mercenary. "Between the shaggy hair and the beard, you're like the poster child for dangerous loners."

"He's leaving the team to become a sexy internet lumberjack,'" Jurgen corrected. "He's got enough hair there now for a serious man bun. Do you have a hair tie?"

Dane chuckled and slapped Valentine on the back. "Twenty bucks says neither of you can get near him with a scrunchie."

He felt his hand curling to strike, and it took a moment to realize he was being unreasonable.

They were teasing. There was nothing wrong with teasing, and from these assholes he should have been used to it. He'd been alone in the house for so long though. Having people underfoot was jarring and made him want to snarl at them until they left. His father, Dietrich, must have told them where to find him, but he was none too happy that they'd bothered.

To other people – even those who knew him well – the house must look as though someone unstable lived there. Jurgen was moving around the great room, throwing cans and cartons into the recycling bin without making any snide comments. Xana had filled the sink with steaming soapy water, and was stacking plates in it to soak. He couldn't remember the last time he had clean plates, let alone clean clothes.

"You have a lot of maps out, Val. Are any of these safe to put away?" Dane asked, gesturing at the pile on the table. He was tactful enough not to mention the ones Valentine had taped to the walls.

Valentine shook his head, clenching his teeth and waiting for his rage to pass. The urge to throw them out of his house was almost overwhelming, but would need help if he was going to stop obsessing. Without intervention, things would continue as they had for the past six months, until he not only alienated himself from everyone but also permanently lost his grip on reality.

"Okay, I'll leave the maps for now, but you need a shower before someone puts you in a zoo." Tentatively, Dane gripped Valentine's wrist and towed him out of the room. He allowed it, and followed the tall blond upstairs to the master bath. When he hesitated in the doorway, Dane turned on the water and helped him strip out of his filthy clothes. Maybe he should have insisted on doing it himself, but he was too keyed up. It wasn't as if Dane hadn't seen him naked a million times.

He hissed and drew a finger along a few of Valentine's more impressive healing wounds and deliberate swirls of scarification. "What the hell happened to you?"

Valentine shrugged. The scarification was just something to do to help deal with things, but many of the injuries had happened during the last episode of Aphrodisia. He couldn't remember all of it, but when he'd come to his senses, he'd realized he'd broken his hand. He'd taken the cast off himself a week ago, and his skin still looked pasty and disgusting. Afterward, when he'd gone back to Jory's last known location, he could feel she was gone, but the metal door to the safe house was pitted as though someone had taken a mallet to it.

Even after the storm had passed, she was still hiding from him. The time apart was difficult enough, but being apart during the days upon days of unsatiated lust was the most disturbing.

Sometimes he recalled flashes of things he'd done during those times, and every last scrap of his self-respect evaporated. Wandering the parking lot of whatever building the Bureau was hiding her in, screaming for her like a maddened animal, didn't leave him with any delusions of control.

Once upon a time, Jory's doctor had told her the episodes of Atypical Aphrodisia would eventually stop, but Valentine didn't hold out hope for that anymore. He was an animal that needed to rut with its mate. When the lust came, he hunted for her. But she was hiding from him, and from the insane need that came over them, convinced he made her weak. They'd been apart since before the rest of her hero team had been murdered. Since the war between heroes and mercenaries had begun. A lifetime ago.

If werewolves existed, he would have felt their pain. Waking up and remembering the crazed things he'd done was both humiliating and terrifying. There was no controlling it anymore.

With Jory at hand, at least it had given him some control over his mind and his lust. With the Aphrodisia pent up inside him and no release, he had nothing but agony and desperation. How was she managing without him? Did they have some sort of cure? Or had they found someone to ease her?

The pacing started again, but he stopped when Dane arched a brow at him.

"Dude, you're naked and you smell like a basket full of gym socks. Get in the fucking shower." Dane urged him in. "Do you need me to help with your hair?"

"No," Valentine croaked. He wasn't used to talking to people anymore. His own voice sounded odd and loud in his ears. Without testing the temperature, he stepped into the walk-in shower and let the water cascade over him. It was almost painfully hot, but maybe he could boil away the chill in his bones. Winter had already been long and cold. It was a miracle he hadn't frozen to death at some point.

"You should have called, you prick. We've been looking for you for so long." His friend had made himself comfortable on the toilet seat and didn't seem as if he planned to go anywhere while Valentine showered.

"No point," he grumbled. The hot water pelted his skin and he groaned as goose bumps rose. Why hadn't he taken the time to do this for himself? It was so good.

"Of course there was a point," Dane snapped. "Like the rest of us not being worried sick, for starters, and having someone here to take care of you when you couldn't take care of yourself."

Valentine didn't bother to respond, but the truth was he was far too proud to have let them see him like that. The next time it happened he'd banish them again, no matter how Dane thought things would go down.

He lathered himself in body wash twice, disgusted by how dirty he was. There was some satisfaction in seeing the mud coursing down him and into the drain, but he couldn't remember why he was muddy. His body was more heavily muscled than the last time he'd looked at himself, and there was no fat on him anywhere. Apparently, obsessive stalking was a better workout than the gym.

"When it happens, no one can be here." On his scalp, the water was almost scalding. He tried to wash his hair, but had to spend a few minutes picking twigs and other debris out of it first. There were mats in his hair. Although it had already been getting long before Jory left him, now it was well past his shoulders. It was going to take ages to comb out. Maybe he would just shave it off.

"We'll burn that bridge when we come to it." Dane didn't seem to get that when he lost control he didn't want an audience.

A few of the newer scarification cuts hadn't healed yet and they stung in a satisfying way where the hot water and soap got into them. Both arms were almost completely covered in scars now, along with a section of his chest. None of them looked infected despite having been coated in dirt.

"Now that the mud is off, those look almost pretty." Dane pressed his lips together and frowned. "I didn't know you were artistic."

"Neither did I." Part of his mind was urging him to be ashamed of the scars he'd left on his skin, but after everything he'd done, he had no shame left.

"That's about her?"

"No." Short lies were the easiest.

Dane was blessedly quiet for a while. When Valentine turned off the water, Dane handed him a clean towel.

"When was the last time you saw her?"

"I don't know. In the fall sometime – just once after she left. What's today?"

"The seventeenth."

"Of?"

Dane gritted his teeth, as though he was pained. "February. You missed Christmas, you know. Your mom is a mess."

Guilt tried to creep up on him as he toweled off, but it was like being told he'd missed it while he'd been unconscious. It sucked that he'd put his mother through that, but he hadn't been in a position to call, let alone visit. A month and a half ago he'd been a monster trying to claw off the window of a safe house.

His friend handed him a t-shirt and shorts out of the duffle bag he'd brought with him, and when he'd dressed, Valentine felt almost human again.

"Xana can tackle your hair," Dane said as he ushered Valentine back downstairs. "Either that or we can shave your head."

The great room looked almost habitable again. Xana was wiping down the counter, but Jurgen was gone.

"He went to get groceries," she replied before anyone asked. "The only thing in the fridge is ketchup and a package of bacon that expired three months ago. What the hell have you been eating?"

Valentine considered the question. "Other than my pride, I'm not sure."

"Well, whatever. We're here now, and you've managed to stay alive this long. Let's get that hair combed out, then we can talk about how you've been dumped and need an intervention."

The anger that never seemed to be far from the surface bubbled up, and he had to slap a mental lid back down on it. "Until the Aphrodisia stops, I can't stop. The Bureau is letting her suffer. Or, if they have a cure, I want it."

"What if no matter what you want, you can't get her back, Val? You don't even know why she left. Not really." Xana patted his shoulder then took a comb from Dane's hand. "You think it was subdrop that made her bolt, but she might have suddenly realized you're a prick."

If only it were that simple.

"I rushed her."

"So what are you going to do to woo her after all this time? What have you been doing to try to win her back? Or are you?"

He bared his teeth at Xana, and she took a step back. "I don't woo." His voice was a growl. Jory wasn't something to joke about. Not with him. Not now. "She's mine."

It was that simple. She belonged to him, and sooner or later he'd take her back.

Chapter Two

It was safe to go out. If it hadn't been, she would feel the usual tug of his presence under her ribs where her heart used to be. Old snow lashed the windows, at the mercy of a cruel wind. It was too cold for new snow. The opportunity to finally go out and do something fun left Jory feeling lost. She wasn't inclined to set foot outside. Even if she chose to go out, what would she do? Her team was dead. It didn't put her in the mood to go shopping.

Half a year of mourning her friends might have seemed excessive to the Bureau, but knowing Arigh had unwittingly given the order that had saved her life – knowing that any of the others might have been chosen to make the phone call that took her out of the alley and harm's way, rotted in her gut. The Bureau called it survivor's guilt, but knowing it had a name didn't make it easier when she woke screaming. None of them had deserved to die like that. Her body still bore the scars, but she still had what was left of her life, while the bits of them the Bureau had found were long buried.

Her team had been her future. She wasn't wired to be a lone wolf.

In some twisted part of her brain, knowing Valentine wasn't watching the house made her feel lonelier than usual. If anyone understood why he kept coming around even though she'd made a show of rejecting him, it was Jory. She tried to convince herself she didn't want him anymore, but it was a lie. Even so, she had to stay away from the man. Being in love with someone didn't necessarily mean they were good for you.

She owed it to her team to make something of her life rather than handing it over to Valentine. She couldn't let herself become weak again.

The dark and cold, though, made it difficult to be strong. It was hard to remember her submission to him, and the dynamic of their relationship, came with a heavy price. Giving up control and letting someone else take care of her lured her the way a siren sang sailors to their deaths.

Beautiful. He was so beautiful. The feelings she had for him so seductive.

But the things that made her soul rejoice left her with little self-respect when the moment had passed. *She* was the problem. His regard for her never wavered, no matter what she let him do to her, but it wasn't enough.

"A penny for your thoughts," Asher said from behind her.

When she turned, he was standing a respectful distance away. As usual, there was a gleam in his bright green eyes that suggested he'd be much closer if she gave him the slightest sign of interest. Like most Atypicals, he was impossibly handsome to other Atypicals. It wasn't that Jory was immune to his charms, but her body and mind knew who owned her, even now.

"My thoughts aren't worth a penny," she said with a small laugh. "Not unless you're interested in my opinions about snow.

"Considering your powers, I'd think you'd love this kind of weather."

She wished she could get away with being rude and telling him she wanted to be alone, but since they'd moved her into this safe house he'd been her only company. It was the first time they'd placed her alone with anyone. Although he'd never said as much, he'd implied he was an undercover operative for the Bureau, and was billeted at the safe house until things cooled off between missions. The only part she wasn't sure about was whether he was currently on duty, both keeping an eye on her and protecting her from Valentine

It wouldn't bother her that much, but she had a feeling another reason they'd chosen Asher would be to…help her the next time the Aphrodisia came. The first time, they'd put her under observation. She remembered the shocked faces on the researchers when she'd been wracked with lust, begging the absent Valentine to let her come. She couldn't take care of those needs alone. Nothing worked but him.

The second time, they'd hooked her up to electrodes and equipment that measured everything from the amount of discomfort she was in to her reaction to certain stimuli. They'd brought in a series of attractive men, like sacrificial lambs, trying to convince her to accept at least one. They didn't believe her when she'd explained that some random dick wouldn't help matters. Of course she'd been screaming at the time, which may have undermined her authority on the subject.

Under the circumstances, she believed Asher was a plant. The Bureau wanted them to hook up more naturally so that the next time the Aphrodisia came it wouldn't be a stranger offering to help her. If it was out of the goodness of their hearts, she might have been thankful, but she knew it was just because they wanted to see what would happen. Being the Bureau's guinea pig wasn't her kink.

As it was, the niggling feeling she'd had all day suggested that the Aphrodisia could break loose again at any time. Or maybe it was the beginnings of a migraine. If Valentine stayed away, there was more of a chance the Aphrodisia would too – his proximity seemed to trigger it more. But he never stayed away for long, and she felt like a bitch for taking comfort in that. His presence was a temptation, but at least she knew that if she really couldn't handle things, he was waiting for her.

*

The wind howled at the window, whipping snow against the pane with a violence that made it sound like stones. Jory threw off her warm duvet, both because it was too hot, and the smell of it irritated her nose. It was clean, but that wasn't enough. It smelled like the sterile cleanliness of a laundry service, which should have been fine, but she longed for Valentine's familiar scent. The wrongness of all of it – the smell, being alone, knowing that for the first time in months he was nowhere nearby – was conspiring to keep her awake.

She missed him. She was madly in love with him even now, after all this time, and she just wanted to see his arrogant face and hear his mocking voice. She wanted to pretend nothing had come between them so she could curl up in his lap on the window seat in their house and have him stroke her hair while he read to her. To talk until the wee hours about books, the universe, and the nature of evil.

When he was lurking outside, the option to open the door was there. With him gone, she was restless and lost.

It was hard to be mad at him for stalking her when it was a mutual obsession. She knew exactly what he was feeling – god, she *felt* what he was feeling. That didn't mean being together was good for either of them.

Irritably, she stretched, the slide of the cotton sheets beneath her waking her senses.

Damn.

She wasn't sure she was strong enough to handle a third round of Aphrodisia without relief. The last time had been shorter than usual. Only four days of agony, and a few more of discomfort, but there was no way to predict how long it might last this time. She grabbed her cell phone from the nightstand, knowing she was supposed to call Dr Gardner as soon as things started, but her finger hesitated as it hovered over the call button. Being hooked up to equipment and monitored like a lab rat made the entire embarrassing experience worse.

It had been hard enough to handle when it was just she and Valentine alone, with no one the wiser, but having an audience humiliated her in ways she wasn't into. Even the time Valentine and his team had tortured her at the private BDSM club had been far less debasing than having a team of doctors and scientists dispassionately observe her as she writhed on a hospital bed, begging for Valentine. At least the people who'd watched at the club had been aroused. That was a logical, natural reaction. Having people watch her and take notes was creepy.

But at least she wasn't being treated like a sex slave and enjoying it.

Sometimes she wasn't sure which was worse.

Not wanting to wake Asher, who slept in next room, she pressed a futile hand between her legs. If he heard her, he might call Dr Gardner. Or worse, he wouldn't. There was a chance they were paying him to be interested in her, but he gave the impression that even if they were, he didn't have to fake it.

Against her will, Jory's mind drifted to the last time Valentine had his way with her. He'd been merciless, and his sexy debaucheries replayed in her head whenever her thoughts strayed to him. Maybe she should have been angry about what he'd done to her, but it had been consensual even if she'd been overwhelmed. The disturbing part had been realizing that no matter how degrading sex with him became, she not only submitted willingly, but she loved it. Heroes shouldn't allow themselves to be sexually degraded, let alone fantasize about it after the fact.

He loved her and she loved him, but they were a disaster.

She couldn't even orgasm without him because he hadn't given her permission. Whether that was the Aphrodisia or just a mindfuck he'd planted in her head was impossible to know.

If he could feel her current predicament and hadn't started to suffer yet himself, he might have been chuckling. If he was with her, he would ask her mortifying questions and demand she answer him. He would touch her just enough to make her wild then pretend he felt bad for her when he was only planning to make it worse. As a lover he'd been a nightmare. Unfortunately, it was the kind of nightmare that came with mind-blowing orgasms and an ongoing desperation to have him inside her, even when the Atypical Aphrodisia had cooled and she was in full possession of her faculties.

It wasn't fair.

Vividly, she remembered crawling by his command, the feel of him following her, tormenting her with the plug he'd shoved deep in her ass. When she cried out in miserable desperation, he'd laughed at her. Had he really laughed, or had her imagination added that? Mockery was such a big part of his personality. The only part that had mattered to her was that he'd eventually give her what she needed. As cool as he played things, he needed her just as much.

The heat between her legs was growing. There had to be some way to relieve it. She touched herself, focusing on the memory of the ecstasy and relief that came with the moment of penetration, knowing he would take care of her and ease the torment for a while. The sound of his growl as he thrust deep within her, taking possession of her body as he already had her mind and her power, the way he whispered the dirtiest things in her ear, the feel of him filling her. Owning her. She thought of the things he'd done once and forced her to like – of the things he hadn't done and she'd dreamed of him doing. Of him tying her out like a dog again, but inviting his team over to see it. Oh god, he'd broken her so thoroughly. The things she wanted now and could never have infiltrated her dreams and her waking fantasies. But none of them could bring her to the point of orgasm. Not even remembering the roughness of his voice when he commanded her to come.

Defeated yet again, her hand fell to her side. She twisted the sheet between her fingers, tears of frustration slipping silently down her temple and into her ear and hairline. There was a creak of floorboard outside her room.

"Jory? Are you okay?"

Fuck, Asher. Quit being available and go away.

"Fine. I'm fine," she croaked.

"Should I call Gardner?"

She tried to say no, but only a whimper came. How the hell did he know?

"I'm coming in."

"No!"

The door opened and Asher stood in the doorway. In the gloom she could almost mistake him for Valentine, with his size and shape, but that was probably why the Bureau had chosen him. He gave off a dominant vibe, but there was no mistaking him for Valentine, no matter how much information they'd given him about her.

Would having someone – anyone – inside her be a relief? From the impression he'd been giving for weeks, she could have Asher immediately, with no strings attached. He was hot, and she was flattered by his attention. Other girls had sex with guys they didn't know that well, and they didn't even have the incentive of Aphrodisia to drive them to it.

He moved closer to the bed.

"It started again?"

"Yes." Her options cycled through her mind at top speed. Do Asher. Tell him to get out. Call Dr Gardner. Call Valentine. Suffer.

"What do you need?"

Fuck. Like she was supposed to respond to that honestly? *Treat me like dirt, say disgusting things to me, use me like I'm your property, then pet me and love me like I'm your whole life.* The image that formed in her mind of that exact scenario came with a complimentary side of Valentine looking sinister.

How could she even think about screwing someone else? Even if this guy was dominant in bed, he wouldn't be evil enough – attuned to her enough – to give her what she craved. Not even if she explained she needed a command to get off. Like she could have that conversation with some random guy. Like her body would respond to anyone but Valentine. And there were no guarantees his power would know how to control hers. She could end up permanently damaging him.

Asher moved closer, and before she could shoo him away he sat on the edge of her bed.

"Don't call Dr Gardner," she whispered as another wave of arousal swept over her.

He smiled down at her, sexy, self-confident. A man used to women responding to him.

Shit. She hadn't meant it as an invitation.

"I –"

Asher's mouth came down on hers, and her eyes widened in shock. He pinned her down, and she struggled beneath him, the heat in her groin flaring in response. Against her will, she moaned into his mouth. An appreciative chuckle rumbled in his chest.

No, no – she was giving off all the wrong messages.

She managed to get her arms up between their bodies and pushed him upward, away from her. He was big compared to her, and didn't move much, although his mouth did come off of hers.

"Asher, I can't…"

"Why not?" In the low light his eyes were almost as dark as Valentine's. Rather than making her want Asher, though, it made her ache for the man who wasn't smiling down at her. "I can see how much discomfort you're in. Why don't you let me help?"

For a moment she blinked up at him, not sure how to explain. As he leaned in to kiss her again, she pushed him back. Although he'd thrown on a pair of jeans, his muscular chest was distressingly bare.

"I belong to him. I can't accept someone else in his place." The words left her mouth, and the truth of them immediately depressed her. Would she never be free of him?

"You don't actually *belong* to him, Jory." His wry smile was apologetic. "That's just a game people play. It's supposed to be consensual. If you're running from him, obviously you don't want to play with him anymore."

The Bureau didn't understand at all.

"It isn't roleplay, Asher. He owns me. I'm sure it seems crazy to you, but even though I'm choosing to be away from him, I know who I belong to."

He sat back. "So why are you getting the Bureau to hide you if you're just going to go back to him?"

Panic gathered in her chest. "I'm not going back to him. We need to stay away from each other."

"So you can be alone forever? You're never going to move on? How is that a life?"

She glared at him. "Oh, so now I need a man to make my life worthwhile? I'm a hero, just like you. I don't need a man to validate my existence."

Asher sighed heavily. "That's not what I said. All I meant was that it's a long, lonely life without someone to share it with. Right now I'm just offering you the chance to see if you can use me to take the edge off. It doesn't have to mean anything. We hardly know each other."

He sat there patiently, giving the impression he'd walk out without an argument if that was what she wanted. The echo of his kiss still lingered on her lips. The man knew what he was doing in that department, at least. The effort of lying still and not squirming with the horrible need building inside her was wearing her down, but she didn't want him to see her weakness.

They stared at each other a long while, and eventually he leaned forward, more tentative than the last time, letting his lips hover over hers. He was giving her the option.

Desire twisted in her belly. She clenched her hands, digging her nails into her palms. A moan tried to escape. She squeezed her eyes closed, forcing herself to breathe deeply.

Asher had a point. If she never planned to succumb to Valentine again, how long was she going to go without human connection? How long until she'd let herself have sex? Maybe she could allow herself the pleasure of kissing a handsome man without having to jump ahead to the future implications. At least Asher was respectful and cared about what she wanted.

When she opened her eyes he was still above her, waiting. When she didn't push him away, he brushed his lips against hers, as though trying to coax her into reciprocating.

Wrong. No. Bad, bad, bad.

She was Valentine's. No one else was allowed to touch her.

She scrambled back on the bed, away from Asher, and bumped her head hard on the headboard.

"No. You need to get out." Fear pierced her. The Aphrodisia was starting to make her desperate, and she didn't know how long she could resist. She didn't want some sort of Valentine substitute, but if he chose to take her arousal as consent, she'd be helpless to stop him.

"If you don't want to do anything, that's fine," Asher said, getting to his feet and holding his hands up in front of him in a gesture of acquiescence.

There was a tug under her ribs.

Fuck.

"He's here." She drew her duvet up to her chin, as though it would protect her from the beast outside the house. "He's here and he knows." Lust hit her like a blow, and she cowered back against the headboard.

"You think he's here? How would he know? He doesn't have an automatic 'Jory's been kissed' detector, does he?" Asher was far too calm. He didn't understand how this was going to go. The other times Valentine had found her, he'd been little more than an animal. This time he was still thinking rationally. She could feel him prowling around outside. He wasn't going to try to claw down the reinforced door. Yet.

There was a scraping sound along her window. Primal terror chased goose bumps along her flesh. The third floor meant nothing to him if he'd come prepared.

"Get out," she snapped. "If he finds you in here he'll kill you." She wasn't sure if she meant figuratively.

"He doesn't own you, Jory," Asher whispered back. He pulled his cell phone from his back pocket and hit a button.

She breathed in short gasps, trying to get her heart to slow.

"He does," she whimpered. "Oh god, he does."

The entire window tore from the frame. Frigid wind blasted into the room. Asher moved into a fighting stance just as a huge spider of rope work slotted a figure through the window and brought it into the room. Jory meant to move to help Asher, but she panicked and, instead, she slipped over the edge of the bed to hide beneath it, like a frightened child.

One booted foot, then the other, stepped from the rope's suspension onto the floor. Tufts of snow fell from the boots to melt where they landed, forming darker splotches in the gray carpeting. Jory held her breath, trembling, clinging to the silly hope that he wouldn't think to check under the bed.

"We have a security breach at Cedar Residence – Valentine Ott has accessed a third-story window and is most likely planning to abduct Jory Savage," Asher shouted.

"Do you narrate everything that happens to you? That would be an annoying habit."

Valentine's voice lanced through her. The sound of it caught her like a hook and tried to reel her closer, out from under her hiding place. She closed her eyes and put her hands over her ears, then pressed her nose to the rug.

What was she, five? She was a fucking hero with a talent for controlling all things winter, and here she was hiding under her bed from Valentine as if he was the bogeyman. Although, to be fair, he was her own personal bogeyman. She'd spent months hoping she'd never see him again. Her breathing rasped loudly in her ears, and her heart banged so hard she was sure he could hear it. It was every nightmare she'd ever had.

There were parts of her innermost self she wanted to forget about, but he was going to remind her.

Enough. Quit being ridiculous!

She would crawl out from under the bed with as much dignity as she could muster, and tell the bogeyman to fuck the hell off.

There was a scuffle, and her anxiety kicked up a notch, freezing her in place. Booted feet walked slowly toward the bed. She held her breath. Her eyes opened so wide they hurt.

Oh god, please make him go away.

The mattress and box spring flipped backward and hit the wall. She screamed, screwing her eyes shut. A strong hand wrapped around her wrist and she was hauled to her feet.

Valentine grinned down at her, a demon about to devour her soul.

She kicked his shin. "Let go of me!"

His dark eyes burned into hers. He didn't look entirely sane.

"Why are you hiding under a bed?"

The grip on her wrist slackened, and she pulled free, then stood and primly brushed off her nightgown, as though finding herself under the bed had been unexpected and unacceptable. Maybe she could say she lost a contact?

"What I do in my spare time is none of your damn business. Now, let Asher go."

The ropes that had the man hogtied in the middle of the floor fell away, and coiled neatly under the windowsill.

Asher got to his feet, glaring at Valentine. The testosterone in the room was stinking up the place. She stepped between them, and looked Valentine in the eye. His brows rose.

"Get out." She pointed over his shoulder at the hole in the wall. "And put the window back. It's fucking wintertime."

Valentine's gaze went from hot to cold in the span of a moment. She shivered, but felt her nipples harden against the flannel of her nightie.

At the edge of her vision, she saw Asher move closer. "You're not welcome here. The Bureau has enforcers on the way. They should be here any minute. Do yourself a favor and get out of here, like the lady said."

"Am I…interrupting something?" Valentine's mouth tiled up at the corner as his gaze moved over her clothing.

"Yeah, I normally seduce men when I'm dressed like this."

"I knew that about you."

His unreadable dark gaze made her guts clenched tight. Then the breeze carried his scent to her. Her senses went berserk. Immediately, she remembered him standing over her, muscled chest bare over his leather fighting pants. Her knees fought her, trying to buckle and make her kneel. She wanted to crawl to him and beg for him to use her mouth. To do whatever he wanted.

"As I thought. You can hide from me all you want, but you can't hide from your own nature."

Anxiously, she frowned at him and shook her head. *Please don't say anything about it in front of Asher.*

"I think you and I need to talk." His voice held both threat and promise. "Maybe we should step outside."

"She's not going anywhere with you, asshole." Asher took a step forward. With a flick of Valentine's wrist, a palm-sized bundle of rope flew at Asher. In flight, the thing spread, grabbing onto Asher's face on impact, like a large angry hand. The hero grunted and tried to pry the thing off, but it squeezed tighter. He grunted in pain.

"Stop! Don't hurt him," she pleaded. "I'll go with you, just leave him alone."

Asher tripped over a footstool and went down heavily, still wrestling with the thing.

Valentine held out a hand, his smile menacing.

"Just talking," she reminded him.

"Agreed."

If nothing else, at least she could formally end things with him, right?

Against her better judgment, she took his hand. Energy flowed from his palm to hers, radiating up her arm and over her skin, prickling, arousing, making her nipples and clit ache. Valentine groaned before he clamped his mouth shut and pulled her toward the window hole.

"There's a staircase."

"Like I give a fuck." He wrapped an arm around her waist. A length of rope scooped them up and carried them out into the night.

Chapter Three

Abducting her had been so much easier without the lust madness addling his mind. It was there – the beginnings of it – creeping in, but it wasn't out of control yet. It meant the difference between trying to knock down a reinforced door and simply removing a window.

Guilt about scaring her and stealing her away tried to sneak in, but the connection between the two of them was buzzing, as strong as it had been before she'd chosen to leave.

His ropes carried them into the woods across from the house then dropped them into a clearing. He should have been cold, but the Aphrodisia kept him warm. In the throes of it, he didn't sleep, barely ate. Aphrodisia was a beast that only cared about being fed, and it didn't want food.

In his arms, Jory was small and sweet. She smelled like everything he'd ever wanted to fuck…or eat. Xana had tried to convince him to do someone else, to see if it would help, but he couldn't bring himself to touch another person, let alone fuck them. He'd had Jory. A substitute wouldn't cut it.

As soon as the ropes fell away from them, he let her go and stepped back. Sharp snowflakes like shards of ice whipped up into his face. Jory's luminous hair stood out from her head, crackling with cold wrath.

God, she was beautiful when she was angry.

"Where do you get off stalking me and yanking me out of my house?" she spat.

He had to force back a smile. "You want me. Maybe your brain isn't happy to see me, but your body is."

A scream of frustration burst from her lips, seeming to surprise even her.

"I don't want you," she snarled. "I don't want you, or your arrogance, or the crappy way you treat me."

"You love all of it until you start thinking you shouldn't." He kept his voice calm, even though the beast was rising, threatening to take over. She was almost naked. A flannel nightie, probably some sort of cartoon panties. Hell, his cock was already hard. He could be inside her now if she'd stop being stubborn.

"Go away," she whispered.

"When was the last time you came?"

"That's none of your business."

None of his business? How could she say that? He tried to hold his mind back from hers, but it reached out against his will. When his power brushed hers, the flimsy barricade she'd built against him dissolved.

"I've missed you, snowangel."

"Don't call me that!" she cried.

He walked toward her. She took a step back, but bumped into a tree and seemed to forget she could go around it. Although, if she led him on a chase through the forest, it might turn out badly for her.

The beast within him growled. As the scent of her arousal reached him, he scrambled to maintain control.

"It doesn't have to be forever, Jory. Eventually this will go away." Maybe the desperate need to fuck would, but his love for her also had a will of its own. And, inconveniently, it had nothing to do with the Aphrodisia anymore.

"Will it? And even if it does, what will be left of me by then?"

'A well-satisfied, cherished submissive' wasn't what she wanted to hear.

"What we share when we're together doesn't take away from you as a hero," he argued. "I don't know why you think it does." He was close enough now that he could smell the other man on her. Jealousy he had no right to flickered through him. Would it be so bad if he pinned her there and kissed her until his own scent covered that bastard hero's?

"That's easy for you to say. You don't have to struggle through living with yourself afterward."

She really didn't understand at all. "Oh, but I do. I have to live with that look of disgust on your face whenever you lay eyes on me. Do you think that doesn't cost me? I haven't second-guessed what I was into since I was a teenager. The amount of loathing you have for me has changed that."

"I don't loathe you."

"Damn the actions, not the man? That's charitable of you."

"Stop trying to make me feel guilty."

"You do it to me all the time, without even having to say a word. You've been hiding from me for months. Am I that much of a monster?" He was. Yes, he was.

The pale blue of her widened eyes haunted him. "I can't be around you. It's not your fault, but you make me weak." She gazed up at him earnestly.

He ached to kiss her, to have the chance to lie in bed and hold her, to talk to her as though they were normal people. To make her laugh. He missed her crazy, artless laugh.

And she thought *he* made *her* weak?

She groaned and leaned her head back against the skeletal tree. The sound made his cock throb unpleasantly. They didn't have much time to talk before he had to get her to safety, away from him and his lust.

"Things between us ended so abruptly that I haven't been able to move past it," he admitted. "I'm sorry I pushed you farther than you were ready for. I shouldn't have relied on the fact that you had a safeword." It had been ages since he'd last rehearsed this, but he hoped the sentiment would be understood even if his words were awkward and rambling. "The last thing I ever wanted to do was betray your trust."

"It wasn't that." She chewed on her bottom lip. "You just showed me what was there, inside me, the whole time. It's a serious flaw – a deep weakness that could be used against me. I have to work at fixing it. Catering to it will just make it worse. Deeper. If you can use my submission against me, who else could? I can't risk that."

"But that's not how it works," he replied, confusion swirling as he tried to see things as she did. "Your submission to me isn't automatically transferable to someone else. Could that guy back in your room even get you off?" He was fishing, wanting to know how far things had gone.

"It doesn't have to make sense to you, it's how I feel." She smoothed her hair back in frustration, but it escaped her hands in wild, unkempt tendrils until she gave up and let her hands fall away. "And my sex life is none of your damn business. I have the right to choose not to submit to you."

"Don't be ridiculous. Of course you have the right to choose not to submit to me. I'm just saying that you're denying a part of yourself that makes you happy. There's no good reason to, other than your pride."

"It *doesn't* make me happy."

Her disgust was a spike in his heart. Suddenly, he just wanted to get away from her, away from her rejection and how much it still wounded him. But men didn't get to run away like small, heart-broken boys. Why had he thought that if they could talk, things would sort themselves out?

"I know you love me, Valentine, but it's not a healthy love. It's built on lust and dominance, and on your desire to own me. Not on true affection."

How could she say that? Yes, those other things were mixed into his feelings for her, but he knew what love was. Maybe he hadn't expressed it well, but his whole life revolved around her now. Nothing else mattered. All he wanted was to build a life with her, and all she wanted was for him to fuck off.

He opened his mouth to apologize for taking up her time, but when he breathed in, her scent shot straight to his brain.

"Run." He closed his eyes, willing her to listen. As he fumbled to force his mind to let hers go, he took a deep breath through his mouth, hoping he couldn't taste her on the air.

"Why?" He heard the snow crunch under her feet, but her voice didn't sound any farther away.

"I'm out of time. You've seen what happens now, Jory. Get somewhere safe."

"Is it worse because I haven't been around to..." she trailed off as though saying it out loud was too crude for her pretty mouth.

"I don't know. Maybe someday someone will write a book that makes sense of this, but I think that not being able to feed the beast forces it to take control."

"When you were trying to claw down the door at my last safe house, were you thinking straight?"

He gave a bitter laugh. "Sure. I always choose to break my hand when I'm trying to pick up hot girls. Cro-Magnon behavior is dead sexy, don't you think?"

"If we don't have sex, you don't just suffer like I do?"

"If we don't have sex, I should probably be locked up. I'm not me anymore. Not until it passes." He swallowed hard, trying to fight down the aggression attempting to take over. "It's not your problem."

When he opened his eyes he'd regained some control, but she was standing right in front of him, her arms wrapped tightly around her tiny frame. Even she had to be cold out here, underdressed as she was.

"The others are waiting for me, back at our house." He realized his slip-up, and hoped she thought he meant that he shared the house with his team, and not that he still thought of the coach house as half hers. "They found me. They'll keep me under control until it passes this time." He drew back, giving her a mocking half-bow. "I'm sorry to have kept you."

"Wait." She put a hand on his arm.

Touching him had been a bad idea.

He backed her against the tree once more, this time holding her there with his body pressed to hers, tension thrumming through him, his cock throbbing against her belly.

"Why don't you listen to me?" he hissed. "When you don't listen to me, things go badly."

She quivered against the press of his body. "Yes, Sir."

"I'm going to let you go now, Jory. You're going to run along home, like a good girl, and hope the Bureau gets here before I lose control." He pushed away from her, and tried to walk away, but his legs wouldn't obey him.

Small, shaking hands lowered to the voluminous flannel skirts of her nightgown. She drew it upward exposing first ankle, then calf, then her pale thighs.

Valentine shook with the effort hold back, feeling like his brain was going to explode.

"If I let you have me just once, would it help?"

If she said anything else he didn't hear it. A ringing started in his ears, as though someone had fired a gun next to his head. He shoved her nightgown up over her hips, only to discover she wore nothing beneath it. For a moment he wondered if Asher had been inside her only moments ago, but he loosened his jeans anyway, knowing the answer wouldn't change his mind.

She kissed him hard, twining her fingers in his long hair, clinging to him. With minimal effort, he lifted her and braced her back against the tree, then plunged into her. He coaxed his way into her with sharp, savage thrusts. She was even tighter than he remembered, and her pussy closed over his cock like a vice. Although he was barely all the way in, she wriggled and fought in his grip. He slowed then stopped. He hadn't meant to hurt her. If he was hurting her, he'd let her go.

The ringing in his ears faded as his pulse slowed.

"Please, Sir," she begged. "Don't."

Her pussy rippled torturously.

"Don't what?"

She screamed again, as though he was murdering her. Teeth sank into his neck, and she clawed at his back.

"Jory! Jory, stop. If you want me to stop, I'll put you down." When he tried to pull out, his muscles locked and wouldn't allow it. Her heels dug into the back of his thighs, pulling him closer, wedging his cock in deeper, until he bottomed out. "If you want me to stop, you have to let go."

"Don't stop. Please let me come," she whimpered piteously. "You're so hard. I need to come so bad. Please, Sir. I'll be good."

The words brought him to the edge, and he fought to hold off. Part of him wanted to make her beg for her orgasm, long and prettily, but her desperation melted his resolve. He thrust up into her twice more then paused, reveling in the feel of being inside her, where he belonged. His mind had wrapped around hers, protecting them both from the unpredictability of her power, groaning as it submitted completely and without a fight.

"Are you going to come for me?"

"Yes, Sir." She panted. "I can't wait. I can't stop."

He felt faint. "Come now," he commanded.

She sobbed once, low and throaty, and the orgasm ripped through her, making her clench around him painfully. Gasping and gritting his teeth, he got through it, the tortured ecstasy of being inside her, hovering on the edge, so near his own orgasm that he shook with the effort of holding back. Her screams of pleasure, and the way she writhed on his cock, made his knees weak. Grabbing onto a low branch to steady himself, he fucked her in long, hard strokes. His balls tightened with months of pent-up desperation. The storm inside him broke from his control, and he pummeled into her, using her the way she loved being used, the way he loved to use her. He came into her, his body reminding hers in the bluntest way of who owned it, his swearing muffled by her hair.

For a few moments he kept her trapped there, between his chest and the bark that was probably digging into her back. In the distance, came the faint sound of vehicles pulling up to the house.

"They're here," she whispered in his ear, as though they were teenagers sneaking around behind her parents' back.

"I guess I should go." He wanted to stay, hoping that this one moment of weakness on her part would mean something more. If he walked away now she might just consider it a mistake, rather than a change of heart, but there was no helping it. "I guess me staying would be a little awkward." The joke fell flat, and he wasn't even sure why he'd said it.

She gasped as he pulled out and set her down on her feet. The poor thing wasn't wearing any shoes. It was a good thing she was immune to frostbite. He pulled her to him, trying to make the embrace good enough to last him forever, in case it was the last. He kissed the top of her head, and she burrowed against him, as though she was thinking the same thing.

"I'll stay away as long as I can," he mumbled into her hair. "But when I can't bear it anymore I'll be back."

"We can't do this again," she said quietly. "Once was bad enough."

"I'm coming back anyway. When I do, you can tell me to fuck off then. I'm not taking your answer now, after I just got you off. It's easy to be brave when you're not desperate."

"I don't want to see you again, Valentine," she insisted.

"I know, snowangel, but I can't be sorry I have no choice." Before she could respond, his rope slithered to him, then twined about her before carrying her off to the edge of the tree line.

When she was within sight of the house, he put her down and let her walk the rest of the way with some dignity – stinking of his use and ownership.

*

Sneaking into his own house was a weird concept, and yet that was exactly what he was doing. Although he probably needed and deserved the lecture Dane would give him, he wasn't in the mood to deal with it.

He toed off his snowy boots, then made his way up to the master bath, torn between taking a shower to warm up, but also wanting to smell like her for as long as possible. He missed her already, and was unhappy he couldn't have spent at least a few minutes holding her, even if she'd just spent the time telling him off.

Tonight had been over too fast and already felt like a dream.

Still undecided about the shower, he stripped then collapsed onto his bed, landing on something hard. What the hell?

There was a grunt and a figure sat up in the dimness. Xana.

"What are you doing in my bed?"

"Jeez. I think you're the first man to ever complain about that. My poor ego is wounded." She edged out from under his elbow. "Something woke me up, and when I came to check on you, you were gone." She flicked on the bedside lamp. "Where the fuck did you go in the middle of the night?"

"Out for air."

She studied him then grimaced. "It must be nippier out there than I thought," she grumbled sarcastically, poking his neck where he could still feel Jory's teeth marks throbbing. "So damn smug." She shook her head at him. "And here I thought we'd decided it was better if you stayed away from her."

"Staying away from Jory would be like staying away from air." He frowned at her. "I might be able to do it for a while, but eventually I'd die."

She sighed. "Why are men in love so melodramatic? You won't die just because you can't stick your dick in a specific girl."

Should he tell her? He'd thought he should keep it to himself, but sparing the others, at this point, wouldn't help them understand him.

"No one knows that for sure," he said, touching the mark Jory had left on him. "From the research I've done, we're the first couple with Atypical Aphrodisia who have tried this hard to stay away from each other. The others stayed together until after it had passed, at least. Most stay together even afterward. There is a possibility that indefinite abstinence could kill me – we already know it makes me temporarily unstable. I could die, or never regain my sanity."

Xana's gaze was stark, worried. "So like a sensible man, you went over there tonight just to tell her that and discuss your concerns? Why am I finding that hard to believe?"

A pile of folded clothes sat on top of his dresser. Valentine sorted through them and found a pair of boxers, then pulled them on. It wasn't as if Xana hadn't seen him naked before, but since she looked like she had no intention of leaving his bed, he thought it would be polite to wear something.

He got back into bed and burrowed under the comforter, now feeling the cold he hadn't outside. His body and mind were enjoying a state of deep calm, but it wouldn't last. "You're right. I just went over to talk to her, but when I got there I realized she was making out with some jackass, so I…made my presence known, and took her for a walk."

"A stroll in subzero temperatures sounds very romantic," Xana remarked dryly. "So your romantic nature charmed the pants off her and turned her into a vampire?"

"She was wearing a nightgown, not pants. And the bite mark is the result of a particularly spectacular orgasm. You can't blame the girl." Valentine settled back against the pillow. As fond as he was of Xana, he wished a different woman graced his bed.

"And yet, despite your cocky exterior, you came back here alone, and I can see you're quite possibly more of an emotional mess than when you left."

He stared at the exposed wood beams of the ceiling, wondering if Jory was asleep. Had she showered, or gone to bed smelling like him? Maybe the Bureau people had kept her up to question her, and were on their way to arrest him now.

"Addictions are like that."

Xana turned the bedside lamp back off.

"You won't get over her if you're harboring hope you'll get back together." Xana sighed. "You may have to fuck her to keep your condition under control, but you have to guard your feelings better."

"I won't get over her until the Aphrodisia ends." Not even then.

"I'm calling bullshit right now. This isn't about the Aphrodisia. If you could be satisfied by having sex with someone else, you'd still only want her." She punched his arm. "One sided-love is pathetic."

His mouth twisted in a bitter smile that Xana couldn't see. "That doesn't mean it goes away."

Chapter Four

The dimmed fluorescent lighting did nothing to make the lab look less clinical. Instead, it just set the stage for the scene of a horror movie.

They'd moved her again, along with Asher. There was something about evil mad scientists who were neither evil, nor mad, that made the experience somehow creepier. Ever since she'd returned to the safe house after she'd been with Valentine, Asher had been treating her like a lab rat that'd had the audacity to bite him. He was a researcher who'd been trying to fool her into believing they were friends. He hadn't turned out to be a hero after all.

The drying electrode goop itched. They'd put a cuff on her arm that automatically checked her blood pressure at regular intervals, and a clip on the end of her index finger that probably served some sort of nefarious purpose. None of them made her feel any less naked than they were keeping her. The sheet that had been draped over her had shifted so many times while they worked that neither of them bothered to readjust it anymore, and it was now half draped over her groin, leaving her almost entirely bare.

Dr Asher, in the pristine white lab coat and with a pen behind his ear, was no longer quite as attractive as he'd been a few days ago. He and Bellan, his partner in crime, only ever left her alone when she slept and when she used the bathroom.

The Aphrodisia had control of her body. She was in pain. They'd pumped her full of meds for the first while – things that made her head muzzy, but did nothing to take the edge off. When the condition was at its worst, she screamed and twisted on the hospital bed while they took readings.

In between, if she was lucky, they let her up to walk around. There was a room with a TV they let her into sometimes, not that she could focus long enough to watch. She was never sure what day it was.

The last time she'd been studied, it had felt like being in a hospital. This time it felt like a shady lab experiment.

"I wish we had the male subject here," Bellan muttered. "This data is more than we had, but without information about his side of things, it's hard to tell what we've got."

Asher shook his head. "It's a publish or die world. We'll never have all the data we want. All we can do is say we'd like to do more research and hope for another grant."

"It's such an obscure condition, though. I doubt we'll get much more funding."

Asher smiled grimly. "Think about it, Bellan. A pretty girl desperate for sex? Even when the bigger journals are tired of the study, there will be investors paying scientists to figure out how to make a drug to simulate the effects."

Jory's skin crawled. She'd considered sleeping with this repugnant asshat? And he'd kissed her. Ugh.

"Let me go."

Both pairs of eyes turned back to her, as though they'd forgotten she was there. Or human.

Asher gave her a half-smile. "We will, after the Aphrodisia passes. We promised the Bureau we'd keep you under observation until then."

She opened her mouth to argue, but the cramping started in her lower belly again. Asher's focus narrowed, and he smiled pleasantly.

"Starting again, is it? Maybe this time I'll try something different."

She didn't like the sound of that any more than she liked the way he watched her, speculation in his gaze.

"We were going to do something other than observe?" his henchmen asked, perplexed.

Asher watched Jory while he replied to Bellan. "Well, every time the subject is at the height of discomfort what do we do?"

"We medicate?"

"Yes, to date. And we've tried every pain medication we have on hand, and ordered several from outside pharmacies.

"Yes." Bellan nodded slowly, his eyes sliding back and forth as though it would help jumpstart his brain.

"And when the subject is in that much pain, what does she ask us for? Pills? No."

Rage prickled Jory, and she fought her bonds. "I'm not a subject. I'm a person. I have a name."

Asher's smile morphed into something more disturbing, and it suddenly became apparent that his interest in her was neither personal, nor clinical. It was based in something more twisted than that.

"Of course," he drawled. "Where are my manners?"

Crap. Did he really just say that? It was the verbal equivalent of rubbing his hands together in nefarious glee.

"You are, of course, Jory Savage. A hero who should be treated like a hero, and not like a little whore who sneaks off to fuck villains who break into Bureau safe houses." The words were venomous.

Bellan stepped forward and put himself between Jory and Asher. "I don't think we should be talking to her like that. She has a point. She's a person, not just an experiment. And it's her body. What she does and with whom is none of our business."

The reminder that he wasn't alone in the room with only a helpless Jory seemed to take Asher by surprise. He pasted a calmer expression over the glimpse she'd caught of his true emotions. Was Bellan going to fall for it?

"No, no. You don't understand," Asher said with only the briefest hesitation. "I've read the reports subpoenaed from Dr Gardner's office. This is what she responds to – what she likes. Believe me, I tried the soft and friendly approach when we were alone together at the last safe house and she doesn't respond to it at all. This is what she needs. She's a sexual submissive. Have you done any reading on the subject?"

Bellan gave a one-shouldered shrug, as though he didn't want to admit to Asher that he was ignorant about anything.

"That's what I thought. I've done extensive research on the subject online over the past couple of days, so just trust me on this. She doesn't want to be treated like a lady. She likes to be roughed up."

Oh god, what the hell had he been reading?

The lust tried to claim her, but she fought it back. She couldn't lose control now, here, when Asher was acting like this and there was no one to protect her.

Bellan's eyes had gone round, but he nodded as if Asher's word was gospel.

"No, that's not how it works," she protested.

"Did you know that sadomasochism was considered a mental illness until relatively recently?" Asher cut her off smoothly. "I'm sure they changed that to be politically correct, but the fact remains that it's a deviancy we unfortunately have to cater to if we're going to help the subject… Jory…with her *interesting* medical issue."

Was it possible the Bureau had decided to get even with her for not accepting any of the teams they'd tried to match her with by handing her over to a man who would beat the crap out of her then rape her in the name of science?

No, they wouldn't have approved this. She couldn't let herself believe that. They were the good guys.

Right?

Closing her eyes, she felt around in her mind, trying to find her power and wake it, but the drugs they'd been pumping into her had taken their toll. Unlike the damned Aphrodisia, her power was dormant.

She was so screwed.

She clawed at the bed's side rails underneath her restrained hands, hoping to find something she could use to hurt him with if he got too close, but she couldn't reach anything. The heat inside her spread outward, creeping up her body until even her skin itched with need. In moments she'd be begging for cock even though they both knew it wasn't him she wanted or needed. The way he watched her said he was going to turn her misfortune to his advantage. It would be her word against his if she went to the Bureau, with his assistant the only witness.

The sheet slid to the floor, abandoning her entirely. Naked and defenseless, she fought, trying to pull a wrist or ankle free to fend him off. He casually slid the extendible end of the exam table closed, and moved between her spread legs, probably waiting for her to beg for him. One of his hands caressed the inside of her thigh and she ground her teeth, hating that her body was trying to react, even though he was touching her against her will.

"Get your hand off me, Asher. I don't want you."

"You will, shortly. I can see your symptoms are getting worse."

Fire burned through her, but it seemed like Asher was the one barely in control of himself. Valentine had said her pheromones when she was in the grip of their condition made her irresistible to Atypicals, but this wasn't just a guy at the grocery store flirting with her.

"No matter what the Aphrodisia makes me say, it's still rape," she snarled.

"You know it's not what I want. I want that on record, Bellan."

Asher's hand inched up her thigh, and she couldn't hold back a squirm. "You'll change your mind shortly. Besides, we've measured what we can while you writhe around alone on a bed. We have to move on to other tests or we won't get sufficient data."

"Substituting yourself for him won't help anyone but you, and as soon as I'm free, or he finds you, one of us will kill you. Is it worth it?"

Asher remained silent, but his hand sliding closer to her privates made words unnecessary.

Her last hope was that Bellan would do the right thing and call for help. He didn't look like he could take Asher in a fight, but picking up the phone wasn't that hard. Yet even though his brow was creased with worry, he wasn't moving to stop Asher or have him stopped. Even if he did speak up or sneak off to make a phone call, would enforcers get to them before Asher took what he wanted? And if they did come, would they stop him? She didn't know what the Bureau had written into his contract, or even what was in the fine print of her own.

Weakness swept over her. She could feel herself babbling as her body smoldered. It was too late now to worry about what came out of her mouth. Loathing Asher only worked for so long before she started begging.

The sound of a fly being unzipped brought with it a shiver of horror. She needed cock, but knew somewhere deep down inside that this wasn't what, or who, she wanted. Sluggishly, her power objected, tried to rise up to protect her body from his invasion, but it fell, crawled, collapsed.

A man's voice cried out.

Her arms and legs were freed.

An animal was screaming.

Something warm wrapped and restrained her.

"We're going to get you out of here, baby girl." A woman's voice. Familiar. Swooping. Movement. A vehicle. The animal sounded rabid. Mad. Darkness.

She fainted or slept, and woke in a comfortable bed. Need nagged her, but she could think, at least. For now.

Day followed night. She was fed. The need became crippling, waned long enough for her to sleep, Asher's drugs making her sluggish, confused, and exhausted. Fire came again. She begged for easing, but she was only held and spoken to with gentle words.

The animal called.

He needed her.

The howls were farther off, like they were coming from behind a thick door.

"He's worse," came a low, muffled voice. Male.

"We can't throw her to him when he's like this." The woman again.

"Of course not. I just wish there was something we could do."

Silence.

Hours. Days?

A door creaked open, waking her. Xana stood there, holding a bottle of water and a straw.

"You're awake!" She strode over to the side of Jory's bed – Valentine's bed – and offered the water to her. "Thank god. We weren't sure if it was the drugs or the Aphrodisia making you so spacey. I'm sorry we took you like that. We didn't know what else to do." Her eyes were wide, worried – not showing any of her usual self-confidence or bravado. "But when we broke in and saw…I don't know if you signed up for that, Jory, but when I saw what he was about to do, I punched him in the face a few times –"

"More than a few," Jurgen said with some satisfaction.

"And put him through the wall," Xana finished, still sounding pissed. "I hope you didn't like the guy. We left them there and called it in to the enforcers, though, so he *should* recover."

"You should have let me kill them," Jurgen muttered from behind her. "The fucking Bureau. After everything else she's been through, they gave him carte blanche? And to drug her powers like that to keep her helpless? It's a good thing Val was coherent enough to explain what he felt in her mind, even if his Jory GPS had us going in circles for a few hours. They never should have moved her so close to the coach house. They probably thought they'd hide her right under his nose. Idiots. Aren't there laws about experimentation on Atypicals in this day and age?"

Jory could hear him pacing, but was having trouble meeting their eyes. She just wanted to curl up and go back to sleep. That whole episode with Asher felt far off, like a bad dream she'd had years before. Thank god they'd shown up when they had.

"Well, now she's safe and she can decide for herself what to do the next time she sees him. You *know* the Bureau reserves the right to experiment on heroes as it sees fit, but…" Xana shrugged. "I don't even know what to say.

I think we stopped him before anything happened. Were you okay with what was going on, Jory? We can take you back there if you want."

She shuddered, but she was angry and revolted, rather than upset. "Hell no. I asked them to hide me from Valentine, not to let researchers grope me, or worse."

"That's what Valentine said, but he's…not well, so it's hard to know how much of what he's saying is delusional."

Not well?

A scream tore the air. Xana and Jurgen both glanced back over their shoulders then turned their attention back to her.

"That isn't him, is it?" Something in her chest flinched, and she pushed herself upright, swinging her feet to the floor. She wasn't sure why she'd said that, because she could feel his distress now as though it was her own. Why was he so much worse off than she was this time? Stupid Aphrodisia. It was so unpredictable.

"You probably shouldn't go in there, after everything else you've been through. You don't want to see him like this." Xana stepped between her and the door, trying to chivvy her back to bed. "Do you want something to eat? You must be hungry."

Jory glanced around now that her head was clearing. It was Valentine's room in the coach house alright, but his bed only smelled like her. She tried to see past them.

"Where is he?"

"Restrained," Xana admitted. "He was bad enough before, but having you so close seems to be making him worse."

She squeezed past Xana and Jurgen, the oversized t-shirt she was wearing rippling around her knees. They followed her, trying to convince her to stay away from him as she padded down several flights of stairs. Inside her, the power still felt dull and sluggish, but even so, it knew where he was.

At the bottom of the steps, she pushed open the basement door.

Bound to the padded wooden X in the center of the room, Valentine thrashed, trying to free himself. Although he was the epitome of hot kinky porn with his leather pants, heavy boots, and torn t-shirt, his helpless rage made her eyes well with tears. Yes, she'd been hiding from him, but her love for him hadn't waned any more than the lust had. Seeing her dominant at the mercy of others, even if it was for his own good, hurt her more deeply than she would have expected.

This wasn't right.

Dane, who'd been sitting in a chair, lurched to his feet, trying to calm his sudden burst of movement. Valentine's black gaze bored into Jory. His frenetic movements made the wood creak alarmingly.

"Out!" Dane glared at Jory and pointed at the door.

She hated that Dane was upset with her, but she had to help Valentine, even if it was just for the time being. She couldn't leave him like this, knowing she was the only person who might be able to ease his suffering. It wasn't fair to her either, but the Aphrodisia didn't care about fairness, only about being obeyed.

Then again, if his reaction to her avoiding him was this extreme, every time they had a cycle of Aphrodisia they'd have to be together, no matter what it did to her self-esteem.

"Maybe I can help."

"For fuck's sake, Jory. You can't have it both ways. You want to get away from him, but then you feel bad and want to help him? Which is it? He's a fucking mess because of you. You have the right to end things with him, but you can't keep stringing him along."

Stringing him along? It was like a blow. It hadn't been her intention but she understood his accusation. If they assumed she was a bitch, why had they saved her? For Valentine's sake? But Xana was being so kind. Maybe she understood how hard it was for her to leave him.

She let her gaze follow the strong lines of his cheekbones and jaw, explore the depths of his black eyes. But he didn't look like he had last time, in the forest outside the safe house. Then, there'd been some semblance of control. He wasn't himself at all anymore. Now guilt and pity were added to the pile of other feelings she had for him.

He screamed for her, his mouth opening so wide she was afraid he'd dislocate his jaw. If she was staying, she needed to get on with trying to help him.

Tears prickled her eyes. God, she loved him. It was easier to pretend she didn't when they were apart. Seeing him suffering like this hurt like hell. Was her well-being more important than his? No.

"I didn't know this would happen to him," she begged for them to understand. "You don't get what it's like, wanting something you're ashamed of. But when I walk away he suffers. It's an impossible situation."

Valentine seemed to be losing more than she ever had. The screaming had calmed for now, but he snarled and mumbled. His long hair hung around his face, making him look as mad as he sounded.

"Being submissive isn't something you need to be ashamed of, but I know you struggle with it." Dane sighed. "What you can live with is a very personal decision and isn't anyone's business but yours. And this? This isn't your fault. It's just really hard to see him…" Dane's voice was rough and thick. Jurgen slid past her and wrapped his arms around him.

"Let me try to help," she murmured, her steps drawn to Valentine as he summoned her without words. "Maybe I can bring him back."

Dane and Jurgen exchanged worried glances, but she knew they'd all abide by her decision.

"I don't like him tied like this. Can you let him go?"

"If we let him go, it may not be safe for you," Xana replied, shaking her head. "If we took that chance and he hurt you, he'd never forgive us. We wouldn't forgive ourselves."

"But…" It just wasn't right. It wasn't her place to be free while he was bound. "Never mind. I'll figure it out. Can we have some privacy?"

As she got closer, Valentine started panting, his eyes feverish. He growled.

A thrill of desire made her whimper. The others had a brief disagreement among themselves, which she ignored then they withdrew from the room.

"We're going to be right outside the door," Xana told her as she paused, her hand on the doorknob. "If things get out of hand, we'll be back in here fast. Don't undo his cuffs, Jory, no matter how weird this feels to you."

The door clicked shut.

His rumble was low.

"Xana said no, Sir. If I let you go, you're going to hurt me."

Evil dark eyes followed her as she approached. His thoughts were nasty and primal, but then so were her own.

"Do you remember me, sir?" Was there anything of him left? There had to be. Trying to talk to him to bring him out of this was a waste of time. This wasn't about talking, but he was like a stranger. Initiating something with Valentine remembering her was difficult enough. Now he wasn't a man, he was more of a beast.

The Aphrodisia urged her forward, recognizing him clearly even though they were like strangers to each other. He was bound, but what if he got free? Wild like this, he could kill her.

She stood, debating, until she realized she was just stalling the inevitable. Screw it.

She let the blanket she wore fall away, and drew off the oversized t-shirt to stand naked before him. The sight of her body made him wrench so hard at the restraints, the wood squealed in protest.

He laughed madly. Angrily. As responses went, it was far from comforting. Visions of him doing serious damage to her played out in her mind.

What could she do that might calm him? Did she seem like a threat?

To appease him, she fell to her knees and knelt the way he preferred when they were alone. She waited until his eyes seared holes in her flesh then she crawled to him. His scent reached her partway through the room – now a mixture of man, leather, sweat and desire. The smell of him permeated her brain. Aphrodisia tried to reclaim her senses, but with him helpless, she couldn't lie back and be his eager victim.

When she reached the space between his black boots, she knelt again and put her palms on his straining thighs. "Sir, may I please take you in my mouth?"

There was no answer, just a watchful silence. She slid her hands to his fly, and freed his cock. It pulsed and twitched. Valentine hissed at her like a feral cat.

What if she couldn't bring him back? What if they needed to hand him over to the Bureau to see if they could find some treatment for him? They hadn't been able to help her, but his team couldn't just lock him away in the basement and hope it eventually passed. Not when it turned him into little more than an animal.

Her need for him urged her on. She opened her mouth and took him in as far as she could, until the tip of his cock hit the back of her throat. There was no taking all of it, but she sucked the best she could with him this deep. Bliss flowed through her as she pleasured him. He was inside her, where he belonged. She sucked and licked, listening to his body, giving him what they both needed. She longed to feel his hands in her hair, but not now. Not yet.

His power, wild and unharnessed by conscious thought, fell on hers like an avalanche, trapping it. In response, her power submitted to his. She lost herself in worshiping the smooth warmth of his cock, moving up and down on his length, her tongue reacquainting itself with him.

Without warning, he grunted and released into her mouth. She struggled and coughed, unable to keep up with his deluge. Warm satisfaction and exhaustion tried to claim her after needing him for so long, but it lasted only a moment before the ache between her legs started again.

Did Aphrodisia mean one of them had to go mad to keep the other sane?

"Mine," he growled.

A word. A real one, instead of just noises. Not her name, but it was better than the trapped animal noises he'd been making. Elation flickered, but was quickly snuffed by reality. A single word didn't mean much.

His dick was still hard, and she brushed her lips over his balls, enjoying the way it made him shudder. She could feel his need deep in her mind, and her own rose to answer it. This situation could have been fun if he'd been himself, although the idea of the punishment he would deliver once she was brave enough to let him go was scary.

"Xana said I couldn't let you go," she explained, as though he'd asked her to. She thought about going down on him again, but it wasn't good enough anymore. They both needed sex, but how could she manage with him tied this way?

Awkwardly, she grabbed onto the top of the X on either side of his head, and found perches for her feet on the wood behind his legs. She rubbed her pussy against him, sighing with the pleasure of feeling him against her, but needing more. A string of garbled profanity fell from his mouth, and he stabbed at her with his body, grunting in frustration when he couldn't guide himself into her.

Carefully, she supported herself with one hand and grabbed his erection, then coaxed him deep inside her, every inch making her impatient for the next. When their bodies were fitted together, throbbing, she stopped, not sure she could go on. Hot chills shot through her, making her shake. She wanted nothing more than to untie him and let him take over. Valentine cried out, and for a moment she thought one or both of them would come. She grabbed the inside of the X and pulled herself tighter against him, struggling to make the position work until she discovered that gravity did half of the work for her.

Her control over the situation was a temporary illusion.

Although he was restrained at wrists and ankles, he pummeled up into her like an animal, barely pulling out before thrusting brutally back in. She clung to her hand and footholds to keep from being fucked off her perch, but his rough use made her pussy ache and burn. His power invaded her, claiming every inch of her as its own. Wood dug into her palms and soles, but the ecstasy of having him inside her made the pain inconsequential.

"Please, Sir, I need to come." The words came out in a pathetic, gasping whine. In his state she didn't expect him to respond, but something shifted in her mind, like a thrown switch. Either silent permission or he was too wild to control her pleasure.

Her body clamped down on his, the grinding friction of his pubic bone against her clit making her eyelids flutter closed. The orgasm gripped her and her legs trembled. A cry of pleasure tore from her lips and his next thrust almost robbed her of her tenuous grip. He bellowed as he found his release, then bit down on the spot between her shoulder and neck like some sort of perverted, sadistic vampire. She screamed, the pain abruptly ending the pleasure of her orgasm.

The door burst open and his team poured in, just as Valentine's teeth eased their death grip on her flesh. Gasping, knowing she should be embarrassed, she pulled off of him and lowered herself to the floor. Valentine's cock had sprung free of her, still rock hard. Come dripped from them both.

"Sorry," Xana mumbled. "We thought he was hurting you."

"He was, but I'm okay," Jory said, she checked her shoulder for blood, but there was only a lurid purple bruise there, rapidly darkening. She grabbed the blanket off the floor and wrapped it around her nakedness. It wasn't anything they hadn't seen before, but modesty hovered somewhere in the background of her mind, reminding her she might regret this later. A sheen of sweat slicked her skin, and her legs felt as though they were going to give way.

Some of the wildness in Valentine's gaze was gone. He watched her – a wary, wounded beast. In her mind she could feel him growing calmer and more sensible, but he needed more of her before there'd be a chance he'd come back to them entirely. His cock pulsed impatiently, and her body was ready to beg for more if it needed to.

"I know he's not himself yet, but I've done all I can with him trussed up like this. I need help to untie him."

Chapter Five

The girl had covered herself. Anger pulsed through him, buzzing in his ears and setting his teeth on edge. The ones who had trapped him moved closer. He watched them quietly, waiting for them to make a mistake.

They untied him. As mistakes went, that one was the best.

"Valentine, we're letting you go." One of the blond men smiled at him carefully. "Stay calm now or we'll have to restrain you again, okay?"

He did his best to hide his disdain for the man.

Nearby he could feel rope coiled, waiting. He flexed his mind, wondering why he'd forgotten about rope, and how it felt. Rope felt good. Clean. Skeins of it wove together in his mind, reminding him of how obedient it was, and how it longed to be commanded.

The girl longed to be commanded too. He wanted only to be buried inside her, but these others were interfering.

When all bonds had been released, he stepped away from the wooden contraption, stretching while he watched his captors. They talked to each other for a few minutes then left the room, leaving him alone with the girl.

He snapped his fingers and gestured, his body remembering the silent language they shared even though his mind did not. The girl's eyes widened, and she dropped the blanket and fell to her knees, cupping her breasts and shyly offering them up to him.

Her white hair billowed around her, drifting and settling slowly on her shoulders like a frost cloud. His gaze devoured every perfect curve of her. No other woman had ever been made more beautifully – more perfectly suited to him.

His mind drooled for her.

Escape would have to wait.

He walked around her, appraising. "Who owns you?" His voice sounded harsh to his ears, but the girl didn't flinch from him.

She hesitated a moment. "You, Sir." It sounded like an admission she hadn't wanted to make, as though she was afraid to admit it, but hearing her say it filled him with satisfaction.

Vague memories flickered of taking her in delicious and humiliating ways. His cock was prompting him to do it again.

"Where were you? Why were you gone?"

"I was scared," she whispered. "I ran away."

"Scared," he echoed. "Why? Do I hurt you?" He moved closer to her. The way she trembled before him made him *want* to hurt her. Her screams of pleasure had been lovely. Her screams of pain would be like a drug.

"Yes, Sir, but you stop when I say 'red.'" A line of worry drew her elegant brows closer together.

"Do I?" A laugh he couldn't control rippled out.

She bowed her head, tilting it aside to expose her freshly bitten neck. She was exquisite. "Why do I do that?"

"Because we love each other, Sir. You told me you love me and you wouldn't harm me."

"Interesting."

Her gaze shot up to his face, her anxiety palpable. "You don't remember me, Sir?"

"No," he conceded, "but I want that pretty cunt of yours again."

The alabaster skin of her chest went pink, and the color crept up her neck to stain her cheeks. It was no wonder he'd claimed her.

But why couldn't he remember what she spoke of?

He pointed at the bed and made a gesture that caused her to blush harder. She crawled to the bed and positioned herself on the mattress, face down, ass up, like he'd ordered.

"What do I call you?"

"My name is Jory."

"That isn't what I asked you."

She shivered. "You call me snowangel."

When he snorted, she hid her face. The lush roundness of her bottom beckoned.

"Tell me – snowangel," he said the name mockingly. Whatever she'd meant to him before, she was nothing now, other than a pretty collection of holes to use. "Do you like having me buried in your ass?"

Her moan of dismay was so very lovely. "You've only done it once, Sir. It h-hurt."

The distress in her voice set his pulse to racing. "Only once?" he asked skeptically. "Why would I deprive myself of this?" He grabbed a handful of ass cheek and she groaned.

"The last time you did it, I ran away and didn't come back," she said quietly.

Irritation flashed, fed by vaguely remembered betrayal, all the worse because he could remember the feeling but not the reasons. "You ran away just because of that? Was it that appalling?"

Seeing no reason to restrain himself from claiming what she was so freely offering, he moved up behind her on the bed and slid a finger inside her pussy, which still dripped his spendings. He smeared a slippery finger over her asshole. She moaned low and shivered for him, but didn't tell him to stop, not that he was sure he would. Slowly, he worked his finger into her, as she whimpered into the pillow.

"Sir, if you're going to fuck me there, could you please use lube? There's probably some in the cabinet."

"I may." Would he even fit? He'd damn well make it fit. "Did I use lube the first time?"

"Yes, Sir." Her voice had gone breathy, and she was starting to squirm again.

"Hmm. Well, it's your second time, you shouldn't need any," he said darkly. "Your body should tolerate me." He held back a chuckle at her sound of distress, and rammed his still-erect cock into her pussy while he slowly finger-fucked her ass.

She sobbed, but held very, very still, her sounds and shudders forcing him to focus on his breathing until the overwhelming urge to come was under control. Not yet.

Without giving her any warning, he withdrew, thoroughly enjoying her gasp of dismay. "Stay," he growled, slapping her ass.

He washed his hands in the sink next that stood in one corner then went to the cupboard she'd indicated. Opening the doors revealed a wide array of bondage equipment, along with the rope he'd felt was there. It took only a moment to make a few selections then return to the girl.

"What are you going to do with those?" She stared at the items he'd dumped on the bed.

"Whatever I like." Although she wasn't fighting or complaining, he manhandled her with unnecessary roughness as he cuffed her wrists and ankles, then clipped both to a spreader bar to keep her in position. Secured, she tugged at the cuffs, testing them, wriggling her sexy ass, obliviously luring him to do what she claimed she didn't want.

Opening the bottle of lube he'd found, he squirted some directly onto her skin. It must have been cold because she squealed and tried to escape with renewed vigor.

He worked one finger back into her, easier now, but it took some effort and extra lube to get a second finger in.

"Please, Sir. Use my mouth or my pussy instead." She sounded so pitiful it made him chuckle. "I'll cooperate with anything else you want."

"You don't want me to use your ass, so that's what I want. Besides, you can't exactly be uncooperative when I have you tied like this."

"Bastard." The whimper that followed the word made his dick pulse in appreciation. "I should have left you tied up."

As he lubed his cock, he contemplated just coming on her ass and leaving her horny. As much as she claimed she didn't want it, the word "red" hadn't passed her lips, and her body was reacting to his enthusiastically, even if her ass was pleasantly reluctant.

He toyed with her a few more minutes then lined his dick up with her ass just as she started to beg for release.

"Noooo!" She gasped. Her body clenched against him.

"That's right," he murmured. "Squeeze tighter, girl. Keep me out as long as you can."

She could only keep it up so long until her muscles automatically relaxed. Wide-eyed distress came at the same moment she realized her body was opening for him whether she liked it or not.

With a bit of pressure, the tip of his cock broached her asshole, and her small keening whines as he invaded her body excited him. Inch by tight inch he persuaded his way in, her sobs almost drowned out by his moans of pleasure. The hot grasp of her ass on his cock forced him to still as his body throbbed with his impending orgasm. The tension in his balls was agony.

"Don't fucking move." He closed his eyes, and eased his power's control of hers, letting the two lace together the way it had been urging him to, even though it felt strange and invasive. The two melted into each other, swirling and combining until it was a bright, pulsating sphere. Sparks of breathless pleasure flared through him. Under him, the girl cried out rapturously. He started to move inside her, and although he was half-insensible, he reached underneath her and stroked her clit.

"Please let me come," she screamed. "Please, Sir!"

"Your body belongs to me," he whispered harshly near her ear. "I'm going to come in your ass so hard you'll never forget who owns you."

The sounds she uttered in response weren't human.

He gave over to the urge to move, pistoning into her ass hard and fast, the slap of his skin against hers loud in the room. He used her body to bring himself to the edge twice, slowing down to nothing right before he would have come.

As he stilled the second time, she screamed and struggled.

"Please! Please!" Her begging was so loud it hurt his ears.

"Please what, woman?"

"Please, Sir, let me come. I'll do anything you want."

Anything? He liked the sound of that.

Catching cruel hold of her clit, he barked, "Come now."

Her body clenched around him, trembling and shuddering, the pain and pleasure combining, echoing in his mind. He crammed his cock in tighter, as deep as it would go, and his come erupted into her, the ecstasy half-blinding him and turning him inside out. She screamed and sobbed through orgasms he lost count of, and he was pleased he'd made her beg for something she'd claimed not to want. The feel of being so thoroughly joined, body and mind, was overwhelming. Sweet and nasty and addictive.

Why had he ever allowed her to escape?

Eventually she quieted and went limp, panting. Her hair was slick with sweat and stuck to the side of her face. She was crying, and from inside her mind he could feel how exhausted she was, and how sore.

Deeply satisfied, he withdrew from her then unclipped the cuffs from the spreader bar. She collapsed onto her side and curled into ball, silent tears trickled over the bridge of her nose to fall onto the bed. Their powers withdrew from each other, and the shock of separation made him grunt in discomfort. He knelt up, watching in fascination as her ass slowly closed up, dripping come and lube. If he decided to fuck her there again, even if it was in a few minutes, he'd probably have trouble getting back in.

Despite the orgasm, his cock was still ready for more. He went to the sink again and washed off, wishing there was a shower in the room.

The sound of the girl's quiet weeping probably should have disturbed him. It didn't.

*

Bleary-eyed, he wandered through the ruins of the big house's snowy foundation, climbing the uneven rocks and balancing on the creaky boards. In the coach house library he'd found a photo of what the place used to look like, back when it was new, before time and the elements had brought it to its current level of decay.

To be safe, he probably should have had it demolished, the old detritus carted away, and the hole filled in, but there was something about the place that pleased him. It was like having a huge jar of buttons or seashells in his backyard. Abandoned quickly, as it had been, and forgotten about, there were always odds and ends to sift through, and peculiar prizes to be found.

This place he recalled vividly. Why didn't he remember people or his history with them? All he got were vague shadows of memory, like a slate that hadn't entirely been wiped clean.

The ruins kept his mind busy while he exercised muscles he'd forgotten he owned. Two weeks of servicing the girl had taken their toll. Walking and climbing used different muscles than fucking, and his legs seized and ached.

He'd left her asleep in the house, knowing she'd probably wake just as addled and sex-starved as when she'd fallen asleep. The rope around her neck would tell him when she woke, possibly even before their mental connection did.

But today, after he took care of her body, he'd need to bring her outside. It was relatively warm out, and she hadn't seen much of the sun for days. She was getting too thin, too pale, and he wondered when this sexual hunger would pass so that they could be free.

But free to do what?

The other people who'd been there, who acted like friends, had left on the second day after the girl had come, saying they needed to go out on a job. But what did he do in life, other than fuck the girl?

Her name was Jory, she's said, but there was no need for names when it was only the two of them. Using her name made her too human. She was already getting under his skin as it was, and it was pissing him off.

Sweet and needy, she looked to him for everything. He fucked her, bathed her, and fed her. He tried to get away with not giving her affection, but she was stubborn. Like a cat who'd discovered a person who hated cats, she was constantly crawling into his lap, bothering him until he petted her out of self defense.

She was…impossible to ignore. It would be difficult enough, considering how submissive and desperate for him she was, but she loved him so fiercely and candidly it was getting more and more difficult to remain aloof. Several times she'd fallen asleep in his lap, curled there like a trusting child, her lashes like whitest down against her cheek. A protective instinct he hadn't known he possessed reared its ugly head.

She claimed they loved each other, but he had nothing but her word, and a general disgust with himself for the flicker of emotion he felt when she told him about other times they'd been together, and things they'd done. She'd even shown him scars on her body he'd healed, but he had no true memory to go with the stories. She was horrified by the scarification on his own body, and had kissed each separate line. But most of her lucid thoughts were gone now. She'd become a needy little doll, pretty and empty.

He made the circuit around the great house, but the snow made it too slippery to go into the basement and spelunk. When he turned to look behind him, he enjoyed the way his footprints marred the pristine white of the low drifts. It made him think of how he'd marked her, body and mind. How he'd tampered with her and she'd allowed it, eager for any attention from him, even if it hurt. The feeling of euphoria it gave him was heady, and he always wanted more. He'd lost track of how many times he'd taken her today alone.

He'd bathed her and tucked her in then watched as sleep stole her away from him, annoyed at his own tender feelings, but even though he could feel she was still asleep, his desire for her was growing again. He wanted to claim her. To mark her more thoroughly.

The toy cabinet in the coach house had several things he hadn't used, but one drawer in particular had caught his interest.

As he entered the room, she stirred on the rug on which she slept at the foot of his bed. The collar he'd made was like elegant lace against her pale skin. The rope that led from her ankle to the bed frame had coiled itself neatly beside her. It was long enough for her to reach the sink, but not leave the room. He didn't permit her to leave the room off-leash, although she was so used to following at his heel he doubted she needed one anymore.

The drawer, when he opened it, held what he remembered, and he withdrew what he wanted. It took only a few minutes to prepare things, and then he lifted the sleeping girl onto the bed. She woke.

"Sir?"

"Hmm?"

She eyed his expression then furtively glanced around, her gaze falling on the side table.

"What are you going to do with that?"

He pulled gloves onto his washed hands then spread her legs. There was the slightest hesitation before she cooperated. It was the first sign of independent thought she'd had in days.

"Just a small piercing. Don't worry, I know what I'm doing." Although he couldn't remember how he knew. He'd simply known as soon as he'd stumbled across the drawer.

Her breathing sped up, and her eyes widened in fear, but there was a quiet acceptance there that stirred his cock.

"Shh," he exposed her clitoral hood, which was exactly right for this piercing. She gasped and her hands wrapped in the sheets. A whimper escaped her and she thrust her hips at him, already seeking relief even though she'd just roused from sleep. He didn't have the heart to tell her they'd have to wait until she healed before he could service her that way again. Maybe this was a bad idea, considering the demands of the Aphrodisia, but he needed to mark her, and it was this or carving his name into her flesh like a barbarian.

"But why?" Her brows were high, but she didn't seem that averse to the idea.

"Because I want to. Spread your legs wider."

Her fear was almost as sexy as the lowering of her gaze and small nod. She opened her legs further apart, giving him an unimpeded view of her softness.

"I trust you, Valentine."

Silly girl. Although she was safe enough in this circumstance. He prepped her and slid the needle-receiving tube into place, trying to ignore her gasp of arousal. If her reactions made him too horny, he could fuck up the process.

"Don't move."

"Will it hurt?"

"Yes, but only a pinch."

Her whine made him shift to ease the pressure of denim on his throbbing cock. He reached out with his power and took hers captive, forcing it to submit to what he was about to do. Somehow he knew the same would work if he chose to impregnate her, and again he had to fight down the urge to put a baby in her pretty belly.

He took a deep breath, held it, then pushed the needle into her delicate flesh. Her wail almost set him off in his jeans.

"It didn't hurt that much," he mumbled, overcome with raw desire as she stared at him in horror.

"You've hurt me worse there," she admitted. "It just – I just…" She shuddered.

"What?"

"I almost came." She caught her nipples between her fingers and squeezed them hard. For a moment he was so distracted by her lust-hazed eyes he forgot what he was doing.

"Stay still, woman." He fitted the piercing with a ring and closed it. A wave of possessive need made him want to throw her down and fuck her immediately, but now he'd have to wait until she healed.

"Do you like it, Sir?"

Not 'can I see it?' or even a glance down to see if she liked it, herself. She only cared about pleasing him.

She was maddening. Addictive. This wasn't how things were supposed to happen.

Gently, he toggled the ring with his still-gloved hand. She moaned and her hips came up off the bed.

"Please, Sir. I need you."

"No sex until that's healed," he grumbled then got to his feet and put the piercing supplies away.

She fell unexpectedly silent. He'd expected begging, crying, maybe some screams of frustration.

When he turned back to her, she simply knelt on the floor beside the bed.

"Sir, you look uncomfortable."

Damn, he was.

"There's nothing wrong with my mouth," she reminded him, her cheeks rosy. She caught her bottom lip between her teeth and squirmed where she knelt.

The woman had a point.

Chapter Six

Sir was asleep.

She crept to the door and peered out. Was anyone else in the house? One tentative foot slid to where the basement ended and the hallway began, but stopped as though she'd stubbed her toe on an invisible barrier.

Stay. Bad girl. Not allowed.

She flinched back and stared down at her too-obedient feet. How could she find clothes and get out of the house if she couldn't bring herself to set foot outside the room? It was hard to stuff down the panic. Her fingers went to her collar. Had it tightened around her neck?

Through a haze, she remembered Sir taking off the ankle rope days ago, but the collar was still on. Would it tell him if she broke the rules? She imagined him waking to find her standing just outside the room, disapproval in the uninterrupted black of his eerie eyes. Fear of being punished, of disappointing him, didn't stop her thighs from growing damp, although it was hard to say what was from her perpetual arousal, and what was the leavings from his most recent use. It had been more than a day since he'd taken her last. It was probably the only reason she was thinking straight – the first time she even felt like a shadow of herself.

If she didn't go now, she might never be strong enough. She was so seamlessly bonded to him it was hard to know what thoughts were her own, and which he'd put there or trained her to believe. He'd used her body, his power, and their connection, to brainwash her, but she'd wanted to be brainwashed. How could serving him and not thinking for herself make her so damned content?

This wasn't what she wanted the sum total of her life to be. She was meant to be more than a come dump.

The first step out of the room made her innards tremble, churn, and squeeze, as though she needed to get to a bathroom fast. She gasped for breath, covering her mouth and nose with her forearm, trying to be quiet. Any minute a big hand was going to grab her from behind. A growling voice would ask her where she thought she was going.

Like a terrified child, she crept up the stairs. As she'd suspected, no one else was there. She hadn't heard anyone moving around in the living room or kitchen for what seemed like days. One more flight up and she was in the bedroom. Her clothing was nowhere to be seen, so she bundled on some of his, rolling pant legs and shirt cuffs, and jammed a pair of too-big shoes on her feet. Clothes felt strange against her skin, chaffing and distracting.

Part of her mind wept, begging her to go back, but she set her jaw and headed for the door. If she stole his truck, he'd have more reason to track her down, so she ignored the lure of the keys on the table by the front door and went back to the kitchen for a knife.

A creak on the stairs stopped her heart. She paused with her hand on the handle of a small kitchen knife, her heart beating so loud in her ears she had to strain to hear past it. The trembling in her limbs made the blade tap against the granite countertop, so she moved a cautious step into the middle of the room, knife in hand. What was she willing to do? How far was she willing to go if he tried to keep her there?

Valentine had changed fundamentally since she'd brought him back to himself. A stranger lived in his body, and there was no knowing what he was capable of. When she'd untied him in the basement, she'd been reasonably sure she could bring him back, but it just wasn't working. She could remain this stranger's sex slave, but he scared her more than the old Valentine ever had. His control over her hadn't waned, but now it was impossible to guess what he'd do with that control.

She'd trusted Valentine, but this man wasn't Valentine.

When the top of his dark head didn't become visible in the stairwell, her heart slowed slightly, and skipped a few beats. Just old stairs creaking? She walked to the door backward, her eyes trained on the basement doorway.

As quietly as she could, she opened the front door and backed out onto the step, closing it behind her with only the slightest click. It popped open again and she stifled a shriek. Just the wind. Sweat beaded on her brow, stung in her armpits, and her neck felt hot.

Carefully, she crunched over the snow-covered gravel to his truck, and slashed two of his tires before setting off for the main road.

*

Having no one to turn to was a cold life. Alone, still fighting off the remnants of her conditioning, she knew she had to avoid people. Involving her parents or Amy – asking them to help, or to hide her – could put them in danger and would make her too easy to find.

As she trudged through the snow in Valentine's too-big stolen shoes, a multitude of crazy ideas popped into her head. If she wanted to avoid the Bureau, and Valentine, there weren't many places for her to go. She thought of calling Xana to see if she had any ideas, but there was no way to know whose side she was on. Valentine's teammates weren't likely to help her behind his back, no matter how strange he was acting. Her teammates would have helped her. They wouldn't have abandoned her to deal with this alone, but they were dead. So very, very dead.

On the main road she got a ride almost immediately. The lone man didn't talk much or ask questions, although he did ask if she was okay when she asked to be let out in the middle of nowhere.

When his tailgate had disappeared, she walked into the woods, wandering, hoping she was far enough away that Valentine wouldn't be able to feel her. Eventually she stumbled across a seasonal road, and she followed alongside it. Maybe it would lead her to a place she could stop for the night. Hours later, a deserted hunt camp loomed out of the darkness, creepy, but shelter nonetheless. Although she couldn't get frostbite, her stolen shoes had given her blisters.

She formed a lock pick out of ice and broke into the place. Would the owners show up tonight? It seemed as if everything had been winterized, but maybe that was wishful thinking. With the woodstove going and snow melted and boiling in a pot, she didn't need much else. Other than food.

There was nothing in the cupboards. Looking for a town was too much of a risk, and she didn't even know if there was one nearby. She had no money, and no ID. Sure, she could catch a rabbit or something with her powers, but then what? She didn't know how to skin an animal or dress it.

Just when she thought she'd have to start walking again, she found a sealed bin above the cupboard that held some cans and dried goods. She opened a pull-tab can of ravioli, too hungry to wait until it was warm. How long had it been since she'd eaten last? Still ravenous, she ate a sleeve of soda crackers, then two granola bars, drank two mugs of tea she made with her boiled water, then collapsed onto the sofa. As the adrenaline from her flight faded, the exhaustion that stole over her made it hard to breathe. Her mind shut down, dragging her into non-consensual slumber.

It was dark when she woke, and she groped around, trying to remember where she was until she burned her hand on the wood stove. The trip back to the sofa to look for the flashlight she'd found before going to sleep resulted in a stubbed toe, but she eventually found it. She added wood to the fire, glad for the warmth even though she didn't need it.

She ate again, remembering the intensity of this hunger from other times the Aphrodisia had passed. It was hard to have an appetite when she could only think of keeping Valentine inside her, but afterward her body always wanted to make up for its lost flesh. Flashes of desire still nagged at her, but they were more manageable now.

There were no distractions past the demands of her stomach. No television, radio, or books. Just her and a lot of time to sit around and think. Circumstances and the choices she'd made had led to her being alone in the world. The only people she had left could be in danger if she went to them.

The Bureau had betrayed her. She was little more than a guinea pig to them now, especially since she wouldn't agree to join an existing hero team. Whatever dreams she'd had for herself were gone. The Bureau wasn't what she'd thought it was anyway. They ran around policing mercenaries, like there was nothing worse going on in the world. Most mercenaries didn't do much she'd consider true evil. It was a struggle for power, not a concerted effort to make the world a better place.

Their negligent betrayal of her meant they could go fuck themselves. She didn't owe them a damn thing. Not anymore.

But what was she supposed to do with her life now? Who was she?

Why was she still alive?

Heaviness stole over her again. She'd almost forgotten about the well of darkness that lurked, waiting for her to remember. It had disappeared while she'd been Valentine's mindless sex slave again, but reality brought back the void. The despair. She had nothing. Was nothing. There was no task left for her to do. She was nothing. Meant nothing.

Her team – Seraphina, Arigh, Vance – they'd hoped to do important work someday. It hadn't happened. As young as they'd been, they'd thought they had all the time in the world to follow their dreams and to make a difference. They were careful, smart, well-trained…and died anyway. So many times, she'd imagined Sera realizing she was about to die, thinking, "Really? Now?

Like this?" It wasn't what any of them had signed up for. They all knew the job was inherently dangerous, but that seemed less important when measured against what they could have done for the world.

It wasn't something they ever covered in the recruitment ads: Join the Bureau, waste your life.

For a long time she sat staring at the faint glow from the wood stove. A small, optimistic part of her tried to pretend she'd been saved from her team's fate for some larger purpose, but the realist in her knew it was a silly lie. There was no grand scheme to their deaths. They were pointless. Just a waste.

But she hadn't died with them. She'd lived. She was the lucky one, right? So many people had told her so, but it was hard to agree. Getting to live with the guilt and the empty, raw ache that never went away didn't make her feel lucky. The devastation of all of her dreams had been the price, and it was hard to know how to go on with the shreds of hope that had survived.

She was a hero without a team. The Bureau rarely sanctioned heroes working alone. Apparently without a team, heroes often became strange, antisocial creatures, sometimes prone to hubris. Without the Bureau behind her there was the option to go rogue, but how did rogues even find out what needed doing? Did they roam dark streets like comic book heroes did, looking for trouble? Did they form partnerships or were they like toddlers, mostly ignoring each other while they played in the sandbox of evil?

And then there was the issue of money.

She had no resources and no connections. She had nowhere to live, no clothes, no food, other than what she'd found in the cabin, which she felt guilty about eating but had no way to replace. The idea of fighting in Valentine's pilfered clothes and too-big shoes made her laugh.

Only a year ago her future had been exciting and bright, like a promise waiting to happen. So much had happened since then, but other than the fact that she was alive when she could have died with the others, none of it had been good.

The desolate wind outside of her stolen shelter spoke to her of death and endings and loss.

There'd been times in her life when she'd felt alone, but she'd never actually been this alone. Maybe her lack of direction wouldn't seem so dire if she at least had someone to talk to. If Valentine had been himself, rather than a stranger he'd turned into, she would've stayed until she figured out what to do. The old Valentine, once the Aphrodisia had passed, would have sat with her by the hour, letting her hash out what her options were and played devil's advocate while she used him as a sounding board. The new Valentine didn't even see her as human.

As much a she couldn't be with him, she missed him, but the Valentine who'd loved her was gone. It made having to leave easier.

After a week, she ran out of food. She slept for two days before she thought to look for rope to make a snare.

She hunted the cabin for rope.

A snare could just as easily be a noose. The cabin had rafters. The kitchen had a chair.

Desperation made her search faster. Nothing. No rope to be found until she remembered the collar around her neck. Maybe it would be fitting to hang herself with it.

Sobbing, she cut the collar from her throat, sawing through the pattern with a pocket knife. She cut her last connection to Valentine into tiny pieces. The cord writhed in her hands, dying for almost an hour before it finally went still. She hugged it to her chest, clutching the motionless strands, grieving its loss. Wondering if it would lead him to her. If he'd even bother to look.

If anyone would.

The rope was too short, but she still had the knife. Maybe she'd die here by her own hand, with no one to find her until spring.

For hours she stared at nothing.

Time to leave.

The day she left the cabin was the mildest it had been since she arrived, and she trudged back through the woods to the highway. The melting snow invaded her oversized shoes until her socks squelched with each step. At the highway, she walked backward, thumb out, ready to dive back into the woods if Valentine's truck made an appearance. It would be just her luck.

The trucker who picked her up was gruff, and lectured her about the dangers of young girls hitchhiking alone, and told her the horrors that could befall them. He wasn't much older than she was, but his tone suggested he was judging her age by her size. She didn't bother to explain that she was older than she looked, Atypical, and far from helpless. His heart was in the right place. She was grateful not to have to fend off any advances.

They parted ways in New York.

She stayed at a no-freeze shelter for a few nights, until a social worker befriended her and got her into a women's shelter.

It started to feel as if no matter where she ended up in life, she was forced into seeing a therapist.

Vanessa, the attractive brunette counselor who always wore a sweater and slacks, seemed too young to have such an important job. She looked younger than Jory.

"If you don't want to share, we can just sit, Rory."

The fake name she was using still surprised her from time to time, even though she'd picked something close to her real name.

"I just don't know what you want to hear."

"It's not about what I want to hear, it's about what you feel like telling me."

Jory pressed her lips together. If she had to do therapy to stay until she found somewhere else to be, she may as well get what she could out of it.

She shrugged. "I'm not safe. I can't go back. What else is there to say?" The Bureau wanted her for a guinea pig. Valentine had lost himself and wanted her for a sex slave. Vanessa thought she had an abusive boyfriend, but there were no services available for someone in Jory's situation, so she let her believe what she needed to.

"No one is saying you have to go back. What you decide to do is completely up to you. No judgment. We have the resources here to set up a new life away from him, if that's what you want, but I don't know if you're ready to make a decision yet."

"I'm not. I appreciate everything the staff here is doing for me. I just – I can't see my family or my friends. Starting over sounds great until you realize what it really means." She drew a shaking breath, and the counselor handed her a tissue, which she balled in her fist. "I could do anything, but that means I have no anchor. What does life mean when you can't be with anyone who loves you?" She choked as her throat tightened. When she put her hand there, the bareness of her neck hurt almost as much as the unshed tears.

She loved him desperately, even now. It wasn't something she could shut off because it was for the best. It was a huge gaping hole in her chest that bled all over the rest of her life.

She tried to tell herself she was being ridiculous, but when it came to this, logic didn't factor in. Amy, her parents – missing them was awful, but at least she could talk to them from time to time from the shelter phones with the blocked numbers. She couldn't tell them where she was, but at least she could hear their voices and know they were all right.

With Valentine, there was no way to check on him.

Vanessa was talking again, but Jory had missed part of the conversation. "It's not an easy position to be in. Just because it's the way things are now, doesn't mean you'll never be able to see your family and friends again, either. But after hearing what you've said, I need to ask – have you been thinking of self-harm?"

Jory opened her mouth to admit it, then wondered how much extra paperwork it would mean for the poor woman. "No."

There was a long silence, as though Vanessa didn't quite believe her. "Well, you know we're here if you want to talk at any time. I need you to contract with me around safety. If you're thinking of hurting yourself, you talk to me before you do anything."

"Okay. You have my word." Whatever that was worth.

"This is a temporary problem, as big as it may seem." Vanessa smiled sympathetically. "I just don't want you to lose sight of that."

Oh, she'd lost sight of *that* weeks ago. Months?

From the ship she was on she couldn't see shore. She didn't even know what direction shore was in.

Her team was dead. The man she loved had forgotten who she was.

There was no ship.

She was drowning and there was no shore in sight.

*

Under a false name, she was able to find temporary work cleaning houses with a few of the other women who were staying at the shelter. The staff found her clothes and shoes to fit, and she was grateful for every scrap of food they put in her mouth.

When she wasn't at work or in mandatory therapy, she watched the news, hoping to find hints about hero work she could do. She needed a purpose. Vanessa said she had to find it for herself in order for it to have meaning.

The only problem was the shelter curfew meant not being able to go out at night. She couldn't miss house cleaning work to do hero work, either, or she'd never save enough to get an apartment – although who would rent to her without ID?

Weeks later, a mom-and-pop pizza place across town gave her work in exchange for a bit of money, food, and a cot to sleep on in the store room. In the restaurant there was a television, and Eugene was passionate about keeping it on the news channel, even though Mari always flipped it to sports when he went out.

Determined to get on with things, Jory started small, dressing in black and going out after the restaurant closed, patrolling the streets. Half of her was afraid Valentine or the Bureau would see footage of her on the news, but the other half was more afraid Eugene and Mari would find out she was Atypical and give her the boot.

Dealing with predators and muggers taught her how to freeze people in place without damaging them past mild frostbite. She moved up to practicing on thieves who targeted the small stores and businesses she could reach on foot. Gone were the days of arriving on a mission in a black SUV, and wearing a fancy uniform. She did sloppy jobs, helping poor families keep their meager earnings safe from even poorer thieves. Growing up in small town suburbia, she'd never seen poverty like this except on television. The work needed to be done – the police did what they could, but there were only so many of them. At times she felt almost as bad for the muggers as she did for the victims. No one had an easy life in that part of the city.

The news, though, was what obsessed her. Night after night came stories about unrest between Atypicals – heroes and mercenaries having standoffs and battles that ended in deaths or serious injuries, often of innocent bystanders. In the aftermath of what had happened to Seraphina, Vander and Arigh, things had only become more ugly.

The explosion that had claimed them was considered the beginning of what was rapidly becoming a war. News reports that used their names as a rallying cry to criminalize all mercenary work and villainized mercenaries, themselves, made her crazy. Her friends had been open-minded and kind – using them as a justification for prejudice was wrong. Maybe Sera and the guys hadn't met Valentine, his team, or the others, but she knew down to her toes that they wouldn't have judged an entire group of Atypicals based on the actions of a small faction. They weren't hateful people – not like some of the hero zealots they interviewed in news reports.

Working alone, time dragged.

There never seemed to be much snow in the city, at least not for long. As the nights warmed, there seem to be more people running around looking for trouble. There was plenty of trouble to be had.

*

The last patron left the restaurant twenty minutes after the posted closing time. He didn't bother leaving a tip, even though he was wearing designer jeans and expensive shoes. Jerk. She flipped the sign on the door to closed and locked the door when he barely had both feet on the sidewalk. Methodically, she cashed out, wiped down tables, and ran the last of the dishes through the dishwasher.

On slow nights, Eugene and Mari left her alone with the tail end of the work, glad they'd finally found an employee responsible enough to let them go home early. With both of them in their seventies, they often complained about their health issues, and their only daughter had no interest in taking over the business. For now, they continued to run things and hoped one day they could retire.

When she had done with all of the necessary tasks, she slid into her room and dressed for her night work. Stretchy black jeans and a black t-shirt hadn't been hard to come by, but it had taken her weeks to save up for the sturdy boots. She'd only had them a week, so they were still stiff. She pulled them on and laced them to the knee, smiling at the idea of how useful they'd be in a zombie apocalypse, if there ever was one. The smell of their leather made her think of Valentine, as usual, but she pushed those memories away.

Weeks ago, she'd thought of tucking her white hair under a hat to make herself less noticeable, too, but the billowing cloud of it had objected. Unfortunately, it meant that on windy nights it flowed out behind her, demanding everyone's attention like an unruly child.

When she'd first started going out on crime-stopping missions, the idea had been that she'd watch for people in danger and help keep them safe. She'd thought of keeping watch over women alone in the street, but the only woman she saw by herself after dark was her own reflection in shop windows. The female sex trade workers stayed close to one another as much as possible and didn't need her help.

Now she would be bait.

By the time she reached the third park on her route she had a blister. Her heel would be hamburger meat by the time she got home, but it was still early and she didn't want to head back just yet. It was warmer out than she'd expected, and she unzipped her jacket, wondering if she should have left it home.

Home? Her room in the back of the restaurant was hardly that, as much as she liked Eugene and Mari. Home was where her parents lived, who she talked to at carefully random intervals from payphones on the other side of the city. For a while Valentine's coach house had almost been home. The house she'd shared with her team had never had a chance to feel like home, although it had been fun. Until they were gone. Packing everyone's things into separate boxes for their families to pick up had been long and difficult, and she never would have managed without Amy there to keep putting her back together when she fell apart.

The subtle scuff of a shoe on the paved path behind her caught her attention. She avoided the impulse to turn around as her heart accelerated. Something rustled off to her left. Two, at least. Were there more? She'd gotten used to fending off advances from men who seemed to think trying to chat up a lone girl in a dark place was going to win her over.

Her hackles rose. If they were Typicals, and there were only two, they wouldn't be much trouble. If there were a bunch of them, or they were Atypical, it would be a different story.

A man stepped into her path. His melodramatic stance almost made her snort, but this wasn't the time for her to find things funny. By the light of the nearest lamppost she could see his hood pulled low over his eyes, obscuring his face. Pretending she thought he was innocent, she moved right, as though she planned to step around him. He blocked her way again.

Power leaked from him in quiet waves. Figures moved to surround her. Six in all, unless more were hiding.

"Pretty little girls shouldn't be out alone at night," the man in her path said. "Didn't your Mommy teach you to be more careful?"

Although it wasn't the first time a man had said as much to her lately, having it come from a fellow Atypical was even more of a piss off.

"I didn't know it was asshole's night out. I hate to break it to you, but men don't own the city just because the sun goes down." She pushed her hair out of her way. "You're wasting your time. I don't have anything you want."

The snicker from her left wasn't comforting.

"Oh, I think you've got *something* we may be interested in," said a man behind her, as he grabbed a handful of her ass.

She managed not to startle or cringe.

Great.

She glanced back at the man over her shoulder. From under the cover of his low hood, a cruel smile was visible.

"A little to the left," she suggested sardonically, as though the old Valentine had spoken through her.

The man paused mid-grope. She clenched her hand into a fist and slammed the back of it against his nose. His bellow of pain broke the stillness of the park, and she heard him collapse to the ground. Maybe it was a bad idea to show them she wasn't afraid, but being assaulted didn't put her in a meek or cooperative frame of mind. It just ticked her off.

"Get out of my way. There's no reason to make this unpleasant," she said civilly.

The man she'd hit was groaning and sounded like he was still down. How did she want this to turn out? It would be nice to turn these men over to Warders, but it would be hard to make charges stick even if she could even get free long enough to call it in. Warders would also tell the Bureau where she was.

All six had power curling around them, lapping at their heels like hungry dogs. Against that many unarmed Typicals she could have held her own, but against six Atypicals the only guarantee she had was that she was in trouble.

"You're going to regret that," someone grumbled from her left.

"I doubt that," she mused, with a bravado she didn't feel. "It was pretty satisfying."

They all started to move at once, circling, making her wish she either had extra sets of eyes, or someone trustworthy at her back. If she was lucky, they'd only kick her ass.

As a pack, they moved in, crowding her, jostling her. They were breathing her air. None of them attacked, but the press of their bodies and their rude grabs almost made her panic. Compared to them, she was so small she could barely see over their shoulders. Her breath came fast, and for a moment she forgot she had the power to fight back, but how much force should she use?

"I'm not someone you should fuck with." She hoped the quaver in her voice was barely noticeable.

A few of the young men snorted.

She shoved the leader, forcing him a couple of steps back, but he was back in place before she could escape through the opening he'd left in their ranks.

"Let me go."

"Not so tough now, are you." His hood had fallen back. A blond with even features Jory would have considered him handsome under different circumstances. The others were similarly attractive, and wore understated name-brand clothing that suggested wealth. Rich boys looking for a thrill?

His hand darted toward her throat, and she let the icy terror she felt leech out through her feet, spreading until it crawled up their legs, sticking them in place from the knees down. One after another they realized they were stuck, no matter how much they fought. It didn't stop them from doing much, other than running away.

Ugh. Dumb move.

The leader's fingers wrapped around her throat, and he leaned close to her. "We're usually gentle with girls your size, but I can see you like things rough."

For a moment the possibilities of what they might do flashed through her mind. She had the sudden urge to whimper and collapse in a heap, or wait for someone to save her, but that wouldn't help anything. Instead, she focused on making the temperature of her throat drop.

"Fuck!" Blondie yanked his hand back and shook it as though burn. "You little bitch." His palm cracked against her cheek, but the slap had less force than it would have if he'd had more room to maneuver and his friends weren't in the way. Someone grabbed the back of her hair and yanked her head back. Two more grabbed her sleeves. She could make certain parts of her body too cold to touch, but she couldn't maintain it for long.

When he reached for her again, she kneed him in the groin. He fell to the ground, his feet still stuck in place. With a few deft twists, she broke the holds on her arms, then tried to leap over the fallen man, but the one with his hand in her hair kept her from running, just as more hands came to help restrain her. She focused on trying to summon ice shrapnel that would burst out in all directions, even though she'd only done it once.

One of the men to her left reached toward her, and dizziness hit. She staggered, but they held her upright. She lolled in their grips, fighting to get her feet back under her, but she was too motion sick even to stand. A man beside the leader pulled him back upright. Where he'd seemed vaguely amused before, now there was cold anger.

For a moment his eyes glowed red. She reached for her power to block whatever he was going to do, but it wouldn't respond. What the hell? It felt like it was stuck in a bubble of sickness she couldn't pop. His power was to take away power? Fear crawled across her skin. The only thing left to do was hit them.

The men were all moving again, their feet freed by her loss of power. They still had her arms and hair, but her legs were free. She kicked out, catching one man in the jaw and one in the nose, but although they fell, others grabbed her legs and they dragged her off the path toward the trees. She struggled hard. If they got her into the tree line, they'd rape her, maybe kill her.

In fear and desperation, she felt for the connection with Valentine, even though she knew he was too far away.

She headbutted a man who was stupid enough to put his face close to hers. That only added to her vertigo, although throwing up might be a good way to disgust a few of them.

"We've seen you moving around the city," the leader growled. "You heroes need to mind your own fucking business. Go save people from a burning building or something, instead of picking on Typicals trying to make a living. Typicals are none of your fucking business."

A stand of trees surrounded them now, screening them from the rest of the park. They pinned her to the ground.

"The entrepreneurs around here pay good money not to have to deal with Atypicals who feel like playing superhero." He knelt across her body. "I don't know where you came from, bitch, but after this you're going home, aren't you?" He slapped her again then grabbed her throat, this time cutting off her air. Eyes bulging, she struggled, but only managed to tire herself out.

He spat in her face, and it hit her cheek and slid down into her hair.

"Don't fuck with my people." Through a tunnel, she watched him, his face gleeful as he snuffed out the lights.

In the thin light of dawn she awoke, freezing, damp, her throat aching. She shook as she rose, brushing off her jeans, glad to find her clothing intact and undisturbed. Lucky, even though all of her muscles ached.

She had to get home. Her shift started at nine.

Chapter Seven

Wind ruffled Valentine's hair, and a stray bit of paper blew past his boots. He was clean at least, but his clothes were ragged from continuous wear. Other than his pack and a few credit cards, he had nothing. Even the truck had been left behind in a parking lot somewhere, doubtlessly towed off to some city impound yard.

Sometimes he remembered to eat.

As he stared through the shop window across the street, the hammering of his heart was almost painful. There she was, mopping the floor like she'd done it a thousand times. As though she had no idea how long he'd been searching for her. With the link between them blocked, she didn't know he was near.

He waited. It was an exercise in masochistic patience.

When she went into the back room, he sat on the sidewalk and leaned against the brick wall of an instant loan place, trying to make himself less conspicuous. Just one of several homeless men within view. The relief of seeing her healthy and whole was more emotional than it should have been. He needed her, wanted her, but the reaction he had to seeing her was unreasonable. Wanting to fuck her was one thing – wanting to hold her, kiss her, smell her, and hear her voice, confused him.

She emerged. Although she was thinner than she had been, she was no less enthralling. He expected her to walk past quickly, her hood pulled low, avoiding eye contact, but she went to a man near the door and handed him something then chatted for a few minutes before crossing to the side he was on.

A few feet from him, a man who'd been stretched out on a dirty sleeping bag perked up as she came near.

"Hey Phil, want some pizza? It's supreme tonight." She smiled at him, offering a flat takeout box.

Leaning back into shadow, Valentine stared. It was really her. He'd had no doubt, but seeing her this close up, almost close enough to touch, was exhilarating. On the breeze her scent drifted to him and he had to stifle a groan.

"You know I love supreme, Rory." The man accepted the folded cardboard from her with a whistle of appreciation. "And it's still hot! Marry me."

"Phil, no offense, but you're old enough to be my grandpa."

"I'm only seventy. Your…slightly older brother, maybe?" He winked at her.

The familiarity and playful banter made Valentine grit his teeth. The woman shouldn't be walking around the city unguarded, especially the way she smelled – like something he desperately wanted to put in his mouth.

Her head came up and she glanced around, like a deer sensing danger at a stream. Tilting his chin aside, he avoided her gaze, using the shadow of the building to obscure his features. Her power was feeling for his, but the block he'd put between their minds held.

"Okay," she said nervously. "I have to get going, Phil. Have a good night."

The man mumbled a goodbye around a mouthful of pizza, and Jory waved and ambled down the street, as though she was in no hurry to get home. Where was she staying? Did she live with someone? And did she really think calling herself Rory instead of Jory was going to throw anyone off?

When she was about a block away, Valentine pushed to his feet and followed, maintaining a discreet distance between them.

She turned down an alley between buildings, and he sped up. Why the fuck was she taking that kind of a chance? Reckless girl.

The alley was dirty, deserted, and stank of rotting garbage and cat piss. The girl walked faster, taking the next cross alley, which was equally deserted, but less unpleasant. It was also a dead end.

Her steps slowed, then stopped.

"Oh," she said, her voice sounding hollow in the trap she'd wandered into. Was she lost?

A cat emerged from behind a pile of refuse, as though it was shocked to see a human, and Jory turned to watch as it scooted past. Her gaze fell on

Valentine, who was only a few feet away. A nervous step backward didn't take her a safe distance from him.

"Oh, uh, I must have taken a wrong turn," she mumbled, her voice faint. She tried to step around him, but the alley wasn't big enough to get past him without coming within arm's reach.

Valentine pulled off his hood. Recognition lit in her eyes, then panic.

"Did I give you permission to leave the house?"

Her mouth opened, but she said nothing. As he closed the remaining distance between them, she stayed frozen, trembling as if she might bolt. God, he wanted her. There should have been at least some guilt about her…reticence…but it only made him want her more.

"I asked you a question," he said coldly.

He snapped his fingers and she moaned, then dropped to her knees so fast she must have scraped them on the asphalt, even through her jeans.

"I'm sorry, Valentine," she said, her voice nearly a gasp. "The way things were between us – I can't stay with you forever and I didn't think you'd let me go."

Would he have if she'd asked? Probably not. For that matter, he didn't intend to now.

"You belong with me," he said slowly, as though she was a small, confused child. How could she not feel what he felt? He pushed her knees apart with the toe of his boot, and her cooperation pleased him. "What could you possibly want that I can't give you?"

She gazed up at him. "Orgasms aren't the only goal I have in life, Valentine. At one time you knew that, and accepted it. You're making more sense now, at least, but you're still not acting like yourself. Even you're not this much of an asshole."

"Did you expect me to be pleased that you ran from me?" He unblocked their mental link. A gasp escaped her as his mind penetrated hers, invading her power, surrounding it. "You'll never be free. Not from me. Not for long."

"Even your mind feels different," she protested, eyes shut. "You're not even yourself anymore. Can you even tell me where we met?"

Irritation flared. A man wasn't just the sum of his memories. "Why does that matter?"

Her eyes flew open.

"You don't even know who I am." She stopped talking when the high pitch of her voice suggested she was about to cry. For a moment she was silent, but continued when she was back in control. "You've forgotten everything about me. About us. The only thing this new Valentine cares about is being serviced. Why don't you go find someone who wants to be a sex slave and leave me alone?"

Guilt at how upset she seemed slid off him. He refused to succumb to it. All that mattered was the deep possessiveness threatening to make him lose control. She was his. She knew she was. Why did she need to be so difficult? No matter what he'd been before, he had a hard time imagining he'd ever been sweet and romantic with her. Not when she made him feel like this.

"What do you want?" she asked. Maybe she was upset, but she couldn't avoid the link forever. Desire lurked in her eyes and flared in her mind. The loop started – his longing triggering hers, and hers feeding his until they were staring lustily at each other. Her chest heaved. "I'll do anything if you promise to go away."

He snorted. "You'll do anything because you get off on getting me off. We both know you love everything I do to you, or you wouldn't beg me for it the way you do. You were *made* to spread your legs for me."

She could easily rise, leave. Or try to, at least. Instead, she reached for him. Her trembling fingers brushed at his zipper. The temperature in the alley rose as he watched her fight the way they affected each other.

"Tell me what you want," he said, turning her question back on her.

"I want to have a life! One where I don't spent all of my time on my knees or on my back. When I die, I want my life to have meant something." And yet, her shaking hand unbuttoned his jeans and drew down his fly.

She was kneeling up now, and he grabbed her wrist before she could slide her hand into his jeans.

"What could be more important to you than being mine?"

"Everything! Being free! Why is that so hard for you to understand?" She was angry, but probably at herself because she was too horny to leave. "I cut your damn collar off my neck. Again! Isn't that enough of a message?"

He shrugged, amused. "It might have meant more if you'd taken out the piercing too." It had been a guess, but her silent scowl suggested he'd guessed correctly.

"I've been too busy to worry about that," she retorted, her cheeks crimson.

"Sure. Next you'll tell me you don't play with it every night and think of me."

"Shut up," she mumbled, turning her face aside to press it to her shoulder.

"It's nothing to be ashamed of, although I didn't give you permission to touch yourself, did I?" He grabbed her hair and she moaned loudly. Why did she always have to be so difficult at first? She wanted this as bad as he did, or worse. "Now," he growled, speaking slowly to pierce through the haze of need that was descending over them. "I asked you what you want. Fuck what you think you *should* want. Tell me the truth."

"I want you to leave me alone." Her whimper shot straight to his already throbbing cock. She reached under his shirt with the hand he didn't have trapped, and let it play over his stomach muscles. "Why do you have to be so perfect?"

"Other than the fact that I'm an asshole?"

"Just make me suck your cock, then go away. Deal?"

"You're going to suck my cock, then I'm going to fuck you against that wall." He flicked a finger. "Because you're a dirty little whore, aren't you?"

"Only for you," she whispered. "I fucking hate you."

"Of course only for me. That and the fact that you hate me is why I can't resist you." He laughed nastily, but mostly at himself. "Once I've filled you with come, you're coming home with me."

"No." It was more plea than statement of fact. "I have things I have to finish here. I can't just leave."

"You don't get a choice." Idiot. The Aphrodisia was already tapping an impatient fingernail on his balls. "Can't you feel it starting, pet? The madness is coming, and I'm going to be buried inside your tight little cunt for the next few days. Afterward, we'll talk."

Miserably, she nodded, like she knew he was right and it was unavoidable. "And then you'll let me go?"

"No, but if you're smart enough, maybe you'll escape again." He pulled his dick out of the confines of his jeans and jammed it in her mouth before she could start arguing about freedom and higher purpose again.

She latched on and sucked as though it was the only thing she'd ever wanted.

*

"So what? You're just going to keep her here forever?" The one called Dane was angry, his blond brows drawn low over his blue eyes.

Valentine followed his gaze to where the girl knelt, naked and collared, as she should be. If what he was doing with his lovely property bothered these people so much, why did they keep coming by?

"You're welcome to leave anytime," he reminded him. "I didn't invite you here in the first place."

Dane leaned against the couch's backrest, running an affectionate hand through Jurgen's hair, as the other man knelt placidly at his feet. "Yes, yes. I know I'm not welcome here, but since I've taken over paying for your utilities and taxes so that you don't lose your house every time you fuck off for months at a time, I don't really consider myself a visitor anymore. You need to take a few jobs with us to pay your bills soon, which means you're going to have to let her go. You can't leave her alone here, captive, with no one to help her if there's an emergency."

"I'm not stupid or naïve. I know how much money is left in my account, and it easily covers whatever I owe you, as well as several years worth of bills. And just because you think she doesn't want to be here doesn't mean you're right. Why don't you ask her?"

Valentine walked to the window seat where he made himself comfortable. When he gestured to the girl, she crawled to him and settled in his lap. He stroked the beautiful, smooth skin of her back and she sighed happily. "Does she look miserable to you?"

The interloper sighed in irritation. "Man, you've got your head so far up your ass you can't even see daylight. Using the Aphrodisia against her to keep her locked up like this isn't fair. It seems like the saner you are, the crazier she gets."

"On the contrary, the worst of the Aphrodisia has passed now, and she hasn't chosen to leave. Do you want me to turn her out even though she wants to stay?"

Dane snorted in disgust. "I don't know what the hell you did to her, but it seems like brainwashing. This isn't the Jory we all know. This is the Jory you've trained her to be."

Valentine raised a brow. "Are you going to tell me you don't train your boy there to meet your needs? The girl has a safeword and can choose to leave at any time. If you don't like that she chooses stay, that's not my problem."

He wished they'd just leave them in peace. His plans for the evening didn't involve company.

"The training I do with Jurgen doesn't erase his personality. He's still the same man. He has a name and he has my respect. It didn't used to be like this between you and Jory. This is weird and abusive, like I've said. Look, I talked to a specialist, and from what she was saying, you and Jory seemed to have the most extreme case of Atypical Aphrodisia on record. She's interested in studying the two of you."

The fierce outrage that stabbed through him caught him by surprise. "After what the last asshole scientist did to her, you dare to suggest she be put through that again? She doesn't deserve that."

"She doesn't deserve what you're doing to her either," Jurgen shot back. "You really aren't yourself, Valentine. I think you need to get some help."

"From what you've said, I haven't been myself since I met her." He shrugged. "So it's gotten worse and I've forgotten a few things – is it really that bad? And if it is, why should I care?"

Jurgen sighed and banged his head on the sofa cushion a few times, but said nothing.

"You, me, Xana, Jurgen – we've been best friends for years. You've always been an asshole, but you've never been evil. With this new you, I'm not so sure. You were the first one to take a stand saying we wouldn't do jobs that were immoral. Now I think you'd do anything, no matter how unethical it was, to keep Jory under your thumb. If she's not here of her own free will, this isn't a consensual power exchange relationship anymore. So what am I supposed to do? Call the enforcers on one of my best friends, and explain he's a kidnapper?"

Valentine sighed and moved the girl off his lap. He rose, went to the door, and opened it then stood there, looking at her. "Dane tells me you want to leave, pet. Here's your freedom. If you want to leave me, go now. If you're feeling shy, I'll go fetch you some clothes." He waited, watching her, but rather than looking relieved or grateful, she looked as if she might cry. "You may speak."

"Have I done something to displease you, Sir? Please don't send me away. Whatever I did, tell me and I'll do my best to fix it. Punish me – I'll do anything, just please don't make me go."

He left the door ajar and walked back to the window seat, taking his spot once again. Hesitantly, she crawled nearer, and when he moved his arm aside in invitation she crawled back into his lap, quietly weeping. He stroked her and shrugged at Dane.

"What do you want me to do? The offer is there. She's choosing not to go. I could order her out, but that would be cruel."

Dane got to his feet and Jurgen did the same. "Fine. You do what you want, but we're going to be dropping by regularly to make sure this is still what *she* wants."

Frowning, Jurgen left Dane's side and held a card out to Jory. "These are our cell numbers, and Xana's too. You call anytime, and we'll be here to get you out, no questions asked." When Jory averted her gaze and wouldn't take the card from him, Jurgen pressed his lips together and put it on the coffee table. "We remember who you both are, even if you don't."

As they left, Jory burrowed her face into Valentine's chest. If they came back with plans to steal the girl away, he'd kill them.

Chapter Eight

Sunlight fell across her closed eyes, warm, turning her world orange red. She stirred, stretched. Every muscle ached, but not as bad as her pussy and ass did. Her nipples weren't faring much better. An ice pack would be her friend, and maybe a painkiller.

Wearily, she opened her eyes and glanced over, already knowing he was there, feeling his mind groping for hers even in his dream.

What did monsters dream of?

Even now he was beautiful. He should have looked innocent and sweet as he lay sleeping beside her, but his expression was a mask of intense concentration. One of his arms was wrapped around her waist, holding her to him like a man who knew his most important possession could be stolen from him any moment.

Or escape from him.

She rolled her eyes. There was nothing she could have done to stop herself from ending up exactly here, with him. That wasn't the issue. The problem was she was now lucid, and could remember most of what had happened, and yet the sight of his hard, naked body made her want to run her hands over him...and maybe her mouth.

She could have him hard in a minute flat if she dared wake him.

It was time to go, though. Now, before she convinced herself to stay for a few more days.

The night before he'd bound her to the bed and tortured her with his mouth for hours, but she was free now.

Free to do the ultimate walk of shame, yet again.

*

Jory's breath came short as she waited, impatient and full of excited anticipation.

The telltale swish of expensive fabric reached her ears. Amy's mother gripped Jory's hand so hard her fingers felt like sausages.

Her best friend's wild curls came around the corner an instant before she did. She was a fairy princess in a slim-fitting dress that flared and feathered just below her hips. Amy's shining brown eyes and tremulous grin made Jory press her free hand to her own mouth. Happy tears brimmed in Jory's eyes and overflowed to slip down her cheeks.

God, if she'd missed this moment, she never would have forgiven herself.

She still wasn't sure how or why she'd broken free of the deep submission in which she'd found herself, or why it had claimed her in the first place. During the wee hours, days ago, she'd woken and the haze had been gone. It was frightening to realize she'd been in deep, unnatural subspace for weeks, without a moment of clarity.

She loved deep subspace as a place to visit, but she also loved being able to have her own coherent thoughts. The milder version was easier to live with every day – where she loved Valentine and served him, and he was the center of her world rather than its sum total. The Aphrodisia didn't seem to offer that as an option, though, and the idea she may be stuck perpetually in that needy, transcendent haze was scary as fuck.

Submission could be beautiful, but not to the point of losing all of her free will and the ability to be self-sufficient. That wasn't for her.

Maybe when the Aphrodisia went away for good, she and Valentine could be together, but under the circumstances she needed to stay away from his evil black eyes and his mind-altering dick.

She pushed aside distracting thoughts of the man before she went crawling back for more. Again, she'd escaped. He'd find her eventually, but hiding from him couldn't take precedence over staying close to Amy and her family. For a while she'd thought it was necessary, but she wasn't going to disappear on them forever.

Now that she'd escaped from him a second time, she trusted herself more. The Aphrodisia kept pulling them back together, but once it passed she could find the strength to leave. She'd done it three times. She could do it again.

As for the Bureau, she hoped they'd lost interest in her.

She focused her attention back on Amy, who deserved her undivided attention today, at least. Jory had been a pretty crappy friend to her for the past year, and yet she'd still chosen her to stand as her maid of honor, rather than one of her more stable work friends, or her cousin.

Like a little girl playing dress-up, Amy twirled once before the mirrors to admire the magical flare of the dress. Her exuberance made her sweet face even more beautiful. Jory's heart ached for her friend's happiness, sharing in her joy, but also regretting how much she'd missed. Here, her best friend had fallen in love and built a life with a man, and she'd missed the whole damn thing. It was like watching the opening scene of a movie, then leaving and coming back when the credits rolled. All the issues that came with being in a new relationship and figuring out how to function as a couple, then learning how to live together – Jory had missed every moment of it, and hadn't been there as a sounding board or a sympathetic ear. Some friend she was.

She hoped Talbot was as good to Amy as he seemed to be, but it was hard to imagine anyone would ever be good enough for her best friend.

"What do you think?" Amy asked, her wide brown eyes hopeful.

"Breathtaking." Jory grinned and wiped tears off her cheeks.

Amy's mother was sitting in stunned silence, her hand over her mouth. Jory hoped like hell she wouldn't burst Amy's bubble, because the girl was gorgeous and this was most definitely her dress.

Her mother shook her head. "Tell them to put the rest of the dresses away. This is the one." She sobbed a laugh. "This was supposed to take all day! I guess the dress is like Talbot. When something is right, you just know."

Jory's tears came faster then, and one of the salespeople offered her a box of tissues. It wasn't time to have a breakdown about Valentine. Today wasn't about her. Seeing Amy like this, though, so happy and settled, made her wonder if her own life would ever be less screwed up.

Not for the first time she envied her Typical friend. Amy always thought having Atypical abilities would be cool, but they seemed to come at a high price for a lot of Atypicals. Like dying, or standing by helplessly as you watched your friends die.

Thank God Amy would be spared all that.

After all sorts of fussing with sizing then choosing a veil, Amy went to change back into the cute blue dress she'd worn to the shop. When she was done, Amy thanked her mother profusely, and they watched as she went with the saleswoman to arrange for payment and a schedule of fittings.

"So you're sure you don't mind wearing turquoise?" she asked as she dropped down onto the seat beside Jory. She leaned on her. "My cousin is being bridesmaidzilla."

"I don't care what color we wear, as long as you're happy. The question is whether *you* like turquoise."

Amy snorted. "You know me. My mom wanted turquoise. Like I care what color the bridesmaids dresses are."

"Ditto."

"We should probably keep our voices down, though. If the staff finds out we're fashion impaired, they may take away our girl cards."

"Whatever. They can have mine if they take my period with it."

"Dude, if my cycle stays on track, the wedding won't land in the middle of shark week. Lucky break, considering I didn't think to check when we picked the date."

"Talbot will be happy he won't have to wait to deflower you."

"Like that would deter him? The man isn't squeamish." She rolled her eyes. "Besides, I only have one orifice left to deflower, and call me a prude, but I'm not letting him fuck my ass on our wedding night." Amy slapped her hand over her mouth and glanced around, but no one was in earshot.

This was one of those situations where a best friend should self-disclose, but the topic brought a wave of arousal, embarrassment and confusion Jory didn't want to be having in a public place. She felt her face heat, and Amy's brows rose.

"Girl, we need to talk."

Jory shook her head. "I doubt I'd survive that conversation."

Thankfully, Amy's mother appeared from around the corner, and waved. "Come on, girls. Let's go somewhere fun for dinner."

"Chuck-E-Cheese?" Amy asked hopefully.

"Amy," Jory admonished, smacking her arm. "You're getting married. You have to pretend you're too mature for Chuck-E-Cheese until you have children to bring as a cover. Besides, after teaching kids all week, I'd figure you'd prefer to go somewhere more grown-up."

"Nope. And I'm the bride, so I get to pick." Amy grinned at her mother, who rolled her eyes.

"Fine, let's go, but when you run out of tokens, that's it."

Amy clapped her hands exuberantly as they hit the sidewalk and headed for the car.

Not for the first time Jory wished she was as fun and carefree as Amy.

Her friend was serious when she needed to be, but was always ready to have a good time. It was hard to imagine whether Amy and Valentine would have gotten along, considering how jaded he was.

Now it was unlikely they'd ever meet.

*

The turn-of-the-century home Xana stopped in front of was a bit of a surprise to Jory. What was it with mercenaries and their fascination with old houses? Reddish-brown brick, a rounded side turret, black shingles, and a veranda and balcony with a black railings gave the impression of sophistication paired with comfort. As they mounted the steps, uneasiness nagged at her. These people had been nice when she'd briefly met them at the BDSM club Valentine had taken her to, but Brock and Brontë were strangers – why would they take her in?

Xana put an arm around her shoulders and gave her a reassuring squeeze. "I know this is fucked up, but hiding you here might just work. Hopefully whatever is wrong with him passes with time like it did with you."

She smiled her thanks at the taller woman, who gave her a friendly wink.

The door opened as they reached it, and a redheaded young woman in a PVC maid's uniform curtsied to each of them. "Hello, ma'am. Ma'am. Do come in. The lady and gentleman are ready to see you in the study, if that would be acceptable?"

Xana nodded. "That would be fine, Rowan." The two of them trailed after the maid as she led them through the house. It was hard for Jory to keep her eyes from following the long line of the girl's seamed stockings all the way up to where the short skirt provided a peek of bare thigh and garters. Jory jerked her gaze away, and found Xana checking her out too.

They entered a formal study that was decorated in the same period as the rest of the house. Two oak desks sat on opposite sides of the room, and every wall held floor-to-ceiling shelving filled with leather-bound books. The dark-haired siblings, Brock and Brontë, were seated in two of the comfortable-looking chairs in a conversation area in the middle of the room. Brock rose to wave them over.

"Xana, Jory… Nice to see you both. Please join us. Can I offer you coffee, tea, lemonade?" He smiled pleasantly, but his cultured demeanor and mannerisms were making Jory feel backward.

They both agreed to coffee. As Rowan poured for them, Brontë made pleasant small talk about the weather. The young woman was the epitome of good breeding and quality, with her chestnut brown hair in a loose chignon, her understated, expensive clothes, and her impeccable manners. She had a hint of an English accent, and Jory thought she remembered Valentine saying that the family had moved to America when the children were small.

Jory felt as if she'd been dropped into some sort of historical docudrama. The only thing that threw off the scene was the way Rowan was dressed, and how she knelt quietly beside Brock's chair when she was done serving.

Before they'd moved past small talk, a tall, muscular, Middle Eastern man with a chiseled jaw entered the room. The guy looked as if he was fresh off the set of a soap opera, and had a dazzling smile, but his gaze slid politely from Jory's and was aimed across the room at Xana almost immediately.

"This is Kade," Brontë said, tucking a stray lock of hair behind her ear.

Jory smiled at the man, but both he and Brontë were surreptitiously watching Xana, who was ignoring them. An unexpected sexual tension buzzed in the room, and Jory's skin prickled. He took a seat, but said nothing.

"So things haven't improved with Valentine, then?" Brock asked. "It's – I can't understand it. I mean, we know what you've told us, but it's so out of character for him. He's always been so self-possessed."

Xana shrugged. "It's the Aphrodisia. It has to be. Jory really wasn't herself for a while either. We were starting to wonder if either of them would find their way back, but if Jory is better, maybe we'll be lucky and get Val back too."

They sipped at their coffee and chatted about friends and acquaintances, surprising Jory with their shared history.

"Didn't Valentine tell you?" Brock asked, when he noticed a surprised expression on her face. "We've all known each other since middle school."

Brontë shifted in her seat as though it had become uncomfortable. "Well, that's a bit misleading. We hadn't seen each other much between middle school and last year. We were surprised to see them again when we moved back and started going to Prospero's."

Jory immediately had a mental image of the sexy BDSM club owner they referred to, with his lean muscle, strong jaw, pierced nipples and long ponytail. Valentine had become territorial when Prospero had shown interest in her, which had excited her more than it should have at the time.

"Are you going to the meeting at the club next week?" Xana asked.

The others all looked pointedly at Jory, as though they were trying to remind Xana she was in the room.

Xana rolled her eyes. "Aren't we hoping for peace? She was there at the beginning. Maybe she wants to be part of the ending."

The others shifted in discomfort but didn't respond immediately. Jory almost felt like excusing herself so they could discuss the matter privately. Instead, she took a sip of coffee and watched the cream swirl over its surface. It tasted fancy, as if it had been bought overseas. For all that she had no use for Val's money, she did appreciate good coffee.

Brontë nodded slowly, and one after the other, the rest of them assented.

"Some of us are working behind the scenes, trying to put the brakes on this stupid fight between mercenaries and heroes," Xana explained to her. "The war is bullshit. Political posturing that's completely out of hand, as you know. There are a few assholes stirring people up, and for a while people were afraid to disagree, but now there's a strong movement of Atypicals from both sides refusing to fight each other. We belong to a faction of that group, actively working as peacekeepers."

Jory's breath caught. There were others? She didn't have to try to figure out how to stop the idiocy all alone? Her throat felt thick.

Xana gave her a grim smile. "Is that something you'd be interested in?"

Not trusting herself to speak, she nodded.

"Okay. They can bring you to the meeting, then." Xana looked at the others. "Don't worry about Val showing up there, or here for that matter. Not yet. He's out of town, and probably won't be back anytime soon. Jurgen tracked him about four hours north then came back. He's…not making sensible choices right now."

They'd told Jory that after she'd gotten away he'd gone silent, then up and left about a day later. Whether he was looking for her or exorcising his demons remained to be seen.

"Let me know if I need to move her. Just call my cell."

Brock's hand stilled where it had been stroking Rowan's hair. He smiled kindly at Jory. "We just got back from Belgium, so it's going to be weeks before we take another job. You're welcome to stay when we do accept something, though, Jory. There's no rush for you to leave. We have plenty of space."

"Excellent." Xana set her mug aside and rose. "Sorry to have to run out so fast, but I have an appointment with a prospective client about a job for the three of us. It's weird without Val, but we're getting used to covering the gap."

"There are always bills to pay," Kade said, startling Jory. He'd been silent until then. He flashed Xana a charming, dimpled smile that moved him again from handsome to gorgeous. Xana arched a brow at the man, and his smile turned rueful. "I know you're in a hurry, Xana, but do you have a sec?"

Her dark eyes went cold, and her expression grim. "I've told you before, Kade, if you want to speak to me, you and Brontë will have to sort things out. I'm not interested in driving a wedge into your group, or screwing up friendships."

Jory took another sip of her coffee and pretended to be very interested in the earthenware cup, hoping they forgot about her and kept talking. It was none of her business, but that didn't mean she wasn't curious. Maybe Kade was interested in Xana, but Brontë was his ex and things were messy?

No matter the situation, it was more fun to think about than the limbo she was living in.

Brontë was frowning so hard Jory was surprised her forehead hadn't cramped up.

"So?" Xana looked back and forth between the two. Her one word held not only command but an implication she felt her time was being wasted by spoiled children.

"We'll agree to your terms," Brontë murmured then glanced up at Xana. "Mistress."

Ohhhhh...oh.

Sometimes she was still slow on the uptake. Then again, nothing about Brontë suggested she'd be into anything kinkier than lying back and thinking of England.

Polyamory was so common in Atypical circles that she had to laugh at her own default assumptions. Growing up with Typicals hadn't prepared her for the realities of living with other Atypicals. She'd always been open-minded, but in this world she was backward and naïve. She really had to stop assuming people were straight and only dating one person.

When it came to her own life, though, the relationship she had with Valentine was complicated enough. She couldn't imagine adding a third or fourth person to the mess.

Xana's expression didn't change with Brontë's words, but it felt as though the temperature in the room had dropped several degrees. "Kneel."

Both Brontë and Kade moved to Xana and knelt. At the edge of her vision, Jory saw Brock and Rowan edge out of the room. When she moved to follow, Xana motioned her back to her chair.

"Stay, if you don't mind," Xana said, her voice bland. "I'd like a witness to this shitshow."

"Sure." Jory looked back and forth, secretly glad she could watch this.

Brontë bit her lip, and Kade's amusement had fallen away.

"You still want to submit to me?"

"Yes, Mistress," they responded together. Side by side, they were so very different – the large, confident man, and the small, prim girl. It made for interesting possibilities.

"I know you wanted me to choose between you, but I won't." Xana paced the room, then returned, looking down at them as though they were a problem that needed to be dealt with. "This is your chance to back out."

Kade's gaze slid to Brontë, but she ignored him and kept looking at Xana.

"I will not withdraw my interest, Mistress," Brontë replied.

For a long moment Kade paused. "I accept your terms, Mistress."

Xana folded her hands behind her back, looking every inch the irritated dominant. Valentine had made that face at her so many times that Jory found herself responding vicariously, hoping Kade and Brontë pleased her.

"You both gave me a list of your hard and soft limits, and I told you what I expect. I am aware there is some animosity between you, but if you agree to move forward, you'll be respectful to one another."

Brontë was already smiling, but Xana held up a hand, apparently not finished.

"And, when I command it, you'll be sexually intimate with each other."

The room went still as both of them seemed to process this idea. Eventually, they nodded, but avoided each other's gazes.

Wow. And she thought her relationship with Valentine was complicated.

"As we agreed, this will be a closed relationship. When you're away from me, I expect faithfulness, and will promise the same in return. If you wish to sleep together in my absence, you must ask for permission."

Kade snorted.

"That won't be an issue, Mistress," Brontë replied.

Xana walked closer to Kade, until she was almost standing on him. "Something about this amuses you?"

"No, Mistress. I just won't be asking to sleep with her," he said. The sour words made Brontë wilt.

Without hesitation, Xana slapped Kade hard across the face. He didn't flinch, but he did avert his gaze. "How dare you come to me saying you've worked through your shit, when you obviously haven't. Why are you wasting my time?" As commanding as Xana was in day-to-day life, seeing her at full dominance was terrifying.

"I —" he began then lowered his gaze. "I apologize Mistress. It won't happen again."

"No, it won't. Because if it does, you won't enjoy the reminder." The threat didn't require raising her voice or more detail to get the point across. A vision of Xana taking a cane to his balls crossed Jory's mind. "I'm taking you both on because you're interesting, but don't assume I care enough about either of you to put up with childish fucking antics. If either of you piss me off, you're both gone."

They nodded.

She pulled two solid bracelets that looked like stainless steel out of her back pocket. "These are a symbol of my ownership. If you want to take them off, you must ask for my permission, unless it's an emergency. If you're waiting for pretty words from me, you'll be disappointed. I'm not that kind of dominant." Without further ceremony, she fastened a bracelet around each of their left wrists. "We've already discussed what we expect from each other, but I'll be back later tonight to start training you to my preferences."

Xana turned and walked away, leaving them kneeling there, gazing after her with worshipful eyes.

Chapter Nine

Dr Matthew Ridlon, the shockingly young Director of Atypical Research, seemed less horrified about finding himself bound to a chair in his home office than Valentine would have expected. Although frustrated and angry, he had himself under control. Maybe the man sensed that Valentine's hold on his temper was tenuous.

"The Bureau doesn't know where Ms Savage is," Dr Ridlon repeated, his jaw firm and gaze unwavering. "The last I heard, she'd fled from the research station. The team lead couldn't explain what happened. An investigation is underway."

"And is the researcher in custody?"

"No." The man frowned. "He and his assistant are telling the same story. That she went wild and ran off under the influence of the Aphrodisia."

"You believe them? Have you even watched the footage?" Were they idiots? Why hadn't they kept Jory somewhere official, like a hospital? Somewhere with checks and balances, where the behavior and methods of the researchers would be under continuous scrutiny. Did they automatically expect two men with no supervision to be trustworthy around a helpless, needy woman? It would be nice to think the world worked that way, but it fucking didn't.

The man pressed his lips together. "The camera in the room went dead, but we can't find evidence of anything criminal occurring. It seems suspicious, but without evidence or Ms Savage's statement, we can't charge them with anything. We'd like to hear her side of things."

Valentine strolled across the room once, collecting his thoughts, but refrained from prowling back and forth incessantly like he would have at home. Acting sane wasn't easy.

"Do you know the current whereabouts of the researcher called Asher? When I went back to the research house on Martha Street, it was empty."

The director looked at him blankly for a moment. "You think Dr Maitland kidnapped Ms Savage?"

Valentine picked up the picture frame on the man's desk and frowned at the photo of the smiling wife and two children. His interest in the picture was obvious enough to make the man shift several times in his chair. He'd never hurt innocent bystanders, but Ridlon didn't know that. Sometimes silent threats were the most effective.

He set the frame back on the desk, angling it so Ridlon could see his family. Maybe their sweet faces would remind him cooperation was good for the soul.

However, instead of looking at the photo, Ridlon was watching Valentine with an odd expression.

"Dr Maitland is at the house on Westbourne now. I wouldn't usually know that, but I was just there the other day." His words sounded distracted, and he shifted in the grip of the ropes again. There was a flush in his cheeks. Was the rope tight? And why was he giving up that information so easily? Either Ridlon thought there was nothing to hide, or he was lying about the location, or he was a coward.

Valentine slid his hand up the man's throat and applied gentle, threatening pressure. Fear and something else surfaced in his eyes. "You'd better not be lying to me. I can always tell what people are thinking."

The man gasped and turned a deeper red, as his gaze shifted away. "You can read people's thoughts?"

He hadn't heard of any Atypical who could do that, a fact Ridlon should have known, but he wasn't going to point that out.

"I'm straight," Ridlon blurted, sweat beading his forehead. "I – please just leave. I told you what you wanted to know. Just get out. I'll forget you were even here." The throat under his hand moved with difficulty as the man swallowed a few times.

Valentine barely managed to keep his surprise from registering on his face. This was an interrogation, not a date, but sure enough there was a very awkward bulge in Ridlon's khakis. The man looked horrified by what had come out of his mouth. Until then, Valentine hadn't really noticed the man was attractive, but he was, especially helpless and distressed.

It would have been entertaining to watch Ridlon struggle through his unwanted attraction to another male. If it hadn't been for Jory, he may have considered it.

He gave Ridlon a cruel smile, and stepped away, inclining his head.

"It's been...enlightening," Valentine said, gesturing vaguely to the tent in Ridlon's pants. "If the Bureau harms Jory again, you'll be getting another visit from me, and it'll be far less pleasant. I know how to hurt people, Matthew, and I know how to make them ashamed they like it."

Ridlon's face went from red to white, and his lip trembled. A dark splotch of precome was gradually seeping through the man's pants. He looked as though he wanted to die.

"I...understand."

Valentine cocked his head to the side and gave the man a considering look. "That would be, 'I understand, Sir.'"

"Oh dear God," he whimpered. Matthew Ridlon could have been the poster boy for closets. "Yes, I understand, Sir."

So adorable. Too bad corrupting a family man wasn't on his agenda. Ridlon had likely spilled everything he knew, even though it could've been fun to spend more time torturing him.

Valentine silently ordered the rope to hold Ridlon on the chair until he was well gone, then he made his way out to his truck.

The fact was that Jory had likely run from him. Why? His 'friends' had told him it wasn't the first time she'd disappeared that way. Xana believed Jory had only come back to him out of pity after the last time. She'd seemed happy with him right up until she disappeared.

Was he that creepy?

Well...perhaps he was, but he could have sworn she'd liked it.

*

For weeks Asher evaded Valentine. Maybe Ridlon had tipped the bastard off, but there was no way to prove it, so he didn't bother paying him another visit to complain. Besides, if Ridlon had told Asher, Valentine visiting again may have been the poor, repressed man's actual goal.

He wasn't sure why hunting for Asher would fix anything, especially since he was relatively certain the Bureau didn't have Jory, but she'd vanished. Following the man gave him something to do other than obsess about why she'd left.

Returning to the house on Martha Street had been a long shot, considering the whole place was dark and no cars were parked in the yard. He took a look around anyway to be sure it was vacant. He'd checked every other Bureau safe house in the state and all of them were currently empty. So either Asher had relocated, or he'd moved back into one of the other houses Valentine had already checked, staying just one step ahead.

Growling under his breath, he got back into his truck. His phone read missed call. Go figure. It was doubtlessly Xana or one of the blond jerks, but the possibility that it might be Jory made his heart kick up a notch. Pathetic.

He'd never know how the slip of a girl had turned him into such an obsessed knuckle dragger. When he thought of her, though, there were echoes of feelings that were either part of his missing memories, or were the product of his imagination. Either way, he couldn't think of her without feeling a sad, lingering betrayal.

For a long moment he stared at the phone in his hand, wishing he had the strength to ignore it, but the red dot mocked him, and he hit the button to check his voicemail.

Stay out of the Asher situation. It's none of your business.

Fuck. It was actually her.

The sound of her voice was like a little snack for his Jory obsession. Having heard it, he couldn't help but want more.

Stay out of it? None of his business? She was his. She belonged to him. Any transgression against her damn well *was* his business.

He put the phone on speaker, and listened to her message again and again, the disdain in her voice stabbing deeper, then deeper yet. Once or twice he let himself believe there was a hint of regret in her tone, but it was gone the next time he listened.

Helpless, impotent rage had him scrambling around his glove compartment, but the knife was gone. He couldn't remember where he'd last seen it. He checked the pockets of his jacket, and his jeans, but it was nowhere to be found. His breath came in short, sharp gasps and the ugly scream that burst from his mouth rang in the small space until his ears hurt. The control he had over himself was so very minimal. Had he always been so unbalanced?

Surely he'd never been the type of guy to obsess over an ex-lover – at least he didn't think he'd been. It was hard to say now. Yet the connection he had with Jory was so strong that her absence ripped at him. Specters of his love for her teased around the edges of his memory, along with her smiling face, and her laugh.

Remembering wasn't good at all. It fucking hurt.

He shoved the few shards of memory into the back of his mind, hoping he was imagining them and that they'd disappear as fast as she had.

Maybe he was a weird, evil stalker, like Xana had accused him of being. Was it stalking when he knew the path he was choosing didn't lead to her?

Just because she chose not to be with him, didn't mean her safety wasn't his responsibility. What if this Asher person tried to hurt her again? He'd tried to force himself on her, and that ate at Valentine more than it should have. By all accounts, she was a strong, capable girl, but she hadn't eliminated Asher as a potential threat to her safety. It wasn't a smart move.

The darker part of his mind laughed.

This wasn't just about keeping her safe. It was about revenge. Asher had known Jory was Valentine's, but had tried to use her anyway. A man didn't let another man have what was his. A debt was owed.

When he'd tortured himself with the message enough, he put the phone back in his pocket, and searched through the middle console for something he knew he hadn't lost yet. The lighter.

It was a cheap one, covered with pictures of cats.

He grabbed the Jamaican rum from the back seat and cracked it open.

There were two options open to him. Get shitfaced and burn himself for a while, or watch the motherfucking house go up in flames.

Fuck it.

The house needed to be erased from the world more than he needed extra scars.

The Bureau would know he was responsible, but he didn't care. Asher needed to know what was coming.

Chapter Ten

It was nice to finally feel she belonged somewhere, even if it was at a kink club surrounded by mercenaries discussing battle tactics. She wasn't sure why the lights had been kept dim. It felt as if a spanking could happen at any moment.

Memories of Valentine letting his teammates do all sorts of naughty things to her in this club played in the background of her mind every time they were there. Looking over at where the scene had happened made her both terribly aroused and yet sad. It was a strange mix of feelings that surfaced when she inevitably thought of Valentine.

Jurgen tapped her knee, and when she turned to him he wore a wicked smile. "*Tsk*. Jory," he whispered, and shook his head. "Being teased by four people couldn't have been that hot. You should really try to pay attention." He gestured up at Brock, who'd been presenting a series of likely scenarios and possible ways to stall or halt fighting between the two factions during a battle. The problem was the group kept coming up with Band-Aid solutions to an issue that needed skillful diplomacy and possibly a time machine.

Jory's cheeks stung with her blush and Jurgen grinned wolfishly at her. Maybe he identified as a sub, but he couldn't seem to resist getting dommy with her. It wasn't fair that she never got to be the boss of anyone. She had just as much power as the rest of them…it was just that when someone gave her *the look*, she automatically melted into a gooey puddle. Once Valentine had called her "profoundly sexually submissive". He may have thought it was a compliment, but sometimes it was still hard to accept, even though she knew it was true. It had been hard not to feel subby around Valentine's teammates ever since they'd tortured her and made her beg to come. How could that not permanently change the dynamics in any given relationship?

At least they treated her like a competent adult with a valuable opinion, unlike the new Valentine.

She forced her mind back to the meeting that hadn't paused just because her mind was in her pants. Maybe she needed to wear a sign around her neck that read "perpetually distracted."

A woman named Delilah took Brock's place next, and gave her report about several places she'd researched where they could practice together without being seen. More than a hundred people were in the room. It was hard to imagine practicing together, or working together. Not all of them could make it to every battle, but if they practiced tactics and formations there was a chance they could throw a serious monkey wrench into this stupid war.

She paid attention, both because she was interested and because Jurgen would tease her if she didn't stay focused. Xana's new submissives, on the other hand, were less than subtle in their distraction, and spent most of the meeting in an attempt to outdo each other to keep their mistress's attention.

Love made people idiots. She should know.

When the meeting was over, almost everyone filed out, forgoing the usual coffee social. The mix of people there – mercenaries, and a smattering of heroes that grew with each meeting – kept things interesting. She'd been introduced to so many of them at this point it was hard to remember who was who. And after all of the stupid stories she'd heard growing up about how selfish and wicked mercenaries were, it was nice to know her friends weren't the only decent non-heroes out there. Most of the mercenary groups were just regular people who'd been born on that side of the divide, raised by parents who'd been mercenaries before them.

Mercenaries were losing their bad reputations with some of the heroes. And with the Bureau acting so shady, the lines separating them had been blurred.

Each side had their own culture, and as she grew closer to the mercenaries, she realized they were more connected to one another than hero groups were. Most of their bonds were organic and family-based, rather than something the Bureau had facilitated. There was something to be said for allowing people to choose their own team instead of being forced into one based on abilities.

The mercenaries had a code, and it was strictly adhered to. There was no need for enforcers when each mercenary took personal responsibility for making sure the code was respected. The Bureau assumed that without authority governing the people, it would cause rebellion and chaos, but really, it just meant people governed themselves and kept an eye on each other. Neither were foolproof. It was hard to say which was better.

"If Delilah and Brock share leadership of the peacekeepers, I think we might just have a chance," Prospero said as he straddled the chair directly in front of Jory. He'd directed the comment to Dane, but if he'd meant to have a discussion with Jurgen's dominant he could have chosen a closer chair.

Dane nodded slowly. "They're good. I know it's been a pain in the ass to get everybody together to practice, especially since there are people from so far away, but I think we need to do it. If we don't practice together and the other groups do, we won't stand a chance. There may be a large-scale battle someday."

The two of them discussed the pros and cons of keeping teams together versus grouping people by ability in larger battles, and soon there were only a few people left in the room. When the conversation wound down, Dane grabbed Jurgen by the back of the neck and excused them both before leading him toward the saltier that stood against a nearby wall.

No one had mentioned there'd be quasi-public play tonight. Not that she minded.

Watching as he commanded Jurgen to strip, then kneel and kiss the tops of his boots made Jory shift uneasily in her chair. Xana led Kade and Brontë to an open space, had them kneel and touch their noses to the ground then started to lecture them about proper behavior during meetings. Dane started to tie Jurgen to the saltier and Jory wasn't sure what to do with herself. Watching a public scene during club hours was one thing, but with so few people around it almost felt creepy to watch.

A few of the others who'd stayed behind were folding the chairs Prospero stored in the back. With a keen awareness of Prospero's gaze following her, Jory rose and went to help the chair-folders. He followed her and her heart sank.

At the last few meetings he'd been hovering. He hadn't made any advances, but she could almost feel one coming. How should she handle this? Things between her and Valentine were complicated. She was still collared to him, at least in her heart. Even as hot as Prospero was, he wasn't going to get anywhere with her.

When he moved right up behind her, she had to hold back a shiver.

"Jory, may I speak to you privately?"

She turned then saw how close he really was and took a step back, bumping into a chair. He wore his hair loose tonight, and it fell like a dark waterfall, partially obscuring his face. Between that, the strong cheekbones, and big brown eyes, he was downright sinful. Wearing jeans and a t-shirt instead of his usual leather pants with his chest bare, he looked less sure of himself. His sensual mouth quirked in a hopeful smile.

Valentine would not like this. Not one little bit. But considering the fact that their relationship had crashed and burned, she didn't know if she should care what he thought. It was just a conversation. It wasn't like she was going to screw the guy.

Briefly, she looked to her friends, hoping one of them would be making mad hand signals to warn her away, but they were busy. Fuck. Prospero knew she belonged to Valentine and BDSM etiquette would stop him from getting too flirty with her.

She nodded, and his smile could have lit the room. Shit.

"My office?" he suggested.

Jeez.

The interest in his eyes may have made her panties disintegrate once upon a time, but he lacked that hint of evil that made Valentine so impossible for her to resist. That and she was still in love with Valentine, even though he'd gone past his normal level of bastard straight to first class asshole.

"No, I don't think Valentine would like that." She folded another chair and added it to the stack on the trolley. "We'll stay in the room."

His brow puckered in confusion, but he beckoned her over to a jumble of couches that had been pushed out of the way to make room for the rows of folding chairs. He was polite enough to sit on the couch across from her rather than trying to sit next to her.

"I thought – I'd heard you and Valentine had gone your separate ways," he said, his grimace just making him look more charming.

"It's...complicated."

"With Valentine? Of course. He's a narcissist and I can't imagine he's good to you. Especially with him half-mad as he was the last time I saw him." Prospero leaned back against the couch and draped an arm across the back.

For a moment, she let herself fantasize about punching him in the eye. Maybe Valentine wasn't perfect, but he was hers, and Prospero was insulting her dominant. She thought of several sarcastic retorts, but he'd only laid out the truth, as he saw it.

"He's as good to me as I need, but yes, things were better when he was well. Until we can sort a few things out, it's better if we stay apart, but we're still committed to each other. At least, as far as I know."

"You haven't spoken to him?"

"No. It's better if we don't see each other right now."

He nodded. "Well, I won't try to get in the middle of that, of course. But if you ever need to move from Brock and Brontë's house, I'm sure he'd never look for you at mine." His brown eyes flashed with devilish amusement. "Although he would probably kill me if you spent so much as a night."

"Well, I could see how he'd feel threatened."

The smile on Prospero's face faded, and the gleam of interest was back, making her drop her gaze in an automatically submissive response. His chuckle and the resulting movement of his well-muscled chest drew her eyes to where his nipple piercings poked up under his thin t-shirt. She jerked her eyes back up to his face.

"Such a good little girl," he murmured in that way dominants were so good at. "No wonder he goes crazy when you disappear."

"I'm not good," she blurted, flustered. Hell, no one had paid the least bit of attention to her before the Aphrodisia had shown up and turned her life on its ear. She really needed to know how supermodels fended off admirers, because the way Atypicals had been acting around her lately she should have been modeling underwear for Atypical Victoria's Secret. Going from awkward and unwanted to awkward and highly sought after left her clueless about how to deal with advances. At least when she was with Valentine people minded their manners.

"I'm sure Valentine makes sure you're a good girl."

Heat crept up her neck into her cheeks.

His pained wince was almost comical. "I apologize. That was crude. You tempt me to indiscretion just by existing. I'm usually much more of a gentleman. I have the feeling I'd be less of one the more I got to know you."

Dirty man. She rolled her eyes at him and he chuckled.

"Are you blaming your wicked thoughts on this poor girl, Prospero?" Xana appeared and sat on the couch next to Jory, signaling for her submissives to kneel in the space separating the two couches.

Relief stole over Jory, who was only too happy to have someone chaperone this conversation.

"You can't tell me you're immune to her," he replied. "If you said you were, I wouldn't believe you."

"It's even harder to resist her after you've tasted her," Xana admitted. "But my own new toys are more than sufficient to keep me from coveting what belongs to others."

Rebuked, Prospero shrugged. "It's better that she's in love with Valentine anyway. I'm too old for such a pretty piece of fluff."

Jory thought of denying that, since the ten years he had on her didn't seem like a big deal, but then realized it would sound like encouragement.

"She's more than fluff, and you know it. If she was just a pretty face you'd have lost interest by now." Xana's gaze was sharp.

Prospero rose and sketched a bow, but winked cheekily at Jory before walking off toward the back rooms.

"Go wait for me by the door," Xana told her subs. They rose and went across the room, Xana watching them until they were out of earshot. "It's your choice you know, Jory," she said, chucking her under the chin. "Things between you and Val are so screwed up, you could take Prospero up on his offer and no one would bat an eyelash – least of all me, Dane or Jurgen. I could tell Valentine things are over between the two of you, and he'd have to understand."

Jory's throat suddenly hurt, and she felt her face twist miserably. Life wasn't fair and all that, but this situation was unbearable.

Sure, the Aphrodisia had brought her and Valentine together in the first place, but being in love with a man who made her a sex zombie was an unexpectedly cruel reality. She could be with him and be perfectly happy that way, but she wouldn't be more than an empty-headed toy. There was a temptation to be okay with that, but she'd always thought of herself as more. Her romantic relationship shouldn't define her as a person, but because of the Aphrodisia, being with him fundamentally changed her.

"I can't be with Valentine, but I can't not be with him," she managed to get out, the words strangling her. "He's...my life."

Xana grunted. "This has got to be one of the most frustrating situations I've ever heard of. You're damned if you do, and damned if you don't." She shook her head in exasperation. "Both of you are going around in circles, miserable when you're apart, but so fucking creepy when you're together. This last time I was afraid your mind was gone for good. You were like a...a..." She gestured vaguely.

"A blow-up doll?"

"Yes! Subspace is great when it happens naturally, but at that extreme level? It's not supposed to be a perpetual state. I mean, if some people are into that, fine, but that's not you. The old Valentine wouldn't have allowed such a huge absence of…self-determination." Xana seemed to realize her voice was rising, because her next words were quieter. "He loved you for you, and loved how intelligent you are, and that you argued with him about things that were important. It made him a better person and it took him down a peg, which he needs. You grounded him just as much as he did with you. But now it's all 'slave do this, slave do that,' and you do it without blinking. Hell, when you called me to get you out, I don't think I've ever been so surprised. I didn't think there was any of you left in there." Xana wrapped an arm around Jory's shoulders, pulled her closer then kissed her forehead. "Thank God we got you back, at least. Now if there was only some way to knock a hole in Val's thick skull and let some light in."

Jory laid her head against Xana's shoulder. It was good to have so many friends in her corner. It was hard to believe she'd ever worried about calling them for help.

"You know, I don't think he remembers anything about the past at all," she admitted. "It's like the Aphrodisia has taken him over and erased a lot of his memory."

Xana sighed and pressed her cheek against the top of Jory's head. "I know, gorgeous, and he's gone missing again. I think the next time we find him we'll have to ask the Bureau to have him hospitalized. He's sliding into villain territory. It goes against everything he stood for, and he's a danger – both to himself and potentially to others."

Tears stung Jory's eyes. Xana was right.

As much as she didn't trust the fucking Bureau, without their help, Valentine might become her nemesis.

*

"We've gotta move," Brock whispered, tapping Jory's shoulder as though she wasn't watching the same scene he was. He still treated her as if she was new and needed protection, even though he'd assessed her at practices and knew what she could do. Maybe it was just a dominant thing.

She crept over the crest of the hill with the rest of her group, impressed by how quiet they were even though there were eleven of them. The hero group's lookout person passed just behind them, where they'd been only moments before. Could he feel the eyes on him as he struggled over the rocky terrain?

How their intelligence people had found out not only where hero and mercenary groups were, and whether one group was planning on interfering with the actions of the other was beyond her. She was glad all she had to do was show up and be ready to stop things from getting out of hand.

The hero's target tonight was Tobias Martin, whom the Bureau had apparently decided needed to be neutralized because of his tactical abilities and their potential use to the mercenaries. The man lived in a secluded farmhouse with his wife and family, and probably thought no one knew who he was, let alone that they'd care to find him. Jory imagined the family asleep in their beds as strangers surrounded the place, over half of whom had been given orders to kill him and take his family into custody.

It was hard to believe that even the Bureau would order something so callous. The man hadn't actually done anything; he was merely on file as being a mercenary and someone who could be useful to that movement. This wasn't exactly fighting fair.

So many times she and Valentine had discussed how groups defined the line between good and evil. But could all these heroes, people who'd come into this work wanting to help and protect, be so brainwashed that they couldn't see for themselves that what they were doing was wrong?

Heroes were tested for their intelligence and their ability to think on their feet, but when she considered all the training they'd had, they'd never been taught to question orders. If anything, obedience had been drilled into them, and she could only imagine the effect was stronger for heroes who'd been raised in the Atypical school system. Just how brainwashed were they? These orders didn't seem to faze any of them, so just how far could the Bureau push the envelope? It was appalling to discover the heroes she'd grown up idolizing were so flawed, and it was terrifying the Bureau's power could go unchecked.

Taking out the sentry might have tipped the heroes off to their presence, so they left the man alone, watching his retreating back until he was well out of sight. They followed the downward slope of the ridge, staying low until they reached the tree line. To their right, heroes were making their way down the road, sticking to the shadows, likely invisible to eyes that weren't expecting them. There were two doors into the house, and one large picture window in the front. The heroes moved through the unnatural silence toward the front door.

"Stop," Xana commanded, from the porch's shadows, her voice ringing sternly through the darkness. She stepped in front of the door and a floodlight blazed to life, illuminating her as if she were a wrathful, leather-clad goddess.

Beside Jory, Brontë murmured, "Just look at her. I'm going to come in my pants."

Between the tension in the air, and Brontë's uncharacteristically lewd comment, Jory almost laughed aloud. Kade gripped her shoulder and frowned at Brontë to silence her.

"Peacekeepers?" the leader of the heroes asked Xana. "You're interfering in Bureau business. Step aside or you'll be taken into custody." The hero group was looking up and down the ranks of the peacekeeper group as they moved into the light. They formed a human wall in front of the house. With half of them in leather and half in spandex, no wonder the heroes were confused.

"No," Xana said, her expression neutral. "Mr Martin has done nothing to deserve this. If the Bureau wants to play at vigilante justice, they're going to have to deal with us."

"We have orders. You're the ones who are playing vigilante!" the man spat, his face florid.

"You know this is wrong. He hasn't done anything wrong, and even if he had, there's due process. He would deserve to hear the charges against him, he would get to have representation, and he must have a trial. This isn't justice."

Wind howled down into the valley. Jory glanced up at the windows of the house, but no lights had turned on. Someone in the house had to have been woken by the noise. Were they watching out the windows in silent confusion, or were they sneaking away into the night? Just when she thought maybe they were still asleep, she caught a glimpse of a child peeking over the sill of the far upper window. Hopefully he or she would wake the others.

Jory and a few others from her team, including Kade and Brontë, joined the human shield in front of the house.

"So you'd let us arrest him?" the hero asked, his tone skeptical.

"Do you have the authority to do that?" Xana asked. "Are you enforcers?"

A man behind their leader shuffled then looked back at someone else, as though this was an argument they'd already had between them. Maybe they weren't all lost causes.

"Well, no, but we have more authority than you do."

"So you expect us to hand him off to you so you can make him disappear?"

Some of the heroes were grumbling, but it was hard to tell if they were angry about what Xana was saying, or they realized they were doing something wrong.

"We don't trust he'll make it back to the Bureau alive, let alone that he'll get a trial. And what would the charges be? We have intel saying he hasn't done anything unlawful. Do you have trumped-up charges ready, in case this mission failed?"

The leader stared at Xana in silence. Two heroes turned away from the confrontation and walked away, back up the road their group had come down. Two out of twenty-something was a start.

"Stand aside or you're just going to get hurt," the man warned, brows lowered. Several heroes took melodramatic threatening stances, their hands out and ready to attack.

Xana's sneer broadcasted her intentions before she even spoke. "Bring it, dickbag."

So much for talking their way out of this.

A blast of preternatural air hit the peacekeepers. They all staggered, but no one fell. The hero leader backed to join their front line, surveying his people to see who had attacked before he'd ordered it. Confused, the other heroes followed suit, throwing a ragged volley of attacks that bounced harmlessly off various shields thrown out by peacekeepers.

They stood there for a few minutes, launching attacks back and forth like some sort of Civil War re-enactment battle, with neither side gaining a foothold. Jory caught sight of several heroes splintering off toward the back of the house, and she nudged Kade and Brontë. They sprinted after the heroes, and she hoped the hole they'd left in the shield wall wasn't a problem. If the heroes got to the back of the house, and the other door, it would only take a minute to bust it down. The little face she'd seen spurred her on. No child deserved this kind of fear.

She turned the corner just as a woman blasted a cone of fire toward her. Kade bowled Jory over, crushing her belly down in the loose soil.

The smell of singed hair. Burnt flesh.

The alley.

The alley.

Seraphina's charred body.

Flesh melting off bone.

Panic gripped her squeezing her lungs until it felt as if the last molecule of air had been squished out of her. She gasped and gasped. Dirt in her mouth.

Kade was motionless on top of her, probably dead.

This was now, not then.

Oh god. Kade.

Why hadn't she been more careful? Why hadn't she kept her shield up?

Her scream was raw and ragged. She wrestled her arm out from under her chest, which wasn't easy to do with Kade's dead weight on her back. She forced herself back under control, hit the group of heroes now trying to get through the back door with a patch of ice that stuck their feet to the ground, rather than freezing them entirely.

They fought to free themselves and she formed a shield of ice between her group and the stuck heroes. Bits of Kade's clothes were smoldering, but he groaned and winced, rolling off of her, but then going still again.

She wanted to cry, but there was no time.

Brontë smacked out the last of the embers on Kade before turning her attention to the heroes, who were still trying to attack.

"Kade, you stay down and watch to make sure no one comes up behind us," Brontë commanded.

He struggled until he was sitting up and nodded. From the amount of scorched flesh Jory could see, he probably shouldn't have done that much.

"It's handy that your shield is transparent." Brontë laughed humorlessly then poked a finger around the edge of the icy thing. A clang of prismatic color and sound burst from her fingertip and concussed into the enemy. The entire group lost their balance, and with their feet still stuck to the ground, they fell. There were audible snaps as a few of them broke limbs because of the odd angle. Jory winced as the screams began.

Fuck. These people were supposed to be on her side. This could have been her, and her team if they'd still been alive. They were just following orders.

Two of the five were struggling to get up, unhurt and furious. Before they could try another attack, Brontë aimed a bolt of sound at each of them that hit with such force they were knocked unconscious.

Brontë grimaced at Jory. "They're going to have headaches in the morning."

"They tried to kill us," Jory said, glaring at the heroes, "and they were trying to attack innocent people, so I don't feel too bad for them."

Not knowing what else to do, Jory rapped politely at the door while

Brontë worked at binding Kade's wounds. Unexpectedly, the door creaked open and a woman stared out the door, her short dark hair sticking up in all directions. She was dressed, and wore boots.

"The way is clear if you want to make a run for it," Jory said simply. "We may or may not be able to convince them to go away." The woman looked at her for a long moment, then nodded. "I was surprised you answered the door."

The woman snorted. "I seriously doubt an enemy would knock. But who are you? Who are they? How the hell did we make so many enemies?"

Jory glanced around, but no more heroes had made their way to the back of the house yet. "The Bureau has decided your husband's abilities are threat to them, because he's not a hero."

"But that's ridiculous," the woman said shaking her head. "He'd never hurt anyone. We're pacifists, for God's sake."

"With the war on, there's no reasoning with them. They seem to have thrown the rulebook out the window. I'd suggest you take your family and hide for a while, at least until this blows over."

There was the sound of sleepy children asking questions, and a man's voice reassuring them. The woman had a pack ready, as though she'd been prepared for this eventuality all along.

Without any more argument, the family followed Jory up into the hills, with her as a shield, and Brontë guarding their backs.

When they were well enough away, and had avoided the sentries, the woman kissed her cheek. Mr Martin seemed stunned, and unable to process what was happening.

"Thank you for this," Mrs Martin said, shaking both of their hands.

"Do you have somewhere to go?" Jory asked, hoping she would say yes. It wasn't as if Jory had anywhere to hide them.

She laughed lightly. "We've lived off the grid and off the land for so long that not having a roof is only a mild inconvenience. We'll find somewhere to hole up until we hear things are safe again." She squeezed Jory's arm and the family made their way into the night, leaving her with the impression that they'd be just fine.

*

When her phone rang, she groped for it, coming awake through a confused tangle of dreams and thoughts. Daylight streamed from the guestroom's window, far brighter than she would have expected.

Day?

She unlocked her phone and answered it.

"Hello?" She sounded groggy even to her own ears.

"Jory... It's me." Amy's voice was barely audible over the din of from wherever she was calling.

"Am I late for something?"

Amy's labored breathing was the only response.

"Amy?"

"Shh. One sec."

Memories of the night before started replaying in her mind, and she craned her neck to see the clock on the pretty wooden dresser.

Mission. Kade patched up at the hospital. Home. Shower. Bed. Now it was about 10 AM. Three hours sleep after a long night.

She sat up in bed, feeling every bruise and ache.

"Amy?"

"Sorry," she whispered, breathless. "I'm at the mall on Second. Are you nearby?"

"Um...I could be." She slid out of bed and rifled through the closet for some clothes. "Was today the day we were shopping for the stuff to make wedding favors or something? Sorry I'm so scattered. My days are all mixing together." The jeans she hauled on were loose, but they'd stay up. Most of her clothes hung on her lately, but stress tended to steal her appetite.

"No, it's not that," Amy whispered. "I was kind of hoping you'd be my superhero on-call." She gasped. There was a crash, and a nearby scream that wasn't Amy's. "There are...villains here, or something. I'm hiding in Nordstrom's."

Fuck. Why didn't she say that sooner? She jabbed the speakerphone button and stripped the jeans back off, hauling on her fighting leathers.

"I'm coming! Be there in five! Text me if you move so I can find you," she barked, adrenaline waking her up better than coffee but a lot less pleasant.

"Okay." The line went dead.

She tugged on her boots and tied them in record time. *Oh god, Amy.* As she ran out of her room, Brock strode into the hall, wearing only his boxers.

"What is it?"

"Atypicals at the mall on Second, fucking things up. My best friend is there." She clattered down the stairs, hoping he'd follow later, not that this was the sort of thing she could imagine mercenaries getting involved in. She got to the front yard and realized having no car was a problem. She was going to have to run, or hail a cab or something. It was hard to slow her brain and problem solve when she was so scared for Amy.

She started running up the road. A few blocks from the house, Brock pulled up in the van with the rest of the team except for Kade. Xana was with them too. Jory jumped in and they sped off.

"I wasn't expecting this much back-up," she said, so grateful she didn't know how to express it.

"What? Why not?" Brock asked, glancing at her with a brow raised.

"Well, this isn't really a mercenary-type job."

The van rang with laughter. It wasn't just Brock, either.

"Really, Jory? Still?" Xana admonished.

"What do you mean?" she asked, feeling sheepish.

"You're a kid with abilities," Brock's slave Rowan replied. "Someone messes with one of your friends. Do you help? Of course. Do you stop the guy taking the little old lady's purse? Do you stop the neighbor who's beating his wife?" She shrugged. "How could you not help?"

They all nodded.

Xana smiled. Together the whole group of them recited, "If you have the ability, you have the responsibility."

Something they'd learned as children? She couldn't remember ever hearing it before.

"Even if you're 'just a mercenary,'" Brontë said slyly, smirking at Jory. "We just don't get credit for it on news reports."

Ouch. And here she thought she'd gotten more open-minded since she'd met Valentine. Old stereotypes died hard. "Touché."

They reached the mall just as Jory was about to have a panic attack. Amy didn't belong in the middle of something like this. No Typical did.

They left the van in the middle of the walkway and headed for the mall entrance. Two ambulances, several police cars and a fire truck were already there, but until the situation was under control, Typical emergency response couldn't do much.

"Enforcers are on their way," one of the officers called out. "You can get in on the first floor now. They've gone up to the second."

Jory waved a hand in acknowledgment, and they moved in, entering through the automatic doors into the mall on-guard and ready to defend themselves. People were down on the floor, hiding behind the foyer fountain and various signs. Brock gestured Typicals toward the exit, and they streamed out to safety.

Not for the first time, Jory wondered at the Typical reaction of hide or run. The runners were long gone. The hiders had probably stayed safer during those initial moments, but now that the danger had moved along, they needed to become runners. There were no casualties that they could see, but bits of display and wall were demolished and smoldering. Nothing serious enough to threaten the building's structural integrity, from the looks of things.

Fatigue dragged at Jory's limbs as they started their silent sweep. She just wanted Amy to be safe so she could curl up in a corner and doze off. Screw everyone else.

Jeez – what kind of hero had thoughts like that? Of course she wanted everyone to be safe, but couldn't these crises happen when she was well-rested?

The adrenaline had only carried her so far, and now she was feeling clumsy and fuzzy-headed. She sucked air, wondering whether she'd find her second wind if there was a fight.

She pulled her phone out of her pocket. The last text from Amy was three minutes old, saying she was in the back room of a jean store on the second floor. Hopefully that was clear enough.

Why the hell were Atypicals attacking the fucking mall, and so early in the morning? Weren't most Atypicals night owls? Maybe this was a group of disgruntled senior Atypicals protesting the rising cost of mall coffee? She fought down a giddy laugh. Fuck, she was tired.

They spotted the lookout on the catwalk near the domed window in the roof, keeping watch. A second man was in a jewelry store to his right, loading jewelry into a backpack.

A robbery? Seriously? Couldn't they just make a threat and grab some gold, rather than bust the place up and scare everyone?

"Dumbasses," Brontë grumbled, shaking her head. It was the closest thing to a swear that Jory had ever heard come out of the young woman's mouth.

Xana chuckled. "Now, now, not everyone is born with good sense. Don't be so judgmental."

"We could still be in bed."

"True." Xana put her hand on the back of Brontë's neck. The girl's eyes fell closed in pleasure, and her cheeks went pink.

Thoughts of Valentine surfaced, and the feelings he inspired when they were together. She banished them.

There could be more than two Atypicals here, and who knew what powers they had? It wasn't time to get distracted and sloppy.

They split up, and Jory took a back stairwell with Xana and Brontë to the second floor to capture the smash-and-grab idiot. The others went up the covered stairwell to the catwalk. Eventually the lookout would see them, and either he'd attack or make a run for it. The five-to-two odds suggested he'd run, but if they were doing something this stupid in the first place, who knew?

"Go check on your friend," Xana ordered. "We've got this."

"No, I'll stay until things are under control."

"If you're distracted, you're just going to get underfoot." Her tone said it wasn't a suggestion. "I think you need to get settled then you can come back and see if we need help sweeping up. If they're robbing a mall, they're dumb as stumps and not very powerful."

Jory nodded and slipped down the hall, keeping to the wall so the sentry wouldn't notice her. The overhang hid the store signs, so she moved along, looking for a store selling jeans. There were several. She tried three before she finally found the one where Amy was hiding behind staff lockers with a female employee.

She'd assumed Amy was safe, but seeing her safe with her own eyes was still a relief.

"You rang?"

Amy rolled her eyes. "Finally! I thought this pizza shop guaranteed delivery in thirty minutes or less."

"You can't rush quality, lady."

Amy climbed to her feet and hugged her. "Ugh! Your leathers need dry cleaning."

"Yeah. Most of that is from last night. Watch my right sleeve, the blood is still sticky."

"Excuse me while I spew all over my savior."

"You didn't specify you wanted someone clean."

"True. If I wanted a clean savior, I wouldn't have asked for you, dirty girl."

Jory snorted. "They sent me to check on you, but I'm going to head back out and see if it's safe yet. Looks like it's just two yahoos busting up the place so they can steal some shit."

"Villains," Amy replied. "And dumb ones. There seem to be a few of those kicking around. Not good enough to get onto a team, but not clever enough to find a paying use for the power they do have." She shook her head.

Living with Talbot probably made this sort of discussion commonplace in her life now. She'd always been smart, but it was weird hearing Amy talk about Atypical things. They'd drifted so far apart in the past months. If life ever settled down, she needed to fix that.

"Stay here. I'll come tell you when it's clear."

The employee agreed wholeheartedly, but Amy raised a brow.

"Fuck that. I'm bored of hiding."

Jory rolled her eyes at Amy, who only mimicked her and moved up behind her.

"Don't worry, if shit goes down, I'm using you as a human shield," Amy whispered.

"Shh."

"Shushing."

The mall was silent except for the Top 20 satellite radio channel being pumped in from the overhead speakers. It was a strange counterpoint to the terror in the eyes of the few Typicals who were still crouched here and there, waiting to be saved or meet their end. They'd probably never hear those songs the same way again.

Jory poked her head out fast then took cover behind the wall. The sentry had been looking right at her. A blast of light blazed past Jory's cheek, and she shoved Amy backward into an open shop doorway.

Fuck. That was close.

"I'll just stay here," Amy said from behind her.

"Do that."

A scream sounded from the atrium. Jory formed a transparent shield of ice, and peeked around the corner again, hoping the shield would survive whatever the guy was throwing at her. Where were the others? They should have neutralized the guy by now.

The man was gone, but movement drew her gaze downward to where he hung by a rope. His neck hadn't snapped but she could hear him choking, even from hundreds of feet away. A dark figure stood alone on the catwalk, rope slithering over his black leather with terrifying effect, the other end of the sentry's noose circling his feet like an affectionate pet.

Oh...my...fuck.

Their gazes locked and everything around them slowed until there was nothing except his eyes and the hummingbird flutter of her heart in her throat. For a moment, she wondered if she'd meet her end, held prisoner by the depths of those glittering black eyes.

"A peace offering." His voice echoed across the empty expanse of air between them.

Something tugged insistently at Jory's arm. In the moment, she'd forgotten all about Amy. She'd even forgotten about the man who swung like an ugly purplish pendulum from the end of Valentine's rope.

"Who the hell is that?" Amy asked, sounding almost as spellbound as Jory felt.

"Take a wild guess."

"Holy crap," Amy whispered. "I can't decide whether I'm terrified or turned on."

Jory barked a laugh. "Welcome to Joryland."

She cleared her throat then cast an ice ledge under the man's feet, to take his weight. Immediately, he started gasping for air and clawing at the noose. "Robbery isn't punishable by death, Rigg."

"He tried to hurt you." The words were the man's death sentence.

This was worse than having a guard dog. At least you could call off a guard dog. Valentine didn't seem to have an off button. She seemed to turn him on all right, but off was a mystery.

Valentine was recalling part of the rope and it slipped upward in his fingers, making the noose tighten again.

She let the connection between them open fully. *You kill him and we're through.* There was no saying how much of that he'd catch, but to her relief, his rope wrapped around the man, and let go of his throat before it strangled him.

Rope slithered, hogtying him. He'd bound her the very same way on numerous occasions. His lip twitched in amusement.

"See you soon."

"I don't want to see you again."

"Liar." He winked then jumped, freefalling from the catwalk.

Behind her, Amy screamed, just as his ropes caught him and carried him away.

Chapter Eleven

"Fuck. I knew it. Why are you spying on me?" As Jory hoisted herself out of the water and onto the pool's deck, the bounce of her bare breasts and curve of her tiny frame momentarily distracted him from her words. Her wet body glistened, pale as snow even though it was mid-summer. Behind her, the pool looked inviting, expensive and well maintained, just like the rest of the house. A high concrete wall, as well as a shortage of neighbors gave him far too many ideas.

"Is it spying for me to look at what's mine?" he murmured, arching a brow as he sat on a lounge chair. "Besides, submissives left unsupervised seem to have a habit of disappearing. What was stolen can be stolen back."

Her pale eyes cut like shards of ice. Did she hate him? Perhaps. Would she let him fuck her? Probably.

She was so very beautiful, and he was pleased to see she hadn't removed the pretty ring he'd put in when he'd pierced her clit hood. Perhaps she'd run off, but that piercing said she still *wanted* to be his.

If it wasn't true, he was willing to pretend.

It was time they stopped this ridiculous game. Either she belonged to him or she didn't. He had no interest in owning a girl who kept running from him. The impulse to take her away by force lurked uncomfortably close to the surface, but he couldn't spend his life tending to a captive. It may be fun to keep her that way for a while, but being her jailer for the rest of their lives sounded like a lot of work. Besides, one of his supposed friends would free her again when his back was turned. He'd tried everything short of killing them to make them go away, but they kept turning up as though they'd been invited.

He leaned back in the chair, hands behind his head. The girl snatched up the folded towel from the chair beside him, and started to wrap it around herself.

"Did I tell you that you could cover yourself, girl?"

She bristled. "I don't need permission, especially not from you. I'm a free woman."

"No," he said. "You're not." Valentine got to his feet and gazed down at her. The way her eyes shifted away from him and she hesitated in closing the towel were perfect. He liked her like this, trying so hard to not submit to him, and yet so obviously wanting to yield.

"I'm free now." This time the statement was said with so much uncertainty it was as though she was asking for his permission.

"If you honestly want me uncollar you, I will allow it," he conceded. "But a week from now, or a month, when the Aphrodisia comes, you'll grovel at my feet, begging me to take you back." He shrugged reasonably, and loved the fury with which she tried to stare a hole in the wooden side table, since she couldn't look him in the eye. "Just because you hate me doesn't mean you don't want me to fuck you."

The blush crept over her skin, turning her from alabaster to all-over pink.

"You love when I bury my cock in your ass too much to give it up."

She was trembling now – angry, embarrassed – but her nipples were hard, and he doubted it was only because she was cold.

"Go away," she whispered. "I don't want to belong to you anymore."

Her words stung, but he chuckled, not about to let her know she was capable of hurting him. It wasn't as though he loved her, right? After all, they'd only been together a few days that he could recall, although he'd been told of much more by Xana, meddlesome as she was. Not remembering what everyone else could made him feel stupid and angry, but for now it didn't matter. He had a toy to play with, and it was time to force some honesty from her.

"You don't want to belong to me, but even now you're shaking. Your body knows who it belongs to, and it's urging you to kneel and beg for me to do horrible, depraved things." He smiled. "But now, Jory? Really? What if someone comes home and finds me tying you up, or beating you until you come?"

Her chest was heaving – her nipples rising and falling jerkily with each uneven breath. "They won't be home until later," she admitted then bit her lips together.

He casually sat back down, as though his cock wasn't pulsing hard in his jeans, begging to be inside her. "So what you're saying is, you'd prefer me to stay."

"I... No. This is a bad idea, Valentine. How did you even know I was here? You weren't supposed to know."

"I've known for days." He smiled faintly. "Why do you keep calling me that?"

"V-Valentine?" she stuttered, running her fingers through her hair.

"That's your name. Or did you forget that too?" He could tell she'd tried to make the last bit sound venomous, but it had come out wobbly.

"No, I haven't forgotten. Why are *you* using it?" He eyed her speculatively. "Ah...you want me to remind you who's in charge, don't you." The snap of his fingers made her jump, but she didn't obey his hand sign to come to him.

"Come here," he said quietly. "Now."

She slunk nearer, her mind and her body visibly at war the entire way.

"Kneel." He'd opted for a verbal command rather than a hand signal, knowing she'd find it harder to refuse.

She shivered violently then sank into the proper position. The cement pool deck would be a bitch on the knees, but that wasn't his problem. Reminders didn't need to be pleasant. He grabbed her hair and forced her head back. Her mouth opened to gasp, but stayed that way, and her eyes hazed with desire.

"Who am I to you, little bitch?"

"Sir," she whimpered. "I'm sorry, Sir. I should never call you Valentine."

He smacked her face, hard enough to correct her, but not hard enough to bruise. She cried out in surprise, but from her dreamy expression, the slap had only shoved her further into subspace.

"No, you shouldn't." He stroked the red patch on her cheek and she leaned into the caress, her eyes teary, but he doubted it was from pain. They couldn't help what they were when they were together. Why couldn't she accept that? "But don't worry. After I'm done with you, I'll leave you alone. Until the next time I want you."

"But what if *I* don't want *you*." Her bottom lip was trembling, and he leaned in and caught it between his teeth. When he let go, she kissed him. The whimper that followed was so tiny and helpless he groaned inwardly.

He wanted to tie her. Hurt her. Fuck her.

The plan had been to talk, but it was hard not to touch.

According to Xana, he and Jory had always had a troubled dynamic, and his interactions with her kept supporting that assessment. He didn't like it. He should probably just leave her alone. He forced himself to rise and walked to the unlocked gate he'd used to get in.

Letting her know he was watching her had been a mistake.

"Don't go," she begged, reaching for him even though he was too far away. "Please, Sir."

Irritated, he sighed. "You complain you don't want to be with me, Jory. You run away, you act like I'm the devil. I hear it's always been like this between us, but the cat-and-mouse routine is getting old. Either you want to be with me or you don't. If it's just pity or the Aphrodisia between us that keeps you from leaving me for good, I'd rather be raving mad and locked in a basement, than have you continue to act like I'm forcing you. We both know you spread your legs for me willingly."

"Our relationship isn't easy for me," she admitted. "Being with you doesn't leave me with much self-respect. Yes, my body wants you, but the rest of me does too, even though I shouldn't. You treat me like shit."

"And we both know you fucking love it." No point in pretending it was a question.

Her cheeks flamed scarlet, and she covered her mouth with one hand.

Unable to resist her, he strolled back, loving the way she watched him approach with wide eyes.

He stopped when the toe of his boot touched her knee. She looked up at him with a kind of horrified reverence.

"You love it," he prompted, needing her to admit she did.

"I love it too much, Sir. It scares me."

Poor little thing. He stroked her hair, and she leaned against his legs and pressed her cheek against the denim.

A bird flitted through the pool area and landed on the wall, then eyed them curiously. Other than the wind in the decorative shrubs, there was no sound, not even of far away traffic.

"When I'm with you I'm a different person," she said. "I don't want people to know how much I crave the way you humiliate me, or how deep my submission to you goes. My family, my friends – they can't find out, but one word from you will make me betray myself, even in front of them."

The snort that escaped him was louder than he'd expected. "Are you worried about me behaving myself at Christmas fucking dinner? I'm not the kind of man you bring to your Granny's."

"No?" she asked sadly. "At one point I was actually your girlfriend, but that was before." Silence fell between them. "Now you expect me to be available whenever you have the urge to do what we do, but you don't care about me as a person. Am I supposed to get the rest of what I need – the care and consideration, and the affection – somewhere else?"

His pride wanted him to tell her to go ahead and see other guys on the side – hell, to get married – to act as if she meant nothing to him except a convenient fuck. But there was a constant nagging feeling at the back of his mind saying he'd regret it.

No matter how much she loved someone else, he knew she'd still fuck him if he turned up and snapped his fingers. He had no love to give her – didn't even want to think about that kind of bullshit – but he also couldn't bear her feeling that way about anyone else.

Possessive irritation fought him for control. He grabbed her arm roughly and pulled her to her feet.

The bag he'd tossed down by the door when he'd entered shifted, and the end of the rope it held slid toward them at his internal command, followed by the rest of the coil.

"What are you going to do to me, Sir?"

"Whatever I want to."

"Of course." She pressed her lips together. "I need more time to think about what I want long term. Even before you lost your memories things between us were complicated, and now you're almost like a different person. I have to get to know you again. Is this new you a good man? Does he have control over himself? Those are questions I need answers to before I jump into anything."

Maybe he wasn't the same man, but control? She had no idea how much control he had. How much of it he exercised trying to leave her alone.

The resistance to his presence had fled, and he could feel her arousal through their connection. How could he convince her he had control of himself other than by showing her? However, she hadn't said anything about having to like his demonstration.

"Shh." He put a finger to her lips, and she caught it in her mouth and sucked, then sighed with pleasure.

Such a little whore for him.

Only for him, she'd said.

Staying in control when she was so determined to make him lose it was a game he enjoyed. It was also one of those games that worked both ways. He slid his finger out of her mouth, tapping her on the cheek when she followed and tried to trap it again. "Are you trying to rush me?"

The guilty duck of her head was all the answer he needed.

"I won't be rushed. I guess you need a little reminder of how things work." She groaned, but didn't otherwise object.

With a firm grip on her wet hair, he steered her to where several o-rings were bolted into the wall. Had these friends she was staying with tied her here before? Jealousy twisted in his belly as he backed her against it. His ropes slithered up her body, and although she gasped several times while she was tied spread-eagle to the rings, she didn't try to avoid being secured there.

"Not the first time you've been tied up here, I see." It was like poking a bruise in his mind. He couldn't help it, even though he didn't want to hear gory details.

"Just because you're an asshole doesn't mean I'm running around the city screwing every Atypical that shows an interest in me." The accompanying glare was adorable, especially since he stood a head taller than her. It also filled him with relief.

Even though she was already tied in place, he gripped her wrists, loving how small and helpless she felt his hands. Why didn't she know if she could trust him? He doubted he'd ever hurt her more than she could bear. She'd never so much as used a safeword with him, even when he could tell she didn't like what he was doing.

He slid his hands down her arms, her sides, and then to her small waist, and encircled it for a moment, marveling how, at her size, she could handle him even at his roughest.

The pool water had already dried from her skin, and she felt cool and smooth under his fingers. So pale, this woman, like snow.

He let go of her waist to trace around her belly button and she tried to squirm back and away. Tickling fingers cruised their way upward, barely touching the firm mounds of her breasts, pleased at how her nipples tightened at his touch, and how she tried to get closer, seeking more. He gave each impatient peak one gentle tug before moving his hands away. Lower, he stroked her thighs – front and back, then finally moving to the insides, teasing slowly upward. As he neared her clit, she strained to spread her legs wider, her quiet whimpers making his cock throb.

To demonstrate his control, he moved his hands away from where they wanted to be, and followed her thighs down to her shapely calves, enjoying the feel of them under his hands then tickling the backs of her knees until she was squirming.

"Please stop," she whined, half laughing.

He looked up at her, and she seemed to suddenly realize how close his face was to her pussy. Her gasp was needy, and she thrust her hips at him. He brought his mouth to hover just before her clit hood piercing, letting her feel his breath, but not touching, no matter how she tried to force herself closer.

When he tired of that game, he spread her labia further apart. Jory groaned in relief.

Silly girl.

He blew a stream of warm air over her clit then lazily flicked his tongue over the sensitive nub, loving the way she opened her thighs wider, silently begging for more. Under his hands, her muscles tensed. Already? He was going to have to be careful if he was going to keep her on edge. He stopped, sitting back on his heels to watch her writhe, tugging at the ropes as though they'd magically fall away.

It took a few minutes for her to calm. When her breathing was almost back to normal, he started again, pretending to ignore the wealth of desperate sounds she made, even though every squeal and moan contributed to turning his balls purple. She reached the edge of orgasm much faster this time, and when she teetered on the brink, shaking with need, he stopped.

Her wail split the silence. "No, no! I was so close. It's not fair!"

"Fair?" His laugh had a nasty edge, but he didn't care. "How you feel right now is how I feel every time we're in the same room. You turn me into a rutting fucking pig, then you run away giggling. Fair would be if I kept you like this for a few weeks to see what it's like."

"Please, Sir. Anything. I'll let you do anything."

He pinched one of her nipples until it was almost flat and she grunted with pain. The sound made his cock twitch. "You'll let me do anything anyway. What else do you have to offer me?"

Her brow furrowed as she considered this, but he quickly grew bored of waiting for an answer. He started again, but this time brushed the tip of his tongue so softly over her clit that her scream went high-pitched – almost too quiet to hear. She jerked forward and tried to impale herself on his tongue, not that the rope gave an inch.

"Please, please…I know I don't deserve it. I know I'm a bad girl." Sweat had broken out on her skin, and he trailed his lips across her belly, enjoying the way it danced and jumped under his mouth.

"You say that, then after you get what you want, you conveniently forget I've done you a favor by letting you come. I've learned my lesson." He clicked his tongue in disapproval, and she sobbed in incoherent dismay.

"I won't forget this time. I promise!"

"No, you won't," he assured her, "because this time I'm getting what I want first, or you don't get to come at all."

A crazed laugh burst from her lips. "I can't come without you anyway, Sir. Do anything you want, just let me come. Please." The please was more of a sob, but he'd take it as an attempt to be polite.

"I have some questions for you, then. If you refuse to answer or I don't think you're being honest, I'll torture you until you're screaming, then leave you here still bound and horny for your hosts to rescue. Do you understand?"

He stood, pulling himself upright using her body. When he stepped back, she looked as though she was about to panic.

"You can't leave me like this, Sir, please!" She tugged at the ropes to no avail, and she gave a brief sob before getting herself under control.

The tart taste of her, mingled with chlorine, lingered on his tongue.

"On the contrary, I could very well leave you like this. Who would stop me? You?" He arched a brow at her and she whimpered most attractively. Why was every single sound she made it so appealing? And why was the smell of her making him crazy?

She wanted him just as badly as he wanted her. Maybe that was the sum total of it.

The adoration in her gaze, though, said otherwise. She blinked up at him with wide, pleading eyes. There was no subterfuge there. Having her look at him as though he was something special, as though he was her entire world, almost made him want to deserve it.

"Who's staying here with you?"

"Your friends, Brock and Brontë, and their team," she gasped out. "How did you know I was here?"

In response, he unbuckled his belt and pulled it from his belt loops. She shuddered.

"Did I say you could ask me questions?"

"No, Sir. I'm sorry."

"Bad girl." He coiled the buckle end around his fist and lashed out twice, leaving raised red welts on the front of each of her thighs. Her breathy cry and moan wound his arousal tighter. It would be impossible to make it through this interrogation without fucking her, but he was supposed to be proving how much control he had over himself.

"What have you been doing?"

"I don't know," she said flippantly, then her eyes widened when she caught sight of his expression. "I mean, I've been hiding from you, Sir. I've also joined a group of Atypicals trying to put an end to the war."

That sounded dangerous. When he frowned, she shrank back and bit her lip, her gaze wary but aroused.

"You're being careful?" he managed to growl through gritted teeth.

"Yes, Sir. There are a lot of us, so it's not so bad. We look out for each other."

Who cared about a stupid war between people they didn't even know – not that he really knew anyone anymore. Why would she even get involved?

"Who've you been fucking?"

"I see some things about you haven't changed." For a moment he thought she'd laugh, but she held it back. "Only you, Sir. I've been a good girl for you. I haven't even kissed anyone."

Possessiveness flooded through him again. Was someone trying to lure her away?

"Who's been flirting with you?"

One of her pale brows rose. "Other than you, Your Creepiness?"

The belt snapped against the flesh of her thighs before she had time to twitch. Her mouth dropped open in disbelief, and a long, silent pause followed before she gasped. She shuddered violently and he gripped the belt buckle until it dug into his palm, while he tried to stem his desperation to shove his cock inside her.

"Sir, you hit the same spot twice," she accused.

Did she really believe that had been accidental?

"Yes, I did. Now answer the fucking question without the brattiness."

She whined. "Only your friend, Prospero, and he backed off as soon as I told him I'm still yours. Don't be angry."

He wrapped the belt around her throat and slid it tight. There was a hole punched into the leather so he could lock it in place to form a collar and leash custom fit to her neck. He didn't lock it, but slid it tighter until she was gasping. Unable to resist, he kissed her trembling bottom lip.

When her face began to turn red, he loosened the belt. She gulped in air, and there was a new, wariness in her eyes. He grabbed her tangled, drying hair in a fist.

"And are you mine, Jory?"

"Yes, Sir." Her pretty mouth turned down at the corners "Still. I miss the way you loved me when you remembered, but I love you anyway."

"Even though I'm a dick?"

"Yes, Sir." There was no hint of amusement in her eyes now, just a confirmation of fact. It shouldn't have bothered him that she thought of him that way. There had been more – he had been more to her in the past – and now he was less. Anger rose, but it was with himself and his missing memories rather than with her.

"Is this the kind of love I gave you back then?" he asked bitterly, sliding his hand between her legs. Her pussy was still slick despite the breeze, and he pinched her clit between his fingers. Her face twisted into a mask-like grimace of pain, and when she gave him the scream he wanted, he let go, but only to wriggle two fingers up inside her. He finger fucked her tightness, his cock painfully aware of what it was missing out on, and toggled her clit with his thumb.

"Please, Sir," she mewled. "Please, I need your cock. I need to come. Please let me come."

He crushed her against the wall with his body, his mouth coming down on hers to make her shut up. If she said another fucking word he was going to go off in his fucking jeans. He couldn't have wanted a woman this badly before in his life. Her mouth submitted to his, meeting every hot kiss with one of her own. When he bit her neck, her cries turned loud and ragged. With the noise, the police could appear at any minute. He didn't care. He'd fuck her while they watched.

But she needed to suffer more first. How he loved to make her suffer.

He knelt again, biting the welts on the front of her thighs as he continued to thrust his fingers up into her wetness, curling them to hit her g-spot. Her raw screams made him crazy but he never wanted the sound to stop. Swiping his tongue over her clit just made the sound louder, and when he sucked it into his mouth, worrying at it with his teeth, he could feel her body poised for a shattering orgasm.

Again, he abandoned her clit. He withdrew his fingers, rose and stepped back.

She writhed, fighting the bonds. "Please, Sir. I can't bear it. I'm going to die."

A cruel smile met her broken sobs, and he wasn't at all sorry as he smeared her own juices down one of her tear-streaked cheeks.

"Good. Now you know how you make me feel."

If control was what she wanted him to prove, this would prove it without a doubt.

He walked out the gate, ignoring the aching bulge in his jeans. The sound of her wretched weeping followed him out.

*

Darkness didn't stop Valentine from punching the peeping tom, wrestling him to the ground, and binding his hands behind his back. In the still night there was no sound except the labored breathing of the man he was sitting on.

It was Asher. It had to be. His own breath came hard and fast. He was angry, shaking, hot.

"Maybe nobody ever told you this," he whispered, his voice harsh with barely contained rage, "but stalking a girl is only sexy if she actually likes you."

The house stayed dark. Inside the connection Valentine shared with Jory, he felt for her frame of mind. She was trying to settle into sleep, but her continued state of arousal was making that impossible.

But she was safe, at least, and unaware of the danger. For now that would have to be enough. Originally, he'd planned to climb into her room and offer to ease her suffering, but finding a stranger watching her window had pre-empted that.

Now that he'd caught him, what the hell was he supposed to do with the guy? He hadn't thought things through that far. If he turned Asher in to the police or the enforcers, he'd get a slap on the wrist. But was Valentine the kind of man who abducted people? Murdered them?

Yes.

For the girl he would do worse.

What would Asher have done if Valentine hadn't been here to stop him this time? If Xana hadn't stopped him last time? His imagination fed him scenarios that twisted in his gut.

Jory helpless. Tortured. Violated. Dead.

To keep her safe, he would do anything.

This man deserved to suffer.

Valentine dragged Asher into the bed of his pickup, hogtied him, and covered him with a tarp. Rousing, shaking off being stunned, the man started to fight. Too late for that.

Valentine got into the truck and pulled away, not yet sure where they were going.

Chapter Twelve

Sitting on the shaded balcony off the library, Jory sipped her tea, wondering why they were drinking it hot on what was gearing up to be a sweltering summer day. For now it was cool enough in the shade of the baskets of hanging flowers, their reds, yellows, and oranges shielding them from the onslaught of the strengthening morning sun. The view of the pool area below them occasionally had her shifting in her padded wicker chair with the memory of how Valentine had left her there the afternoon before.

Horny, bound, she'd spent ages in increasing discomfort, humiliated and hoping like hell he'd come back and fuck her so hard she'd forget everything, like he'd forgotten. The ropes had eventually dropped to the ground, and she'd wandered back into the house where she'd curled up alone in bed, wishing Valentine had been there waiting for her there. Even if only to mock her.

She'd woken in the night feeling as though he were near, but he didn't come to the door or the window. Since then, a knot had twisted in her stomach. Something was wrong. Against her better judgment she'd called his phone, but he didn't pick up. He hadn't called her back, either.

Brontë was curled up in the seat opposite her, reading a novel, but although Jory had one to read too, reading wasn't the same without Valentine around.

His reading tastes were eclectic, and it hadn't taken long until they'd started reading together, lying in the window seat in a sweet tangle that sometimes became sexual and impatient and naked.

The last time they read together, it had been before she'd lost her team, back when she and Valentine were still together and happy. Cari Silverwood's

Take Me, Break Me had been difficult to read aloud. Blushing, she kept needing to stop and compose herself.

"You're not reading very fast today," he'd teased. "It makes me wonder if you secretly want a man to lock you in his basement, like Klaus does to Jody."

"Shut up!" It was an interesting fantasy, but not something she'd ever want to have happen to her. She started to read again, but then stumbled over a particularly dirty part.

He chuckled. "You beg me for cock often enough that reading that word aloud shouldn't make you stutter. Are you trying to draw my attention to the spider gag idea? I could have one here by tonight."

"Shh," she admonished, glaring at him playfully. "You're interrupting."

"I could interrupt you more thoroughly," he offered.

"Then how will we know if Jody ever escapes Klaus's evil clutches?"

"I'm more interested in finding out if Klaus manages to keep what's his." His voice had taken on a seriousness that made her shudder.

Had he been fantasizing about keeping her against her will even then? Probably. He'd always insisted he wasn't a very nice man. She just hadn't listened.

Not true.

She'd known, but she'd also liked it. To an extent.

"I can hear you not reading from here," Brontë said, smiling, her gaze still on her book.

"Sorry. I'm probably being distracting. I'll go in." She put her cup on the table and moved to rise, but Brontë waved her back into her chair.

"No. Stay. I can honestly say I've read the same chapter twice and I'm not seeing a word." She sighed and snapped the book shut.

"Xana?"

Brontë nodded, grimacing. "I never thought I'd be the kind of woman to let my interests narrow so far, but I can't seem to think about anything else. I've had a crush on her for so long. But look at me. I never thought I had a chance."

Jory considered her friend for a moment. As always, Brontë was impeccably dressed and coiffed, as though she was on her way to spend the day at a country club. She had a quiet, self-effacing beauty, with a fresh face and pink cheeks, and eyes that often sparkled with mischief when she became more comfortable with a person.

"I don't know what you're worried about. You're hot."

Brontë's gaze shifted to one of the flower baskets. "I'm pretty, maybe. I'm also tame. Uptight. But Xana is…she's like a hurricane – all power and terrifying beauty. I'm more like a spring drizzle – just enough weather to mess up your plans. She's so far out of my league. I spent years just watching her. I don't even know how to flirt."

The sentiment was eerily similar to how she felt about Valentine. Someone as backward as Jory never should have had a chance with someone like him. The only reason she'd caught his attention was the Aphrodisia. It was hard to imagine what she would have done if she'd met Valentine through friends or through the Bureau, and he hadn't been so forward with her. She never would have been self-confident enough to flirt. As for Brontë, she wasn't as much of a dork as Jory was, but it was true that her prim reserve wasn't something that matched Xana. Luckily, people didn't need to be the same to be interested in one another.

"Oh, I wouldn't say she's out of your league," Jory said. "The two of you just have very different personalities. I do admit that the day Xana brought me here and I realized something was going on between the two of you, I was pretty surprised. And then throwing Kade into equation – that threw me for an even bigger loop."

The laugh Brontë responded with was more of a groan. "I know. What a mess! If you would have told me six months ago that I was going to agree to be in a poly relationship I would have laughed out loud. And with Kade? No way. We've known each other for too long and there's always been an underlying tension between us that neither of us could figure out the reason for."

It was none of Jory's business, but Brontë seemed to be in an uncharacteristically sharing mood, so it was now or never if she wanted to pry a little.

"So what happened to change your mind?" Jory took a sip of her tea. "I know I shouldn't ask, but staying here with all of you has piqued my curiosity."

"Well," Brontë began, "it's pretty embarrassing, really. This is the twenty-first century, and I'm a feminist even though I'm submissive. I understand and embrace the concept of sexual liberation, and yet somehow when it comes to dating someone new or even expressing interest I get completely tongue-tied. If a dominant doesn't initiate things with me, I'll just wait and hope. It's ridiculous." She plucked a sugar cube out of the dish in the old fashioned tea service and popped it into her mouth, her eyes narrowing impishly. It was probably the least ladylike thing she'd ever seen Brontë do without Xana there to give her an order.

"With Xana though, like I said, I knew she was too good for someone like me." She rolled the sugar cube between her teeth, and sighed. "And the fact that she's a woman…" Her cheeks went pink.

"You'd never been with a woman before?"

"No." She laughed self-consciously. "The idea of trying to attract her, or…*serving* her if I ever got the chance, was even more daunting." Her blush turned from pink to red. She sipped her tea then shook her head ruefully. "Then a few months ago, when Kade mentioned to my brother that he had the hots for her, I was heartbroken. You know him. Big personality – in a lot of ways better suited to her. With him taking an interest, I knew my secret hopes of her miraculously noticing me were going to come to an abrupt and pathetic end. The idea that she might be around more, and I'd be forced to see them together, was a hard pill to swallow." Her face drew down into an expression of stoic misery.

Had Kade known about the attraction Brontë had harbored for Xana? If so, him deciding to put the moves on her wasn't very kind, especially since teammates were supposed to have each others' backs.

"Before you go thinking Kade is a horrible person," Brontë said, holding up a dainty hand, as though Jory had spoken the thought aloud, "no one knew how I felt about her. I hadn't even told my brother." She tucked her feet up underneath her. "It was a fantasy I'd kept to myself knowing there wasn't a chance in hell it would go anywhere. But still not an easy fantasy to walk away from. But if Kade was going to belong to her, I was going to have to get over it."

There was an invisible tug at her mind, and Jory longed to check her phone but she didn't want Brontë to think she was boring her. If Valentine sent her a message, her phone would vibrate, but it was hard not to just sit there staring at it and willing it to ring.

"They started hanging out at the club and I could tell she was charmed by his attention," Brontë continued, seemingly oblivious to Jory's struggle. "I felt like I was going to shrivel up and blow away. Doms always like Kade. He's fun and wild, but also obedient. He's into service, too, and he's good at a lot of things. How can someone like me compete with that? He could fix her car, carry heavy things, re-shingle her roof…and he knew how to please a woman in bed. Plus, he's hot, and I was never sure whether Xana would seriously get involved with a woman or if she just played with them." Her thin shoulders drew together, and Jory felt protective of the girl, even though they were about the same age. There was just a sweet vulnerability about her that made Jory want to shield her.

"Yes, he's charming and helpful, even with me," Jory agreed. "So I can imagine he'd hold a serious attraction for a dominant. So things were going well between the two of them, and then what? Obviously something happened because he doesn't have her all to himself. But it doesn't sound like you were part of his plan, either."

"Ha! No." She offered Jory more tea, but Jory still had half a cup. "I'm still not quite sure what happened, myself. I'm too shy to ask. All I know is that we were all out dancing and drinking one night, and things were looking hot and heavy between the two of them. Typical masochist, I was watching them, and the next thing I knew Xana was standing in front of me. She asked me to dance with her. I probably should have said no, to be fair to Kade, but I figured just once wouldn't hurt, and I wouldn't want to be rude. So there I was, drunk, trying so hard to behave myself and not say anything inappropriate." She shook her head and rolled her eyes.

"And then?" She probably shouldn't have been so eager for details, but Brontë's relationship was still all new and shiny and full of hope. She missed that in her own life.

There was a twinge under her ribs and suddenly Valentine's emotions were loud in her head. Rage was eating at him from the inside, his frame of mind explosive. But where was he and what the hell was he doing? She pushed away the feeling, trying to block it. His emotions were so all over the place lately and it wasn't as though she could do anything to help him.

"Xana didn't say anything about it to me, but when we got back to the table, she looked at Kade and told him if he wanted a collar, he'd have to convince me to take one too." Her laugh was short, still amazed. "I don't know why. She wanted us as a package deal, and wouldn't take one without the other. I – I don't know who was more horrified. I didn't know she was remotely interested in me, and there was Kade looking like she'd shot him in the chest. It's hard to know what her motives were. My guess is Kade was too cocky, and she wanted to take him down a peg, and that I'm a charity case who was in the right place at the right time." Her face reddened, along with her eyes. "We had the job in Berlin right after that, and hadn't been home long when she showed up with you."

What a horrible position to be in. Thinking someone she adored offered her a collar out of pity? The instinctual reaction would be to say no, but it would be hard to turn down that kind of chance. Knowing Xana though, and how seriously Valentine's whole group took their D/s, she doubted that pity was a motivating factor in Xana's decision. Sure, Xana had probably enjoyed messing with Kade's head, but she wasn't the type to offer someone a collar unless she was damned serious about them.

There was a point where Jory had hoped to impress Valentine before he realized he was slumming by dating her. It had been a horrible feeling, but at least the idea he'd collared her out of pity hadn't crossed her mind.

Poor Brontë.

"So you see why I'm not asking Xana why she collared me. Now that I've been with her, I'm a lost cause. What if I ask her, and she tells me it was to teach Kade a lesson? I'd die." She swiped at her tears with the heel of her hand. "Being in love with someone who doesn't love you back is pathetic." She laughed at herself then stopped abruptly, gazing over Jory's shoulder, her gray eyes round. The girl dropped to her knees so fast that, for a moment, Jory thought she'd fallen out of her chair.

Jory turned slowly. Xana was standing on the other side of the screen, and as she slid it aside to step onto the balcony, her brow arched.

Shit. How much had she heard?

"Am I interrupting?" Xana's mouth quirked. "Rowan let me in and said you were reading up here."

Jory nodded. "It's a beautiful day for it."

Xana sank into Brontë's chair. The girl rearranged herself so that she was kneeling prettily at Xana's feet, her floral sundress making her seem far too innocent for the energy zinging between them.

"Yes. Lovely." Xana was watching Brontë, dark eyes hungry. Brontë was staring at the woven grass rug beneath her knees, unaware of Xana's appreciative gaze.

"Mistress, would you care for some tea?" Brontë asked. "Or I could fetch you something else?"

Xana tugged a strand of hair loose from Brontë's chignon and twirled it around her finger. "I'm not one for tea, girl, but could you find me some coffee?"

"Yes, of course!" she said, sounding eager to be of service.

Jory had never even thought of fetching things for Valentine when they were together, and wondered if that had disappointed him. If anything, he'd spent their time tiring her out in other ways, then fetching things for her while she recovered. Did that make her a bad submissive?

"And I need to speak to Jory privately for a moment, so could you leave us alone for ten minutes?"

"Yes, Mistress." Brontë leaned down and kissed the toe of Xana's boot, then rose gracefully and went into the house.

Jory watched Xana watch her go. When she'd gone, Jory frowned at Xana. "How much did you hear?"

"More than she'd be comfortable with."

"So you know…"

"That she thinks I collared her to teach Kade a lesson? Yes, but I already knew." She snorted. "Don't look at me like that. You've known me long enough to know that despite my faults, I'm not unnecessarily cruel. I wouldn't do that to any sub, let alone her. And if you think Brontë is a delicate little doll, you're mistaken. She's tougher than even she realizes."

Jory had to agree with her there.

"I was actually interested in Brontë before Kade made his own interest known. They're very different submissives with different appeals. Lucky for me, I don't have to choose between them." Xana leaned back in the chair, the arrogance with which she took up space so like Valentine's that Jory had to stifle a laugh. They'd grown into dominance together, so it was hard to know which of them had influenced the other in their mannerisms.

"So if that's the case, why don't you tell her?" Jory asked. "She's really unsure of where she stands with you."

Xana sighed in exasperation. "Think about it. Do you think me telling her will fix anything, or will she just blow it off as an empty reassurance? The only way I can prove that I'm honestly interested in her is by showing her. It'll take time, but if we're compatible, I can keep showing her for a very long time."

Jory wanted to argue, thinking even a small reassurance would be kinder than none, but then when she thought about how she'd reacted to Valentine when he'd done the same, she had to admit Xana was right.

"Well, as much as I like to chat about my relationships –" Xana grimaced. "I'm actually here because I was hoping you'd heard from Valentine."

Under Xana's gaze, Jory could feel her cheeks burning.

"Busted."

Jory bit her lip, and nodded. "He showed up here yesterday when everyone was out." She stopped herself from saying more. It was humiliating enough without having to relive it by giving Xana the gory details.

"What did he want?" Xana asked then held up a hand. "Wait. Don't answer that. Stupid question."

"No, he just showed up to torture me and fuck off again. He said he'd known I was here for days." Jory kicked off her shoes and folded her legs underneath herself. "He's kind of closer to being himself. At least he's not acting all feral like he was before."

"Oh, so he's back to just being a dick? Other than the fact that he can't remember much?"

"Yeah, but there's something off about him."

"Something?"

"He seems less…controlled." Jory shook her head. "No, not controlled. It's hard to explain. There's just something about him that gives the impression he's different inside. Like he'd do things the old Valentine would never consider doing."

"To you?" Xana stiffened and her brows slanted downward. "Did he hurt you, little girl? I'll kick his fucking ass if he did."

"No, no. I'm all right. He didn't cross that line." She frowned at Xana, then into her now empty teacup. "Today, though, I can feel how angry he is. Something is eating at him and he's close to losing control. If the wrong person pisses him off, he'll slit their throat."

Xana grunted out an impatient breath. "That motherfucker will be the end of me, I swear to God. Well, what you're feeling matches the message he left on my phone last night. I forgot the stupid thing on the coffee table and didn't hear it ring."

"What did he say?"

"Oh, he left some bullshit story about hooking up with a girl and not to bother him for a few days. He sounded pissed. Even as weird as he's been lately, his words and his tone were a complete mismatch. I went by the coach house this morning but there's no one there."

A stab of white-hot jealousy plunged through Jory, even though she knew it probably wasn't true. He hadn't been with anyone but her since they'd met. She usually got echoes of how he was feeling, but considering how he'd left her yesterday, a seed of doubt crept in. Maybe he'd been hard up and angry enough to look for satisfaction elsewhere. Maybe if he had, it would be for the best.

Sure.

If that was true, why did it make her want to punch something?

Considering the feelings she was reading from him today, though, so clear and strong, if he had picked up she should be more concerned about rescuing the person rather than being jealous. When she focused her attention back on Xana, the mercenary's wry smile banished the rest of her doubt

"Really, Jory?" She rolled her eyes. "Do you think I would have announced that so bluntly if I didn't know it was complete bullshit? He may not be running on all cylinders, but he might be even crazier about you now than when he had his memory intact. He's utterly obsessed with you. Part of the reason why I came by this morning was to make sure you were here, and that he hadn't grabbed you when no one was looking."

Jory covered her eyes momentarily, ashamed by how weak she'd been when he'd shown up, and how long it had taken her to fall asleep. "No, that was yesterday. And as you can see, he left without me. But whatever he's doing, and wherever he is, I think he needs someone with more control to intervene. He's...not well."

Xana swallowed hard, and her eyes shone. It was hard not stare. As much as Jory knew Xana loved the guys, she'd never seen her tear up.

"It's time," she said simply. "He needs to go to the hospital. We keep putting it off, but he's become too unpredictable. I'm afraid he's going to do real harm. He seems almost normal again, but I think it's an act." She leaned forward and rubbed a hand over her face. "This isn't the guy who was our moral compass not so long ago. It's bad enough he's forgotten all of us, but forgetting himself is worse."

Was it time to send him for help? Probably. Jory leaned her head to one side and pressed at a tight muscle in her shoulder that was running up her neck to give her a headache. "You're right. He's kind of himself, and yet he isn't. It's like he's pretending to be Valentine."

Xana sighed. "He's changed. Old Valentine never had an evil bone in his body, but this new guy? I'm not so sure."

Rage flooded through Jory, and she gripped the armrest of her chair. Behind the rage came adrenaline, violence, a surge of almost sexual satisfaction, and then cycled back up into rage. He was beating someone. The thrill of livid adrenaline stole her breath.

"What was that?" Xana asked, alarmed. "Something is going on with Valentine?"

"We need to find him." Jory drew a steadying breath then exhaled shakily. "We have to go now." She lurched to her feet, knocking over a flowerpot.

"Bad?"

"He's going to kill someone."

Chapter Thirteen

The bastard crawled through the smear of his own blood, his panicked scrabbling reminiscent of the way a cockroach made its bid for freedom after the first or second crushing blow. Valentine didn't host even the slightest of sympathies for Asher, and the terror leaching from the man was beautiful. It wasn't the same sexual high he got from being around Jory but it was orgasmic nonetheless.

Here, there were no safewords. Hours and hours had gone by. He'd controlled himself at first, but it was getting harder to do. Every violent act tempted him to do more. To rush. But he didn't want to rush this.

The man would die. Slowly.

He'd hurt Jory. Treated her like a lab rat. Tried to rape her. Then he'd tried a second time.

Valentine wanted blood. The raw connection to Jory throbbed like a rotten tooth. Made his head ache.

Asher howled in agony as Valentine dug his fingers into one of the man's pressure points. It was giving him a high. This was different than fighting, and brought its own set of enjoyments.

"Please, please," the insect kept whining. "I'll never go near her again, I swear."

"No. You won't." Neither of them would. There was no need for Valentine to raise his voice. He had the man's full attention.

Step by measured step, Valentine followed Asher's wet, gritty progress as he slithered across the floor. The blood trail he left was a lopsided Rorschach Test. A giant butterfly's snow angel in a spill of red wine.

Snowangel. The word gave the situation a deeper sense of urgency. A memory flickered, teasing, then disappeared.

"I didn't know she was yours," the man pleaded. "I didn't understand, but I do now. I'll do anything you want. I'll leave the country."

Valentine drew back his foot, swung, and the toe of his boot met Asher's ribs with a satisfying crunch. Asher screamed, a wounded animal. He rolled on his side and curled in a ball, clutching his ribs, trying to keep his organs safe with his thighs. Like that would save him now.

The wet gurgle of Asher's breathing through his mashed nose was the only sound in the room other than Valentine's quiet footfalls and the snick as he opened his pocket knife. So far he'd only used fists and boots, but it was time to move on to more interesting things. Valentine crouched beside him, irritated by the way the man cringed, eyes closed.

"Didn't I tell you to keep your eyes on me? How will I know when to stop if I can't see your eyes?"

"Just stop now. Please. I've learned my lesson. I'll never touch her again. I'll never touch any woman again." The way he was whimpering into his knees made his voice almost inaudible. Valentine was tempted to kick him in the balls just let him know he'd left himself open, having not curled up tight enough, but that would speed things along too quickly. That kind of pain would leave him unaware of his surroundings for too long.

The knife was trying to lure him into hurrying. He itched to slice into Asher's skin, to make him scream in agony. How dare this insect touch her, hurt her? She was his, and his alone. No one touched what was his without his permission.

What this insect had done was inexcusable. She'd volunteered to be the subject of research, from what Xana had told him, but to pin her down and study her as if she wasn't a sentient being, as though she was of no importance past the condition they shared?

She was so much more than that.

Perhaps Valentine treated her like an object at times, but he owned her, and she mostly enjoyed it, at least in the moment. She had a word to make him stop. This bastard hadn't given her a way out, and then after she'd been rescued, he dared try to capture her to do it all again?

He deserved to suffer. He deserved to die.

His ropes curled around Asher's wrists and ankles then pulled him out of his protective ball, splaying him flat on his back. He was sobbing in desperate terror, but rather than filling Valentine with empathy, it made him wonder if that was how Jory had felt when she was at the man's mercy.

Another flash of rage came. He gripped the knife to plunge it into the man's heart. What if Xana and the others hadn't found her in time? It had been a close call, she's said. Anger blurred his vision, and his knife hand shook as he held himself back. What felt like snaps of electricity shocked along the top of his head. This rage was too big to hold. He needed to let some of it out.

He rested the blade against the base of the man's throat and pressed, scoring the flesh, drawing a line of blood. The insect shrieked, as Valentine drew the knife all the way to the neckline of his t-shirt, then quieted to sobs as he changed his hold on the knife and cut the garment away.

Other than the bruises, Asher's torso was almost a blank canvas. The hairless chest and smooth muscle willingly accepted the letters he carved as the man's screams filled the room. When he stepped back and looked at his handiwork, it was all quite legible, even with the blood oozing. It hadn't taken long, even considering the fact that he'd had to revive Asher several times. It wouldn't be fair for him to sleep through the ordeal. It wasn't the neatest work – he'd misjudged how much room he'd need to carve "rapist scumbag" and so the 'ag' had wrapped around the side of Asher's ribs.

At least when the authorities discovered the body, they would understand the man hadn't been an innocent victim.

He paused. Jory deserved to finish him off herself, but she wasn't the type to take pleasure in that kind of violence. For that matter, she probably wouldn't have approved of him doing this much, let alone finishing the job.

For a few minutes he paced, watching Asher bleed. It still wasn't enough.

Not for Jory. She deserved so much more than what either of them had done.

It was time to free her.

But before he withdrew, she needed to be protected from this man. If Asher was stalking her, it meant he was planning to hurt her again. He was an immediate threat to her safety. As the man who'd collared her, protecting her was Valentine's job. But should he untie the man and give him a fighting chance, or should he finish him off while he was trapped and helpless, like Jory had been?

There was no way the man deserved an honorable death, but maybe he'd tortured him enough. With no one else there to rein him in, though, he wasn't sure he would feel the 'enough' when it happened.

Enough. The word rang in his head, but in her voice.

If he was doing this for Jory, maybe he shouldn't do it in a way that would horrify her. Maybe he'd already gone too far.

Valentine lifted the knife is the air, pausing so that Asher's last moment would be filled with the helpless knowledge that he would die. As the knife arced down, Asher screamed.

A frigid blast knocked Valentine sideways.

Company.

Chapter Fourteen

Her hesitation had almost made Valentine a murderer. The crimson spray and smear of his victim's blood painted the basement laboratory, as though Valentine were a vampire toddler making blood pies. Baptized in blood, he stood looking directly at her, the calculation in his gaze draining the last of her hope.

No matter how bad things had gotten, she'd never given up the hope that somehow they'd get him back. But this? There was no coming back from this.

"I stopped," Valentine said. A laugh rippled up out of him. The humorless sound chilled her soul. "I stopped for you, Jory."

"You weren't going to stop," she accused, feeling gutted. "I saw you. You were about to murder him!"

"Well, yes." Valentine watched her, black eyes glittering. "For you. To keep you safe. You trusted him, and he hurt you," he said simply. "Asher was outside the house, trying to catch you again. I thought I should kill him."

Asher? That...swollen-faced mess was Asher? She fought down bile.

God, he'd been outside the house? She felt dizzy and wished she could sit down.

"Even if you need to kill him, you didn't have to torture him first!" Dane shouted, anguish in his voice. "What the fuck, Valentine? You need help, man. We can't fix this for you. We can't fucking fix you!"

Asher writhed in his bonds, gurgled, mouth opening and closing like a fish flopping around the bottom of a boat.

"What was I supposed to do?" Valentine gesticulated with the knife, and the drops of blood that flew off the blade splattered his face. He didn't seem to notice. "The Bureau won't do anything. I won't wait for him hurt her again.

She's mine." His gaze shifted back to Jory and the possessiveness there made her shiver. Was there something else there – a glimmer of himself?

But as soon as the lucidity was there, it was gone again. His black eyes narrowed with pent violence as he looked down at the mess of human on the floor. Brutality rolled off him, overwhelming Jory's senses. She put a hand to the wall to steady herself, and stepped into the room, but her foot slipped in blood and she almost went down.

"Please," Asher gasped, his voice raspy and brittle. "Jory, call the enforcers. He's crazy."

Part of her pitied the man, but part of her wanted to take the knife from Valentine's hand and finish the job. How dare he try to rape her, then stalk her, and then ask her to save him? What if Valentine hadn't caught him? Would she be tied down now, in this very room, at his mercy again?

Could she say vigilante justice was wrong when she'd been doing it only a few months ago? She'd been deliberately wandering the streets and parks looking for predators. Even her work with the peacekeepers could be called vigilantism. But how far was too far?

When she'd first started training to be a hero, in her mind good and evil had been polarized and distinctive. It had been such a naïve, comfortable delusion. She may never have questioned any of it if she hadn't met Valentine.

But this was different. This was evil. Even if his motivation had been to protect her, this was so far past wrong she didn't know how to fix it. She'd known he was a sadist – she'd seen it in his eyes often enough – but this was like a horror movie.

She wanted to excuse this. Excuse him. She'd always wanted to believe that deep down she was a good person, but her instinct was to protect Valentine. If they killed Asher then hid his body…

Bile rose.

How had she gotten to the point where she was considering this?

"We have to get both of you to the hospital," she said.

"No." He stepped between Asher and the rest of them. A long rattling sigh came from the body that lay behind Valentine's boots. Silence descended.

Oh god, they were too late.

"Valentine, you have to let us take him. If he dies…" Her voice squeaked and stalled. "They'll never let you out of jail. Let me try CPR."

"Jurgen called the Bureau hospital," Xana told her. "The ambulance should be here soon."

"He has to die!" Valentine snarled. "He'll never stop until he has you. He'll lock you in his basement and experiment on you and rape you. He needs to be put down like a fucking rabid animal."

She shook her head, edging closer, trying to see if Asher's chest rose and fell.

"No," she said, faking calm. "The enforcers will bring him in. There'll be a trial."

"For what? For hanging around your friend's house? For keeping you the way the Bureau told him to?" Valentine's voice rang strangely hollow against the rows of medical equipment.

She did her best not to look at the table she'd been strapped to, once upon a time.

"You know they've got nothing on him. They'll just let him go. He's obsessed with you and he's not going to stop."

At any other time that statement might have made her laugh, coming from him.

He spun the knife in his hand, ready to stab rather than slash. "This is just how it's got to be, Jory. You need to be safe. This way you're safe from us both."

Fuck, he knew he'd go to jail and he thought it was for the best?

"Valentine, no!"

"Both of us need to be euthanized, Jory." His laugh was bitter. "I'm not much better than he is, and I'm tired." Dark eyes went dead. "I catch flashes of the past, but that's all I ever get. Those memories will never come back. I can't live with that anymore."

He crouched beside Asher's body, knife ready, and Xana rushed him. Valentine pulled a handful of rope from his pocket and flung it at Xana. It latched onto her face, making her stumble and cry out. She went down hard in a puddle of blood.

"I have to make you safe." His knife hand rose in the air then the blade flashed toward Asher's exposed throat.

Jory's hands automatically flew up in a defensive gesture, as though the knife's edge was coming for her. Valentine's gaze pierced her, and he was in her mind, boosting her power. Cold deeper than anything she'd ever made before burst from her palms, burning her skin. The blast caught him full in the face. He crashed back against the wall, and struggled to his feet.

The ice shroud shattered, and he staggered and lurched, clutching his head. His face frosted over, contorted with pain, lips blue. Horrified, she watched as he went to his knees.

What had he made her do? Paralyzing dread crept through her every muscle. She felt faint. Her knees buckled, but she stayed up through sheer force of will.

Nothing she'd ever done had hurt him before – not like this.

"Valentine!" She ran to him as he crumpled to the floor. "Oh god, don't you fucking die."

He stared into nothing, eyes unseeing, breath frozen in his lungs. As stiff and dead as her heart.

*

Part of her watched, far away and impassive, as she screamed and wept. She'd fallen. Blood, cold and sticky, congealed on her clothes, in her hair. But not his blood. There was no mark on him. Still and perfect, Valentine lay on his back, uninjured except for the delicate blooms of frost that had formed over his unseeing black eyes.

The muscles in her legs didn't want to work, and she couldn't see the point of standing anyway. Jurgen had forced her away so Dane could do CPR, but she kept creeping closer, looking for signs of life.

Inside she was desperate, prodding at Valentine's mind, searching for anything, recklessly poking at the icy part of him that was no longer him at all. It refused to yield, frostbiting the tendrils of her mind and power that dared touched it. Vacant. Frantic, she searched her mind for their connection. She found it, severed, dangling, bloody. There was a slack in her mind where the connection had been, and its lack threw everything off axis. Shock. Like someone had ripped away one of her limbs.

The ambulance came. A second. A third.

Trying to force her way into Valentine's mind, she barely noticed as they loaded her into one. They were bringing her back to the Bureau. None of that mattered anymore.

Cold, the synapses quiet, she hammered at the doorway to his mind, hearing the empty echo behind it. His body was abandoned. He'd left her behind.

Something inside her broke, and Jory's soul drained from the severed connection, following Valentine into whatever oblivion he'd gone into without her.

*

No matter how hard she wished to die, her body refused to obey.

The realization had been grim, but slowly, as she came back to herself, it was undeniable. The grief seared, burning away parts of her she hadn't known she could live without. She surfaced and sank. Faces had appeared. Xana, Jurgen, Dane, her parents, Amy. Strangers in lab coats prodding her, jabbing her. Everyone talking in low tones – bees buzzing in the vast chasm of her hollow, colorless world.

A smell, chemical, disgusting, intruded. The buzz and hum of machines. Lights shining bright even through her eyelids.

"Shock," a woman had whispered, "and some sort of brain damage on the scan, but it wasn't a bleed."

"Brain damage?" A man. Upset. Loud.

They were nothing, those words. A soap opera playing out, with her the sedated spectator. Her head pulsed like a fresh burn, despite the haze from the drugs, but it was her chest that hurt more – a rending agony that made her want to claw past her ribs to make it stop.

The dead ones got peace. It was the living who suffered.

Voices in the room. The ones she wanted. The ones who would punish her for her sins. Her parents and Amy would defend her to the last breath, but the others – no, they would never betray his memory and forgive her. She needed them to make her bleed.

She squinted against the brilliance, forcing unwilling eyes to slit open.

A warm hand clutched hers. Xana. Her attention was elsewhere, though, on Jurgen.

"No change?" Jurgen came closer, brushing Jory's hair back as though he'd done it a million times.

No, no, no. Why were they doing this? She was the enemy now, not their friend who was injured. Things weren't supposed to be like this.

"Not since an hour ago," Xana murmured, her voice resigned. She gripped Jory's hand, keeping it warm. That grip – she recognized it. She had tethered Jory with that grip, and slowly forced her to return.

Valentine had invaded her dreams, waiting for her somewhere quiet. He was waiting and she was dallying here.

She'd never deserved his long-suffering patience, and yet in her was a kernel of anger that he'd finally given up and gone. But maybe, if there was a later, he'd tell her exactly how much of an idiot she'd been. She'd only meant to wait out the Aphrodisia, to see what they could have together once it passed. Like a fool, she'd thought they'd have time. If it hadn't been for her stupid pride, he wouldn't have lost himself. He wouldn't have lost his way and taken Asher, and she wouldn't have had to stop him.

He'd only been trying to protect her. Maybe when he'd seen the horror on her face he couldn't live with it.

I killed the man I love to save the man I hate.

The memory of that last moment replayed in graphic detail, stabbing her in the chest over and over again.

Dead...dead...dead...

His beautiful eyes, blank and frost-etched. She remembered that final thrust of power. It hadn't come from her. Somehow he'd fed extra power to her from inside her mind. He must have known what it would do, but how did he know he could do it? And why?

When he'd come to see her by the pool, he'd seemed...not happy, but typical for the new Valentine. Arrogant, pleased to have the upper hand. Irritable.

Had he been depressed? Had she said or done something to trigger this?

Why use her to kill himself, leaving her to hold this huge burden of guilt? It spoke of anger at her. Of blame. Or maybe, for some unknown reason, he'd thought it was right he die by her hand.

"I'm awake," she interrupted the conversation flowing around her.

She was so tired of fighting.

Of life.

Of living without him.

If she could make them see reason, maybe they would kill her too.

*

Not only was she not his next of kin, according to the Bureau, but the hospital staff tried to keep her out when it wasn't visiting hours.

She didn't listen. Maybe she didn't deserve to be near him, but he didn't deserve to lie alone in that room for hours every day, hooked up to machines that wouldn't let his body die. He had visitors during visiting hours, as did she, but two hours a day left long stretches of silence.

At first the nurses caught her and turned her away, but she persisted, acting confused and agitated. Damaged. Eventually, one by one, the staff gave in.

Where was the harm? She'd heard them argue among themselves. He was dead anyway. His body just hadn't figured that out yet.

It helped that she, herself, had been diagnosed with brain damage. The doctor had told her nothing could be done to heal her, but she'd felt around in her mind and the only difference she could find was the bloody stump where she and Valentine had been joined. Now there was a total alien solitude – the absence of sound, of life.

The quiet at the end of his hallway was different today.

A man sat in the chair next to Valentine's bed. He was older, but there was something around the eyes that reminded her of Valentine at his cruelest. His father? He didn't even bother looking up when she entered the room. At first she thought he hadn't heard her, but the alertness in his body language soon suggested otherwise.

"Hi," she said. "I'm Jory." Would he even know who she was by name, or that she'd been Valentine's…girlfriend?

"Oh, I know who you are," he intoned icily. "We've met, but you were unconscious at the time."

For a moment she stared at him blankly, and he finally met her eyes.

"You are not now, nor will you ever be good enough my son," he said, without a hint of apology. "As unremarkable as you are, he showed a single-minded dedication to you that he never had for anything else in his life, so I helped where I could. So really, all of this is my fault." His mouth set in a hard line, which seemed to be the natural expression for his facial muscles. "If I'd let you die with the rest of your team, you couldn't have done this."

The words were a shard of ice jabbed into her heart.

The same thought had been on auto-repeat in her head since it had happened. If she'd died with her team, Valentine would still be alive. Hearing it come out of someone else's mouth finished her.

She inclined her head, accepting his statement for the truth it was, then padded back down the hall.

It didn't matter that she'd only meant to stop Valentine from killing Asher. It didn't matter that Asher had lived, and would mostly recover. Her good intentions wouldn't spare Valentine anything.

Eventually Asher would leave the hospital and go on with his life. If she'd let Valentine kill him, Valentine would be in jail, or institutionalized, but there would have been hope. In jail or in a psych hospital, he would have lived. He might have recovered.

Now, she never would.

*

"You have to get up," Xana grumbled.

The bed changed positions, but she didn't care.

Outside, the sun was out, and she watched impassively as birds scooted between trees.

"Do you think he'd want this? For you to blame yourself and just lie here and let yourself waste away? For fuck's sake, Jory, no one blames you for what happened except you."

The words came to her through a dark tunnel. They spilled over her, skimming past as her body tried to remember how to breathe. She wasn't sure why it bothered.

The warmth behind her shifted, the arm around her torso adjusting more comfortably. "Come on, good girl," Jurgen whispered. "You can't leave us too."

A shallow breath shuddered through her, and her eyelids drooped shut.

"If she wants to die, why are you two trying to stop her?" Dane said, sounding both emotional and exasperated. "If something happened to Jurgen, this is exactly how I'd be. I'd do it myself, instead of wasting away, but it's her life, and her choice. You can't force her to live."

"We lost him, we're not going to lose her too!" Xana cried. "She's all we have left of him, you stupid ass."

"So you're making her stay out of selfishness? How is that fair?"

Voices were raised again, but she didn't bother thinking past the arms around her. The wrong arms, the wrong scent, but when Jurgen or Xana held her at least she was less alone. The raw end of the connection throbbed like a migraine that never went away. The drugs they kept pumping into her didn't take the edge off. There were no drugs to fix what was wrong.

No drug would wake him or make him whole again. He was dead, but he wouldn't die. There was no way to grieve him or let him go. There was only holding him, lifeless in her arms, wondering if it had hurt when she'd murdered him. Wondering if he'd seen what she'd been about to do, choosing to die rather than live with her betrayal. He'd been trying to protect her, like he always had. There was no morality for him when it came to her. She was his, and protecting her had been as important to him as keeping her. More.

He'd been so beautiful and fucked up, but he'd been hers as much as she'd been his. Going on alone would be the biggest betrayal. She couldn't do it.

She'd kissed him and told him she'd never give up, but she was a fucking liar.

Chapter Fifteen

Going on was like learning to swim in tar.

Weighed down, she couldn't breathe, but the others slowly pulled her back from the brink. At first it had been against her will, but slowly they'd convinced her that leaving wouldn't be fair to the people she abandoned.

Her parents and Amy were worried sick, and came as often as they could, but it was Jurgen who'd convinced her. The man shone patience and love into the darkest corners of her. Eventually he'd made her stand on her own again.

Xana had tried to boss her into staying.

Dane seemed unsure of whether she'd made the right choice, but only because he couldn't imagine living without Jurgen.

The day they released her from hospital, she had a panic attack and had to be sedated. Baby steps. They were all living at Brock and Brontë's for now, the two teams melding into one. Amy and her parents were hurt she hadn't chosen to live with them, but the team understood her better. Understood what she'd lost.

Thank god no one shied away from talking about Valentine. She needed the stories to bridge her realities – to reassure herself that he existed in the hours she wasn't at his side.

She spent mornings at the hospital, in bed with him, listening to the Kink Monsters. Now she knew every word to all of their songs, and would sing to him even though she had a singing voice like a parrot with laryngitis. She was forty pages into reading him Brontë's copy of Orwell's *1984*, and thinking she needed to take another sip of water, when she heard the scuff of a shoe.

"Are you here again, Jory?" Valentine's mother, Emma, stood in the doorway for a moment, leaning there to look at her.

"Yeah. I was just reading to him. We used to read to each other all the time, but Mr Lazy here used to take a turn. This is hard on the throat."

The older woman laughed, and put the cloth shopping bag she'd brought with her on one of the chairs. One of the nice parts about his family being rich meant that his room was comfortable, and after so long, it hardly felt like a hospital room at all.

"I brought some clean socks. I thought I'd wash his hair today, at least."

"I'll help." It was probably unnecessary to say, since she always did.

Emma nodded then pulled back Valentine's bed sheet and changed his socks. "Dietrich wants to move him home, but I think that would make visiting less comfortable for everyone else."

Jory felt her eyes narrow, but she glanced down at the book. She loved Valentine's mother. Even though their first meeting had been an awkward nightmare, she'd still been the epitome of grace and good manners. His mom seemed to love the fact that she was sticking around, and didn't care that Jory wasn't the kind of woman her husband had wanted for their son.

"I know you and Dietrich got off on the wrong foot. He's a good man. He just has strong opinions, and he's fiercely protective of Valentine. They were always butting heads, but he's his favorite son."

"Valentine said good things about him." Jory cast back in her memory for anything nice he'd ever said about the man.

Emma snorted. "Don't lie to me to make me feel better, peanut."

Embarrassed, Jory gave a half-hearted laugh. "Well, he did save my life. No matter what kind of relationship Valentine had with him, I won't forget it."

"It was the right and decent thing to do. You don't owe him a damn thing." Emma pulled the sheet back up to Valentine's waist then folded her arms. "Even if you hadn't been our son's significant other, it needed to be done. This whole war is ridiculous and I don't know how he ever got mixed up with it." She shook her head in disapproval, brows lowered.

Jory chose not to respond, and busied herself putting Valentine's worn socks into the bag.

"I won't let Dietrich move Val home. He gets better care here, and even if he never wakes up —" The words caught in her throat. "It's more comfortable here for him. Anytime he visited us in the past few years he was always in a rush to leave. I'd like to follow his wishes as much as I knew them." She dabbed her eyes with her sleeve, then pasted on a brave smile.

"Besides, I'd be worried you'd be uncomfortable and stop coming. Then who would I play cards with?"

She sat at the small table and beckoned Jory over, pulling the ubiquitous pack of playing cards out of her purse. Methodically, she got the cards ready for euchre.

"Is it strange that I was lying awake last night regretting that I won't get to see you two get married?" His mother smiled sadly. "Probably. I'd hoped for a million grandbabies, but our son, Pascal, doesn't want children. I always thought Val had plenty of time."

It was no weirder than her thought the other day that she might still be able to have his baby. She's heard there were situations like this where women had been artificially inseminated, but she didn't know if it would have made him happy or not. It wasn't as though they'd actually agreed to start trying to have a child together. Doing something like that without him being able to consent felt wrong, even if his mother might have agreed. The temptation to bring it up surfaced, but she kept it to herself. They'd talked about babies a lot, but it had been vague discussions about the future. She wished they hadn't waited.

Emma was staring at Jory over her hand of cards. The penny dropping in the other woman's mind was evident.

"No," Jory said firmly.

She nodded, and the light in her eyes snuffed out as quickly as it had appeared. "It was just a thought, but you'd already considered it, I see."

"Without his permission? I can't." At least not now. Not yet. Maybe never.

She doubted he'd begrudge her a child, considering the circumstances, but it was all conjecture. It was something she'd have to think about. Sometimes right and wrong were so intertwined they were impossible to tell apart.

They sat in silence for a moment, deep in thought.

"If you ever change your mind, let me know. I'd set you up so you never had to work another day in your life." Emma laughed at herself. "The words of a forlorn mother with all sorts of money and no one to fill my days with. Dietrich and Pascal are busy with their work, and I just wait and wait for days that will never come now." Her hand reached for Jory's. "At least I got you out of all this. I always wanted a daughter."

They sat there uninterrupted for a long time, their cards forgotten.

*

370

"I still can't believe you're here." Amy's pretty face shone, even though Jory had walked through the door of Amy's parents' house an hour before.

"Like I'd miss this?" Jory grinned, curling a ribbon. "It kills me that your wedding favors look like they're for a kid's birthday party. It's just so..."

"You and me?" Amy arched her brow as she stuffed some candy necklaces and Fun Dip into a yellow happy face coffee mug then handed it to Jory.

"Yup." She put the mug in a precut cellophane circle, drew it up then tied it off with ribbon. "Where did Cari go? She curls ribbon better than I do."

"She went to pick up Chinese food with my mom, I think. She may make better ribbon curls, but when she comes back it might be better if you took over, considering." Amy's cousin was hilarious, but had seemed a bit unhinged since she'd downed a few glasses of Champagne. "I'm not sure we're all going to make it through the evening if she keeps talking about how pissed she is at her husband with those scissors in her hand. She was waving her arms around and I was starting to wonder if I'd be walking down the aisle with an eye patch."

"You'd look pretty badass with an eye patch."

"Oh, I'm sure, but it might not be Talbot's favorite look." She laughed, and Jory's gaze lingered on her friend's one slightly crooked tooth.

The sight filled her with a slide show of memories – of Amy with her hair in pigtails, Amy wearing her favorite Green Day t-shirt, of that time she'd given herself a bob that had gone terribly wrong, of her first date with Talbot that was supposed to have been Jory's first date with him. And this place, with its '70s wallpaper and the pleasant and comfortable smell of...Amy's house. Maybe it was the fabric softener they used? How many times had they covered this very table in glue and sparkles? Tonight felt like the culmination of every crazy craft they'd done together over the years – as though they'd been training their whole lives for this moment.

Jory kept going back and forth between elation and wanting to cry. She was so, so happy for Amy. This was life. These little moments that seemed so mundane, and yet were so momentous. It was a demarcation between what had gone before and what would come after. Neither of them would change because of making wedding favors, but both of them had changed so much recently that it amazed Jory how they could just be here like this, like them. Like they were twelve and their biggest problem was whether they'd bombed a history test. When the hard choices were about which starter Pokémon to choose.

"Do you have any idea how much I love you?" Jory asked.

"Not as much as I love you, jerkface," Amy replied, meeting her gaze. "If you died, I never would have gotten married. How could I have chosen someone else as my Monster of Honor?"

"I know." Jory smiled sadly. "You told me. I'm sorry I put you through that."

Amy held up a hand, not finished her lecture. "If you weren't around, I would have gone to my grave a spinster, and that would have all been on you. Just remember that."

"Yes, ma'am."

Her best friend swallowed down a small sob, then got herself under control and flicked a lollypop at her.

"When we were thirteen you promised me you'd never die." Amy's expression was dour. "It was a pinky promise, bitch."

"Yeah. That's what finally tipped the scales for me, you know. Leaving you. Between you and Jurgen badgering me, I had no chance of slipping away."

"I was so pissed when I ran out of sick days and had to go back to work. Remind me to kiss Jurgen again if they come to the wedding."

"They're coming. They wouldn't miss it." Jory smiled. "They're going to be my escorts."

She had no idea how their old friends would react to her merc friends, but she was so far past caring that the idea was only vaguely amusing. They'd already met her parents and Amy, so after that nothing really mattered. Valentine meeting them would have made her nervous, but now she'd have told them the gory details of their relationship herself if it would heal him. Every damned detail. It had all seemed like a big deal before, but she couldn't remember why anymore.

"How's Valentine?"

Jory shrugged. "We argue a lot less than we did before I killed him, but he's being difficult about coming to your wedding." He was still completely unresponsive. No hope. Not the flicker of an eyelid or a twitch of his finger. Being glib when people asked after him was the only defense she had.

"I wish he could be there. The priest could have caught you doing kinky shit in the bathroom, and my whole wedding could have been a scandal." Amy sighed. "When you go back to the hospital later tonight, you tell him that if he doesn't show up at my wedding I'm not sure he and I can stay friends."

Jory put down the mug she was wrapping and went around the table to hug her. "I'll tell him. He would have loved you, you know."

"Hmm...maybe not." Amy kissed her ear. "Men don't take kindly to threats."

"Talbot takes them from me all the time."

"He knows they're meant affectionately. Although telling him you'd disembowel him if he was late getting to the wedding was probably over the line."

"Nah." Jory pulled away, feeling as if she'd been leaning on everyone else too long. It was time for her to be there for other people again too. The last thing Amy should be thinking about tonight was comforting her.

"True. He's got a good sense of humor. He knows you're kidding."

"So not kidding." Jory tore open a packet of Fun Dip and dumped it into her mouth.

Amy snorted and gave her a shove. They were wrestling on the kitchen floor when Amy's mom and cousin walked in the door. Neither looked surprised.

*

The room was quiet and dark, the gentle beep of the heart monitor a reassuring sound in the background of her thoughts. She'd rolled him onto his side like the nurses had showed her, to keep him from getting pressure sores, then shut off the lights and slotted herself in front of him. Atypical hospitals were so much more pleasant than Typical ones. Doctors with powers meant far less in the way of equipment and tubing. She could almost pretend he was just asleep.

She caught herself before the tears fell. Letting them start sometimes meant they didn't stop. There had been enough of that today.

"I'm going on a mission with your team tomorrow," she confessed. "It's a bit weird. I know I can never take your place with them, but they need help, and I have nothing to do except lie around feeling guilty, so I agreed."

She took his wrist and carefully pulled his arm over her, as if he was holding her. She laced their fingers together and pulled his hand firmly against her chest, where all of the empty feelings came from.

"Today was fun. Lots of people were here. Your mom blew out your candles. If you wake up, there's some cake left." She smiled to herself. "Don't worry though. I wouldn't let Xana put the party hat on you, Sir."

The rise and fall of his chest against her back lulled her, and she wished he'd smell more like himself again. Antiseptic was a good thing, but it masked him to her senses.

"Your mom told me that when you were little, you used to stick your fingers in the frosting at other kids' birthday parties if you were left unsupervised. I could totally see that. I wonder if our kids would have done stuff like that. Probably." She laughed. "I think I ate half the candy that was supposed to go into Amy's wedding favors a few weeks ago. Our kids would be menaces."

She let her own familiar silence close over her. If he could hear her, he probably wished she'd shut up. It had been a very busy day. The nurses had been nice enough not to kick them out when they'd promised to keep it down and they'd bribed them with cake.

Slowly, her mind drifted. Valentine's hand twitched in hers. It happened sometimes, but the doctors had told her it didn't mean anything.

She lay frozen, listening. The last time he'd moved, he'd had a seizure. They'd almost lost him, but she'd shrieked at the doctor, demanding they resuscitate him despite the Do Not Resuscitate order his father had signed.

Against her hair, his breathing changed. Panic surged. She reached for the buzzer.

Valentine's arm tightened around her, weak, but not a twitch.

Maybe? Or maybe she was asleep, or just plain crazy.

Carefully, she shifted over and looked back at him.

Black eyes gleamed, half-lidded, in the darkness.

Chapter Sixteen

She stared at him, the pale blue of her gaze a cold lake for his aching head. Her snowy hair was wild, pluming around her face like a torrent of frigid mist. Every perfect angle of her face broke his heart. He wanted to ask what she was doing there, but when he opened his mouth nothing came out. Maybe it was better not to speak and break this spell between them. Even if they were frozen like this forever, staring at one another, it would be enough.

Behind him, he could hear the insistent beep of a machine. The bed was hard and too small for them both, but he wasn't about to complain about that. A scent of some sort of noxious disinfectant clung to the room, irritating his senses. What he wanted – really wanted – was for her to press her back against his belly again, so he could feel her warmth and inhale her scent, exquisite and…Jory.

God, he loved her, but what the hell was he doing in a hospital, and why was she visiting him? She must have changed her mind about him, at least a little, if she was in his bed. Or was she the one hurt?

Anxiously, he tried to reach for her face but his muscles wouldn't obey. Not her then, him. An accident? A battle? Fuck, he was tired. Why couldn't he move?

"Valentine?" she whispered, voice shaking. Her face twisted and she sobbed so loud it must have hurt her throat. "Oh God." She touched his face. He blinked, but she didn't disappear. Not his imagination. "Don't talk. I'll call the nurses. The doctors. I don't know. Someone needs to look at you."

Staring at him, tears on her cheeks, she groped awkwardly for something behind her. "Am I hallucinating?"

He frowned, and she made a strange, strangled noise, like a watery laugh.

375

She touched his face again then cupped it between her hands. When she leaned in and pressed her lips to his, he tried to kiss her back, but why was she kissing him? Didn't she hate him?

Had he woken up in an alternate universe? He was in no hurry to wake from this, if it was a dream.

"Oh god, I didn't kill you," she whispered, kissing him again.

Footsteps. Several people had entered the room, but he couldn't turn to see who. Jory rose from the bed, and he tried to grab her hand to pull her back. He needed her to stay close. His muscles refused to obey him. Panic tried to set in, but the way Jory was looking at him – as though him waking had made him amazing and perfect – would do for the next few minutes.

"Is he really awake?" Jory asked, eyes wide and pleading, as if she wanted them to check and tell her she was right.

Two nurses rounded the foot of his bed. They stared down at him, brows raised.

"I'll get Dr Zeffer," the taller one said then bustled off so fast he barely saw her go.

"Mr Ott, you've been in a coma." The remaining nurse's voice seemed loud. "The doctor is just down the hall. She'll be glad to see your eyes open."

Jory hovered behind her, staring at him, her pale face paler than usual. "Is he okay?"

The nurse smiled at her kindly. "Jory, hon, don't get your hopes up."

"He's thinking, I can tell. He was looking right at me. Oh shit, your mom!" She pulled out her phone, and made several calls, still staring at him gleefully. The one time he dared close his eyes, she barked his name like a command, and looked relieved when he opened them again.

Jory was too far away. Why had she called all these people into the room? They were standing between them, and he wanted her close again.

A pretty young woman in a blouse and skirt arrived, her high heels clacking with each step. "Mr Ott? I'm Dr Zeffer. Look at you waking up and throwing my whole ward into a tizzy." She clucked her tongue in disapproval, but grinned widely. "How are you feeling?"

"Jory," he managed to mumble, watching her past the doctor. His throat felt raw, his mouth unfamiliar.

Jory screamed. "I told you!" she said, triumphantly. "I knew it." She took a step toward the bed. "Me? Do you want something, Sir?"

Sir? She was sir-ing him in front of all these strangers? This had to be fucking Narnia, or something. His mind felt ponderous, like his body.

He forced reluctant fingers to move in the gesture for "come," and even though he hadn't been able to raise his arms to make the signal, she was on the bed with him in a heartbeat.

The doctor chuckled and shook her head. "Mr Ott, if she didn't wander off while you took your nap, she's not going anywhere while I examine you." She walked back to the other side of the bed, since Jory was between them, and the nurses helped him turn to lie flat. He was poked and prodded and told he'd be sent for a CAT scan.

Croaking one word at a time was exhausting, and he felt like nodding off, but struggled to stay awake for Jory's peace of mind. She kept touching him as if she was afraid he'd disappear, quiet tears leaking down her cheeks. He wasn't sure what she was upset about.

Dr Zeffer put her hands on either side of his head then closed her eyes. Power pulsed through his mind, unfamiliar and alien, but benevolent. "I can't believe this. I never would have guessed." She laughed in self-derision. "Well, way to keep me humble, Mr Ott. Jory told me not to write you off, and she's proven us all wrong. You've proven us wrong." The doctor patted his arm, as though they were good friends. "Don't overtax him, Jory. He's going to be weak and need more sleep. I know it'll make you nervous when he drifts off, but he should wake again without any issues. The cryogenic stasis his brain was in seems to have cleared. He'll need physical rehab, but his brain is looking healthy enough."

"Three months wasn't enough sleep?" Jory asked desperately, her tone joking, but her expression earnest.

Three months?

What the fuck?

No wonder his body didn't want to obey him. What the hell had happened? He thought back to the last job he remembered, or even the last thing, and bits and pieces came back but his last clear memory was a couple of months after she'd bolted, after he'd pushed her too far, too fast.

"We can start your physio as soon as we get you cleared for it, but there'll be no rushing," the doctor warned, as she headed for the door. "No rushing!"

*

Valentine woke, head aching, and breathed slowly through the pain. Jory was curled against his belly in his tiny hospital bed, right where she needed to be, but there was no saying how long they'd be allowed to stay together like this. When they moved him to the psych floor, they'd probably start making her leave after visiting hours.

He felt for her in his head, but the link between them was still severed, and was like hamburger at his end.

So many stories they'd told him of what had happened and things he'd done. How he'd forgotten everything and gone off the deep end. So much that came back only in vague shadows of memory.

Enforcers had been stationed outside his door ever since he'd awoken three days before, even though he was weak as a kitten. They said he'd almost killed Asher because of what he'd done to Jory, but even though he had no recollection of any of those events, he had to admit he would do it all again if he felt she was in danger.

Torture wasn't really his way, but he wished he could remember doing it. Maybe it would settle the part of his mind that wanted to see the man suffer for what he'd done to her. Asher had apparently made a full recovery, and had been relocated. Valentine's feelings about that were less than charitable, and he could see the same war play out in Jory's expression when she'd told him. Even now, he fantasized about tracking him down and finishing the job.

The Bureau had heard both sides of the case, and interviewed him for hours. He'd told them he was horrified by what he'd done. They seemed fooled, but still thought he needed psychiatric assessment. He probably did, but that didn't mean he was feeling cooperative. All he'd be able to tell the Bureau psychiatrists was that he didn't remember anything, which sounded sketchy as hell.

He kissed the side of Jory's neck, loath to lose her again so soon after she'd come back to him. It was crazy that she'd stuck around through all of this, although he was probably a better boyfriend when he was unconscious. She'd taken care of him, gotten close to his mother, had become best friends with both his team, and Brock and Brontë's team.

At times when they were alone, she told him of a few of the interactions they'd had when he hadn't been himself. He'd asked her forgiveness for some of them, but it was difficult to know which ones upset her, especially since the flashes of memory made his dick hard just like all of her furious blushes did. It was like having to apologize for something he'd done to her in an erotic dream.

And there had been more, he knew, that had happened between them –

things she was too shy to say aloud. He could see those secrets lurking behind her eyes. What she was withholding would have to come out sooner or later, if they were going to fix things between them.

He still couldn't believe she wanted to.

The tip of his finger slid over the rope collar she'd let him put on her before bed. The satisfaction he'd gotten from the simple act of collaring her again had made him grin like a fool for the rest of the night. It was sloppy work in a few places, but it would do for now, until his power was fully restored.

She was his again. She admitted she always had been. It was more than he could have hoped for just a few months ago.

There was no way, if there were scores kept somewhere by a higher power, that someone like him deserved her. He'd always felt that way, but now it was even more obvious. A few darker parts of him had been unleashed on the world for months, but he was capable of things that were so much worse than what they told him he'd done, and those options beckoned to him like they never had before.

Guilt tried to surface, but it was a vague feeling. At one time, Jory had made him almost good – had swayed him to sway his team – and now she seemed to be having a similar effect on Brock's team, and on this whole mixed bag of mercenaries and heroes that they were forming.

Jory was a beacon of light uncovering people's good intentions, but he wasn't sure she could purify him again. He wasn't sure he wanted her to. His conscience seemed to have died somewhere along the way, and the only thing holding him in check was the fear of losing her. She'd changed him before, and maybe it would happen again, but right then, in the darkness of his room, he knew he was missing the things that made a man good.

The only good part of him left was Jory. The fear of losing her again was his conscience.

Maybe the drugs they kept pumping into him made him philosophical and morose, but he didn't feel like the same man he'd been.

In her sleep, she wriggled against his erection. He groaned, caught between lust and overwhelming affection. How could one woman inspire him to be his best, and yet his very worst?

He slipped his hand up the front of her baggy t-shirt, and ran his palm over the silky softness of her skin, cupping the globe of one breast then the other. Her nipples hardened at his touch. She stirred and whimpered. What was she dreaming of?

He missed having intimate access to her beautiful mind.

What would happen when they could eventually have sex again? She hadn't mentioned it, but they both knew without their old connection, if she lost control, she might freeze his dick off.

Whatever. They'd experiment. Slowly.

She woke, mewling, and ground her ass against him. "Please, Sir," she said, her voice sweet and sleepy.

"Please what, snowangel?"

"Please use me. It's been so long since you used me." She arched against him languorously.

If only he could. At this point pinning her down and taking her would have to be a goal he set for himself in physiotherapy. "You know I can't."

He slid her loose track pants down the curve of her ass, and she shuddered and pressed back against him. "I know." She sighed. "That doesn't mean I don't want it. Maybe if you stay still and I do the work? I'll be careful."

God, if she kept wiggling her ass like that, he'd get off before he got inside her. "How would I be using you, if you were taking what you wanted from me?"

She moaned quietly. "I don't know. You can pretend you're doing the work and I don't really want it?"

"Like you ever don't want it from me?"

"Mmm." She pulled down the front of his boxers and squirmed until his cock was nestled between the globes of her ass. "Do you know that you found me and forced me to give you a blowjob in an alleyway? You used my mouth and called me your dirty whore."

He considered apologizing, but he wasn't sorry. Then again, from her squirming, she didn't seem to be sorry about the incident either.

"Are you trying to say you're not my dirty whore?" he whispered harshly in her ear.

She shuddered. "And you tied me up in the pool area at Brontë's house, and you teased me and left me so needy. I was naked and stuck there, squirming, until your ropes finally let me go. Anyone could have seen."

"Maybe I should bring you to Prospero's club and do the same thing. Then you'd know for sure people were watching."

She whined, and his cock started throbbing as hard as his head.

"Have you slept with Dane and Jurgen?" The question had been bothering him for days, but not because he was jealous. Only because he didn't want her hiding things from him. Hell, he owed them for keeping her alive for him to come back to. When they touched her now, in passing, he could tell there was familiarity there as if they knew her more intimately than they had before. It wasn't something he wanted them to tiptoe around. They'd thought he was dead.

"What? No!" she said, appearing genuinely shocked at the idea. She wasn't that good of an actor so he was inclined to believe her. "Why would you even ask that?"

"I've seen how they interact with you. Since I woke up, it's like they've all taken you as their own."

"No, it's not like that. When I was bad – really bad – they wouldn't let me slip away. They came and held me and talked to me and badgered me until I was so annoyed I snapped out of it." She laughed bitterly. "I didn't want to snap out of it. We're close very close friends now, but only friends."

"Uh huh. You don't think Dane and Jurgen fantasize about pinning you between them and convincing your little body to take them both?"

She shivered. "What? I-I doubt that's true."

"And that would leave your mouth for me. Would you cry and choke on my cock while they used your other two holes, pretty girl?"

"No! I don't want them to use me. I'd safeword."

Like hell she would. If he ordered her to submit to it, she'd let them, and she'd probably love it.

He grabbed his cock and guided it between her slick thighs. "Sure you would."

"I would!"

She squirmed, her thighs tensing around his dick and making him grunt with the effort not to come right away. His gaze was drawn downward to the roundness of her bottom and he watched in fascination as she tried to get herself off by rubbing against his cock. She tipped her hips forward, then arched back, until he was poised at her entrance then wriggled until he was lodged deep within the grip of her pussy.

"The three of us would fill you so full of come you'd be dripping for days."

"No, Sir," she whimpered. "Just you. Please, just you."

"But you'll let them fuck you if I insist."

"Nooo," she cried, moaning as she thrust back against him and he bottomed out.

Fuck, she'd squeal so loud with all of them inside her. He hadn't fucked a girl with his friends in years. Seeing her between Dane and Jurgen earlier that day – each of them with an arm companionably around her waist as they teased her about something – had triggered the thought of triple-teaming her with them. The idea had lingered, and had become more detailed and fascinating.

Besides, if he died before her someday, or lost his mind again, he wanted her taken care of. Maybe with their mental connection broken she'd be able to orgasm with other men, if they could figure out how to control her power when she was aroused. Braiding her hair, like he had their first time together to keep her power in check, might be enough. It was braided now.

He thrust into her, feeling his muscles trembling with fatigue already. The head of his cock bumped her g-spot, and both of them were already breathing hard.

"Don't come, little Jory. You might lose control."

"I know, Sir," the words dripped with regret. She struggled on his cock, trying to fuck him harder without having enough leverage.

He pressed a kiss to the nape of her neck, then bit her, unable to resist. She mewled then froze. Before he could pull out, her body milked at his cock. He spilled into her, groaning as she cried out in pleasure.

Fuck.

He needed to pull out – couldn't make himself to do it.

A stab of pain flashed through his head, then another as his body continued to come into hers. Jory hissed, and through his own red haze, he saw her press her palms against her forehead.

The raw ends of their connection touched, and his bones ached hollowly along with that part of his mind. The link knit together, itching, healing. It hummed to life, making reaching for her unnecessary. They were plugged in, the connection a live wire arcing in the rain. Like Frankenstein's monster, dormant parts of his mind flared awake.

Aphrodisia sealed the connection tight – their minds dog-locked. It hadn't been gone at all, it had just been waiting for them to screw to get the connection back online.

He felt for her and it was all there again. Every damn bit of it.

"No," Jory whispered.

"Fuck," Valentine agreed.

"I thought now we'd have a choice. That we'd get to choose to be together."

He kissed the side of her neck. "I know. I'm sorry."

"Are you?" she murmured.

"For you."

"Not for yourself?"

"I would choose this, and you, every time."

"But the link and the Aphrodisia were finally gone." She sighed, but the sound was relief rather than disgust. The pain quickly ebbed for both of them, leaving a feeling of well being behind.

He'd assumed the link returning would have upset her, considering how long and hard she'd tried to fight free, but he could feel her spirits lifting just as his own were. She was…happy. Almost jubilant, even if she didn't want to say it out loud. Neither of their lives should have centered so intensely around one person, but without the connection he'd been lonelier than he could even describe. Maybe it was the same for her.

"Without it we could have had normal lives," she mused. "A normal relationship."

"We're not normal people, Jory. Why would we want normal, when we could feel this?" He let his power slide into her mind, covering hers, stroking it, binding it to his will. It purred for him, and she quivered in his arms, panting. Even though it caused so many issues between them, there was an intense intimacy to being in her head rather than just her body.

He thrust his cock into her, but the muscles in his legs were approaching their limit. Sleep was trying to steal over him.

"I think we have a few days," she said, sounding disgusted. She had to be talking about the Aphrodisia. It gnawed at the edges of his consciousness, warning of the voracious sexual hunger it would bring. "Maybe three before things get ugly."

One. No more than one.

"Tell them what happens when you don't have access to me, and ask for Dr Gardner. She knows all about us. Well…some of it. I guess she'll see the rest. The Bureau wants data on us together. And there was a specialist – I can't remember her name, but Gardner will probably know it." He could feel her mind racing through information, but he just wanted to feel her come one more time before he let his exhaustion win.

"I know, sweetness. Hopefully my body will be strong enough to handle it."

"Well then maybe I'll get to boss you around for a while," she said smugly.

He tangled his hand in her hair and she whimpered, melting into him.

"Over my dead body."

Chapter Seventeen

If Valentine knew where she was, he'd kill her, but it wasn't her fault. He seemed to want her to walk away from things like this, but it wasn't in her nature, even if it would please him.

Jory ducked a bolt of something that sizzled, dove under some merc's legs, and military crawled toward the teenage girl cowering low against the sidewalk. Was the kid hoping the bike rack would keep her safe?

"Hey!" Jory shouted when she got close enough for the girl to hear her.

The young girl's gaze snapped to her, but she got the impression being noticed by an Atypical didn't give her peace of mind.

"Come on," Jory called, holding out her hand. "Let's get you out of here. Stay down."

The girl shook her head, pressing further back toward the convenience store. "No. Just leave me here."

Pavement heaved under Jory's belly, and she rolled aside just as a hole opened where she'd been. Fuck. These jerks weren't paying attention to the Typicals on the scene at all. She'd managed to get six people out of harm's way, but the girl and an older man were both stuck in the crossfire. She'd tried to save the older man already, but he insisted Jory help the girl first.

And the damage around them? Atrocious. This wasn't a movie where a hero could throw a car through a store window without repercussions. Insurance companies only covered so much, with acts of war often not being covered by most policies. And the government couldn't afford to keep fixing the infrastructure Atypicals destroyed during a pitched battle. Water mains and roadwork were expensive. Every time one of these battles happened, it made the whole lot of them look like an irresponsible group of troublemakers, even though some were trying to stop the others from making such a mess.

She crawled forward, glad for the leather that protected her knees from the stones and broken glass that bit into her palms. Anyone who thought being a hero was as glamorous as they made it out to be on TV was a dumbass.

"Come on," she prompted, but the girl only shook her head and squeezed her eyes closed. Playing possum wouldn't fix anything. "Do you want to die here? I can't get you to safety if you don't cooperate."

The girl grimaced, peeked at her then nodded. "Fine."

In real life, Typicals were rarely grateful about being saved. Atypicals were considered the problem, even if they weren't the same Atypicals who'd caused the problem in the first place.

"Come on."

The girl crawled alongside her, yelping every now and again. Glass had to be embedding in her exposed skin and even digging through her clothes.

"Why don't you freaks just leave normal people alone?" the girl complained. "Go to a deserted island to fight so the rest of us can live in peace."

A barrage of blasts made it impossible to answer her, but they crawled on until they got behind the large brick post office, where they met up with a few people who'd stuck around to help after she'd rescued them.

"Take her and leave the area," Jory recommended. "It's too dangerous to stay here." She surveyed the surrounding buildings, worried pieces were going to fall and crush them.

She waited while they ran down the street toward safety then turned back to the battle to look for the gray-haired man she'd left behind.

As she searched, she refused to let her gaze stray to the woman lying dead in the street. She knew she was there, body twisted, her face a rictus of pain, frozen in death. She looked so much like Jory's high school history teacher, she'd checked twice to make sure she wasn't her.

The poor woman. Someone would miss her, whoever she was. Had she left behind children? A dependent parent? A career where she helped the community? Later Jory would go out of her way to find out, just because she felt obligated to know, but the sightless eyes of all of those she hadn't been able to save still haunted her.

Stubbornly, she headed back into the fray, searching for the man. His leg was bent at an awkward angle, which meant she'd have to drag him. Maybe she could build a travois out of ice and pull him behind her – it would jostle his injuries less. But at his age? He had to be about eighty. Even if she got him safely out, there was no saying he'd survive the broken bone.

Battles brought so much ugliness.

When she reached the spot where she'd seen him earlier, he was gone. She cast her gaze over the tableau of destruction, and caught movement. Jurgen had removed some of the man's gravity and was floating him out, already almost to safety. Thank God. She exhaled in relief then tried to decide what to do next.

"Rime!" the urgency in Dane's voice made her whip around, but before she could do more than look, she was cocooned in something warm and soft – her head free, but her arms and legs trapped. She over-balanced and fell, barely managing to avoid hitting her head, then saw Dane get the same treatment.

A wiry man with dark hair bared his teeth at her. "Ahh." He chuckled. "Leader of the peacekeepers. Prettier than I expected. With that hair you're easy to pick out."

"I'm not the leader." She frowned at the man, wriggling her hands and trying to freeze the silk that bound her, but when she managed to do so, it was as ineffective as it was on Valentine's ropes. "Why are you people even attacking downtown? Angry about not finding a good parking spot?"

"We figured if we started some mayhem, your people would make an appearance." He threw her over his shoulder and stalked off. She tried to fight, but her teeth were her only weapon, and she couldn't bite through his fighting leathers.

"Catch yourself a new pet, Lonomia?" a woman asked. "Looks a little young for you."

"She's not for me. Caligo wants to talk to her."

Jory flopped on his shoulder like an overgrown salmon, but only succeeded in winding herself as he carried her from the area. Down the street, he entered an abandoned drycleaner's storefront. He set her down on the front counter, as if he was going to pay to have her cleaned.

A small woman with brown hair and a wide mouth walked in not long after, followed by six or seven large men.

"This is Rime?" The woman raised a skeptical brow. "I thought she'd be…bigger. And older. How old are you, girl?"

"I have a nine o'clock curfew and I don't want to get grounded again, so can we hurry this up?" Jory gave the woman her best Valentine-is-unimpressed glare.

"Not even going to beg for your life?" Her mouth twitched. "My name is Caligo. I'm one of the leaders of the Mercenary Free Army."

"I'd say I was charmed, but I'd be lying."

The woman snorted, but her eyes sharpened in interest. "Fearless, mouthy, immature. Typical peacekeeper. Nice collar, by the way."

She refused to be embarrassed by it anymore, and only stared back at the woman, unperturbed.

"Who do you belong to?"

"Does it matter?"

"It may."

Jory sighed. "Rigg owns me."

The woman, Caligo, grunted, and Lonomia took a respectful step back.

"You are the one we were hoping to find then."

What in the ever-loving fuck did these people want? "I'm not one of the leaders of the peacekeepers, if that's what you're thinking."

Caligo paced from her, to the door, and looked outside, clasping her hands behind her back. "Not so much a leader, no, but a catalyst. A symbol." She turned and pinned her with a cold stare. "You were there at the beginning. You were supposed to serve as an example, but instead of dying like a good girl, you became a rallying point. Your existence has caused civil unrest, where it was supposed to teach the Bureau to mind their own fucking business. Creating a third side to the equation wasn't supposed to be the result of that attack."

Jory pushed aside the memories of her teammates. She'd been so worried about Valentine lately that Arigh, Vance, and Seraphina hadn't come to mind much during the past few months. Moving on felt horribly disloyal, but Dr Gardner had told her it was part of the healing process. At least she could think of them now without curling into a ball and crying.

"We just want peace between the two sides," she growled, her ears still ringing with adrenaline. "Typicals need to be protected, and everyone else needs to settle the fuck down."

"So you don't think the mercenary groups need to be disbanded?" Caligo asked doubtfully. "They say you're calling for an all-out ban on mercenary work."

"What?" She frowned at Caligo. "Are you serious? My dominant is a mercenary, and so are most of my friends. And even if I hated mercenaries – which I don't – why the hell would anyone listen to me? I'm a nobody newbie hero and at this point I'm rogue."

"So you're saying this is all rumor?"

"Yes. Haven't the peacekeepers been sending representatives to speak to your group?"

Lonomia looked meaningfully at Caligo and jerked her head in Jory's direction. He moved to Jory's side and whispered something she couldn't hear, and the cocoon fell from her like paper streamers. Relieved, Jory gave Lonomia a nod and slid off the counter to stand on her own feet.

"No." Her mouth twisted like she'd eaten something sour. "No one has said much. They've spoken to some of the other groups, but all we've heard so far is rumor from teams who've spoken to other teams."

"So your solution was to start destroying things and killing people in the hopes we'd show up?" The words probably weren't very diplomatic, but an innocent Typical – possibly more than one – was dead because they couldn't figure out how to get the peacekeepers a fucking message? "What the hell is wrong with Atypicals? All we want is for everyone to start minding their own business and leave Typicals alone and safe."

Caligo pushed her hair back, frowning. "Well, there's always collateral damage in a battle. It's unfortunate, but not unexpected."

She shook her head slowly in bewildered disgust. How could people be this shortsighted? Maybe no one had ever explained things to her. "Not many years ago, the Typicals were still killing us off. If we keep looking like villains to them, eventually they'll start questioning our humanity again. I don't know about you, but I prefer not having to worry about getting hunted down and destroyed."

The grunt that was Caligo's answer wasn't agreement, but it also wasn't denial. "We all know the history," she said, glancing briefly at Lonomia. It was hard to tell what their relationship was to each other. They didn't look alike, but that didn't mean anything in some families. They also might be husband and wife, or good friends. Teammates, surely. "It's hard to believe that all the rumors we've heard are unfounded. We've heard the Bureau has secret plans to shut us all down, and they're using you people to trick mercenaries into working for them. So what – they assign the young, pretty ones to make us change sides?"

Lonomia raised his brows. "I'm sure she could make me change sides if she tried hard enough."

"Hell, if she smiles at you the wrong way you'll mess your leathers, old man."

"You'd know, *cara mia.*" He winked at Caligo, who rolled her eyes.

Jory studied the man again and this time noticed the metal collar around his neck. He inclined his head, as if he was acknowledging their shared status as submissives.

"No one is trying to convince anyone to change sides. We just want to restore peace, for everyone's sake. Both sides are in the wrong."

"Oh, so we're supposed to sit back and let the Bureau sniff around in our business?"

"No. Their limits of power need to be discussed and negotiated, and voted on legally. The Bureau shouldn't threaten and overstep, and the mercenaries shouldn't kill people to make a point."

The woman sighed heavily. "True. We weren't involved with happened to your team, by the way. In cold blood like that." Caligo shook her head. "I mean, I've killed in the heat of the moment, but to plan out their murder?" She grimaced. "Those actions weren't something I would have sanctioned. There seems to be a whole lot of people talking for other people lately. We're getting tired of waiting for the answers we ask for. We contacted the Bureau four times in the past month to ask about their new policies, and no one even returned our calls. Guess we're not fancy enough to deserve answers."

"Yeah, I've been hearing that from a few people now. That's not right. We're planning to meet with the Bureau representative in the next few days – Rigg knows one of them personally, and he came to pay his respects when he found out he was in hospital."

That had been an odd situation. Valentine couldn't remember meeting Dr Matthew Ridlon, but apparently they'd had a long conversation at the man's office and the man now seemed desperate to be useful. He had no power to negotiate with the mercenaries, but he knew people who did.

Something had been there when Ridlon had looked at Valentine. Lust? Submission? After Ridlon had left, Valentine denied seeing it, but he was still distracted by the Aphrodisia even though the last of it had passed a week before.

"Well, you do that and get back to us." Caligo adjusted the leather pouch attached to her thigh harness.

"I will."

"We're going to find out who the dead woman is and see that her family gets some money to help them out. Zygo didn't see the poor thing until it was too late." Her gaze was regretful. "You, of all people, should know we're not monsters."

Jory nodded. "If you run out of patience again, just leave a message for me with Rigg's team. Someone will know how to find them."

*

"You have to sign me out before we leave," Valentine said ruefully.

Jory raised her brows. "I know."

They'd already been over that, but she suspected he was excited to be going out. Lord knew she was excited to get him the fuck out of here.

"I feel like a damn library book."

"Good," she said, leering. "I plan on dog-earring you later."

"Pervert."

Jory smiled giddily and straightened Valentine's tie. She couldn't wait to get him out of the psychiatric hospital. The staff were great, but seeing him cooped up here had been difficult for her even though he'd been full of a deep and steadfast patience. He'd spent the time reading and working out when he wasn't in therapy sessions, and the confinement didn't seem to bother him.

He always looked so out of place in the hospital, but even more so today. Gone were the jeans and t-shirt. The Valentine before her was a sinfully delicious male model in a tailored tux, long hair slicked back in a ponytail. His appearance was incongruous with the drab hospital bed he sat on, in the drab room. She'd done up every button of his shirt, teasing herself with it, slowly hiding the broad chest and lean muscle. She was pretty sure it was a crime to cover up a man who looked this good.

This overnight outing might be the end of his stay, if tonight's pass went well. The court and the Bureau's psychiatric review board had agreed that what Valentine had done to Asher had been caused by temporary insanity, from the Aphrodisia, and that he wasn't criminally responsible. The therapy he'd completed, and his willingness to cooperate had the Bureau psychiatrist discharging him much faster than any of them would have thought possible. Between Asher being alive and well, other than the chest scarring, and Valentine having been comatose for months, they'd been lenient.

They'd move back to the coach house, with his team looking in on them. She was going to miss living at Brock and Brontë's, but she was excited she and Valentine would have some privacy.

"Did you pack your overnight bag?"

"One more motherly peep out of you and I'll turn you over my knee right

390

here and now," he growled. "Or maybe I'll take you to the nursing station and spank you there. Some of them need to see what happens to people who disrespect me."

A knot of embarrassed desire formed in her belly. It was hard to remember not to coddle him, but he wouldn't stand for being treated like a baby.

"Show me what you're wearing under that dress," he commanded.

"What?" she squeaked. She'd hoped the turquoise, cocktail-length gown was modest enough not to pique his interest, but as soon as his gaze had settled on the neckline, she'd known there'd be trouble. It showed a generous amount of cleavage, and Valentine's gaze zeroed in on the swells of her breasts every time she drew a breath. He was going to bite her there sometime before the festivities were over, and there'd be no way to hide the mark. She could only hope it wasn't before photos.

"Are you having trouble understanding English today, little girl?"

"But Sir, we're going to be late. I have to get to Amy's on time for pictures."

"I won't ask again."

The 'or else' didn't need to be said aloud.

Damn. Every suit fantasy she'd ever had danced through her head. If she didn't hurry up and show him, her panties would be drenched from the idea of him punishing her, and then he'd touch her and...and...

She sighed and lifted the hem of her dress, staring at the wall behind him and hoping to hell no one walked in.

"Pantyhose? You know I don't like pantyhose." His disapproval made her want to peel the dumb things off, but it was part of her outfit.

"Amy bought us all the same color hosiery so we'd match, Sir."

"Later tonight I'm going to take a knife and cut them off of you." A cold statement of fact.

She shivered, trying to slow the racing of her heart. The anticipation of having a night with him alone at his coach house was far too distracting. It was Amy's big day, but as much as she was looking forward to it and had been for ages, part of her wished she and Valentine could disappear for part of the afternoon.

She was never going to be able to function through this, and almost everyone she knew was going to be there. His appraisal of her said the wedding plans for today were inconsequential, and that he had other, better ideas.

"I'm standing in Amy's wedding today," she said, reminding them both that those plans carried precedence over anything she wished he'd do.

"Yes, I know. Otherwise I would have skipped the suit," he said, his eyes gleaming. A smattering of frost blooms still etched his black eyes. "But after the wedding, you're all mine."

"But…" She shifted where she stood, finally looking at him, but not daring to drop the hem of her dress back into place. God, he was beautiful and he knew every damn button to push – as if he had a catalogue of her turn-ons and wasn't afraid to use it against her. As her gaze slid from his sexy expression, to his broad shoulders, down to his French cuffs with the cufflinks and his big hands, she started to hyperventilate. "Sir, can I come?" she blurted.

"Now?" He chuckled, and her blush crept up her neck to burn her cheeks.

"I-I need to be able to concentrate."

"All I did was tell you to show me your pretty panties, Jory." He smiled an evil smile. "I like the birdies."

"They're bluebirds," she pointed out in a small, high voice.

"Of happiness?"

She bit her lip and nodded, and Valentine groaned.

"Quit looking so edible. We have places we're supposed to be."

"Do you *really* like my panties, Sir?" She drew a shaking breath and moved to stand between his knees. "You could…put your hand in them if you wanted to."

"Fuck."

Mmm…Valentine swearing usually meant he was struggling to control himself.

There was a stretch of silence as she waited impatiently for him to touch her.

"Do you need a spanking, little girl?"

"Anything you want, Sir," she murmured hopefully. "Over your lap, or I could bend over the bed?"

He groaned. "No. Behave." Firmly, he set her away from him, then rose and walked out of the room, slinging his bag over his shoulder. Like a sad puppy she followed along, trying to think of ways to seduce him before they reached Amy's place.

The staff at the nursing station teased them good-naturedly as she signed him out, and they got into the elevator.

"Please, Sir," she whispered as the elevator door closed. "Just one orgasm and I promise I'll be good until we go to your house tonight."

"You'll be good until we get *home*, because I said so," he corrected. "And it's home, not my house. You live with me, not with Brock. Not with Jurgen or Dane or Xana."

"You want me to move in with you? You don't want to take things slow, Sir?"

"No. Life's too short for that bullshit," he said. "I don't do coy, other than when you're playing hard to get."

"I never play hard to get! And I'm not coy."

He snorted, and she attacked him with kisses just before the elevator door slid open.

"Down, girl," he said smugly, ungluing her from his chest, then tugging her out of the elevator and past grinning guards.

"Bye, Mr Ott! Have a good evening!" one of the guards called. The sentiments were repeated eagerly by the second, who rushed to open the door for them. Only Valentine would have the guards at the psych hospital calling him mister and acting the part of the well-paid doormen at an upscale condo.

They got to her car and he held his hand out for the keys.

"You don't even know where she lives!" Jory objected, squinting against the noon sun. Amy and Talbot had beautiful weather. Her best friend had been a bundle of nerves before Jory had left to pick up Valentine, but hopefully her cousin had helped her hold it together during the forty-five minutes she'd been gone.

"I'll drop you off for the pictures at her parents' house, then I'll go to Brock and Brontë's. Scout's honor."

She snorted. "Like you've ever been a Scout."

"How do you think I got so good with rope?" He winked slyly.

Immediately, she pictured a teenaged Valentine tying up a teenaged Jurgen while teenaged Dane watched. Her teenaged self squirmed at the thought. Knowing they had history sometimes gave her interesting fantasies about them. The one time they'd played with his whole team at Prospero's dungeon hadn't helped banish those ideas from her mind.

He kept teasing about sharing her with his friends again, filling her head with dreadful ideas. She'd possibly watched a few porn clips where women got triple teamed, and it had only terrified her more. Where did a girl even put so much penis? The guys in the videos weren't quite so well endowed as

Valentine, either. She could barely handle anal, for goodness' sake.

"Sir, you're not really going to share me, are you?"

"Hmm." He buckled his seatbelt then started the car, watching her expectantly until she buckled up too. When she had done so, his attention shifted to driving. She felt bad when she realized how long it had been since he'd been behind the wheel. He loved to drive.

She stared ahead trying not to ask again. Had he forgotten she'd asked? Had he even heard her? Knowing him, he might just be fucking with her, but then again maybe not. He was an unpredictable man.

In silence, he wended his way through the congested streets to Amy's, never asking for directions. Of course he'd know where her parents and best friend's parents lived. Creepy bastard.

He parked out front then pulled her to him roughly, kissing her hard and thoroughly. When he let her go, she was gasping. He uncurled her fingers from their grip on his lapels.

"Get in there before I grab you by that pretty hairdo and make you choke on my cock."

"But, Sir?" she insisted, needing an answer. He couldn't be serious about letting them fuck her, right? He was too jealous to share. He'd said so before.

But then he'd let them touch her, and he'd been dropping hints for weeks now.

He narrowed his black gaze at her, the strong line of his jaw looking determined.

"Soon. Not tonight."

Not *tonight*? That supposed to make her feel better? His expression held no hint of teasing.

None.

Oh fuck, she was doomed.

She squirmed, but got of the car like a good girl, because that was what he seemed to be expecting.

"But, Sir," she objected, looking at him through the still open door. "I don't want…" She couldn't say more because guests were milling around the yard, probably waiting for the photographer to arrive.

"Does what you want matter, Jory?" he said in his quiet way.

Dampness pooled in her underwear.

"No, Sir." It was what he wanted to hear, even though they both knew it wasn't exactly true. She had a safeword, but she didn't know if she'd use it, even for something that scared her this much.

"Go play with your friends now, snowangel." The corner of his mouth quirked sinfully upward. "We'll talk later."

Chapter Eighteen

The park setting had been perfect for the light-hearted ceremony. They'd had a warm late autumn day, comfortable even though it had been forever since Valentine had seen much sun. Children and adults and balloons were everywhere. At first he'd been surprised by the bouncy castle and cotton candy machine, but it turned the wedding into an occasion where everyone spent the day laughing.

It was like a family picnic in formalwear.

Jory's friend, Amy, was radiant. She hosted the celebration with the smooth effortlessness he imagined she used in her classroom. Her man, Talbot, was entertaining and down-to-earth, and today he couldn't seem to stop smiling.

But it was Jory who drew the eye, with her white hair and pale skin, her ice blue gaze and full lips. Everyone else seemed to be watching her too, and Valentine wondered how the hell he'd landed such a woman.

Through the ceremony, the receiving line, dinner, and speeches, he tried to remember to be polite and make conversation, but it was hard not to stare at her and imagine releasing her glorious hair from its pins, and kissing her perfect face. The smooth column of her neck, unmarred and collarless for today, mocked him, and the dress she wore revealed the kind of cleavage that begged for his hands or teeth.

With Jory standing at Amy's side all day, it was far too easy to superimpose the white dress onto her, and imagine her as the bride. His team, all dressed up and presentable, had been teasing him about just that for the past few hours, thinking they'd piss him off or freak him out, but it wasn't working. Instead, it was making him consider something he'd rarely given a passing thought to until now.

Weddings had always seemed like an archaic notion, but now he understood it. At one time, being surrounded by a girl's friends and family would have made him desperate to escape, but Jory's people were pleasant, and he loved hearing all of the affectionate and potentially embarrassing stories from her childhood.

"I'm sorry," Jory murmured to him after the first dance was over and the party started to loosen up. She held an untouched glass of wine, as she had been all evening. "Pretty soon, if you don't take control of the conversation, they'll tell you all about my imaginary friend, Keziah. I don't know if our relationship is strong enough for that yet."

"Interesting. I need to hear all about that."

She shook her head ruefully.

"Don't be sorry. I'm enjoying myself." He took the glass of wine from her hand and set it aside. "You should dance with me."

"Dance?" She laughed. "First you're making charming conversation with my parents and Amy, and now you're going to do something frivolous like dance?"

"Is that so surprising?"

"There was a time you told me not to expect this from you. Normalcy. A relationship other people could see that wouldn't shock them."

He led her onto the dance floor to the strains of the unfamiliar tune, and took her in his arms, loving how she felt there. "Both of us can fake being normal for the people we love. You've seen me do that with my mother and Pascal."

"True."

"You can't succeed in life without knowing how to fit in and hide your secrets."

She tipped her head back and gazed up at him, and he could feel the tension of the day leaving the lines of her body.

"Do you have secrets from me, Sir?"

"Some," he admitted. "But only because some of my kinks might scare you."

"Am I too vanilla for you?" she asked sadly. "Am I holding you back?"

As if she could even wonder. "No, not at all. Things between us are always evolving, and I find you, and your progress as my submissive, completely fascinating." He kissed her, and they stopped in the middle of the dance floor, his lips pressed to hers in a chaste yet satisfying moment of public claiming.

"You seemed so hell bent on leaving me, once upon a time. What changed?" A moment of terror seized him. "Or are you waiting to break things off until after I've recovered?"

"No!"

"Why then?"

She smiled sadly. "Well first, I almost killed you. You being dead for three months put things in perspective. Second, this you – the real you – is much nicer than the you who didn't remember me."

He raised a brow at her. "So I'm just less of a dick now, so you're counting your blessings?"

"The dickishness, plus the kink, added up to something I couldn't handle," she admitted. "You have to remember that when we met, we didn't understand the Aphrodisia. I was practically a virgin, and I didn't know anything about kink. You're not exactly a training wheel dominant."

"No?"

"You're more of a Tour de France dominant."

"I am not," he protested. "I'm barely even kinky. I just like to tell you what to do."

She snorted. "Bossy, kinky…whatever. You've turned me into a pervert now too, so I can handle it."

He kissed her again, because he couldn't help it.

"Oooh," a small voice crowed.

He broke the kiss and looked down to see Amy's flower girl staring at them in fascination. Amy had said something earlier about the child being one of her cousin's kids. Children and babies were underfoot at every turn, and they were all hopped up on the candy from the wedding favors. He got the feeling Amy and Talbot were going to have a houseful of their own wee ones before long.

"You like her!" the flower girl observed, difficult to hear over the music.

"Yes," he admitted. "I like Jory the same way your cousin Amy likes Talbot."

"Are you going to marry her?"

Was is age appropriate to tell the kid he was planning to lock Jory in a tower?

"Bella, that's none of your beeswax," Jory said, blushing prettily and rolling her eyes at Valentine as the girl laughed and lost interest in them, running off to twirl around and around in the middle of the dance floor.

Not sure how to break the awkward silence, Valentine started dancing again and the song transitioned to something he was pretty sure came from an old Disney movie.

Why not discuss this subject? They'd been together long enough to at least talk about it. "Did you ever used to dream of getting married when you were a little girl?"

"Me? No," she said, a bit too quickly.

He snorted and waited for her to recant.

"I mean –" She shrugged as if it was a silly discussion. "I thought I might eventually be married and have a family, but I wasn't one to plan out details of a wedding and picture myself as princess for a day."

That he believed.

"It's not important to me though. It's not something I need."

He leaned down to whisper in her ear. "Maybe you can't picture yourself as the princess because deep down you know you're the slave."

She groaned and pressed closer.

"You'd marry me if I commanded it," he said, faking some bravado he wasn't feeling. "You'd let me plan any kind of wedding I wanted."

"Valentine!" she admonished, drawing away and looking scandalized.

"That's seven times you've called me that today."

"So?"

"That'll be the number of cane welts I leave on your ass tonight."

"But in vanilla situations calling you…that…can't be avoided!"

"That's not my problem."

"You suck, Sir."

"Eight."

"Oh!" she pressed her lips together before she made it worse, and he chuckled as she glared. "You can't dom someone into marrying you. That's just not right. If we ever decided to take our relationship in that direction, I'd expect a real proposal, and the choice to accept or refuse without punishment."

"How adorable."

She scowled. "This isn't a joke."

"No, it's not."

"You shouldn't tease me about things like this."

"I'll tease you about whatever I please, but I'm not teasing now. We need to talk about this eventually. This, children. Those sorts of things."

She buried her face against his shoulder. "You haven't even been discharged from the hospital yet."

"I didn't say it would happen tomorrow."

"Yes, I want to get married and have kids eventually."

"My kids," he growled.

"Yes, beast…I mean, Sir." She grinned up at him, her luminous face mesmerizing. The idea of having his babies seemed to make her happy. Hell, it made him happy. "That is, if you can get me pregnant. My power may not allow it."

"Your power will do what it's told, where I'm concerned. You're lucky I didn't put a baby in your belly when I wasn't myself."

"You're lucky I didn't ask the doctors to artificially inseminate me when you were in a coma," she shot back. "Your mother offered to sign the papers."

He blinked down at her, his mouth open, but he couldn't think of anything to say. This had to be the first time she'd ever shocked him.

"You wouldn't have," he finally said.

"I would have. I almost did."

The idea that she'd considered doing such a thing – that he meant that much to her – hurt, but in a good way. She'd wanted to keep part of him alive so badly she'd considered bearing and raising his child alone. A child he never would have known about. Never would have met. It was hard to decide if he wanted to punish her or kiss her.

"Crazy girl."

"Where you're concerned, Sir? Very."

*

The Bureau boardroom they'd been escorted to was as nondescript and depressing as the occasion warranted. Valentine and his team sat at the conference table with the leaders of the peacekeepers, the leaders of two of the larger organized mercenary groups, the Director of Atypical Affairs, and some of its other representatives. Dr Matthew Ridlon was also there, and had straightened his tie about eleven times since Valentine had walked into the room. It didn't appear to have made the man any straighter, at least not the way his hungry gaze kept drifting to Valentine.

A heated debate raged between the Bureau and mercenary reps. It was good that the peacekeeper reps outnumbered those for the other groups.

They needed all the influence they could muster.

Jory leaned over to whisper to him. "So what happened between you and Ridlon?" she teased.

"Who knows?" Valentine smirked at her. "But if I'd slept with him he wouldn't be making eye contact like that. I'd have taught him better manners."

Jory, and Xana, who was seated to Valentine's left, both chuckled silently.

The current Director, Anderson Wick, was red in the face. "So you're saying that you don't think the Bureau should have any jurisdiction over the actions of mercenaries? That's absurd, Ms Nordskov."

Jurgen's mother, Alett, who was spokesperson for the mercenaries, leaned back in her chair, jaw set in the stubborn line that meant she'd reached the limits of her patience. She was done with Wick's bullshit. She'd honed that look on Jurgen and the rest of their team during their teenage years.

"The Bureau is comprised mostly of mundane Atypicals, appointed by the Typical government," she pointed out. "Why should we allow our laws and our way of life to be dictated wholly by people who have no real understanding of what we do, or what we need? We're policed like criminals, taxed to the gills, and yet it's the Bureau that has a higher rate of corruption than any other group of Atypicals." She sipped at her water, but cut Wick off before he could start a rebuttal. "The heroes are your puppets. Except for a select few –" She gestured to Jory. "Most of them can't think for themselves. They're a mindless tool you use to oppress the free thinkers of this world. The free thinkers won't kowtow to you and will never become your tools, Director."

Wick drew in a long breath through his nose, as if someone had trained him how to find calm in these situations, but he had no experience with putting it into practice. He gave the impression he was a man who wasn't used to being challenged.

"So you think we'd all be better off if this was like the Atypical Wild West?" he asked, his voice loud. His lack of self-control made him look weak, especially in the face of the placid calm radiating from Alett. "We tried that early on, remember? Atypicals were hunted down and euthanized like an invasive species. We're trying to show the Typical population that the Bureau can keep Atypicals under control, but instead of cooperating so we don't all get exterminated, you and your people keep acting out to show you won't listen to us. You're like a bunch of cranky toddlers stomping around breaking toys just because you can't jump on the couch. There must be *rules*, Ms Nordskov."

Alett straightened her already correct posture and looked down her nose at Wick. "We're not children in need of your direction, Director. To us you're an oppressor trying to dictate our way of life. Our actions weren't bothering anyone until the Bureau decided to start cracking the whip and issuing orders. Mercenaries don't take orders. We're not heroes. We negotiate and fulfill contracts that offer mutual benefit. You can't scare us no matter how big your stick is." She arched a brow, letting the bit of innuendo sink in.

Wick's cheeks reddened.

"If you want cooperation from free thinkers, you have to involve them in the law-making process in meaningful ways. You can't say 'thou shalt not' without explaining why and having us sign off on it. We're not trying to make murder legal. We're not trying to enslave the Typical population. We just want to be left to our own devices in matters of business. We have a code and we police ourselves far more effectively than your enforcers ever could."

"If I could interject at this point," Delilah, the co-leader of the peacekeepers began, "Maybe we should move back to the items on the agenda. It's good to work on a mutual understanding, but there are a few pressing issues we wanted to cover today."

Valentine looked back and forth between the mercenaries and the Bureau reps. Would they ever be able to understand each other? They had completely disparate points of view and ways of life.

It reminded Valentine of when he'd first met Jory. It was as though they'd been raised on different planets. Wick had grown up immersed in the Atypical school system and was so heavily indoctrinated into Bureau culture that critical thinking might be permanently beyond him. Jory had been raised with Typicals and had only learned the Bureau propaganda at Atypical cultural school on weekends. She'd been taught the Bureau's laws, but she'd had enough space away from the culture that it hadn't become engrained. It hadn't taken many discussions on the subject before she'd started questioning things on her own. Smart cookie. Atypicals everywhere would be better off with someone like her as the Director, rather than Wick.

Under the table, he felt for her hand, and she squeezed it once before batting him away. *Not now, dear, I'm trying to look professional.*

"No, you know what? I think we're done here." Wick stood, surprising his people, who scrambled to gather their things. The meeting was scheduled to take another two hours, at least, but apparently he was done talking. "It's apparent Ms Nordskov and her people didn't come here to discuss things in good faith. We're the government. We control the people, not the other way around."

"No," Alett shot back. "You're supposed to be our representatives, not our masters. Maybe one of your Bureau lawyers can explain that to you."

"You people will do what you're told," he bellowed, "or you'll be incarcerated like the dissidents you are." The man was so full of rage he looked like he might have a stroke. "Your assets will be seized and your children will be taken away and raised as law-abiding Atypicals." He slammed his hand on the table, glaring.

The Bureau reps to either side of Wick were stony faced, but Ridlon and two of the others looked shocked.

"You can't do that," Alett growled. "No way the Feds would agree to that."

"Oh, but they have," Wick said, having regained some of his composure. Now his smile was smug. "This issue is costing them money hand over fist, and it's causing turmoil both nationally and internationally. I was given leave to do anything, up to and including putting those solutions into motion."

They stared at each other in silence.

Well, fuck. War it was.

There was no way the mercenaries were going to bow to a scare tactic, and Wick had to know that. He was forcing them into an all-out civil war. But why? To see that the mercenary way of life was destroyed?

Now Jory was clutching Valentine's hand, a mix of horror and rage roiling in her mind. He lent her some of his own calm. With all of the work she and the others had been doing to fix this shitshow while he'd been in hospital, she'd been hopeful that this meeting would settle things.

Alett stood as well, her power swirling the still air into wind around her, but well under her control. "I'm sorry it has to come to this, Director," she said coolly, unsurprised. "I had hoped this was a venue for us to mend fences rather than adding barbed wire to them." Her smile was mirthless. "I'll advise my people on the Bureau's stance, but you must understand that I am their *representative*, not their master."

Without replying, Wick turned and walked from the room.

Jory opened her mouth to say something, and both Delilah and Alett shook their heads at her, making the mercenary hand signal for listening devices. As he thought to whisper an explanation about the gesture, she nodded curtly. It was strange knowing she'd been working with mercenaries so much since they'd been apart that she actually knew things he didn't know she knew.

They surrounded Alett and Delilah, acting as their bodyguards as they left the building. Until recently the measure wouldn't have been necessary.

Ridlon followed them out to their transport vehicles, waiting politely until the leaders were safely inside and had driven into the distance.

"Just so you know," Ridlon said, addressing all of them, rather than just Valentine, "it's not all of us. Wick's faction and the assholes who suck up to him have an anti-mercenary stance that's extreme and outdated. There are some of us who would join the peacekeepers if we had any skills to offer, and if it didn't mean losing our jobs."

Dane moved to him and clasped the man's hand in thanks. Even coming out to talk to them was a bad political move for Ridlon. It was gutsier than Valentine would have expected.

"I'm glad to know not everyone hates us."

Ridlon nodded grimly then turned and went back into the building, casting an almost covert glance at Valentine over his shoulder.

When he was gone, they got in the SUV.

"Valentine," Dane called from the driver's seat.

"What?"

"So when the mercenaries band together and demolish this place, are we saving your boyfriend?"

"Be nice!" Jory admonished. "It's not his fault his bosses are idiots, any more than it's his fault he has the hots for Valentine."

Dane and Jurgen chuckled.

"You really need to teach him not to make so much eye contact," Xana teased. "I know you allow it from Jory, but if you let all your submissives do it you're going to lose your dom card."

"He's not my submissive!"

"Oh, but he wants to be." Jory shot back, her expression mischievous.

"I'm not in the market for another one." Valentine smacked her shapely, leather-clad thigh. "The one I have is enough of a handful. If he wants a dominant it won't be me."

Through their connection he could feel the tension in Jory's body. Her joking was a smokescreen for how she was really feeling. The meeting had rattled her, and he wished there was something he could do to fix all of this so she could stop worrying. She'd need a good beating later if she couldn't calm the hell down. The tension in the SUV was thick, but none of it touched Valentine. For him the outside world still felt surreal.

There was silence for a few blocks, and the façade of amusement died away well before the next words were spoken. That meeting had been a fucking mess. People were going to die, and they wouldn't be able to stop it from happening.

Chapter Nineteen

Steaming water poured over Jory, relaxing muscles that hadn't done anything more taxing than reading. Valentine had been keeping watch over her all day, tense, protective. The night before had been the worst battle they'd seen yet as peacekeepers, and even though she hadn't been hurt, the amount of death – the gruesome aftermath of the battle – had shaken them all.

The mercenaries hadn't taken well to Wick's threat. The two sides were bent on destroying each other. There was no resolution in sight, especially with Wick at the helm at the Bureau. His sycophants were weak, but numerous, and they were afraid. After so much bloodshed, some of the other radical anti-merc bureaucrats were almost ready to negotiate, but Wick and his people vetoed any and all attempts to schedule a meeting.

All day Jory had hidden in novels. At noon she'd laid them aside to pay attention to Valentine, but he'd insisted she keep reading, curling around her and holding her, sometimes reading over her shoulder rather than picking a novel up himself. A few times she'd wriggled against him in invitation, but although he'd groaned and pressed against her, he soon stopped her and insisted she relax.

She'd be more relaxed if he put out, but he was being stubborn for some reason.

"Are we going somewhere?" she'd asked, when he ushered her into the shower after dinner.

"No," he said.

When she'd tried to find out what was going on, he'd pressed a towel into her hands and turned her toward the bathroom, swatting her ass as she went.

She washed everywhere she could think of, but didn't know what else to do. Obviously he had some plan for her tonight. When she got out of the shower, one of her long, white flannel nightgowns was waiting, along with a pair of cartoon frog underwear.

Ah, he wanted his old, sweet Jory back tonight. A dominant could only do so much to his submissive before she stopped being quite so easily shocked. Hell, he'd only made her blush a handful of times today. Maybe he felt like he'd corrupted her too far?

When she'd dried and brushed out her hair, she padded toward the living room, looking for him. She'd expected to hear the television, but the house was eerily silent.

She walked into the room and found him standing there, dressed in jeans and a snug t-shirt, his hair still damp from showering on the main floor. Going to him, she wrapped her arms around his waist.

"You're dressed? Are you…going out and leaving me here?" She looked up at him, confused. Cold detachment filled his dark eyes – Valentine at his most dominant. She shivered and mentally reached for him. There was a firm lid on something in his mind, but it was hard to tell whether it was anger or arousal. Possibly both.

Was she in trouble for something? If so, what?

"I already told you we're not going anywhere," he admonished, "but I've planned a surprise for you."

Her first thought was a movie night, but the tenor of his mind was too…wicked, as though he was planning something dastardly and was more than half hoping to freak her out.

"A surprise, Sir?"

"Hello, kitten." The deep voice behind her made her whip her head around. Jurgen? But not like she'd ever heard him before. Silky…evil…seductive. He and Dane both, and they'd moved up silently behind her.

Oh…fuck…

"Uhh…hi." She turned and backed into Valentine as the two huge blonds crowded her into him. Trapped – she was trapped by a huge wall of muscle-bound men, and they were planning to…

Oh my god…

"You've known us for a while now. You're not afraid of us, are you, sweetness?" Dane trailed a finger down her cheek.

She trembled, struggling not to run screaming into the night. "Valentine?"

"You didn't like playing with them the last time?" Valentine asked, his tone teasing. He knew damn well she'd liked it.

"There were rules then. Limits," she protested.

He chuckled, the rumble vibrating against her upper back. "There are new rules now."

"What are the new rules, Sir?"

"Dane and Jurgen know. They'll follow them."

"I don't get to know?"

"It's enough that they know. You may negotiate rules of your own now, if you wish."

She stared back and forth between the two men who could have starred in Viking recruitment posters. All three of them were huge – especially compared to her – and seriously hot. But did she really want to go there with Dane and Jurgen?

Jurgen's blue eyes narrowed alarmingly. "Don't you want to play with us, little girl?"

"I…uh…" Her heart was fluttering and skipping beats, and she hoped she'd conveniently swoon.

"Shh. No need to be so frightened." Valentine stroked her hair. "As always, it's your choice, snowangel. I can send them home just as easily as I invited them over."

Both of the other men watched her, their eyes hot. At one time she'd thought Dane didn't like her much, but when Valentine had been in the coma, Jurgen had explained it was because as a fellow dominant, he was trying to be respectful of Valentine's claim and property. From Dane's expression now, and the tension that played through his muscles, she could tell it had been the truth. Jurgen had never had to hide his attraction, both because he was a submissive and because he had special status with Valentine, having been his first lover.

"How come you all get to boss me around? You're a submissive, just like I am, Jurgen. What if I wanted to try domming you?"

The way his brow arched suggested that hadn't been part of the plan. After a moment, he shrugged and looked to Valentine.

"I'd be interested in watching that." Valentine's deep voice rumbled from behind her.

Shit. She felt as if she should have done some research online before suggesting such a thing out loud. It wasn't really an idea that turned her on, but it just felt unfair that in this scenario *everyone* seemed to think they'd get to boss her around.

"And I don't know how I feel about…" She looked from one of the lusty males to the next. "…you know."

Valentine smiled patiently. "You'll have to be a little more specific."

"Uhh…"

"Protection? You've mentioned you don't need it because of your powers, but we'll use it if you prefer."

"No, not that. I meant…you know…"

"Being tied up, being spanked, sucking cock, watching Valentine with one or both of us…" Dane suggested.

She felt her eyes go wide. That idea hadn't occurred to her, but now that he'd brought it up…

"Oh, I'm perfectly fine with watching the three of you together," she said hastily. "Hell, I'll find a tarp and oil you all up myself."

"Watching men do naked oil wrestling is one of your kinks?" Valentine asked, looking amused.

She grinned. "Oh hell, it could be."

"Look up Turkish oil wrestling on YouTube, sweetness. You're welcome." Jurgen winked.

Valentine's expression turned cool, as if he didn't want Jurgen encouraging her to lust after strangers on the internet. The man made no sense. Jurgen and Dane were fine in real life, but people she was never going to meet were a threat? Silly man.

"Quit stalling and tell me what you're not okay with," Valentine ordered. "Whisper it to me if you need to."

She turned toward him and bit her lip, and he traced along her jawbone with the pad of his finger. He leaned in, and she put her lips next to his ear.

"I mean…all of you at once…in every…orifice," she explained in a hesitant whisper.

"Ah," he said, as though he should have thought of it himself. She had a suspicion he just wanted to make her say it. Bastard. "We know what we're doing when it comes to DP. We'll be careful with you." He hadn't whispered.

She hid her face in her hands, but it did nothing to shut out the sound of three low, evil laughs.

"I love the way she blushes," Jurgen said hungrily.

"Such a sweet little toy you have, Valentine," Dane agreed.

"Is it a hard limit?" Valentine asked her seriously.

A hard limit? Well…no. Not after the bastard had kept bringing it up. Now the stupid idea turned her on. And here were men she actually liked and trusted. They weren't the type to do nasty things to a girl and then tell people she was easy. But still, the idea of playing with all of them at once was scary. She had the chance now, though – would she be an idiot not to try it?

But today? Couldn't they reschedule for a few weeks from now, when she'd braced herself and gotten really, really drunk?

They were watching her, all of them looking amused. They wouldn't make her do anything she wasn't okay with at least.

"Well," she said carefully, "maybe we could try."

And what was it with dominants and embarrassing people? Were they all like this? And why the hell did it have to turn her on? She wished she could bring herself to turn and stalk off, but Valentine would spank her for being rude.

"She likes to pretend she doesn't like anal," Valentine explained.

Jory lifted her hand to smack him, then panicked and pretended she'd just meant to brush her hair from her eye. His impenetrable stare said he wasn't fooled and she was lucky he was overlooking it.

"That's okay, I hate it too," Jurgen told her, wincing sympathetically.

"Like hell you do." Dane snorted.

Jurgen glared. "Well, I did in the beginning."

"Point taken, but that was in high school," Dane replied, gripping the back of Jurgen's neck. Jurgen leaned against him affectionately. "Like Val said, though, if we do decide to try DP we'll be careful with you, sweetness. And we know what we're doing."

Jory believed them for some reason. It wasn't as though either of them would have trouble attracting women, and both of them together? Hot damn.

She highly doubted they'd done that with Xana, but then again, what did she know? She was still so inexperienced and vanilla compared to the rest of Valentine's team. Did they think she was being a big baby?

"Okay," she mumbled, before she could chicken out.

"So you said you wanted to try domming Jurgen first?" Dane asked, hauling the advancing Jurgen back by the collar of his t-shirt.

"Fine," Jurgen growled. "What do you want, woman?"

Dane cuffed him. "Be an obedient little bitch for her, or I'll beat you myself."

Jurgen bowed his head sullenly, but then winked at Jory. She couldn't imagine being so…high spirited with Valentine, and he barely ever spanked her. Did Dane spank Jurgen? She doubted it. It was hard to imagine the big man putting the other big man over his lap. She'd watched Dane beat Jurgen with all sorts of things more times than she could count. Thankfully, hardcore beatings didn't seem to be one of Valentine's big kinks – although maybe he held back for her?

With animalistic smoothness, Dane took a spot in their almost king-sized window seat where she'd been reading only an hour ago. Valentine joined him.

"Do you want help," Dane asked, "or do you want to play with him alone for a while?"

"Uh…" She gazed up at Jurgen, who'd become one of her best friends, and tried to ignore how damned big he was. This was too weird. "We'll just use 'red' as a safeword?"

"Sure," Jurgen replied, like she was being exasperating and slightly adorable. Maybe he'd never need one with her, but rules were rules.

"I'm not sure what to do," she admitted, looking to Valentine for suggestions.

Valentine smiled as though secretly amused. "Well, when you fantasize about making someone do what you want, what do you imagine?"

She'd never really thought about dominating someone and he knew it. *Damn it. Think harder.*

"Um, I could get him to kneel?"

"Okay, so tell him, not me."

"Kneel," she said, aiming for a basic "bossy Valentine" tone of voice. The effect might have been ruined by her pretty white nightie because Jurgen was smirking at her as he slid into one of his über-masculine kneeling poses. His expression was cocky, sexy, and not at all submissive. From experience, she knew that Dane would slap his face hard for even thinking of making that face, but she and Jurgen both knew she was just using this whole charade to stall.

"Jory, may I pleasure you?" he asked, his gaze scalding her. Jurgen was always a little flirty with her, because Dane and Valentine permitted it to a point, but this was different. This was the promise of a hot guy doing absolutely anything she wanted, and having permission from both Dane and Valentine to tell him to do it. The idea of doing naughty things with Jurgen while their dominants watched felt very, very…naughty.

Focus, woman. She thought about commanding him to do this or that, but the three of them looming over her, all virile and dangerous, had been so hot and scary she was still jittery.

"Yes," she replied. "You can pleasure me by crawling to the window seat. And take your shirt off first."

He lifted a brow, but inclined his head. One-handed, he tugged off his t-shirt by the back of the neck, revealing his broad chest with the silver hoops in his nipples, banded muscle, and sexy amount of blond chest hair. It was hard not to let her gaze follow the narrow trail of hair that led down his belly into the waistband of his jeans, and harder still to not stare at the bulge there. The curve of his lips said he saw her trying not to check him out, and loved that she couldn't help it.

He crawled toward the others, but the only excitement she derived from it was from the anticipation of what her next command would be. That and he had a hot ass, and he moved like a predator.

Damn, this was going to be good.

When he reached the window seat, he stopped and knelt back in his former position, waiting patiently for her next command.

She gathered up the bottom of her nightgown and crawled up onto the seat, sitting next to Valentine, who was watching her the same way an adult would with a child doing something grown-up and hilarious. As though he was struggling not to laugh and hurt her feelings.

"Is it true that you were the first one to give Valentine a blowjob?" she asked.

Jurgen nodded.

"How old were the two of you?"

The two exchanged a look.

"Teenagers," Valentine replied. "You don't need to know the exact numbers, but you should know he started it."

"You're the one who brought over the porn," Jurgen objected. "I just said you could try my mouth if you wanted."

Jory shifted in her seat, suddenly too warm, and checked Dane's expression. He was chuckling.

"I still regret I was home sick that day," Dane grumbled. "I had the hots for them both, and would have been more than happy to watch if I couldn't get in on it."

"So we're going to play Twenty Questions?" Valentine pushed his hair back from his eyes. "I think you're stalling, snowangel."

"Hey!" she complained. "This is part of what I want."

"Part?" Jurgen said hopefully.

"Well, what I'd really like you to do is –" She didn't want to say it out loud, and wasn't sure how pissed Valentine would be.

"Women," Jurgen muttered. "Let me guess. You want to watch."

Jory could feel the blood rushing to her cheeks, but she held Jurgen's gaze. If she looked away first the game would be over. And they both knew this was just a game. Jory would probably never get to be in charge again.

Dane shrugged. "It's a two-way street. Like we wouldn't watch her with Xana, or little miss Brontë."

Jurgen nodded in concession. "True."

Valentine's cool gaze assessed her. "You honestly want to watch me fuck Jurgen?"

"What?" Her mouth opened in surprise. Well, it wasn't like that would be difficult to watch either. "No! Well, maybe someday. I just meant I wanted to watch him…you know…go…" She pointed to Valentine's fly, blushing hotly.

Valentine grabbed her by the hair hard enough to make it hurt. Against her will, her eyelids closed and she shuddered, her arousal spiking. "If you want to play dominant, you're going to have to fake it better. Either make an effort, or it's our turn." When he pulled her close and kissed her deeply, it occurred to her that he was cheating and trying to throw her off, but her protest was a small, very needy noise.

He let her go after a long moment, but she was panting for breath. A sound made her tear her gaze away from Valentine to where Jurgen still knelt obediently at the foot of the window seat. Had he moved closer? He had.

She frowned at him. "I don't think you want me spanking you, Jurgen. You'd better behave." Her breath caught, shocked at her own temerity.

Irritation flashed in his eyes. Hell, she was botching this. Maybe she should have trying dominating someone small and cooperative first. Trying to control a muscle-bound man almost twice her size was hard to wrap her head around. She knew women did it all the time, but for her it was hard to stay in the right headspace

"I want to watch you give Valentine a blowjob," she said, proud that her voice didn't waver. She looked from Valentine to Dane, who both shrugged indifferently. She turned back to Jurgen.

"That's nice," Jurgen replied.

She snapped her fingers. "Up. Now." Between the glare and her pointing at the window seat, he finally obeyed, although she suspected Dane had given him a warning look to back up her command.

"Straddle his legs and unzip his jeans."

Jurgen looked to Dane, who nodded.

Hesitantly, Jurgen crawled over top of Valentine where he lay, half reclined, leaning back on pillows. Valentine watched as Jurgen pushed up his t-shirt, then unbuttoned and slowly unzipped his jeans. The intense eye contact between them made her squirm. By the time Valentine's fly was all the way down, Jory's throat was dry and her underwear felt as if they were melting off.

Jurgen reached into Valentine's jeans and slid his hand down to coax Valentine's erection out. He was seriously hard, so his bored expression was an act. The fact that this was turning him on turned her on even more. Jurgen began to stroke Valentine's thick cock in his hand, and Jory struggled to remember to breathe. She pressed her thighs together, trying to take the edge off of her arousal.

"Is that how I taught you to suck cock?" Valentine growled. "There's a difference between a handjob and a blowjob, bitch."

Jory startled at the reprimand, even though the comment hadn't been directed at her. The fact that it had been directed at Jurgen was even hotter than him saying it in the first place.

Chastened, Jurgen leaned down and touched his tongue to the base of Valentine's cock, then drew it upward to the tip. Jory scooted down on the couch cushion to watch up close, and Jurgen circled his tongue over the head of Valentine's cock, sparing a sexy, narrowed glance at Jory.

"Oh my god." She groaned.

Jurgen winked at her, then took Valentine's length into his mouth, and sucked, his eyes going half-lidded in pleasure. Valentine grunted, his hands twisting into the pillows. When Jory glanced up at him, he was watching her, and his gaze was ferocious.

"Maybe you should help him, little girl," Dane whispered.

When had he moved from Valentine's other side to behind her? His big hand trailed up the back of her calf, shoving her nightie higher.

Jurgen shifted over, and left the shaft of Valentine's cock available for her to work on. There was no way she could stick with just watching anymore.

She joined Jurgen at his task, their mouths working together, moving over Valentine's hot length until his thighs strained beneath them. The pleasure he felt was being fed to her through their link, overwhelming them both with the sensations of two hot mouths and his need to come. Someone's hand was in her hair, and Dane's fingers were following the elasticized leg of her panties, and he was making small noises of pleasure in her ear. She squirmed, wanting, but too shy to ask Dane to get her off, even if he could. Although with Valentine present, maybe it would be possible.

She moved toward the head of Valentine's cock, and when she got there, Jurgen's mouth met hers, his tongue swirling over the tip just as hers did. They kissed each other around the sensitive head, sucking, licking, the wet sounds making her giggle just as Dane ground his hardness against her ass. The barrier of their clothing frustrated her. Dane slid his fingers down the front of her panties, and she whimpered as he insinuated his finger into the top of her cleft, then massaged there with two fingers and slowly moved downward to her aching clit.

Jurgen tugged at the ribbon that tied the top of her nightgown closed, then slid one hand into the loose neckline. He groped for a breast, and slid his palm over it, groaning in pleasure. A twinge shot from her nipple to her pussy, and she accidentally squirmed her ass back against Dane's erection. His rough fingers trapped her clit and she started to pant, feeling dizzy and confused.

How had this situation gotten so far out of her control so fast? She didn't know. All she knew was that one word from Valentine and she'd come so fucking hard.

"Stop."

That hadn't been the word she'd been hoping for.

She quivered in frustration, shoving her ass back at Dane, needing to come so bad she didn't know how to process her arousal anymore. Jurgen was watching her, just waiting for permission to take what he wanted from her. He arched a brow at her and his tongue came out, tracing a vein in Valentine's throbbing dick. Hypnotized, Jory shuddered violently.

"Jurgen," Valentine growled in warning.

Dane grabbed one of Jurgen's nipple rings, and her friend's expression shifted from chastened, through pain, to ecstasy.

"She's ready to be a cooperative little girl now," Jurgen gasped out when Dane let go. "So why are we stopping?"

"Because I said stop, and I hold all the cards in this situation," Valentine said smugly. "Besides, you really want to keep going with this vanilla shit?"

"And it's hard not to come with two people who know you so well blowing you?" Dane chuckled.

"You shut up." Valentine grimaced at him. "One more fucking moan out of Jory and I would have embarrassed myself."

Dane grinned. "So what do you suggest we do to her?"

"What? That's it? My turn is done all ready?" Jory pushed her hair back out of her face and wiped her mouth on the back of her sleeve. She struggled to sit up, but Dane was lying on the back of her nightgown. Nighties were comfortable and pretty, but right then she just wanted to strip out of the hampering thing. "How is that fair?"

"How fair do you honestly want this to be, Jory mine?" Valentine asked, buttoning then zipping his jeans. The tip of his cock still jutted visibly from the top of his waistband until he pulled down his t-shirt to cover it.

"I think I want to try domming all three of you at once."

The identical looks they gave her forced her to cough to cover her laugh. Apparently they were getting impatient. For what, though? There was only one of her! How were they all going to dom her at once? Take turns? Rock, paper, scissors?

"Maybe next time," Valentine said indulgently, urging her off the window seat and onto her feet. "If you like playing with them maybe Dane will let you borrow Jurgen again."

Next time? This wasn't just going to be a onetime thing?

Jeez. There was nothing stopping them from doing this to her whenever they wanted to, except for her own objections. If she could come up with any.

"May I undress your girl, Valentine?" Jurgen asked, his gaze far less polite than his words as he followed Jory off the seat.

"The nightgown doesn't do it for you?" Valentine asked. "It makes me want to do terrible things to her."

"You're such a fucking pervert, Val." Dane chuckled.

"That goes without saying," Valentine replied. "Go ahead, Jurgen. I know you've been wanting to do this ever since we played together at Prospero's."

Jurgen turned her so she was facing the others, and drew the gown slowly upward, baring her calves and thighs. Rather than feeling shy, she was impatient. She'd been right on the edge of orgasm, and all she needed was for Valentine to touch her. Instead he lay there like a sultan waiting for the entertainment to start.

"So beautiful," Jurgen murmured to her as he drew the garment over her head.

"Hell, is it just me or did she get even hotter since the last time we saw her naked?" Dane said, making a blush prickle her neck and cheeks again.

"Is she wet?" Valentine asked. "You should check."

Ugh. He knew she would be, but he still enjoyed embarrassing the hell out of her.

Jurgen laid aside her nightgown and she saw a muscle in his jaw tic when his gaze fell to her painfully hard nipples. He was polite enough to move his gaze back to her face after a brief moment.

"Did playing with us make you wet, Jory?" He stepped closer, almost standing on top of her, crowding her, making her feel tiny again.

She gazed up, past his big chest and nipple piercings, and nodded at him.

"Use your words," Valentine said sternly. "Don't be rude or you'll be punished."

Damn it. Why did he have to love embarrassing her so much?

"Yes, I'm wet, Jurgen." She swallowed nervously. "But I guess Dane could have told you that."

"We have different opinions sometimes," Dane said from where he reclined against the pillows next to Valentine. "It's best if he checks for himself."

She rolled her eyes. Jurgen tapped her face – gently – but it still made her gasp. Who'd have known he had it in him?

"Don't disrespect my dominant, little girl."

"Sorry."

He grunted, and the sternness in his blue gaze made her whimper. This was not the same Jurgen who liked to cuddle her and bake cookies with her. He was always hot, but this version of him made her want to squirm.

"Fuck, I love that sound," Dane's voice rumbled. "Jurgen rarely makes it."

Jurgen, the supposed submissive, was staring down at her and looking awfully switchy as far as she was concerned. "Don't move or I'll spank you." Jurgen's sensual mouth was set in a hard line.

Had he spanked anyone before? It wasn't fair that Jurgen dominating her already felt more right than her trying to dominate him. He'd been kinky longer, so maybe that was it.

He drew a finger along her collar bone and trailed it down between her breasts, raising goose bumps along her skin as they meandered their way down to her panties, but rather than venturing inside them, his hand stayed over the thin fabric. His fingers moved lower, tracing her slit back and forth, tickling her at first then pushing the damp fabric to form to her. Her clit was still sensitized from Dane's touches, and every time Jurgen's short fingernail bumped over it she gasped at the flash of heat, even knowing the touch was coming. She shook with the effort to stand still and be quiet, and not to cling to his arm for support.

She looked to Valentine, feeling awkward, and as if she was being disloyal just standing here letting Jurgen do things to her, but he watched with hooded eyes. Through their connection, his arousal slid over her, making her shiver. There was no hint of jealousy tingeing it – these three were far too used to sharing.

"Please," she whispered, no longer sure to whom.

Dane stood, pulled off his shirt, and rose from the seat to stroll to them. "Please what, kitten?" He moved behind her, and caught her wrists, then trapped them in one hand, holding her still for Jurgen even though she hadn't been trying to get away.

She tested Dane's grip, but he only laughed. His breath stirred the hair on the top of her head, and his bare skin brushed against her back.

She hoped he didn't really want an answer to his question. She pretended he didn't.

"Why are you so wet, Jory?" Jurgen asked.

"Um...from my shower?"

"If it's from your shower, then why are you only wet here?"

"Why is your dick hard?" she shot back, tired of dumb dom questions only meant to embarrass her.

Dane grabbed the back of her hair. "Watch your tone, girl." Between his grip on her wrists and her hair, she was completely stuck. Completely, deliciously stuck.

Jurgen's eyes gleamed, and he finally ceased torturing her clit. Unfortunately that meant he had two hands free. He caught her nipples between his fingers and squeezed them hard enough to hurt. She sobbed, arousal making her press her thighs together, trying to relieve the ache.

"My dick is hard because I've wanted to fuck you since we met, sweetheart, and now I'm allowed to do whatever I like." His voice was harsh.

"Please, Jurgen. That h-hurts."

Valentine groaned, and Jurgen's lips parted, his blue eyes hazing with lust. Dane's hard-on was pressed against her ass. Again.

Damn it. Watch what you say in a roomful of fucking sadists.

She watched the sensual set of Jurgen's mouth as he pinched and twisted at her nipples. The pain sent jolts of sexual energy through her, and she squealed and wriggled in Dane's grasp. It was hard not to think about kissing him around Valentine's cock.

But he was hurting her, and she couldn't escape. He kissed her and she tried to jerk her head away, but he only kissed her harder, taking her mouth roughly, his hands getting more violent with her nipples, until she was gasping and screaming against his lips. The pain-corrupted pleasure was terrible enough, but he wedged his leg up between hers. She rubbed shamelessly against his thigh. Harder, gentler, he tugged, a gentle brush of fingers, excruciating pain – her mind couldn't keep up. Her body spasmed, trying to come, but there was only drawn out, endless need.

"Please let me come!"

But all he could give her was torture. Dane had let go of her hair, but his hand snaked down to her ass, squeezing, exploring. His fingers strayed to the cleft of her ass and she was helpless to stop him as the tip of his finger brushed over her anus. She squealed, fighting, but she was helpless against the large men, who had no trouble keeping her right where they wanted her.

"No, no, no," she whimpered continuously as they forced her to feel all of it – to take what they gave without any hope of release. Her body filled with the pressure, the need, but it only ratcheted higher and higher until she thought her chest would burst from the fluttering of her heart. With her mind, she felt for Valentine. His entire psyche throbbed with arousal. She caught sight of him but he was still sitting in the widow seat, watching, not even touching himself.

"Stop," came his cold voice.

Her blond tormentors both stopped immediately. They withdrew, taking seats to either side of him, both of them staring at her as if they'd eat her alive if he would only say the word.

She wailed, but stayed where they'd left her, even though she only wanted to crumple to the floor. Maybe have a screaming tantrum.

"Touch yourself, Jory."

"But that won't fix anything!" she shrieked.

"I don't care. Do what you're told."

She was crying now, tears searing her cheeks, making her face wet and itchy. Humiliation heated her face, and she felt like an idiot. Probably looked pathetic.

"Slide your hand into your panties." The statement was a threat, and she knew it. If she didn't cooperate he'd make this ten times worse before he let her come.

Sullenly, she did as she was told, the smooth, familiar feel of her fingers on her body after the roughness of both Dane and Jurgen's touch was much less exciting.

Peeling her sodden panties away from her pussy made her gasp. Her nipples were throbbing and burning and she'd have bruises there tomorrow. Jurgen and his cruel fingers.

She moaned as she ran the tip of her index finger over her pierced clit hood, so close to orgasm, but so far without Valentine's permission to come. It wasn't fair at all. Wasn't she a good girl? Weren't good girls supposed to get rewarded?

She sniffled, feeling lonely and exposed and stupid, playing with herself as the three of them watched. Their gazes didn't say she looked stupid, though. They were watching as though she was the best porn ever. She was so horny she was pretty sure she'd die. Again and again she reached the edge of orgasm, hovering there, then having the sensation diminish just enough to keep her from going over the edge.

Tears dripped off her chin. Some had hit her breasts and were drying there, cold. Her fingers worked, feeling so damn good, but she was starting to get raw as she tried desperately to break past the control he had over her mind. Another orgasm built, crested then ebbed. A moaned sob escaped her.

"Please," she cried. "Please, Sir. I can't." She fell to her knees on the gritty hardwood, glad it hurt enough to distract her from the pressing need between her legs. "I can't come and I'm so sore."

"Get up and take your panties off," Valentine said, his voice gruff. "Quit being a baby."

Shaking, she pushed herself to her feet, then pulled her panties down and let them fall. She froze with them around her ankles when she saw the ferocity in the men's eyes. She swallowed, afraid, covering her pussy with a shy hand.

He signaled, and when she hesitated, he arched a brow at her. She moved her hand away, and averted her gaze from her tormentors.

Ropes slithered out from under the sofa, and she stumbled back, shaking her head. "No...please, Sir. No more." Ropes always meant torture, never quick orgasms. Why did he have to be so cruel?

The ropes caught her around the waist, the arms, the legs, and in one swooping motion they flipped her upside down. They suspended her from one of the open ceiling beams in the center of the room, spreading her legs wide, and leaving access to her entire body. Blood rushed to her head and she swung there gently, glad she hadn't eaten a lot tonight. She felt ridiculous and vulnerable but at least they couldn't fuck anything more than her mouth in this position.

"New art?" Dane asked, walking up and patting her bare inner thigh. She couldn't close her legs, stupid rope. "Love what you've done with the place."

"I was thinking we should get one of these for our apartment," Jurgen mused, "but since Valentine doesn't seem to mind sharing, we can just borrow his." He bit the front of her thigh, sending a shock of sensual pain straight to her pussy. He spread her labia as though he owned her and had done so a million times. "You're getting sore?" he asked her. "Such a pretty little ring you have here. Hmm. You're all red. Poor girl." He flicked her clit hood ring with the tip of his tongue, making her shudder, then attacked the sensitive bud with the most grazing of licks. Again. Again.

She sobbed.

"Fuck, I love how you taste."

She tipped her hips toward him, wanting more even though he couldn't help her come, but needing his cruelty even if it was just going to end in more frustration. He paused between each lick, and she howled for him, writhing in her bonds. Her head was throbbing from all of the blood rushing to it and she could hear her heart beating in her ears.

"It really does sound like she's sore, doesn't it?" Dane remarked. He stood behind Jurgen, unzipped his submissive's jeans and pulled out his rock hard shaft. Dane stroked Jurgen's cock right in front of her mouth, then pried her mouth open and made her take it deep. She choked and Jurgen groaned, his grip on her tightening, digging into the soft flesh of her bottom. His hips eased back, giving her back her breath, and she did her best to suck on him, the position making it awkward.

"Fuck, Jory," Jurgen groaned, thrusting shallowly into her mouth as he kept teasing her clit with his tongue.

Breathe, suck awkwardly, breathe, choke when saliva went up her nose. Dane – at least she thought it was him – bit the back of her thigh. She gasped and fought, but remembered not to bite Jurgen. He pulled out of her mouth, breathing hard, and gripped his balls in a white-knuckled hand, struggling for control.

Dane's teeth released her. "Is your poor little clit still sore?"

"Yes," she whimpered. "Can I come? Please?"

"You know I can't fix that for you, sweetness." The bastard didn't sound sorry. "All I can do is make it worse. Are you sore here?" He left a trail of kisses along her ass cheek. It tickled but it felt good, and she sighed.

"No, Dane."

He bit, of course. It went on longer than the last bite, and her mouth fell open in incredulous pain, only for Jurgen to shove his dick into her mouth again. Her shriek was muffled by Jurgen thrusting his cock in deeper, cutting off her air. She gagged then gagged again before he let her breathe. Dane stopped biting, and licked the spot he'd injured then trailed his lips over her ass toward her pussy. For a moment he and Jurgen fought for space – one tonguing at her clit and one at her entrance, but moving back toward her perineum. She froze. Hands gripped her, holding her still.

She whimpered, their mouths on her torturous, sucking, flicking, tasting. Jurgen's cock withdrew and Valentine's shoved into her mouth just as Dane's tongue flicked over her asshole. The shameful thrill of pleasure made her want to hide her face.

Fuck – why hadn't she said licking her there was a hard limit? Too late now.

Clenching her muscles to try to keep Dane away from there just made him use his hands to pry her ass cheeks apart. She objected around the bulk of Valentine's cock and tried to squirm away, but she didn't have leverage, and didn't know how to use the rope to control the movements of her body. He licked her there, exploring every secret part of her, as she moaned and gasped, unable to tell him to stop. Valentine had done it to her a few times, but rimming was weird and wrong and made her so horny she was ashamed.

She screwed her eyes shut, trying not to like it but crying out, partially in disapproval, but mostly in a desperate plea to come. Jurgen's mouth latched down on her clit, sucking in long hard bursts as a blunt-tipped finger worked its way into her needy pussy. Valentine was facefucking her from off to one side, leaving room for Jurgen to work, and she found herself deep in a haze of submissive lust, giving up her objections and letting them do what they wanted. Jurgen's pumped his finger in and out of her pussy, and another finger started to prod at her bottom.

"Fuck," Dane grumbled. "You haven't used her ass in a while."

"Hang on, this is too awkward. Let me take her down." Valentine pulled his cock from her mouth and she gasped in big lungfuls of air. The other two withdrew their fingers and backed a step, then the ropes dropped her and Valentine caught her with practiced ease. Blood rushed away from her head, and for a moment she felt dizzy, but he didn't put her down. He strode toward the stairs, with the other two following close behind. She caught a glimpse of Dane's grin and she buried her face shyly against Valentine's sexy shoulder. Upstairs meant the bedroom…and the bed.

What the hell was she doing?

"Why couldn't you have done this when I was being controlled by the Aphrodisia?" she grumbled. "Then I'd have an excuse and I wouldn't have to think about it."

"Sorry, snowangel. I had to have clear consent for this, at least for the first few times."

The first few times? Oh jeez.

Jurgen tossed the duvet off the king size bed. Valentine laid her on the sheet before stripping off his jeans and stretching out next to her, and Jurgen did the same on the other side. Two naked men was a lot to wrap her head around. When Dane came in from the bathroom he'd didn't waste any time getting naked too.

In a moment of panic she tried to vault over Valentine and off the bed, but he caught her around the waist and dragged her back. They crowded her, skin sliding against skin, hard cocks prodding at her.

"Do you really want to stop, Jory?" Valentine asked.

She shook her head.

"Do you want us to chase you?" Jurgen's smile wasn't comforting.

Chase her? She frowned at them, but they were watching her like starving beasts.

"Whoever catches her gets to choose which hole they use?" Dane suggested. "But you can't use your connection to find her."

So much for rock, paper, scissors.

This time, when she scrambled over Valentine, she moved faster than he did. She flew down the stairs to the sound of men cursing and laughing.

"If no one catches me for three minutes, you fuck each other and I just watch!" she shouted over her shoulder.

They gave her about thirty seconds' head start before they followed.

She could hear them prowling down the stairs, slowly, like the killers in a horror movie. Their footfalls were so loud they had to be trying to freak her out. She yanked open the door to the basement to throw them off, kept running into the kitchen, trying not to make any sound, feet bare and silent on the hardwood. Where the hell could she go? Three minutes was a long time, especially in this house. She hid behind the counter, inching along toward the door out to the yard.

The guys had split up and gone quiet. She could hear careful footsteps and squeaking boards in different parts of the house over the pounding of her heart. How could she win with three-against-one odds?

Someone was in the living room, and she'd heard someone go down the stairs to the basement, but where was the third?

Crouching, she ran to the French doors leading to the backyard. She paused with her hand on the knob and wondered if she really wanted to go out into the dark, naked and alone. Well hell, there were no neighbors and she wasn't going to win without cheating a little. They'd never actually said she had to stay inside.

The French door squeaked as she opened it. For a breathless moment she paused. A footstep sounded nearby.

Fuck.

She shoved the door open the rest of the way and pelted into the yard. Someone was close. Terror lanced through her, spurring her to run faster through the chill grass. She whipped past shadows, wondering if they concealed men, her ragged breaths burning her throat. Feet thudded loudly on the ground behind her. If she threw a blast of cold behind her she might get away, but the guys were as naked as she was. The last thing she wanted was to be responsible for giving a guy a frostbitten dick again. And she was scared, and that always made her power unpredictable. What if she really hurt him, like she had Valentine?

Was it close to three minutes? Who was behind her? What would he do when he caught her?

She tripped on something and she went down, skidding on her hands and knees in the wet grass. She tried to scramble away, but a heavy naked body came down on hers and pinned her to the ground. Cold grass squished against her belly and thighs, chilling her almost as much as the knowledge that she had been caught and now they were going to do whatever they wanted.

She kicked out, but didn't have enough space to do any damage. The chest against her back vibrated with his chuckle, and his hard cock was slotted into the crack of her ass.

"I get first choice," Valentine said, sounding pleased with himself.

Two pairs of feet were in her line of sight. "I got here second," Jurgen said smugly.

"I'll take her any way I can get her." Dane laughed breathlessly. He must have been the one in the basement. "Just happy to finally have permission."

Valentine bit the spot between her neck and shoulder. "I'm taking her ass."

"I want her sweet little pussy," Jurgen said, his pleased tone suggesting it had been his first choice anyway.

Dane knelt next to her in the grass and traced his finger along the seam of her lips. He smelled like soap, but she nipped his finger rather than politely opening her mouth.

"Hellion," he grumbled. "No wonder you and Jurgen get along so well."

"Can we go inside, at least?" she begged. They weren't actually staying out here, were they?

"No. Obviously you wanted a nature fuck," Valentine admonished. "We were in a nice comfy bed but you decided the backyard would be more fun."

Oh god, they were all going to use her out here in the dirt, like some sort of fucking animal.

She tried to buck Valentine off her back so she could run back into the house, but he barely budged. Instead, he grabbed the hair at the back of her head again then forced her forehead to the grass. He rocked against her ass then swore.

"Damn. Did someone bring lube?" Valentine laughed, most likely because none of them had pockets in what they weren't wearing. He sighed heavily. "Come here, Jurgen."

When Valentine let go of her hair, she turned her head to watch as he sat up, straddling her thighs. Jurgen went to him obediently and gasped as Valentine took his cock into his mouth. It was the hottest fucking thing she'd ever seen. Dane went to stand behind his submissive, running his hands over his body while Valentine worked Jurgen's cock in his fist, licking and sucking on the head, then deep-throated him without gagging. Jory wished she could flip over and watch without giving herself a sore neck, but getting to see this was worth taking some ibuprofen later.

Hot damn. Valentine was better at giving head than she was. She'd wondered once whether it were possible to give a blowjob in a dominant way, but after watching Valentine's smug oral mastery of Jurgen's cock, the answer was an emphatic yes.

Valentine pulled away, pumping his fist almost cruelly as Jurgen groaned, coming all over Jory's lower back. Valentine gave the tip of Jurgen's cock one last lick, and Jurgen shuddered, his eyes closing in pleasure.

"Good boy." Valentine swatted his ass. "Now lie down."

Jeez. Her bastard bossed everyone around. No wonder he was impossible.

She could feel Valentine sliding through the come Jurgen had left on her back, then he coaxed her up to lie on top of Jurgen warm, muscular body. He was a bit smaller-framed than Valentine, and moved faster when they fought, but he was still built enough to make her feel like a pixie about to get used by some big, evil men.

And why did they all have monster dicks? Had it been a prerequisite to get onto their team?

Several girls she could think of would trade places with her in a heartbeat, but she was too scared to enjoy the anticipation.

She and Jurgen stared at each other for a moment, but then he threaded his hand through her hair and pulled her down for a kiss.

"Don't be afraid, snowangel," Valentine murmured, dropping a kiss on the back of her neck. "We'll be careful."

The feel of Valentine sliding his cock up and down the crack of her ass was reminding her body just how needy she'd been earlier, and the rocking motion made her pussy rub along Jurgen's rapidly rehardening cock until they were all grinding against each other, their hands and mouths exploring.

Dane returned from somewhere – when had he left? He got down next to them, lying on his side and joining in on the kissing and touching. So many hands. So many mouths.

When she was panting and whimpering again, Jurgen pushed her higher on his body for a moment, freeing his cock from between them and positioning himself at her entrance.

"I've been waiting so long for this, Jory," he whispered to her, his gaze earnest as he broached her. She backed to meet him, but he slowed her with his hands on her hips, controlling, possessing. Maybe he was on the bottom, but he was the one in charge. He groaned in pleasure, stilling when he was all the way in. His hips bucked once, like he couldn't help it, and she could have sworn she felt her damn cervix hit the back of her throat. The hiss of his slow, controlled breaths seemed loud in the silence.

"Fuck. It's a damn good thing Val just got me off, or I'd already be done. I want to do this forever." With a hand wrapped around her throat, he fucked her, staring into her eyes and refusing to let her look away.

Jurgen who'd been there for her when Valentine was in the hospital. Jurgen who'd insinuated he and Dane would be glad to have her as theirs if Valentine had never woken again. It had all been discussed with him in the weeks afterward, and Valentine had been happy she'd been taken care of rather than being jealous.

He was moving inside her now, and his eyes said this wasn't just sex for him, and he was making her whimper with each stroke of his cock. Could they have real feelings for her?

At some sort of signal from Valentine, Jurgen reluctantly stilled. A finger prodded at her ass, slicker than expected, and he coaxed it into her.

"You're lucky Dane has a soft spot for you," Valentine whispered over her gasps. "He went back in to get you lube. Be a good girl and thank him."

"Thank you, Dane," she whimpered, turning her head to look at him.

The man in question kissed her, taking over her mouth while Jurgen nipped at her ear. A second finger joined the first in her ass. She already felt stretched impossibly full, and Valentine honestly expected her to take his cock? It was true she still didn't like anal, even if he made her enjoy it against her better judgment.

When it was the tip of his cock rather than her fingers, she couldn't help but clench in a desperate attempt to keep him out.

Beneath her, Jurgen moaned. "Fuck, that felt amazing. Whatever you just did, Val, do it again. I think her pussy just tried to crush me to death." He pulled out of her almost completely, letting Valentine work on her.

"My little bitch thinks she's going to keep me out," Valentine replied. "Keep fighting it, princess. You know I love it when you don't cooperate."

"Hurry up and get your cock into her ass," Dane complained. "I need to get my dick into this pretty little mouth, but I don't want to get bitten." He rubbed his thumb along her bottom lip.

Gradually, Valentine coaxed the tip of his cock into her protesting body. He was too big – just too damned big. Even for anal, with just him, she found him too big. When he pulled out she was hoping he'd give up, but he just added lube, then tried again, stubbornly rolling his hips, inching into her, forcing her body to take him too. Deeper, deeper he worked himself, opening her body to him.

"You think you get to keep me out of your body when you let him in?" he growled. "You're mine. Always. No matter who else is using you with me. Am I clear?"

It ached, but he made her take him. Hips met her ass and she cried miserably into Dane's mouth, not sure when he'd started to kiss her. Just as her body got used to being full with Valentine, he slid an arm between her and Jurgen, lifting her hips. Jurgen repositioned himself and Valentine forced her body down, a bit at a time, filling her so achingly full, until their cocks were both plunged deep.

Jory, stunned, felt as if her eyes were bulging both from shock and the ache. Both men were panting, cursing under their breath.

"Damn, she's tight," Jurgen complained. "You don't fuck her enough."

"Shut up or I'm going to come," Valentine bit out.

"Uncomfortable?" Dane asked, brushing a lock of hair from her eye.

She could only whimper in response.

"That's a lot of cock, isn't it?" He kissed her nose, and his fingers laced through hers. "They'll start moving in a sec, and it won't be so bad."

Yeah right.

They were touching her, kissing her, turning her on, distracting her from the mind-blowing sensation of pressure. She stopped feeling as though she was going to cry. Valentine eased back and thrust in, his movements so tiny at first she wasn't sure the action was deliberate. He backed off and held her still to meet his careful movements, but just when she thought she was getting a handle on things, Jurgen started to move beneath her, grinding up against her clit. The two of them got more coordinated, then rougher, stealing her breath, their quiet moans and curses filling the cool night air.

Her mouth dropped open as she tried to process all of it. Trapped between them, a receptacle of their lust, she could do nothing but feel them moving inside her, huge and aching and stuffed so full. Her throat emitted one long whine that she couldn't seem to stop. They controlled her body, working their brutally hard cocks in and out of her sore holes. Her connection with Valentine opened wide, feeding his sensations into her mind, making her feel his pleasure at being clutched so tightly in her ass while Jurgen kept moving in the way that rubbed relentlessly against her clit.

If she wasn't so afraid agony was imminent, she would have come right away. But what if they lost control when they came? What if they hurt her?

Something damp bumped her bottom lip. With effort she pried open her eyes. Inches from her mouth, Jurgen was licking Dane's cock, but it was her face he was watching, his expression euphoric. Tentatively, she kissed Jurgen around the head of Dane's shaft like they'd done with Valentine. Dane, lying on his side next to them, cupped her chin encouragingly and groaned with each tentative lick. She took the head of his cock into her mouth, sucking, closing her eyes again as her fear melted, replaced by a torturous pleasure.

They were using her body, cocks pistoning in and out, grunting their bliss. It was so fucking good. Sweat slicked her body, but every nerve was awake, goose bumps creeping along her skin, even into her hair. Valentine's breaths on the back of her neck, his elation, the pride he felt in sharing her body wound her arousal tighter. She felt like a thing – something less than human, to be consumed for their pleasure.

Why the hell did she love this?

She rode the edge of an orgasm forever, the tight heaviness in her groin all-consuming.

"You're a stubborn little thing, aren't you, princess," Jurgen snarled, digging his fingers into her hips as he thrust harder, like he was on the verge of losing control. "I can feel every twitch of your tight little pussy, but you're just not going to come for us."

She struggled between them, sobbing, needing the permission Valentine was withholding. Too horny for too long, her arousal hurt, the knot in her lower belly so tight as she felt Jurgen's cock quiver inside her pussy, as Dane's cock throbbed in her mouth. They were panting, trying to stay in control. The way her clit was crushed against Jurgen, edging her, made her want to scream in frustration.

"Does my poor baby need to come?" Valentine whispered in her ear.

She wailed, unable to answer with her mouth full of cock. Dane was fucking her mouth, and she tried to suck, but the angle and her moans made things sloppy. Saliva dripped down her chin and her face felt soggy between that and the tears. His hips jerked spasmodically, and then he was coming down her throat in thick, hot streams. She gagged, eyes flying open as she swallowed and swallowed, desperate to breathe.

"That's a good girl," Jurgen crooned, watching her with hungry eyes. "Swallow it all." He licked her bottom lip where it was still wrapped around Dane, and then his body arched beneath her. Deep inside her pussy his cock jerked. He swore, and she cried out in pleasure as her clit was crushed harder between them.

She was going to die. She was going to fucking die if she couldn't come now.

"Oh fuck…come!" Valentine barked hoarsely in her ear as she felt his cock start to jerk in her ass.

For a long moment everything froze as his permission sank in.

The tension in her body snapped. A scream tore from her throat just as Dane's cock pulled out of her mouth. Valentine and Jurgen began pounding into her, driving her orgasm higher and harder. The pleasure hurt even more than their rough hands as they forced her body to submit to their storm. Every muscle in her pussy and ass tightened and throbbed. She wept with pleasure, coming with a shocking intensity that left her stunned, feeling small and insignificant and at the mercy of their big bodies.

She rode the aftershocks for a long time after the storm passed, and they held her through them, petting her, kissing her, kissing each other. So many hands, it was hard to know who was doing what. She closed her eyes again, not caring, happy that using her had brought them pleasure. The smell of their satisfaction permeated the air, and she wished she could just wallow in it there with them for days.

Eventually they pulled out. A shocking amount of come leaked from her, making her feel used and dirty, but she'd braced herself for that feeling, even as exhausted and emotionally spent as she was.

They took care of her, lying together in the grass, holding her and stroking her, making her feel as though she was some sort of sexual savant because she'd managed to take all of them.

The men teased each other good-naturedly, and snuck kisses from her and each other as Valentine carried her inside and up to the bathroom to draw her a bath. Dane and Jurgen went to shower, and Valentine got into the tub then laid her on his chest. He cleaned her gently, whispering words of love in her ear.

Later they slept, all four of them, a cozy tangle of arms and legs in the king-sized bed. She slept soundly despite Valentine's promise that when they woke they'd all use her again.

Chapter Twenty

Mechanically, Valentine shoveled food into his mouth.

The buzz of the diner and murmur of the television were comforting, lulling him in his bone-deep exhaustion to the point where he was contemplating pushing his plate aside and resting his forehead on the table to sleep, just for a few minutes. Jory had curled up next to him on the hard wooden bench with her head in his lap. She was gazing up at him, her little fist balled into his t-shirt. Some of his toast had ended up in her hair, but she didn't seem to care. Then again, they were sweaty, filthy, and for most of the night, they'd been assaulted by far worse things than breakfast food.

Further down the table, Dane and Jurgen spoke quietly. Xana was coaxing Brontë to eat. The girl looked shaken, but Valentine hadn't gotten the story yet. Kade kept hovering, making sure no one needed anything even though he had to be just as tired as everyone else. Rowan was dozing on Brock's shoulder, looking far too sweet to kick ass like she did when she was fighting.

They'd all left their jackets in the SUVs, but they weren't fooling anyone. People in the diner were giving them wide berth, and for the first time in his life, that bothered him. Being a known Atypical always came with the awkward sideways glances from Typicals, but he didn't have patience for the leeriness in the restaurant today.

Both teams smelled acrid, like smoke, but not from a campfire. Maybe the stench was just stuck in his nose, but he had to shower before he even thought of crawling into bed.

He rubbed at a smudge on Jory's forehead but it didn't come off.

The television got louder, and the people around them fell silent. Jory sat up, and suddenly everyone at their table was wide awake.

Wick's voice, distorted by the television's crappy speaker, filled the room. Valentine whipped his head around to see the man on screen, standing at a podium.

...day and night to complete work on the schools, and we are pleased to open the first of them today.

There was a smattering of applause from onlookers on television, but the people in the diner were silent.

This afternoon, the removal of children from Atypical mercenary parents will begin. If any of you believe your Atypical neighbor or friend may be functioning in a mercenary capacity, it is your civil duty to report them to the authorities. Tip lines have been set up, and all calls will remain confidential.

A phone number flashed onto the screen, crimson and foreboding.

Impotent rage filled him. It was too late to stop this. There was nothing they could do to go back in time and keep this from happening.

It is our duty to ensure that all children are raised as law-abiding citizens. The unrest we've all seen in our cities, in our neighborhoods, and even in our own backyards, has shown that mercenaries are unfit to raise good citizens of this country. The cycle of violence needs to end with this generation, and the Bureau has determined this is our best hope for future peace.

The scene cut to people sitting at a news desk, discussing legalities, and debating the civil rights implications.

"My God. They're really going to do it," Jory said under her breath. She clutched at her stomach, as though to ward their future babies.

"I have to help my sister hide the boys." Kade leaped to his feet, and his chair momentarily rocked back on two legs before righting itself.

Xana and Brontë rose immediately, gathering their things. Xana cast Valentine a look and he waved her off. As if he needed help paying for this breakfast?

"Call if you need us," he said.

"Small and quiet is better for this," she murmured. They left quickly, followed by stares from some of the other patrons.

The elderly server came back, but when Valentine extended his hand to take the check, she crumpled it.

Mind whirling, he couldn't make sense of the gesture. He braced for a tirade, but the woman's face was grave rather than angry.

"I know you." She pointed at Jory and gave her a sad smile. "I read that you're a peacekeeper now."

"Yes," Jory said, tension forming lines around her eyes.

"Breakfast's on the house. You need your strength so you can stop the Bureau from doing this," the woman whispered, her eyes swimming with tears. She shook her head. "Our next door neighbors went into hiding last week, with their little ones. They're like family."

She patted Valentine's arm and wandered back to the counter to grab the coffee pot before any of them could thank her.

Valentine shut his eyes, embarrassed and trying to think of what to say to the owners before they left. Insist on paying? No, that would be insulting.

He felt like an imposter accepting the gesture. They were wrong. None of the people at their table were heroes. They were just stupid, weary Atypicals trying to protect their way of life. Trying to cling to hope.

Hope was waning fast.

*

All around Valentine, people's fighting leathers creaked, but the scent couldn't block out the stench of singed hair, sweat, and fear. He was tired – of fighting, of worrying, of being angry. Battles and skirmishes blurred together in his mind until they were a jumble of movement and flashes of light. His own pain and the cries of the fallen.

The Bureau had taken the children.

The Bureau had demanded this Atypical war.

Indigenous leaders, as well as a host of other Typical groups, protested the Bureau's continuous construction of residential schools for the children of mercenaries. Most Typicals were trying to ignore that it was happening.

The children, one by one, were snatched from playgrounds, from beds, from the arms of their mothers – some no more than four years old. Heroes guarded the new schools. The children never saw the sun, for fear their parents would "abduct" them.

The Senate was in an uproar. Protests were getting more violent. During the past week alone, several Typical protesters had been killed by heroes while trying to breech the school walls.

Mercenaries and peacekeepers discussed raiding the schools, but were too afraid the children would get caught in the crossfire.

The government, swayed by popular opinion, urged the Bureau to close down the schools again – especially in light of the social upheaval, but the Bureau had been prepared for such an eventuality, pointing out laws, and clauses, and loopholes that made it impossible for the Typical arm of the government to shut them down.

The Bureau, always thought of as a branch of the federal government, had slipped its leash and no one knew what to do about it. They had declared martial law over the entire Atypical population, and even the Senate couldn't stop them.

The case was in courts, but could take years.

Although the media tried to paint all mercenaries as evil, the fact remained that the majority of people didn't think children should be pawns in a political game. It had been a bad PR move, but the Bureau didn't seem to give a fuck about public opinion. Not anymore.

The ground around Valentine was littered with resting fighters, groaning in pain and exhaustion, panting for breath, passing water flasks from hand to hand. The heroes had retreated, but the respite would be brief. They'd be back.

Their ranks had been reinforced with men and women in plain clothes – defector heroes who'd forsaken their spandex when their morals had been challenged. Maybe the Bureau considered them traitors, but to Valentine, and many others, they were the real heroes.

"These pointless battles aren't getting us anywhere," Jory grumbled. "What does this accomplish? It's just a pissing contest."

"Yup, stupid," Xana agreed. "Maybe we're cutting their numbers, but they're cutting ours too." She pulling Brontë closer and used some of the water from her flask to clean soot off her cheek. Kade had collapsed at Xana's feet after shedding his jacket and t-shirt, apparently unashamed to show the telltale whip marks on his back.

He might have been better off with a more tolerant dominant. Xana didn't let him get away with anything and he tended to be challenging.

Valentine was still having trouble processing the idea that Xana had taken submissives. Real ones. He'd missed the beginning of their relationship, and it still felt as if someone was going to admit they were just pulling a prank on him. But Xana had never been a good actor – she was too direct for that. And to watch her trying so desperately not to fall in love with them was comical.

Sucker. She'd teased him about Jory for so long, and now she in the same position. She'd decided she didn't want a relationship just in time to fall in love. Twice.

The lines of combatants shifted, and everyone got to their feet. How or why they were fighting in a field made no sense. How would they know when the battle was over? How was this going to get the children back with their families?

Jory shook her head, grimacing in disgust. "We need to have another meeting. This is stupid."

"I'm not even sure why we're here." Dane laughed, dropping an affectionate kiss on the top of Jory's pale head. "To die in vain?"

"Drastic times call for drastic action," Jurgen muttered. "We need to stop fucking around and hit them where it hurts."

Fear vied for space in Valentine's irritation. Something had to change, but some of the more radical mercenaries were suggesting things that would stoke the fires of war rather than solve things. People were angry, to put it mildly, and becoming extreme.

"We're not kidnapping their children," Valentine said flatly, zipping his jacket.

"No," Jurgen agreed, "but if they assassinate my mother like they've been threatening, they're going to fucking pay."

Before Valentine could respond, they were swallowed by the battle. The rush of spandex-clad heroes funneled, forming a wedge that plowed its way forward into the ranks of the mercenaries and peacekeepers, step by hard-won step. Why?

Somewhere out there, Delilah was at the helm, her orders coming down to them through their commanders. From their vantage point, though, it was hard to tell what was going on.

Valentine and Jory fought shoulder to shoulder, with Dane and Jurgen covering Jory's other side. Xana and Brock's team had their backs. The nine of them were learning to function as a unit and were getting sent on specific assignments together more and more often. Nine was a large and unwieldy number for merc jobs, but this was war.

The two lines blurred into each other. Jory's opponent repeatedly broke from her freezing attacks, stopping only briefly before bursting free. Her razor-like ice shards glanced off harmlessly, and still he was advancing. A punch to his own mouth landed before Valentine could dodge aside.

"Quit watching Rime!" Dane barked at him. He ducked and grabbed his own adversary's fist as it jabbed for his face, narrowly avoiding the knife it held. An arc of electricity crackled from Dane to the other man, and the hero dropped to the ground, convulsing a moment before going still.

Valentine spun away from the mountain of a man in front of him, and blocked the knee to the groin headed his way. Jory's attacker bobbed up into the air, flailing, and Valentine threw a length of rope at him. It constricted around the man's neck, turning his face purple before his eyes rolled back. Jurgen restored the man's gravity, and he plummeted back to the ground, taking out the two men behind him as his unconscious form landed on top of them.

"Will you two fuck off and let me fight my own battles!" Jory snarled, blasting Valentine's man-mountain with ice razors. The man fell, screaming, clutching his bleeding face. "You're just making everything more chaotic if you don't mind your business. If I need help I'll tell you!"

Behind them, Brock was chuckling. "You see, my dear? It's a dominant thing."

"Yeah?" his slave, Rowan, shot back. "Well you're all sentimental idiots. Being my dominant doesn't make you a better fighter."

"Yes it does, but only because you're an excellent sparring partner," Brock replied. "Remind me to beat you for insolence later."

The wedge of heroes hammered into them harder, and soon they had no breath the waste on banter, and no time to waste fighting each other's battles.

*

"Well, that was a complete shitshow," Xana said, downing the rest of her beer.

Valentine took a sip of his own and sighed, just happy to be sitting still with Jory at his feet.

The nine of them sprawled on the mats and equipment in Brock's gym, freshly showered. Brock was also freshly stitched. His woman was good with sutures.

"No talking about work!" Dane reminded Xana, lobbing a second bottle at her head, which she snatched neatly out of the air. She hadn't even taken her feet down off Kade, whom she was using as an ottoman.

"We need to talk about it," Xana said sourly. "Alett has her head on straight and so does Delilah, but we need to talk about how we're going to end this. They need ideas just like we would if we were the ones in charge. And with Brock and Jory on our team, we get proxy say through them."

Between their family connections, and the fact that the war had started with the murder of Jory's team, as well as Valentine's connection to Ridlon, they kept getting invited to negotiations and meetings.

"This bullshit has to stop," Brock agreed. "We keep fighting the same battles against the same people. No one wants a bloodbath, but I'd be surprised if they didn't start ignoring the codes and bringing guns to pick us off. These battles aren't doing much other than wearing everyone down. A few die, or are incapacitated, but it doesn't solve a thing." Brock stripped Rowan down to her panties, apparently not caring that other people were watching, and coaxed her up onto the massage table. He rubbed oil between his hands and smoothed them over her back. She grunted in pleasure as he started to work the knots out of her muscles. Everyone watched the massage as if it was a TV show.

Watching made Valentine want to remove Jory's clothes and feel the softness of her skin under his hands. From his seat on the weight bench, he leaned down over her shoulder and unzipped her hoodie, and let it slide from her shoulders. He peeled off her fitted t-shirt as she half-heartedly tried to stop him. She gave up all pretense of objection when he started to massage her shoulders.

Brontë was watching them shyly, and he wondered if she was a voyeur or if she was interested in Jory. Or maybe it was simply a desire to watch something other than her brother touching his woman. It had to be an awkward situation sometimes, but they all seemed used to it.

Xana chuckled, and her hand dropped to rest on the back of Brontë's neck where she leaned against Xana's chair.

The girl shuddered.

"Should I strip you too, Brontë, and show my teammates what's mine?"

"If it pleases you, Ma'am," the girl replied, her cheeks reddening. She curled in on herself like a wilting flower.

Xana grasped the girl's chin, pulling her upright until she knelt respectfully where Xana wanted her. "You're very beautiful, Brontë, and a pleasure to look at."

The two of them stared at each other a long moment, and eventually Brontë groaned and nodded. "Thank you, Ma'am."

"Good girl. Now I'll only have to spank you for making me wait for your response."

"Yes, Ma'am." Her voice was so pained and quiet it was surprising she didn't melt into the floor entirely.

Dane sighed contentedly. Jurgen's head was in his lap and Dane stroked his hair, the two of them at the point of yawning and struggling to keep their eyes open.

A wave of emotion washed over Valentine as he watched the two of them together. What kind of friends stuck with a man through all the shit he'd put them through? And 'friends' was such a pale word. The amount of time he and Jory were spending with them had re-solidified the relationship between the three men. They'd gone back and forth from friends to lovers to friends so often over the years that being with them again was as simple as breathing.

He missed Xana, but she had her hands full with her submissives, and they'd settled on a closed relationship. For now. Xana was still interested in Jory, he could tell, and hinted sometimes about wanting to watch her with Brontë.

Such a big, lovely mess.

Fighting-wise they were turning into a cohesive unit, but relationship-wise they needed to figure things out. Thank god Brock and Rowan were completely monogamous.

"I still say we take out the Bureau's main office," Dane muttered, almost to himself. "It makes a statement.

"All those innocent people?" Jory asked. "Sure Wick will be in there, but what about middle management people, and support staff? What about Ridlon?"

Valentine let his hand drift down to cup one of Jory's irresistible breasts and she glanced up at him, her gaze already turning soft and submissive. It didn't take long to put her in that headspace.

"We're not proposing mass murder," Jurgen reassured. "We can make sure no one is inside."

"And you think that will be enough?" Kade asked, his voice strained. His arms and legs shook, but he was steadfastly refusing to safeword, as usual. It was hard to imagine it was even comfortable for Xana, considering her footrest was experiencing a mild earthquake. "It's just a building."

"The other choice is to cut the head off the dragon." Jurgen sat up and stretched. "The problem with that is there's no saying the dragon isn't a hydra. Neutralizing one man may not fix the problem."

"Neutralize him how?" Xana asked. "Assassinate him? You know that goes against the code, Jurgen. Was Evil Valentine starting to rub off on you?"

Valentine felt his mouth twist wryly, and Xana smirked at him. The room fell silent for a moment, but no one jumped in to back Xana up, even though she was right. It had been a long battle, and people's morals were slipping.

Time to test the waters. "I have a hard time believing Ridlon would be as bad as Wick, and he has growing popular support as a moderate," Valentine said. "Wick's lackeys only seem to have balls when he's out front doing the barking." He closed his mouth before he said anything too crazy.

Would it be an evil act to assassinate a man perpetrating so much evil? Maybe.

Maybe he still didn't have his head on completely straight. Maybe Evil Valentine was alive and well.

"Yeah, and if Ridlon got Wick's job, you know he'd fall at your feet if you snapped your fingers." Jory's cheek curved, giving away her smirk even though she was facing away from him, out into the room. "We wouldn't be dealing with someone who hated us."

As much as he didn't want to talk about Ridlon's crush on him, he was grateful to have his words glossed over.

He wrapped his hand around her throat and she melted into his grip like a ragdoll. Would throwing her on the floor and fucking her right here be so bad?

"Are you saying you want a playmate, snowangel?"

She only whimpered.

"If we came to visit, that would be four cocks, kitten," Dane pointed out. His math skills were impeccable.

"It wouldn't be about me," she pointed out. "It's my Sir he wants. And if it meant getting those children back to their families, I'd give him a fucking hall pass."

Xana snorted. "So Valentine's dick is going to save the world? Somehow I knew it would come to this someday."

Jurgen nodded solemnly. "No surprise there."

Dane arched a brow at Valentine. "And the sword Excalibur will deliver them."

"I didn't know your dick had a name, Sir," Jory said innocently.

"Should have picked a name she could pronounce when her mouth was full of it." Jurgen chuckled. "I'm not sure how to spell *ghwgaggguh.*"

They sat in quiet contemplation for a while. There were no easy answers.

Xana took her feet from Kade's back. "All right. Now that we've solved the war, I have a girl who needs a spanking. If I take her leggings down here she might faint." Xana got to her feet and snapped her fingers. Her submissives rose – Kade unsteady on his feet, and Brontë blushing hard – and followed her from the room.

"Fuck, I thought they'd never leave," Brock grumbled. His massaging hands moved lower on Rowan's now well-oiled body. He drew her sodden panties down her legs, then let them drop to the floor then massaged her ass while Valentine and the others chatted.

Jory's quiet intake of breath drew Valentine's attention from Dane's detailed overview of explosives and the availability of components. Automatically, they followed her gaze.

Brock was in the middle of pushing Rowan's legs apart.

"See? You were too noisy and poor Jory couldn't help but notice." Brock ran a slick finger down the cleft of her ass, and they had a clear view of her horrified expression as he pressed first one, then two fingers into her anus. "You wanted them to watch."

"No, Master!" she mewled, gasping. Her hands wrapped around the edge of the table, but she wasn't trying to get away.

Jory's breathing turned ragged, and she pressed against Valentine's grip on her breast, begging for more. Dane and Jurgen seemed to be having trouble deciding which show was more interesting.

"You love when people watch us," Brock growled.

"No," Rowan whined. "Please take me upstairs, Master."

Jory turned and looked up at Valentine with concern. "Should we go?" she whispered, brows drawn together.

"This is their thing," he whispered back. "She may be a slave, but she has a safeword and likes to pretend she has no choice."

Her pretty lips formed an "o" of enlightenment, and she turned back to watch.

"Did you listen to me when I told you to get behind me tonight?" Brock asked.

"No, Sir," Rowan admitted. "I – I didn't want Jory and Xana to think I was a wimp."

"What happens when you don't listen, little slave?"

There was a long pause, and her face paled. "Things I don't like, Sir."

"You hate when I fuck your ass in front of people, but you're the one who broke the rules." Brock clicked his tongue in disapproval.

"No," Rowan wailed. "Please, not in front of them, Master!"

"Yes, in front of them. You're lucky you get lube."

Jory turned around to glare at Valentine. "Is there some kind of dom training school all of you go to or something?"

"You should see the uniforms," Dane said, winking at her.

"You got cranky about me trying to help you tonight, come to think of it," Valentine observed, loving the way she stiffened in apprehension. "Maybe I should do some punishment anal on you too."

"We could help with that," Dane offered. "We could take turns." He and Jurgen both leered at Jory, and she backed against Valentine to get away from them.

Rowan cried out, and their attention was drawn back to the massage table, where Brock was pressing his cock into Rowan's pinned and squirming body.

"No, Master, please! It's too big!"

"You always say that and yet you take it for me anyway."

At Valentine's feet, Jory was tense and still. He caught her nipple between his fingers and slowly crushed it. She shuddered so hard he contemplated giving her the order to come just to see if she was that close.

"You were a bad girl tonight, Rowan," Brock growled, thrusting into Rowan's ass with a viciousness Valentine doubted he, himself, would ever use with Jory. "You need to listen when I tell you to do something, even if you don't want to – especially when we're fighting. It's my job to keep you safe."

The girl's only response was the steady stream of tears that had started up.

Valentine shifted, his rapidly hardening dick getting uncomfortable.

"If you'd obeyed me, you wouldn't have gotten that burn on your arm." Brock drove into his little slave again and again, her gaze quickly hazing over and her mouth going slack.

"I'm sorry," she whimpered. "I'm sorry. I'm a bad girl."

God, Valentine could handle watching people fuck all day, but listening to a girl cry and beg made him crazy. But why suffer? He grabbed Jory by the hair and dragged her between his legs.

"Is there something wrong, Sir?" she asked, biting her lip and looking up at him innocently, as though she had no clue what he wanted.

He smiled at her, then eased the zipper of his jeans down and freed his hard-on. "You can complain if you want to, but I lasted longer than Dane."

Jory glanced over to where Dane had Jurgen trapped beneath him. Dane was fucking his submissive's face almost as ferociously as Brock was going at Rowan's ass. Battle adrenaline was always messy to work off.

"I never get to watch the end of porn with you around." Jory sighed, as if he was a trial to her. She was laughing as he forced his impatient cock into her mouth.

Brat.

Chapter Twenty-One

"What are you doing?" A self-conscious laugh bubbled from her, and she covered her mouth then realized she should be covering other parts of herself, instead.

Steaming water poured from the waterfall showerhead and sheeted down her body to wash down the drain in the stone floor. The sweat and soot from battle had been washed away several minutes before, but with the weeks upon weeks of battles they'd had, she was in no hurry to leave the comfort of the state-of-the-art shower Valentine had installed. Between the shower and the huge tub, their bathroom was now her second favorite place in their house. Her first was still the window seat in the living room.

Valentine moved the camera away from his face, revealing a sexy grin that only made her blush harder. "When I got out and saw you in there…well, this is your fault."

"Yes, Master."

His expression switched from playful to dangerous. "Don't call me that."

He claimed to hate it when she called him that, but it also seemed to turn him on. After hearing Rowan use the word so much, Jory had gotten over her initial aversion to it. Honestly, it defined their relationship better than the milder Dom/sub terminology.

Although maybe she was a little too bratty to be a slave.

Giddy nervousness erased the loose muscled relaxation the shower had wrought. "Yes, Master. Sorry, Master."

Valentine laid aside the camera and reached in to shut off the water. He crowded her back until her ass touched the cold stone wall. She yipped, and moved closer to him, clinging to his muscular body, still damp from his own shower. His erection pressed against her belly.

"Do you *want* me to master you, woman?"

She didn't answer, only turned away from him and rubbed her cold ass against his cock.

"You're looking for trouble today."

"Noo…"

"True. You're not looking for trouble. You *are* trouble." He grabbed her roughly by the arm and pulled her out of the shower enclosure, then dried her with a towel.

When he was done, he shoved her belly down on the bathroom counter. She waited, wondering, more eager than she should have been. He'd done this to her brain, though – made her love never knowing what he'd do next.

"Wet spankings hurt more, Jory."

"Uh huh." She shivered, her body melting into the chill of the stone countertop as she arched her back and offered her ass. Anticipating the sting of his hand. Wanting it the way most women would long for a kiss.

The pain never came, and when she looked back at him, he was taking pictures again. She pouted at him, and deep in his chest he made a sound of pleasure.

"What's the matter, snowangel?"

She went up on tiptoe, shoving her ass out further, giving him a better view of her pussy. He could rarely resist that kind of invitation from her, but she had to be careful not to get too pushy or he'd say no out of principle. "I want *you*, Master, not your camera lens."

Ignoring her request, he made the hand signal for her to kneel and present. Sighing gustily, she did as bidden, kneeling on the stone floor in the middle of the slate gray-on-black spiraling mosaic.

He manhandled her, moving her this way and that, taking photographs, changing the tilt of her chin, taking more. Her nipples ached for him, and he kept touching her. The touches were sensual, lingering, maddening, he seemed to be in no hurry to give her what she now desperately wanted.

"I need to talk to you," he eventually said, walking away.

"Talk?" She was a short step away from begging. The last thing she wanted right then was to have a fucking chat.

He lowered himself into the smaller window seat he'd built in the bathroom, and signaled for her to crawl to him. Her knees rejoiced that he'd opted for smooth stone. Strange as it was, one day when she was too old to crawl for him, she'd miss doing it. Her bastard would probably even make her crawl when she was heavily pregnant with his child someday, but the idea did nothing to turn her off.

How far she'd come since she'd met him. At one time, the feelings she had for him would have frightened her, but now submission was normal. They were surrounded by other people like them. None of the submissives were taken less seriously as fighters even if their dominants were habitually overprotective.

It all just fit.

When she reached the seat, she knelt between his knees. Valentine stroked her damp hair, and she laid her head contentedly on his thigh, although her gaze strayed to the hard-on he seemed woefully set on ignoring. She brushed her mouth against the top of his thigh, fascinated by the way his balls shifted in response.

"Behave, Jory."

"Behaving is boring," she said to his cock, who seemed less interested in talking than its owner was. The camera was in her face again, snapping pictures. She pouted at him through the lens, which only made him chuckle.

"As effective as it sometimes is, using your spoiled little girl voice isn't going to get you what you want right now."

She considered biting his leg, but decided it wouldn't go over well.

"Try it," he suggested mildly, laying the camera aside. "Putting you on orgasm restriction for a week will be good for you."

"I'm being have!" she growled.

He snorted then tapped her cheek in warning, and she rubbed against his hand like a cat.

"Come on, pay attention. It's not time to be all cute and subby. I need your brain working."

"Then let me get dressed and don't keep me on my knees."

"Nice try."

"Then get me off again and maybe I'll be able to concentrate."

"Again? Aren't you still sore from earlier?"

"Not sore enough," she grumbled.

"I'm not beating you or fucking you until I choose to, so quit trying to force my hand."

It wasn't his hand she had her hopes set on. "Fiiine," she said with a petulance she never would have used if he hadn't been in a playful mood.

"What do you want to blah blah blah about?"

The slap connected with her cheek, and she slipped deeper into the subby abyss she never seemed to crawl all the way out of anymore.

"Don't take that bratting of yours too far, miss," he admonished, his black gaze harsh and glittering. The frost flecks almost entirely gone now. "It's cute when I'm in the mood, but you're playing a dangerous game."

"Sorry, Ma – uh, Sir." She rested her forehead on his knee. Something had been bothering him since the night before. She could feel it through the link, but he hadn't wanted to discuss it before now. "What do you want to talk to me about? Am I really in trouble or something?"

"No." His voice was gentle, as if he'd forgotten her testing behavior already. "I'm struggling with a decision, and I need your advice."

"My advice?" She knelt up straight to look at his face, but his head was tipped back against the window and she couldn't see his expression.

"Yes." He husked a laugh that sounded as if he was making fun of himself. "Lucky girl. You're not only my submissive, you get to be my therapist."

"You never have to worry about that. You're my therapist, too."

For a long while he was silent, and she could almost hear the whirr of his thoughts from where she knelt. She waited, concerned, but not wanting to push him.

"When we met, I was worried you were going to try to change me. You've done that, but you didn't even have to try." He scrubbed a hand over his face. "But I also have… There are dark parts of my mind. Parts I don't let you see. Maybe you saw some of it when I went mad from the Aphrodisia, but even then, I doubt I told you everything I was thinking. I'm different than before we met, but if you were hoping to make me a *better* man, I don't know whether you accomplished that."

Valentine always had strange moods, being as introspective as he was – as they both were. But some days it was hard to know what was going on behind those fathomless eyes of his.

"I don't need to make you a better man," she began cautiously, not sure what his point was. "You are what you are, and I have no need to change you. That's how love works."

He gazed out the window for a moment, out into the trees or the yard. Maybe at the ruins of the great house. It was hard to tell from where she knelt, but knowing him, he wasn't focused on the scenery anyway.

Finally he sighed, as though resigning himself to something. He shook his head. "You're too good for me Jory."

The urge to make light of the conversation probably wasn't helpful, so she held her tongue. What was going on with him? She should have figured things out before now. Yes, they'd been busy with all of the battles and negotiations lately, but his welfare was more important to her than any of that.

He was still so troubled sometimes, even though things had been good between them. The shadows inside him were deep and sinister.

Maybe it was simply his nature.

Every day she tried to swallow some of that darkness – took it into herself to make it more bearable for him. Even so, he struggled under its weight, sometimes so smothered he couldn't see light. The scars he'd left on his body when they were apart were more about him than they'd ever been about her. She traced a few with the tip of her finger, as she often did, accepting them like she accepted everything else about him.

What did she care about the plight of the world if he was suffering? Maybe it was wrong to feel that way. It scared her, but knowing it was wrong didn't change it.

"Is there something I should know?"

His attention returned to her, full intensity. "I have a problem which might be easily solved if I do something quite unscrupulous. So the question is…do the ends justify the means?"

"What's this about?"

"It's best if you don't know."

She didn't know what to say to that. "Well, sometimes the ends do justify the means, but it depends on the situation. Without more information I don't know what else to tell you. You'll make the right decision."

His thumb brushed her cheekbone, and the tenderness of it made her heart feel lighter. "The only thing stopping me from doing this is you."

"Because?"

"Because your opinion of me means everything."

Tears pricked her eyes, and she could feel her face getting hot and blotchy. "There are very few things I wouldn't forgive when it comes to you."

"What would be unforgivable?" His muscles and tone were tense, and his brows were lowered over his troubled expression. Very upset, but why?

"Tell me. I won't tell anyone, and then you'll know how I feel about it for sure."

"It's not a matter of trust, Jory. It's just better that you don't know." He laced his fingers through her hair, letting the strands slide through his loose grasp. "I have to make the decision, then hope that if you find out what I've done, you won't despise me."

"This thing you're doing…are you risking yourself?"

"Yes."

"For me?"

"Yes." His dark eyes hardened. She could tell in that moment he'd made his decision. Could tell she wouldn't like it.

Foreboding twisted in her belly. She wanted to rail at him – grab him and shake him and make him tell her what he planned to do, but she knew he wouldn't. They'd lost each other more times than she could count, and now that things between them were finally resolved he was going to do something crazy again. She just knew it. Other Atypicals got to be happy, but not them.

All they got was pain.

*

The concussion made her bones hollow. The air shook. Trembled. She felt lightheaded. Faint.

They watched in silence as the structure crackled, rumbled, sagged, shadow within shadow in the darkness. It crumpled to the ground like a domino house, collapsing in upon itself in a tidy heap. Even knowing the building had been empty of people, it still made her skin crawl. This attack had been a message, but none of them were stupid enough to think this was enough to end the war.

This might just escalate things.

Valentine stood behind her, his body supporting hers and lending it strength while his presence calmed the panic that threatened to overwhelm her.

It wasn't every day a hero attacked her government.

Sure, she'd been fighting against heroes with the mercenaries and acting as a peacekeeper in negotiations, but, in her mind, blowing up a building was a serious step into villain territory.

But children were dying. They'd run out of time to negotiate with an organization that had no interest in being reasonable.

The first had been a thirteen-year-old girl who'd fought the Bureau's abduction of her and been hurt in the process, dying later from her injuries. The second and third were young boys – brothers – who'd decided to escape a residential school and had died during the attempt. When their family got their bodies back for burial there'd been bruises upon bruises, which the Bureau dismissed as the result of punishments received for difficult behavior.

The spies they had in some of the schools reported that things were exactly as the peacekeepers would have expected. Raised to be critical thinkers, the older mercenary children weren't buying into the Bureau's attempt to reprogram them. The younger ones were just scared and missed their parents.

"Maybe this will make them reconsider," Valentine said, brushing hair from her face and looping it behind her ear.

"Or maybe it'll just piss them off."

"That's a serious possibility." Xana sighed.

Dane, who'd done or directed all of the work, was still grinning like a kid at Christmas.

As for Jory, there was no feeling of accomplishment. There was only a soul-deep exhaustion that no amount of sleep dispelled.

*

Valentine threw her to the ground and covered her with his body.

The sound of gunfire echoed through the air, crisp and final.

Guns? They'd brought guns to an Atypical battle? Heroes never used guns. Hell, mercenaries rarely did.

"We need to withdraw!" Valentine shouted. It was hard to tell if he was yelling at her, or the others.

"What will withdrawing do?" Jurgen said, belly down right next to them. "If we run now, all we're doing is showing them we're afraid."

People were on the ground all around them, but it was hard to tell if they were ducking gunfire or if they were dead or hurt.

Valentine rolled off of her then shoved her toward the stand of trees behind them. They crawled, taking cover behind a knoll as gunfire cracked and bullets whizzed overhead. Harsh, dappled light poured through tree limbs, reminiscent of a UFO abduction scene from a fifties movie.

The ground shook with the violence of explosions impacting nearby. Grenades?

This wasn't just an Atypical battle anymore, this was a war – the grim kind that got Academy Awards, where everyone died at the end. There'd be no winning, just varied degrees of loss.

The hopelessness of the situation made her eyes sting. There was no easy solution. This battle was just one in a string of so many she'd lost count. They were getting more brutal. Neither side would admit defeat.

Not until every Atypical was dead.

Chapter Twenty-Two

The old colonial home sat silent and forlorn in the misted, dawn light. It kept watch over the manmade trout pond, unaware of the hooded figure that ghosted up to its side door.

Two security guards were unconscious, but there was no knowing for how long.

Upon entering the door code, the man slipped inside, making his way up creaking stairs, past oil-painted ancestors and graceful statuary, to the master suite.

His own breathing deafened him to everything but the creak of his fighting leathers. Even hours later his nostrils stung with the stench of burnt hair. His eyes ached, and his muscles shook in exhausted protest. All he wanted to do was go home and sleep until it was time to die. All he wanted was for her to be safe. For this to be over.

The beastly evil that plagued his every step sniffed the air, all too aware it would see freedom, if only for a moment. It wanted out. It always did. The only question was whether he'd be able to leash it again when he was done.

He moved into the bedroom to find the target asleep, snoring lightly in his antique bed. Sleeping soundly, as though he wasn't the most hated man in the country.

The short knife felt slick in his grip. He switched it to his left hand for a moment, rubbing the palm of his right against his filthy leathers.

He stood beside the bed for a long moment, trying to think of who to pray to. No deity he could think of would forgive him for this. Neither would most people.

Instead, he turned his thoughts to the dead.

The innocent children.

Delilah, leader of the peacekeepers, who'd died only hours ago.

Jurgen's mother, Alett, not dead, but lying still and pale in her hospital bed, barely clinging to life. She'd come to accept Jurgen and Dane's relationship only weeks ago, and was finally working to heal things with her son. With the extent of her wounds, he might lose her.

Then there was the other face – the one he didn't want to think about. Stubborn, proud, now devoid of expression. Peaceful in death as it had never been in life. Sightless eyes staring. Had it only been an hour ago?

He hated him and loved him, hated him again for dying before they could fix things between them. Angry the man hadn't even tried. Hadn't returned his calls. He'd never been good enough for him, no matter what he did. No matter how hard he tried he couldn't be Dietrich's clone.

If only he hadn't hesitated. If he'd done this weeks, or even months ago when things had first started to escalate. How many more people would they lose if they didn't act now?

Maybe it wouldn't stop the war, but it would slow it while the Bureau scrambled to replace its leader. It would bring some symmetry back to the world. Perhaps his father hadn't started the war alone, but Valentine assumed he'd been part of the planning. Being there when Jory's team was killed was damning. Valentine didn't need to know how deep his involvement in that had been.

His father had been involved. His woman had suffered. His father had died.

This was for Valentine to do – to wield the evil he'd inherited from his father for the greater good. It was right even as it was wrong.

A shiver of repressed elation rolled through him. The blight on his soul terrified him, but he was aware of it, keeping it in check while he passed judgment on himself. It sickened him that he had to do this, and yet the drumming of his pulse wasn't disgust. So much anger buried – senseless rage that had no clear reason. It had always been there, along with his passion to dominate and to inflict pain. But this was different. It was wrong.

Murder didn't come with a safeword – didn't make his cock hard. But killing this man would bring him pleasure.

If he could like this, how could he ever trust himself around Jory? What if his perversions did branch out to encompass this someday?

What if he craved this again and again? Became a serial killer?

Too late to turn back now.

Holding his breath, he slid the blade of his dagger between the man's ribs, the weapon cutting through flesh with a sickening ease.

Anderson Wick awoke screaming, flailing. Desperately, he tried to knock Valentine's hands away. He pinned Anderson to the bed and held on, staring into his eyes, refusing to allow himself to look away as the last spark of life fled. Refused to let himself enjoy it. This was a job, nothing more. This was just a fucking job.

When he rose, covered in blood, he stood for a long while, gazing down at the untenanted body. Wondering why he was numb.

Knowing he had one more stop to make before he could sleep.

*

"I was worried." Jory's voice was barely a whisper as he slid between the sheets. The bed made her look even tinier than she was, not much bigger than a pillow.

He didn't respond, not knowing what to say. There was only an aching numbness. The room was cool on skin he'd purposely scalded in the shower. No water was hot enough.

"I know you said you wanted to be alone, but you were gone for a long time."

Her body spooned behind his, warm and alive, reminding him that there were things other than death and the maelstrom of his own thoughts.

Eventually her breathing became deep and even. The way her arm draped over his chest protectively, as though she could shield him from the big, bad world, made him ache. Asleep, she nuzzled against the back of his neck, her breath warming him, the Ice Queen melting the icy shield he'd thrown up. It was all that stood between him and a shitload of ugliness he didn't want to feel, but breath by breath, she made his defenses thaw.

"I had to do something," he whispered, knowing she wouldn't hear.

"*The* thing?" she asked, surprising him. Not asleep after all, just giving him space. The feel of her lips moving against the back of his neck made him sigh with unexpected pleasure he didn't deserve.

"Yes."

She pulled away then shoved down on his shoulder until he turned onto his back. Insistently, she snuggled into the crook of his arm, bringing a faint smile to his lips. The smile had been brief but still felt wrong, so hard on the heels of what he'd done, and so soon after losing his father. But without a word she brought warmth and life where there'd only been despair and death.

"I know what you did. You can talk about it or not, but it's not a secret. Not between us."

Suspicion flared. She couldn't know, at least not yet. Maybe she'd guess after seeing the news. Now, she was just fishing for information.

"Yes, I left my mistress very tired, but she was happy."

"Don't try to cover this with a lame joke. You're hurting right now, about Dietrich. The rift bothered you and he was too stubborn to let it go. Alett was there with him at the end, at least."

The memory of his father's face after death was still too raw. That thought he stowed away, locked it up to deal with it later. Maybe after he slept a week. There'd be time for anger and ranting and depression, but he couldn't even begin to process what it meant to lose the man he'd always measured himself against, and had always felt inferior to. Then he'd been involved in killing Jory's team and starting a war. How did a son forgive his father? His father was dead, but memories of his childhood kept replaying in Valentine's mind. He'd been a hard man, but he'd had tender moments. Those were the ones that hurt.

She paused for a long time, probably waiting for him to emerge from his thoughts and come back to her.

"And after the battle... It needed to be done, but no one else had the balls to do it. It had to have freaked you out. I'm guessing you went alone too." She trailed her mouth along his jaw, and he sighed. "But you're home safe. I was worried that if you went you wouldn't come back to me. You don't have to put on a brave face. Talk. Cry. Scream. Use me. Beat me. Just tell me what you need."

Did she honestly know?

"Why would I be freaked out?" he said coldly, realizing the way he'd pulled her close betrayed him even if his voice had been devoid of emotion.

"Your father is dead and you just murdered a man in cold blood. I'd say you have every right to freak out." She levered herself onto his chest, and laid her head against it. Liquid dripped and he realized she was crying. He squeezed her, wondering if this was the point where she'd leave him again — now that she knew the exact nature of the monster he contained, barely captive, in his soul.

Slowly, he slid his hand up and down her back, letting her cry as he wondered what to do. He had nothing left over to give her.

"Why are you crying, Jory?" he whispered, finally.

"Because you won't," she said, voice shaking. "Because you need to and you won't."

He rolled her onto her back, angry at himself for being so broken but knowing better than to blame her. She let him wipe her tears away, with the fingers that had held the knife, knowing his calluses probably scraped her skin.

"He was an evil man," she said, "but it still must have been awful."

It had been, but more because of what he'd had to admit about himself.

"I just want to forget." He pressed his forehead to hers. "I don't know how I feel about any of it. I think I'm angry because I couldn't think of any other way, but there's too many layers on top of that for me to sort it out."

Impatiently, he nudged her legs apart and got between them, not knowing he wanted sex until he was hard and inside her.

She grunted and struggled beneath him, shoving at him playfully as though she was trying to escape. He pinned her down and punished her with his cock, working the edge off his feelings with her body. Being inside her, and joined to her mind to mind, made him feel as though he might live through this. As though he might have reason to. She weathered his violence, crying out, writhing, giving him the fight he wanted, biting his shoulders and his throat, taking his sexual aggression and not asking for anything from him, not even release.

When he was done, she curled into a ball, and he wrapped himself protectively around her small form. He'd probably made her bleed, but the satisfaction he could feel echoing back at him through their connection said she didn't mind in the least.

"You're such a good girl for me."

"I love to give you what you need."

How many women would even care to help him feel better after he'd done something so heinous? How could he ever deserve her?

Gradually their breathing synchronized. His heartbeat slowed and the tension drained from his body.

"Such a good girl," he murmured, feeling like she'd drugged him.

"Only for you, Master."

"I hate it when you call me that." His dick started to stir again, and he had the urge to grab her throat, but he was too tired to even keep his eyes open.

"No you don't," she said, her words slurred by exhaustion. "And you know that's what you are to me, no matter what I call you."

For a moment he forgot everything else except his pretty ball of fluff, sleepy and warm in his arms. Maybe things would be okay. Maybe he wouldn't get caught and spend the rest of his life in jail.

"Master?"

"Yes, love?"

"You need to go see Ridlon."

"No." He grunted. "I don't."

"Why aren't you talking to him now – strike while the iron's hot?"

"I tried earlier. He wasn't ready to hear it," Valentine muttered sourly. "Shit."

"Yeah. I think it's best if you talk to him tomorrow. He has a…hard time concentrating on business when I'm in the room."

She snickered. "Well, you can't blame the guy."

"I'm probably going to sleep longer than you, so bring him something to eat when you wake up."

"I don't even know where he lives! And why am I bringing him food?"

"He's tied to a beam in our basement."

"What!" She tried to scramble up, but he held her tighter.

"I tried to talk to him," he murmured, "but the man can't think past his hard-on."

Jory covered her eyes with her palms, as though it would make Ridlon magically disappear from their dungeon. "What if he calls the enforcers after we release him?"

"You know he won't."

Shit. What a fucking mess. There was no way Valentine's father would have approved of how this war would be won, but it would mean a hell of a lot less bloodshed than the traditional route.

"Okay, Master. But when you wake up we need to talk limits."

"We're just talking to him," he objected. "I'm not fucking him. I'm not even going to dom him."

"Not even if it'll save the world?" Her laugh was short. Humorless.

He meant to say something glib, but darkness nipped at his heels. Finally, he allowed it to swallow him whole.

Chapter Twenty-Three

The strains of one of the Kink Monsters's instrumental songs, as performed by a string quartet, reached her ears. It quieted the crowd into silent expectance. Jory's white gown flowed around her like purest snow, dappled here and there with black embroidery to symbolize the stain he'd left upon her soul, like ink on a fresh sheet of paper.

Most people fought their demons. Today she would marry hers.

She stood in the mosaic foyer of St. Thomas Cathedral, staring at the doorway into the cathedral, proper, and wondering if she could bring herself to walk through it. Although she tried not to think about it, in a moment she'd be wading through a sea of strangers all silently judging her.

"Well, I know you're not getting cold feet about Valentine, so what's that face for?" Amy's own expression was blank. "Trust me, I'm frowning at you, but if I do it for real all the foundation the makeup artist put on me will crack."

"Did Valentine put a crotch rope on you before you left the house this morning?" Jurgen asked innocently.

"You shut up," Jory growled.

"Poor baby." He chuckled. "You want me to bring you to the cloakroom and help you take the edge off?"

"Men!" Amy smacked him with her bouquet of dark red roses.

He snickered and moved to kiss Amy's forehead, but she held up a staying hand. "No kissing my porcelain, mister."

"I bet your husband doesn't hesitate to kiss any bit of you, or you wouldn't have needed the extra dress fittings." He waggled his eyebrows, and she smacked him with her bouquet again. This time one of the roses came away bent at an awkward angle. Jurgen snapped it off for her, then put it on a small side table.

"You deflowered me! In church!" She clutched her chest dramatically, making both Jory and Jurgen laugh. "But yeah, when Jory chose this dress, triplets weren't in the forecast." She patted her huge belly, grinning impishly. "By the way, Talbot said to tell you that if any of them are blond, you're paying child support."

Jurgen leered at Amy, because it was part of the running joke between them.

His expression made Jory's mind flash back to him being buried deep in her ass only two nights before, smiling down at her just like that. She felt her face heat, and of course Jurgen just had to notice, which meant they were now both thinking about it.

It had been an interesting night.

Valentine and Dane had bossed them into do all sorts of things to each other while they sat back and watched. Jerks.

Jurgen winked. He was also a jerk, because he'd enjoyed it so much. She was still steadfastly pretending she'd hated it.

She tried to banish the memory, but it played through to where all three of them had been inside her, controlling her body while they used her for their own pleasure. With thoughts like this, and the feel of Valentine's shifting rope creation with its sodden knot positioned just over her clit, pressing, rubbing, making it hard to think of anything but sex, she was going to burst into flames as soon as she reached the aisle.

From the pallor of Amy's face, Jory could tell she was tiring. She'd have plenty of time to relax while she listened to the service. Jory had arranged for Amy to sit.

Triplets. She couldn't imagine it for herself, but was looking forward to helping Amy.

Jeez. If she got pregnant someday, she might not know which of her teammates the baby belonged to.

"Jory," Amy grumbled, actually frowning this time. "Why the hell did you let him put a crotch rope on you? It's your wedding day!"

"Thank god my dad forgot his boutonniere in the car," Jory whispered back. "But my parents will be back any second, so keep your voice down, woman!" They all glanced behind them at the door to the parking lot, but her parents, Leah and Eric, weren't in sight. "It was cool Valentine's mom planned the whole wedding. It made her really happy and helped distract her from mourning, but it's a little more vanilla than Valentine would have liked. The rope I'm wearing was supposed to be our secret, but I guess he told Jurgen."

"No. I could just tell by the look on your face." He chuckled. "It's a very specific look. Like when –"

She glared at him affectionately. "Didn't I tell you to shut up earlier?"

The click of Mom's shoes on the cathedral's outer stairs sobered the mood quickly. The fun had to be less improper with her around.

"Sorry," her mother whispered anxiously as she and her father ran into the foyer, red cheeked and breathless. Dad's boutonniere was in place. "Here you are marrying a rich Atypical man, and of course it's your poor Typical relations holding up the show."

"Oh, stop it, Mom." Jory grinned, squeezing her arm. "I needed to take a breather before walking the plank anyway." She saw Jurgen's mouth twitch, and she gave him a quelling look.

"See you in there." Jurgen placed a chaste kiss on her cheek and went in to take his place with Valentine.

Jory picked up the second bridesmaid bouquet – the one with the red-and-black ribbon she'd had made to represent Seraphina – and handed it to Amy too. Her best friend took it and nodded to her.

It was wrong that Amy had never gotten to know Sera the way she'd gotten to know Jory's other Atypical friends. They would have been hilarious together. The three of them should have been here today – Sera, Vance, and Arigh – laughing and joking, full of fun. Full of life. Enjoying each other, and the free bar later. She missed them like hell, and knew that would never fucking change. She'd invited their families, but they'd all declined with long, heartfelt letters. The wounds were still too raw.

The music ceased, leaving the cathedral in silence.

"We're up!" Amy gave a little hop that Jory prayed wouldn't break her water. She was due anytime now, and the babies were big enough that their chances of being healthy were excellent, but still.

"No jumping!" Jory and her parents all blurted.

Amy rolled her eyes. "I'm fine." She leaned in to whisper in Jory's ear. "Just don't shift around too much during the service. It'll make the rope feel a hundred times worse, trust me." Her best friend laughed evilly. She had become much more worldly since she'd started hanging around Jory's kinky

Atypical friends. Amy grinned at her then disappeared through the doorway to join the rest of the wedding party, more graceful than any woman smuggling a family-reunion-sized watermelon had any right to be.

Her father pulled her veil down over her face, misting everything she looked at.

They moved up to the doorway after a few moments, pausing as Jory's heart crawled into her throat. Her anxiety wasn't about marrying Valentine – she never doubted him, or them. Not anymore. And she understood that people needed hope, now that the war was over. Their wedding had become a symbol of peace between the factions of Atypicals, and the guest list had been a million miles long.

Being the center of attention at a wedding with almost a thousand guests was the issue. Who the hell had a thousand guests at their wedding?

Her parents escorting her down the aisle felt completely surreal, as if she was watching a movie on a snowy television, and none of it was happening to her. The huge crowd, in all of its finery, was eerily silent.

The black fighting boots she wore under her gown made no sound on the runner. Everyone had tried to talk her out of wearing them, but she needed the reminder today. This life – her new and happy life, full of hope and plans – had been built upon the rubble of a devastating war. Their path to the future was painted in suffering. In the blood of innocents and loved ones.

Wars could end, but no one won. Not really.

They walked past Matthew Ridlon, the Director of Atypical Affairs, and his wife, Mizuki, who sat with other dignitaries near the front, looking uptight and formal. Jory wasn't used to seeing Mizuki wearing anything other than the leather dominatrix gear that drove Matt crazy, and it was weird seeing them sitting side by side, looking all vanilla, rather than him fawning at her feet. Ever since Valentine had convinced Matt to talk to his wife about D/s, they'd been hanging around Prospero's with them. Mizuki had taken to domination in a fast and slightly terrifying way.

Despite what Xana had predicted, it wasn't Valentine's magic cock that had ended the war, but his willingness to do what no one else would stoop to. Without Wick, the wind had been knocked out of the Bureau's sails.

Several of the old guard mercenaries and heroes had died during the last few battles, and with them most of the old grudges. Without people like Wick and Dietrich, peace had become possible. Alliances had been forged, and the sullied heroes and righteous mercenaries were on more even footing in the eyes of the Typicals.

She walked the gauntlet of their wedding party – Xana, Brontë and Kade, Dane and Jurgen, Brock and Rowan, Amy and Talbot, and Valentine's brother, Pascal. Dane and Jurgen might have been smiling more widely than the others, but she tried not to look at them, or see Dane's wink, so she wouldn't blush. Dane loved teasing and embarrassing her almost as much as Valentine did.

Jory's father and mother stopped at the end of the aisle, and when her father lifted her veil, they each kissed one of her cheeks.

She could feel him. She knew he was there. She'd been avoiding looking his way.

Jory worked up her courage and peered up at Valentine from under her lashes. The custom black Armani with the black shirt made him look just as cocky and dangerous as his mercenary leathers did, but it was her eyes that gave her pause. Evil, evil black. Eyes that didn't belong in a church. Eyes that spoke of lust and sin.

And love.

That was there too, but she couldn't think of that now – not while she was working so hard to keep herself from falling, sobbing, at his feet. Her relief made her want to scream and laugh and cry. After all of it – all they'd been through – she hadn't trusted they'd get here. Not even the day before, while they finished the last few errands. Not even last night in each others' arms.

So many things had conspired to keep them from this moment that she kept waiting for the other shoe to drop.

She should have known, though. Should have trusted that the stubborn bastard would never give her up. To get her here he'd fought. He'd refused to die. He'd murdered. There was so much blood on his hands, and so much of it had been for her. Because he loved her and wanted to keep her safe. And he wanted to keep her. Forever.

"You're here." He reached out, offering his hand, and for a moment she saw a flicker in his dark eyes, as though he was convinced she might run screaming from the cathedral. Go back into hiding. Change her name. "I wasn't sure you'd come."

Maybe she shouldn't have, but she wanted this, and him, more than anything.

She took his hand, and together they turned toward the altar.

Maybe he was a monster, but he was her monster.

She was unafraid.

Acknowledgements

First and foremost, thank you to my critique partners, who continue to demonstrate how much I don't know about writing. Justice Serai and Cari Silverwood, my life would be very different if you hadn't taken me in when you found me alone, wandering the internet. Thank you for helping me through these books, and with holding my hand through my usual Don Music moments *cue me banging my head on the piano keys*.

Thanks to Justice Serai for standing by me throughout all of my cover art moodiness, and for creating the cover I ultimately needed for this book. I still want to lick it.

Also, thank you to my lovely beta readers, Janine Gardner, Christine Benoit, and Heimy Roa for taking the time to read for me during the books' rougher stages. Without you I wouldn't have been sure readers could handle Valentine at his most dickish.

Thanks to our street team, the Badass Brats, for being my sounding board for various parts of this work. I love you all.

Thank you to my editors, Lina Sacher, Justice Serai, and Nerine Dorman (Vampire Queen of the South) for having patience with my dangling modifiers and smutty sex scenes.

And finally, thanks to my family for not caring when I overcooked your chicken nuggets and ignored the cleaning. You'll never know how much I value your love and patience. With any luck, you'll never read this book.

About Sorcha Black

Sorcha Black writes kink romance, both alone and co-written under the name Sparrow Beckett. When she's not writing, she's generally avoiding housework and planning her next tattoo. Sorcha lives in Canada with her husband and their horde of witty children.

www.sorchablack.com

Made in United States
Troutdale, OR
04/28/2024

19502870R00266